OFF WE GO

A NOVEL
(Based on Actual Events)

COLONEL (RET) PETER A. DONNELLY

This is a work of fiction and was written and intended for entertainment purposes only.

The views expressed in this book represent the personal views of the author and are not necessarily the views of the Department of Defense or of the Department of the Air Force, the Department of the Navy or the Department of the Marine Corps.

INTRODUCTION

The Global War on Terror was my generation's World War II. The events of September 11, 2001 were our Peal Harbor. Initially, America didn't knew what a Global War on Terror was going to be like, who we would be fighting or how long it would last. I remember telling my wife when I deployed in November of 2001 that I didn't know when I'd be back. I told her it could be two years, thinking of how long soldiers were gone when they deployed to Europe or the Pacific during WWII, or maybe a year, like tours in Vietnam. Hundreds of thousands, maybe millions would eventually serve in Afghanistan and Iraq over the fifteen plus years since it began. At the publishing of this book, we're still there. But the initial response was literally a handful of soldiers, sailors, Airmen and Marines sent to Afghanistan and surrounding countries who, by luck of the draw or fate, were called to be the first to avenge the attacks of 9/11 and fight the Global War on Terror. These first few would have to figure it out for those that followed; they would have to come up with answers to all of the questions. For all that fought, for all that experienced and lived through these historic events, this novel, this story, is like any of the thousands of stories that started on 9/11. This is a glimpse into how it all began and culminated with the first combined conventional and Special Operations battle in the Global War, Operation Anaconda.

I deployed seven times downrange to Afghanistan and Iraq from 2001 until I retired in 2014. Most of the rest of those deployments were more complicated, more sophisticated, maybe more significant, but there has always been something for me about that first foray out the door. Maybe it was because we were less prepared, less sophisticated, and maybe more optimistic. There was also something different about going to fight when smoke was still rising from ground zero, the place where the Twin Towers previously stood tall, and having grown up in New Jersey, a place I'd personally been to several times. I don't think I ever felt the same on subsequent deployments; I know I didn't, because it always seemed it was about something else. Eventually, the deployment mechanism became a big machine and you got on the conveyor belt and you went when it was your time or your unit's time and if you made it back, you got back in the machine, back on the belt. Going was always monumental and important, but it wasn't like it was two months after 9/11.

That's why I wanted to write a story about that time.

THE BURDEN

War changes all its participants; the willing and the unwilling, the perpetrators and the victims. Each leaves the experience uniquely changed; some are ultimately affected; they die. For the survivors, there are those that have faced death or have seen death, and those who have caused death. For the military, that's part of the job; it's a duty. It is a legally mandated requirement that soldiers, sailors, Marines and Airmen must obey: the legal order to kill. There is a pre-established rationalization that comes with the order to kill people and break things. That experience, unlike that of the victims, is usually absorbed; tucked away and dealt with by the killer, emerging once in a while to weigh heavily when time or deep thought erode the rationalization. The heavy weight is the gravity of taking life, perhaps many lives. You've become a killer. For the rest of your life – you can suppress that reality. You can change jobs, you can change the color of your hair, you can change your address, you can change your name – but for the rest of your life, you'll always be a killer. For the professionals, those killings can bleed together and become a number; one, two, a dozen, a thousand, or they can haunt individually through the specific details of how each occurred, how each death was dealt. Those of us that survive eventually come home. The distance may be great, and time may pass, but it doesn't diminish the impact when you remember. Memory erases that time and distance, you go back, and it becomes your current reality. No matter where you are or what you are doing, remembering makes you feel like you did when it happened. In your head it doesn't feel less real, you just know how each remembrance turns out. When you remember it, it's the same as when it happened the first time, or the second. Every time you remember it, it happens again; over and over. You kill over and over, and you can't forget. The remembering makes it fresh. You relive it. It becomes a memo-reality. You go through it over and over. After a while the rationalization you used to help you kill doesn't work anymore: for God and country, for freedom, duty, clean kill, valid target, good mission, confirmed, militant, terrorist, insurgent, time sensitive target, high value target, kill or be killed, TGT 001B01... Now you wonder, is it just? Is it sin? You can't talk about it. You can't explain it. Who'd understand? What do you do?

You deal with it. Your country expects you to bear that burden; it's supposed to be heavy. Your country expects you to accept the honor of bearing it and to deal with it.

PROLOGUE

LEGACY

The last thing that went through Jack Gillespie's head before he hit the ground at 120mph, besides fragments of his helmet and some rocks, was the thought of his poor wife having to deal with his death. The alarm went off that day at 0400, 12 Jun 1960; Jack reached over to the nightstand and smacked the top of the clock to shut it off. He moved his hand to the right, feeling for the radio, found it and turned it on. A commercial for a car dealership was on the local station; the salesman was screaming about "great deals and huge savings." For the first few seconds since he'd awoken, he'd forgotten this wasn't a typical duty day. He quickly remembered it was 4am and turned the radio off, wincing as he did, hoping he hadn't woken Natalie. She would usually sleep through the first few seconds of the alarm clock, but would wake and listen to the music with Jack. He knew it was going to be hard to get up. He'd been out late with some of his fellow officers the night before and they'd hit it hard. He lay still for a moment but caught himself before he nodded off. Letting the covers fall forward back onto the bed, he swung his legs ninety degrees and lowered his bare feet to the cold hardwood floor. He leaned forward and jackknifed up to a standing position with his eyes still closed, his feet felt swollen and his knees cracked on the way to straight. "Damn," he said out loud. He heard Natalie breath in deep then sigh. He cracked and snapped, moving forward in a jerking, rusty-mechanical motion toward the bathroom. After taking a piss, he flushed and gave a count of three before he stepped into the shower. Natalie got up to make his breakfast like she always did, no matter what time it was. He preferred she didn't get up but appreciated that she did.

Jack got out of the shower and started shaving.

"Shit," he said out loud, feeling the steel blade of his razor slice into his skin. "What a way to start the day." Natalie pushed open the bathroom door.

"Ouch, that looks like it hurt," she winced with

1

sympathy in her voice.

"A bit."

"Here's your breakfast" Nat balanced the plate on the edge of the sink.

"Thanks Hon," Jack replied, once again containing his slight annoyance. Nat always brought Jack his breakfast wherever he stood: the garage, the porch, even the bathroom. But he realized she'd just gotten up at O'dark-thirty to make him that breakfast; where it was served, he thought, wasn't all that important.

Jack Gillespie was an Army Captain in the 1ˢᵗ Brigade of the 82d Airborne Division stationed at Fort Bragg, North Carolina. He was a paratrooper; an airborne infantryman, 28 years old and a West Point graduate. Jack was somewhat famous within the Army for his actions during the Korean War. He played a pivotal role in the counterattacks during the battle that became known as Pork Chop Hill, he was barely 21 at the time. He killed a bunch of Chinese soldiers defending his position, some in hand to hand combat. The rest of his squad was killed. He excelled in academics and played in the defensive secondary on the football team. He met Natalie while at West Point. She was from Upstate New York and they met when she was a waitress at a local restaurant and she knew from the minute she laid eyes on him that Jack Gillespie was the best thing that would ever happen to her. The prospects in her hometown for a bright future and great husband were bleak. Jack just looked to her to be alive and positive.

The planned parachute jump this morning was more of a morale event than anything else. The Chaplains were sponsoring it and the call went out for all the "pay-hurts" and "pay-losses;" soldiers that would lose or have already lost their jump pay for that quarter due to not jumping often enough. Each active jumper was required to jump once each 90 days, but a soldier could jump "backwards" and "forwards;" jumping once for the previous 90 days and again for the next 90 days. Jack was one of the ones that needed the jump. He finished dressing and lacing up his highly polished jump boots and walked over to the desk to eat his breakfast. Right on top of his eggs and toast was a folded paper napkin, Jack could see through the paper enough to tell it had handwriting on it. He picked it up and unfolded it.

Good luck babe — Be Careful! — I love you.

The note had three hearts drawn at the bottom of it, Jack could tell it was written with eye-pencil and reading it helped the now cold food go down easier. He grabbed his rucksack and headed downstairs. Natalie was waiting at the bottom in her robe with a cup of hot coffee. Jack took a sip, handed it back to her, put down his ruck and gave her a full-up hug. He wrapped both arms around her and squeezed, just enough so she knew he meant it. She returned the hug with her one free arm. Jack picked up his ruck and opened the front door.

"I love you," Nat said. "Be careful."

"I will. I love you too," Jack replied over his shoulder.

He walked down the front sidewalk to his green '50 Ford pickup parked at the curb. He started the motor and leaned forward enough to be able to see out the passenger window to wave goodbye to Natalie. She waved back and flipped the porch light on and off a couple of times as he drove away. Jack drove a couple hundred yards and turned right and headed down Reilly Road toward Pope Air Force Base. He got to the gate just off the Butner-Reilly intersection and slowed to a stop at the guard shack.

"Good Morning," Jack said to the Airman guarding the gate.

"Morning Captain." The Airman waved Jack on and saluted. Jack returned the salute and drove through the gate and on toward Green Ramp, he glanced down at his watch, making sure he had plenty of time to make the "show time." Green Ramp was the area near Pope's runways where airlift aircraft assembled. All airborne parachute jump operations were conducted from Green Ramp. There were other ramps, named with other colors, but if you were airborne, the one you knew was Green. Normally Jack would have reported to his unit or whichever unit was running the jump and ride to Green Ramp on the "Cattle Car," a rickety contraption used to haul troopers to Green Ramp from Fort Bragg. It was a series of trailers rigged with seats towed by a truck. Troopers had fallen out of the

Cattle Car on several occasions during Jack's current tour of duty. Jack's battalion commander had told him to make his own way to Green Ramp since none of the other battalion troopers were jumping and he wasn't going to set up transportation support just for him. Jack approached Green Ramp and could quickly tell there weren't as many vehicles, buses or people as there should have been. The show time was in ten minutes. He pulled into the parking lot and parked close to the mock-doors, an apparatus set up to look generally like the inside of an airdrop aircraft. Jack's mood lifted, just knowing he got to do this for a living. Paratroopers would practice actions-inside-the-aircraft before they would head into the pack shed to rig up. The pack shed was a warehouse-sized building where all the jumpers for the day's mission gathered and rigged up for the jump. Jack parked and went in where two noncommissioned officers stood just inside the door.

"Good morning gentlemen," Jack said as he neared the NCOs.

"Morning Sir," they both replied.

"What's going on?" Jack stuck his rolled up hat in the cargo pocket of his trousers.

"The jump's been slipped for three hours. Winds are out of limits and not expected to improve until later this morning or maybe this afternoon," replied the senior of the two NCOs.

"Okay thanks. Are we supposed to check in with somebody?"

"You just did Sir. Captain Gillespie, I'll mark you down," the NCO said, noting the name tag on Jack's uniform. "You're cleared off until o-eight hundred."

"Roger, thanks. See you gents later."

Jack drove back onto Fort Bragg and parked in front of his house. The recently painted door stuck a bit when he pushed on it and made a loud crack when it broke loose, he winced. He left the lights off and tried to climb the stairs as quietly as possible. He got undressed and moved to the bed in the dark, but as he got close to the bed one of the floorboards of the old house creaked.

"Hon, is that you?" Natalie asked in an excited tone.

4

"Yeah babe, it's me. We're delayed. I'll reset the alarm and catch a few more winks."

"Ok babe, great." Natalie rolled over onto her back.

He sat on the edge of the bed. "Watch your eyes." Natalie pulled the covers up over her head. Jack turned the end table lamp on, reset the alarm to seven o'clock, and turned it off. Nat pulled the covers back off of her head, and snuggled up against him.

"You know," she said in a provocative tone. "We shouldn't waste this opportunity."

Jack arrived back at Green Ramp ten minutes before the new show time, like he always did. As soldiers showed up for the jump they dropped their rucks and helmets at the edge of the parking lot near where the primary Jumpmaster, the soldier in charge of the airborne operation, stood and would verify the manifest. The JM gave the mandatory briefs and controlled all of the activity leading up to and including actions inside the aircraft, right up until the paratroopers jumped out the door. The manifest was a list that held all the necessary personnel information required for the jump and all the jumpers were listed in "chock order" – the sequence they'd go out of the doors. It was also used to verify an individual had actually jumped. Since it involved money, the government required a reliable audit trail. Everybody paid attention during the manifest call. Master Sergeant Warkowski was the Primary JM for this jump. He stepped up to the briefing platform.

"Ok listen up for manifest call," he barked. "After your name is called go to the end of the mock ramp and get your ID, dog tags and helmets checked by one of the secondary jumpmasters. Johnson!"

"Kevin W. 4265," the soldier responded. The standard operating procedure was for the primary JM to call out the jumper's last name by position. The jumper would confirm by responding with his first name, middle initial and the last four of his social security number.

"Stephenson!" the Master Sergeant continued.

"William A. 2264," that jumper replied. The calls and

5

responses continued for several minutes.

"Gillespie! Check that, Captain Gillespie!" the Master Sergeant barked again. "Sorry, sir."

"John E. 2526." Jack walked around the crowd toward the end of the mock ramp. He held his ID card and helmet in one hand and had his dog tag chain looped through his right belt loop, dangling by his side. He handed his ID to the JM; the JM reached for the dog tags and compared them to the manifest. He then handed the ID card back to Jack and took his helmet. The JM inspected the inside of the helmet, looking at the webbing, ensuring that it was good to go. He connected the chinstrap, let the helmet fall, holding onto the chinstrap and lifted it up and down, jerking it a few times, ensuring it was in good working order.

"You're good Sir," were the first words uttered by the JM.

"Thanks." Jack moved out of the way to let the next jumper in the long line take his turn. Once everyone was complete, Master Sergeant Warkowski directed everyone to split up to continue with sustained training based on which aircraft they were going to be on. Sustained airborne training was the process of going over the actions the jumpers would go through inside the aircraft; "hooking up" attaching the parachute static line to the aircraft, actions under the parachute canopy like "slipping" maneuvering the parachute while descending and the parachute-landing fall, the "PLF." The chutes Jack and his fellow jumpers were using for this mission were virtually the same ones used since before World War Two.

Warkowski moved to the center of the mock ramp. All the jumpers crowded around in a tightly packed semi-circle, staring at him intently.

"Ok, listen up! The first items I will cover are the points of performance. Your first point of performance is proper exit; check body position and count. Jumpers hit it!" All the jumpers took a small hop forward on one foot, simulating departing the aircraft, then straightened their legs and leaned forward at the waist as they counted collectively, "1000 – 2000 – 3000 - 4000…!"

Warkowski continued. "Upon exiting the aircraft, snap into a good tight body position. Keep your eyes open, chin on your chest, elbows tight to your sides, place your hands on the end of the reserve, with your fingers spread. Bend forward at the waist keeping your feet and knees together, knees locked to the rear and count to four thousand. At the end of your four thousand count immediately go into your second point of performance, check canopy and gain canopy control." All the jumpers reached their arms up in the air, grabbing the imaginary risers of their imaginary parachutes. Two troopers dropped their arms down at their sides and shook them out, thinking Warkowski wouldn't notice,

"What's wrong with you two?" he climbed down off of the briefing platform and moved toward them with a purpose. They immediately looked up, heard and saw the JM's reaction and snapped back into the imaginary parachute position. Warkowski got in their faces and spoke in a soft tone. "Okay kids, you better get energized right fucking now or I will PT you until I puke. You'll be running around the flight line with a reserve in each hand pumping away like you're a loco-fucking-motive. Am I going to have any more problems with you two hippie wannabees?"

They both responded in unison: "No sergeant."

"When jumping the T-10 series parachute, reach up to the elbow locked position and secure a set of risers in each hand, simultaneously conduct a 360-degree check of your canopy. If, during your second point of performance, you find that you have twists, reach up and grasp a set of risers with each hand, thumbs down, knuckles to the rear. Pull the risers apart and begin a vigorous bicycling motion." The jumpers reached both hands behind their heads as instructed and pulled in opposite directions, like they were pulling the backs of their heads open; at the same time they slowly pumped their knees to simulate the bicycling motion.

"When the last twist comes out, immediately check canopy and gain canopy control. Your third point of performance is to keep a sharp lookout during your entire descent. Remember the three rules of the air and repeat them after me: always look before you slip."

"Always look before you slip." The group responded verbatim after each of his directions. "Always slip in the opposite direction to avoid collisions! And the lower jumper always has the right of way."

Warkowski continued through the technical details of the jump operation, covered what the jumpers will do once they hit the ground, putting their weapons into action, collecting the gear and moving on to their primary missions. Then he covered what to do if something went wrong.

At this point for some reason Jack thought to himself how much he enjoyed this. Even though the prep seemed mundane and fairly painful, he couldn't imagine himself being anywhere else. He recalled that it was like when he played football. Practice wasn't generally fun, but it was going through it with his buddies that made it something he enjoyed. They went through all the crap together and it made them closer. He thought that it was even truer here, now, with jumping. Anyone of them could burn in, hitting the ground at high speed, but none of them ever thought of that. If anybody ever really thought about it, who would ever jump out of a perfectly good airplane?

Warkowski went over the procedures for a "towed jumper," the unlikely situation when the jumper's static line doesn't break and the jumper is hanging from it, out the door, banging against the side of the aircraft. He covered malfunctions; total malfunctions and partial malfunctions. During a total malfunction the parachute provides no lift capability at all and the jumper falls like a rock. The only way out of those is to pull the reserve parachute. For partial malfunctions a failure of some type occurred during the parachute deployment and the parachute could provide some lift capability and the jumper falls like a lighter rock. There were other ways out. In some situations, a jumper should activate his reserve parachute in others, he shouldn't. The jumpers listened, but they hadn't seen a demonstration of these partial malfunctions since jump school and most relied on the fact that the parachutes usually worked the way they were supposed to. He also covered entanglements.

"If you should enter another jumper's suspension lines, snap into a modified position of attention. With either hand protect your ripcord grip and rip cord handle and with your other hand attempt to weave your way out of the suspension lines the same way you entered and then slip or turn away. If you become entangled and are jumping the T-10 series parachute, the higher jumper will climb down to the lower jumper using the hand under hand method. Once both jumpers are even, you will face each other and grasp each other's left main lift web with your left hand. Both jumpers will discuss which PLF to execute."

Two jumpers near Jack simulated the "discussion" they'd have regarding which direction to execute their PLFs.

"I say ole chap, shall we execute a right or a left PLF this morning," said the first soldier.

"Bloody hell, a left PLF sounds smashing..." the second replied.

Jack heard them and thought it was funny, but also realized the jump brief was no time to fool around. He saw one of the JMs heading in their direction, no doubt to rip them new ones, so he stuck his hand up and got the JM's attention, pointing at the two, indicating he'd take care of it. The JM nodded back, leaving the situation to Jack. "Hey soldiers knock that shit off and pay attention!"

Both soldiers replied with a crisp, "Yes sir!"

As Jack moved back to his position, he let out a barely audible, "Bloody hell..." The two didn't look back at Jack, but they both smiled.

Warkowski continued detailing all of the bad scenarios that could possibly happen and concluded with how to get out from underneath your canopy if you land in the water. After the instruction, all the jumpers were rotating their arms in a swimming motion. Warkowski directed the other JMs to head to the PLF pits and ordered the jumpers to commence their practice PLFs. After his last PLF, Jack dusted himself off, grabbed his ruck and went into the pack shed. Everyone assembled in jump order along a series of long wooden benches. Jack placed his ruck, which weighed about 65lbs, in his spot on the floor in front of the bench. Since this was a morale and admin jump no one was jumping weapons. Normally all jumpers would also have a weapons case to contain their M-14 rifle, but not today. Jack put his helmet on and went back outside to draw his main parachute and his reserve. The reserve parachute was much smaller than the main chute. The reserve had a ripcord on its right side, a canvas carrying handle on top and another on its left side, opposite the ripcord. Jack's turn came as he moved toward the flatbed truck with wire cages on top containing the parachutes. He held up his right arm toward the soldier passing out the chutes. The soldier on the truck had been scanning nametapes as he handed out the chutes. He saw Jack's,

"Hey Captain, are you Jack Gillespie?"

"Why yes I am. Why do ask soldier?" Jack alternated looking at the soldier asking the question and another soldier assisting him standing at his side. The second soldier was also confused.

"JD what the hell are you doing? Just pass out the chutes," said the assistant to the soldier passing out the chutes that just asked Jack his name.

"Sir, my First Sergeant said to tell you he said hi and to have a good jump if I saw you." He put the chute down on the deck of the truck and put his hands on his hips.

"Ok, that's great. Who's that?" Jack realized they were holding up the never-to-be-interrupted flow of jump operations and was now visibly anxious, as he looked over his shoulder at the growing line behind him. The soldier leaned over and picked up a different chute that was leaning against the sidewall of the truck bed, positioning the chute over Jack's arm.

"Sir that would be Sergeant First Class Matt Foley."

"Huh, I'm not sure I know him, think I've heard of him. Anyway, tell him I said thanks." Jack took on the weight of the chute on his shoulder and moved on.

Jack peeled off to his left and headed to a second flatbed truck that had the reserve chutes. He grabbed his reserve and headed back into the pack shed. Dropping his chute on the bench, he began to undo the "rigger roll." The rigger, the soldier that cared for and repacked the parachutes, organized the harness and waist strap, pulled all the adjustment straps tight and wrapped everything into a neat bundle, thus the rigger roll. When he got his main chute sized up he propped it up on the bench, put his reserve on top of the bench and rested his aviator kit bag, the large canvas bag used to store all the chute pieces and parts once they hit the ground, and helmet on top of the reserve. Jack BS'ed with a couple of the soldiers and officers he recognized as they all waited for the next phase of the jump op. Jack was pleasant and people genuinely enjoyed talking to him.

"Ok, let's start getting it on," Warkowski yelled. It was time for everyone to rig up and get inspected. Jack went back to his place on the bench and got with the jumper in front of him to "buddy rig." Two jumpers would work together to get their gear on, helping each other put on their chute, attach their rucks and get ready for the Jump Master Parachute Inspection, JMPI. After Jack and his partner, the jumper behind him, rigged up they stood by waiting for their turn to be JMPI'ed. One of the JMs approached Jack. Jack stood up and put on his helmet, stepped forward and positioned his hands on top of his helmet.

"You ready Sir?" The JM asked, already having started the inspection.

"Yep," Jack replied. The JM moved to a position squarely in front of Jack.

"Open your rip cord protector flap," he commanded. Jack reached around his gear and opened the ripcord protector flap, a thick piece of hinged fabric rimmed with Velcro that covered the hardware that held the reserve parachute together and housed the business end of the reserve ripcord. The JM moved his hands toward the right side of Jack's helmet and began the inspection in earnest. Jack stared at the far wall of the pack shed and scanned around the enormous building. He wondered what all the other jumpers were thinking about. He'd done this before, many times over the years, and he knew some were scared, some were nervous, some were bored, some were excited but overall he sensed a collective calm. Everybody knew what was coming and most got into a groove since it's all inevitable. The aircraft *is* going to launch, you *are* going to get airborne, and you *are* absolutely going to jump. There are very

11

few decisions left to be made once the bird gets airborne. The last one is the decision not to jump. That's a big one and you would have to have a damn good reason to make it. So, you are going out the door. What had been going on was just one of the lengthy, necessary steps that leads up to the point when the paratrooper "puts his knees in the breeze." Jack had gotten out of the habit of praying since Korea, but going through jump school reintroduced him to it and now it became a part of his pre-jump routine. He thought about the jump, what his responsibilities were, how it would go, but he also thought about the what-ifs, if something went wrong. Today he felt calm, said a few sets of Hail Mary's and Our Fathers, and then just relaxed.

"Hold, squat," directed the JM. Jack lifted his rucksack and reserve chute up as high in front of him as he could and bent at the knees and squatted to allow the JM to check his leg straps.

"Recover!" the JM barked out, having finished the inspection and cleared Jack to sit back down on the assembly bench, "You're good sir. Have a good jump." The JM slapped Jack on the backside.

"Thanks," Jack said, showing his appreciation by making eye contact with the JM. "I'll see you on the drop zone."

When Jack was done he sat back down in his position on the bench, took off his helmet and rested it on top of his reserve. He took a deep breath and closed his eyes. This was one of the points during jump operations that Jack took the time to mentally throttle back. Not quite dozing off, but just sitting quietly, thinking, and sometimes not thinking at all. For him all the jumps felt about the same. There was a lot of time for thinking; he never really thought about the danger or risk, just everything else. This morning he was thinking about Natalie back in their bed, sound asleep, oblivious to all the activity going on, all the preparation. Then he started thinking about the follow on mission, his leadership role and the expectations of his commanders and of his men. He'd do all right, he thought to himself. He felt calm.

"Everybody up." Warkowski kept the jump machine moving. Airmen positioned next to each of the metal garage doors on the flight line end of the pack shed started pulling on their connected chains and the doors opened up, daylight streaming in. The C-123 Provider aircraft were all lined up with their tails facing the pack shed. All the troopers struggled to their feet, weighted down with their chutes and rucks and began to head out the doors in their respective lines. Each trooper moved forward with a kind of a waddle. Most of the jumpers' rucksacks were heavier than Jack's and hung down from about waist level, preventing the normal gait of a leisurely stroll. One of the Airmen that opened the pack shed doors, grabbed a clipboard and led the first chock out to ensure they'd be able to cross over the correct entry control point onto the flight line. The jumpers were lined up in "reverse chock order," loading the last jumper first toward the front of the aircraft. The first jumper would board last, positioned next to the troop door at the rear of the aircraft. Jack was number three on the left side, so he was third to last in line. The lines accordion'ed out and Jack started to move forward toward the doors; as he cleared the edges of the doors out to the flight line he looked left and right. He could see the dozen C-123s with their engines running. The C-123 was a two-engine cargo and airdrop aircraft, which could operate out of modern airfields but could also land on austere dirt strips, the mainstay airlift aircraft of 1960. The jump was being supported by the local 464th Troop Carrier Wing aircraft and crews. The Wing had a great relationship with the paratroopers of the 82d Airborne Division, of which Jack intended to be a lifetime member. The corresponding twelve lines of troops moved toward their assigned aircraft. Some of the troopers were already climbing the ramps by the time Jack got out of the pack shed. About one hundred feet behind his aircraft Jack felt the hot exhaust and prop wash from the engines. He tried not to breath the burned-aviation-fuel-smelling hot air too deeply as he got closer to the ramp. When he started up the ramp the soldier in front of him, jumper number four, tripped and fell straight forward because he couldn't bend a knee to thrust one of his legs out to counter his forward momentum; they were held back by his ruck. He couldn't reorient his arms fast enough to break his fall. He hit ruck – reserve chute - helmet. Everyone around him heard the helmet impact, even over the engine noise. Jack moved around to his side to help pick him up, grabbing one arm while the aircraft loadmaster grabbed the other. Once the jumper was erect it was obvious he'd hit hard and was dazed. Jack and the loadmaster guided him over to his seat against the side of the aircraft. They spun him around and lowered him into his seat, each one holding him by the hand and letting him lean back then sit down. One of the JM's saw what had happened and was already on his way over as Jack and the "load" were helping the dazed trooper.

"What the Hell Airborne?! Were those feet recently issued!?" he shouted. The dazed jumper looked in the JM's direction, expressionless.

Jack put his hand on the JM's shoulder and leaned in toward him, his head turned slightly away. "Hey jumpmaster, let's keep an eye on this guy. I was right behind him and he went down hard and bounced off his brain-bucket."

"Yes Sir, I got it" the JM responded. "I'll give him the once over before we give the 20-minute call."

"Okay," Jack replied. The JM turned back toward the front of the aircraft and started counting jumpers as he went forward. Jack noticed a slight disapproving shake of the JM's head and wondered if that was for him or for the clumsy jumper. All 60 jumpers were strapped into their seats, mostly looking straight ahead, some with eyes closed and heads back against the seat webbing. The loadmaster, the Air Force Airman in charge of the back of the airplane, was conducting his checks and had to move back and forth throughout the length of the aircraft. With a full load of jumpers with combat equipment, he had to walk across their rucks, legs, shoulders, or wherever he could plant a foot. This was understood by all and part of the routine. The public address system crackled on. It might as well have been in a foreign language as distorted and electronic sounding as it was.

"Attention, standby for the safety brief," it blared.

For about five minutes an unbroken string of all but inaudible noise, punctuated with high-pitched squeals and snaps, intermixed with the sound of the four running Allison engines

14

spinning their four-blade props.

"Sir, do you have any idea what they were saying?" Jack's jump buddy leaned in toward him.

"No, except the part that if we didn't either do or not do what they were telling us to do or not do, we'd die," Jack replied.

The soldier looked up at him with a serious expression. Jack looked back at him with an equally serious face, then smiled. The soldier got the joke, smiled for a second, looking forward and then got serious again and turned back to Jack and said, "No seriously sir, what did they say?"

"Don't worry about it soldier, just do what everybody else does. Hey, I'm your jump-buddy. I'll watch out for you," Jack said in as reassuring a tone as he could manage, screaming over the engine noise. Just at that moment the engines revved. It was now their aircraft's turn to join in the "elephant walk" – the slow progression of the aircraft to the runway hold line. As they taxied jumpers would check their seatbelts, chinstraps, adjust their earplugs, shuffle their rucks to give spots on their legs a break from the weight. Some would offer their neighbor's gum or chewing tobacco. The aircraft smelled of a combination of puke, AVGAS, farts, BO, testosterone and fear. The primary loadmaster got one of the other "loads" to help him carry a jug of water around, offering it up and down the aisle. It was tough to maneuver it but most of the jumpers took a drink. They taxied for a good ten minutes and then a loud grinding noise came from underneath the aircraft as the brakes were applied. The aircraft reached its hold position. Jack's aircraft was number five in line. Once the first aircraft got the green light for takeoff, it'd only be a few minutes until it was their turn. Jack always said a few Our Fathers and a few Hail Mary's at this point. He'd say a few more once the doors were opening and they were all standing waiting for the "green light."

He closed his eyes and put his head back. "Our Father, who art in heaven…" he recited to himself.

"Okay, here we go!" Yelled the jumpmaster. He sat in the furthest aft seat and leaned as far forward as he could with his seatbelt on and screamed, "All the Way!!"

Everyone, including all the Airmen whose careers were

focused on working with and supporting the 82d Airborne Division, shouted back over the revving engines with a booming "AIRBORNE!" The aircraft lurched forward as the brakes were released; the whole mass of bodies in the back of the aircraft was pushed toward the left as they made a hard right turn onto runway 23. The pilots now pushed the throttles forward to maximum thrust. All onboard got pushed toward the back of the aircraft as it accelerated. Some put their arms behind their heads or across their chests and grabbed the seat webbing to hold themselves upright. It only took about 30 seconds before the nose of the aircraft pointed skyward, then there was a drawn-out shutter as the wheels started to lift off the runway. They were airborne. The gear doors clunked closed behind the retracted wheels and the nose pitched up slightly higher and everyone could feel the aircraft accelerate a few more knots. After a few more seconds the nose started to level off and everyone adjusted to sitting up straight. The aircraft formation was going to make a low-level entry into the drop zone for the assault. It would take about 20 minutes to form up and then start heading to the low-level entry point. This part wasn't a lot of fun for most paratroopers. Every training mission was in preparation for combat, even on a currency jump. It cost a lot of JP4 fuel to fly these missions and the Air Force needed to get its money's worth in training out of each one of them. The crews would descend the formation down below 500 feet, simulating evading enemy radars and anti-aircraft-artillery, known as AAA, "triple-A". They'd hug the nape of the earth and execute "gun-jinks," a maneuver where the pilot pulls the aircraft up and pushes it over in order to complicate the enemy gunners' targeting solution, and standard evasive maneuvers. Once over the drop zone they would actually have to climb to get the troopers out. To the paratroopers in the back, it either equated to an exciting rollercoaster ride or an aggressive weight-loss program – usually the later and the stench of puke has a way of begetting more puke. Not many of the jumpers were excited about the next 45 minutes.

The formation was ready to descend. At this point the crew turned off the air conditioner. It was hot. A final reminder to secure loose items and tighten seat belts was given over the PA system; no one understood it, but knew based on routine that's what was said. The crew determined it had reached the entry point and both pilots pushed forward on their aircraft control yokes. Everyone in the back of the aircraft became weightless for a few seconds when the aircraft nose went from horizontal to pointing at the ground. Jack thought to himself that this crew was aggressive. After about 30 seconds the pilots started to "dish out" the aircraft – leveling off at about 300 feet; pushing everyone down into their seats. At this point, 80-pound rucks weighed 160 and heads slumped forward from the increased weight of the troopers' helmets. Now the fun began. The first maneuver was a gun jink followed by an evasive maneuver to the left and then back to the right. The aircraft then turned to the right and descended, leveled off followed by about a two-minute-long series of gun-jinks. The soldier right across from Jack blew first. He had a pathetic look of helplessness on his face right before his face exploded with a stream of manila colored vomit. Luckily for Jack, unluckily for his jump buddy, the vomit hit the soldier to Jack's right. The shower of food-particle-shrapnel sprayed the young soldier's reserve chute, face and helmet. He went next – he had to. He tried to pull out the airsickness bag the crew chief had passed around before takeoff, but he'd stuck it up in the top of his helmet and couldn't get the chinstrap undone fast enough. Justifiably, at that point of inevitability, he aimed his puke at puker number one, sprayed him across his shoulder and right side of his face. There were more eruptions up and down the length of the aircraft. The crew chief got a thumbs-up from the loadmaster to do what he could to keep the physiological incidents to a minimum. He passed around a plastic bottle of water – nobody cared about germs – and passed out more puke bags; nothing helped. The end of the low level route eventually came. It was a tough one but the crew got great training. There was an imperceptible sigh of relief when the aircraft began its gradual climb. The JM and assistant JM stood up and talked with the loadmaster. They looked at each other's checklists and nodded. The JM then squared off facing the front of the aircraft on the left side while the assistant JM

17

mirrored him on the right., their arms cocked backed, hands with open palms retracted into their armpits. They nodded and faced forward; simultaneously shooting their arms straightforward, fingers spread and shouted, "Twenty Minutes!" They extended and retracted their arms and outstretched fingers twice to indicate 20. The rear of the aircraft where the JMs and the loadmasters were positioned became more active. Checklist items were accomplished and preparations were made. The loadmaster caught the JM's attention and held his open hand out, level with the deck of the aircraft and in front of his mouth and made a blowing motion across his hand, like he was blowing him a kiss; he was passing on the wind readings he was getting from the cockpit over his headset intercom. He moved his head back and forth in that position and then held up eight fingers – the winds were eight knots. A few minutes later the JMs positioned themselves as before and this time shouted, "Ten Minutes!" At this point the actions became continuous. Checking and double-checking continued.

About four minutes later, "Get Ready!" shouted both JMs simultaneously.

"Port side personnel stand up!" The primary JM commanded. All jumpers on the left side of the aircraft echoed the command as they struggled to their feet, buddies helping buddies. After the long sit and the rough ride it was a relief to stand. Legs were shaken, crotches adjusted. Once everyone stabilized the assistant JM yelled, "Starboard side personnel stand up!" The starboard side jumpers echoed the command and also struggled to their feet.

"Hook Up!" Both JMs directed. All jumpers disconnected their static lines from the carrying handle of their reserves and hooked into the static line cable overhead. The jumpers steadied themselves with one hand against the outboard bulkhead.

"Check Static Lines!" Came the next call.

"Check Static Lines!" Came back the echoed response from the troopers. Everyone double-checked that the opening of their static line snap hook was facing the outboard side of the aircraft and that it was properly routed over their shoulders; it was then the responsibility of the jumper behind to check the routing of the static line for the jumper in front. If it was good, the jumper in the back would give him a tap on the shoulder or helmet.

"Check equipment!" The next command was barked out and echoed back. Everyone now did a final equipment check, ensuring all their straps were secured and they were ready to go.

"Sound off for equipment check!" Again echoed back by all the jumpers. Starting from the front of the aircraft, the last man in the stick, the group of troopers that would jump together, slapped the outboard butt cheek of the trooper in front of him and yelled, "OK!" and repeated the slap and call out on up the line, one jumper after another.

"Ok, ok, ok, ok, ok, ok, ok, ok, ok, ok," until the first jumper stomped his foot forward and put his arm out with an open palm toward the JM and sounded off.

"All ok jumpmaster!" said the first jumper. The jumpmaster slapped his hand signifying the check was complete. Now everyone stood with one hand holding their static line, properly securing it with two fingers' worth of a loop sticking out of the bottom, elbow up and arm positioned slightly forward. Once the "GO" command was given, spacing would be determined by extending the static line arm to create distance between the jumper behind and the jumper ahead. The aircraft lumbered along and having done this many times, Jack knew everybody was doing one final check inside their heads. He knew some thought about what could go wrong, some thought about the mission once they hit the ground and some just thought about hitting the ground.

"Standby!" The jumpmaster said. He made a motion to the first jumper with both arms pointing to a spot on the deck just short of the open door and helped position him. Jack was number three, so he could see out the door and he had a direct view of the lights. The light was red.

He figured he had time for one more, so to himself he started, "Our Father…" The light turned green.

"GO!!" the jumpmaster yelled and slapped the backside of the first jumper; he leaped out the door, both hands on his

19

reserve, slightly bent at the waist, and he was gone. Number two was out right behind him and then Jack. He barely had to take a step, planted his left foot and jumped out the door. As he cleared the edge of the door the prop and windblast hit him and turned him toward the tail of the aircraft. As this was happening he saw the first jumper streaming along the side of the aircraft with his arms down at his sides; hung – but it was a flash.

Jack was counting, "1000, 2000, 3000, 4000…" nothing… "5000 – shit!" Jack reached for his reserve ripcord on the right of the reserve, he grabbed the reserve handle on the left, pulled the ripcord, and it slipped out of his hand. He grabbed again, pulled… knife-edge sweep… again…again…*Poor, sweet Natalie…* was his last thought.

CHAPTER ONE

CAREER DECISIONS

Pat Donovan was conceived in May, 1960, the morning of the day his father burned-in on the Sicily drop zone on Fort Bragg, North Carolina. His mother, Natalie moved back to New Jersey and eventually remarried. Her new husband, John Donovan, the only father Pat ever knew, was an interesting, fun-loving guy who took good care of her and their other two children. He was in the Army and had also served at Fort Bragg as a rigger; the soldiers who pack the parachutes for jump operations, which is where he met Natalie shortly before Jack's death. John was by all accounts a great guy, loved by all, as was Pat's biological father, so he was told – over and over again. On several occasions he was reminded that he wasn't half the man Jack Gillespie was and on several others people pointed out to him that he wasn't half the man John, his adoptive father, was. John's background contributed a lot to Pat's decision to join the military, as did the legend of the father he never met. Natalie's deep but mostly contained resentment of how she was handled, gently but quickly assisted off of the post shortly after her husband's funeral ensured she would never support him joining the Army.

Pat didn't share that resentment. He learned over time of Jack's history and thought about it more and more as he got older. He had a pride he couldn't explain and was enamored with the military. Like all kids growing up in the 60's he played Army. He and his brother John and his sister Dawn, she played the nurse, and all their friends waged constant war in the woods next to their house. They all played sports too, but Pat loved to play war. Pat's Uncle Patrick, his namesake, served in the infantry in WWII with the 276th Infantry Division during Patton's historic push into Germany. His Uncle Pat never talked much about the experience, but Donovan admired him and that he had participated in such a monumental event. There were also several occasions where it was pointed out he couldn't hold a candle to his Uncle Pat either. When the time came, the Army was the first service he looked into. He loved airplanes and flying but wanted to join the Army. He wanted to prove himself, mainly to himself, and it seemed like the Army offered plenty of opportunities to do that. He talked to recruiters about flying helicopters. Whatever it was he did, he didn't want to be one of many; he wanted to stand out. John Donovan never tried to sway his son one way or the other; he loved him and trusted he'd make the decision for himself. John spent two tours in the Army one at Fort Indiantown Gap and one at Fort Bragg, a portion of the second in the stockade.

Pat eventually decided on the Air Force during his senior year at Lebanon Valley College in south-central Pennsylvania. He chose LVC for the physics and electrical engineering program, but also to play football. He loved football and played little league, high school and through college. He found honor in it and loved the danger and risks and the opportunities to be brave. He also loved the camaraderie. By his senior year he was done with his major, took a bunch of electives and played ball. He also did a lot of what he also really enjoyed doing – drinking with his friends. He had plenty of free time, too much. He'd gotten into a couple of nasty bar fights but luckily he was never one of the ones the police hauled in. He and a couple of his buddies got drunk and broke into the dining hall late one night. They grabbed rolls and bread; everything else was locked up in coolers. As they were heading for the door they'd pried open, a Security Guard spotted them. Pat and one of the other two, Randy, ran left and the third, Rob, ran right. The college had a little jail and Rob spent the night in it. The next morning he was brought to the Dean who put the word out that Rob was going to be suspended if the other two perpetrators of the Dining Hall robbery didn't come forward. By noon Pat and Randy were standing tall in front of the Dean's desk. The Dean was a good man and cut the boys a big break and put them on probation; he even let Pat finish out the football season.

It was about that same time that Pat started trying to figure out what he was going to do when he graduated. Once he'd committed to the Air Force they let him fly all right, but in the belly of a B-52. It was the early '80s and America needed

"SAC-trained-killers," as members of the Air Force's Strategic Air Command were known. These men would man the bomber fleet poised to wage nuclear war toe to toe with the Russkies. Despite what Pat Donovan wanted, the USAF needed him to be a bombardier, also known as a radar navigator, on a B-52. He didn't get to man the controls or even have a window, but he did get to fly. His job was to guide the aircraft, manage, arm and aim the weapons to hit their targets; he was good at it. His first duty assignment was in the 325th Bomb Squadron, 92d Bomb Wing, Fairchild Air Force Base, near Spokane, Washington. He loved the area and excelled at his craft. The unit had all of what Donovan loved, drinking, sports, women and training for war. He won several annual command-wide Bombing Competitions and got "best bombs" in all of the unit's Operational Readiness Inspections. These were a big deal. They were the test SAC put their bomb wings through – doing well at one got the Wing Commander another star; not doing well get them fired. Donovan advanced rapidly and moved through every position he could hold. He upgraded ahead of his peers. He got cocky. He started pushing the limits of "crew rest," the regulation mandating time off before and between flights and the "bottle to throttle" rule – eight hours bottle to throttle meant eight hours of not drinking before takeoff. He never busted the rule, but used it to maximize his drinking time, but he did stay on top of his game as far as his leadership was concerned. He was handpicked by the squadron commander to fly the annual airshows, and he did, six of the eight years he spent at Fairchild.

Nika Kassymbek was born in Tashkent, Uzbekistan, in 1976. She grew up outside the city with her parents and sister Ulyana and brothers Uktam and Aaqib. Nika was the oldest and Aaqib was the youngest. Uktam was three years younger than Nika but they did everything together. They went to school at the same time and when they became teenagers together they got tired of their life in Tashkent and were anxious to find out what else the world had to offer. Nika saw her parents struggle day to day to put food on the table and survive with the bare necessities. She knew she had to get out and maybe she would be able to help her family when she became rich and famous. She put all her energy toward her English classes and studied after school and late at night with Uktam. She went to every American movie she could and worked on her accent. Her desire to leave clouded her judgment and her desire for something better led her to fall in with "dishonorable people," as her mother called them. Uktam was equally driven but wasn't ready to act on it the day Nika left. She had met a man; someone named Yusef. Yusef was a young man known in the area as a man with "options." He was a "traditionalist" and sported a long beard. He was political and had strong opinions about everything, especially that the West was the root of all evil. Yusef and Nika started spending time together; more like Nika was around Yusef and whatever he had going on. She was one of many young girls and boys that Yusef kept around him, employing them in various schemes and businesses. He promised Nika access to the world. He was true to his reputation; one night Yusef had talked Nika into crossing the border into Kazakhstan, for the "opportunity of a lifetime." With a bad combination of too much vodka and hope, Nika crossed the border and her life was changed forever. She never had a chance to say goodbye to her family; only Uktam knew of the possibility of her running away someday, but he thought he would have gone with her. She left that night in April of 1992 and it was several years before her family knew where she was; she never told them what she was doing. After that night she never heard from Yusef again. She spent several years in Russia as a "hospitality girl" as an imitation American. She was beautiful, tall for her age, blonde-brown hair, caramel brown eyes and the body of an athlete. She spoke in English or used a phony accent, speaking in Russian or Uzbek with an American accent. After a few years her handlers became bold and wanted to expand their market share, and they thought no better place than the USA. Shortly after they set her up in the US near Los Angeles, she escaped and after a few weeks made her way to boring Watertown, New York, and because of or despite her looks and accent she landed a job at a small bar. She Americanized her name to Nikki.

She made enough to rent an apartment and the first night she spent there alone was like she'd just been let out of prison. She had no fear, no worries; everything was quiet and calm. That first night in her own, small dank apartment she rested, really rested for the first time since she was a little girl. One late night when she was coming back from the bar as she was unlocking her apartment door she noticed something out of the corner of her eye, off to the side of the porch. She saw movement and realized it was a kitten with its head stuck in a McDonald's bag someone had thrown over the fence that surrounded the apartment. It rested up against the porch and the kitten was busy going after whatever leftovers were inside.

"Hey kitty," she said softly. The kitten started, backing out of the bag hissing, its back bowed up. "Hey there little one, it's ok, it's ok." The kitten softened its posture and slowly started moving toward Nikki's outstretched hand. It nuzzled and rubbed its tiny head against her.

"It's ok little one, come on," she said and picked up the kitten. She now had a friend. She brought the little cat into her apartment even though pets weren't allowed, and took a washcloth, wetted it with warm water and rubbed down her new roommate. As she stroked the kitten she got a good whiff of him; he stank.

"Stinky. That'll be your name little fella," she said as she held him up in the air. "I'm Nikki and I'll take care of you."

0800, 26 Dec 2000, Paris, France, Café Pierre. It was an unusually warm day and the café had opened up its outdoor-seating. A tall dark man sat alone at the far table on Rue Madeleine. The waitress approached and asked, in French, what the man wanted. In French, he ordered a café au lait and a croissant. He read the newspaper. On page one the story was about the suicide car bombing three days earlier in Ninovia, Georgia. The story described the carnage, how a vehicle laden with explosives drove into the central market and detonated, killing 46 people and wounding 117. The waitress came back with the customer's coffee and croissant.

"Would you like anything else?"

In Arabic he said, holding up the front page to her, "This was me. I did this. I zip tied the sheep's hands to the steering wheel and his feet to the gas pedal and made sure he knew if he didn't do this, I would kill him right there and then slaughter his entire family. Of course the sheep did my bidding and now he is glorified." He giggled and put the paper down, paused and then said again in Arabic, "I know you don't understand me, you French cow. Your country too will soon be cleansed. Now remove your stench from the range of my nostrils."

She looked confused. "I don't understand."

In French he replied, "I apologize. No, thank you. I don't need anything else; this is perfect." Yusef sighed, shook his head and took a sip of coffee. He would depart for America later that day.

CHAPTER TWO

WATERTOWN WATERING HOLE

Donovan, like everybody else in the military, had heard of the reputation of the 10th Mountain Division. He worked with an Air Force enlisted man at Langley who was an Enlisted Terminal Attack Controller, the modern day term for a forward air controller, who had actually been stationed at Fort Drum. After talking with him, and considering that Fort Drum was about five hours from his folks in New Jersey, he figured why not? He submitted the necessary paperwork and since being an Air Liaison Officer with the Army was a less than desirable assignment for an Air Force aviator, he got the posting within a day of his request, which was fine with him. He passed through New Jersey and stopped in to see his family for a few days before heading up to Fort Drum. They were glad he was closer; still five plus hours away, but closer than across the country in California, Washington or Colorado.

Donovan had picked up two dogs while stationed at Fairchild: Buck, a big, lovable black lab and Steve, a yellow lab. Steve was much older and starting to have medical problems. They were all best friends and Donovan spent most of his off duty time making sure Buck and Steve were happy. Donovan was happy if he was with them and they were happy if they were with each other, and with Donovan. They'd go on long walks, camp, swim, whatever he thought Buck and Steve liked to do.

After a few days Donovan headed up to Watertown to look for a place to live. He found a house in Evans Mills, just west of Fort Drum. Donovan reported in to the unit after a week in the area in early August of 2001 and started his training. It was obvious to the guys in the unit that Donovan had a bit of a chip on his shoulder. He seemed to always be conscious of any type of challenge to his knowledge or physical prowess, or drinking ability. He never admitted to it, but the latter was the one he seemed to be proudest of. To Donovan, at this new unit, in a new career field, everything seemed like a challenge. He went out with some of the guys bar-hopping in the evenings and that became a competition too. They'd drive to the post and park their cars, take a taxi to a bar, and a second bar, then a third and fourth before taking another taxi back to the post where they would sleep on the floor of the squadron. They'd drink some of the local brews and ultimately turn to shots. Donovan had an affinity for tequila; he loved tequila and it didn't have the same negative effect it did on his buddies. They would shoot Jack Daniels, Jameson's, Bushmill's or Jägermeister, but when the tequila came out Donovan was in charge, so he always went for the tequila. On one of the nights in late August they were running their routine, the group ended up in the bar where Nikki worked. That night would change everything.

Nikki had another friend besides her cat Stinky: Jodie, who had been her friend since Nikki showed up in Watertown. They eventually found several things they had in common, one of which was they both had grown up in a maelstrom of abuse and neglect. The consequences of that fact drew them close together, alternately comforting each other through their respective trials. They hung out together and if they had nothing to do, which was often, they'd do it with each other, usually smoking and drinking, way too many cigarettes and pot when they could get it. They dated the same type of men, always losers, and then they'd take care of each other through the aftermath of bad relationship after bad relationship. Nikki was pretty but tried to hide it while Jodie was plain and a bit frumpy but always acted like she was a runway model even though she preferred to dress like a lumberjack. And, although the product of a rough childhood and struggling with alcoholism, she always had a smile on her face. She actually carried off how she came across pretty well, usually, and she was the one hit on as often as Nikki. It was her self-confidence, or acting like someone with self-confidence.

Jodie came to see Nikki at the bar during the first week of September as the low sun shot a blinding ray of rare Upstate New York sunshine into the bar. The three old men hunched over their beers turned to see through squinting eyes who was coming in.

"Hi sister!" Jodie skipped up to Nikki.

"Jo-Day! What's up sexy?" A big smile came onto Nikki's face as she continued to wipe down the bar.

"Not much. Just thought I'd see how the other half lives."

"You mean the half with jobs?"

"Ouch! Little early to be giving me shit isn't it? We haven't even had a beer yet."

"Nah, it's never too early, you ought to know that by now," Nikki quipped. The door opened again, the three men pivoted on their bar stools, squinting at the door like before. Jodie spun her stool around completely, not stopping and coming to a halt again eye to eye with Nikki. She'd spotted a tall, young, dark haired man with the quick glance.

"Ooh, who's that?" Jodie asked, leaning in toward Nikki. Nikki looked up with one eye, keeping the other closed against the sun as the door swung back shut and brought the comfortable darkness back to the bar.

"Beats the shit out of me. Never seen him before. Sure not from around here."

"Yeah I know. He looks like he's got all his teeth and hair and weighs under 250 pounds."

The man approached the bar and sat down next to Jodie off to her left side.

"Hi, how you doing gorgeous?" he said to Jodie.

"Who? Me?" Jodie pivoted her head left and right, then pointed at herself.

"Yes you! How are you? What exciting things have you done today? What have you got planned for this evening?" He rested his elbow on the bar and his chin in his hand.

"Shiiittt who are you, Prince Charming?" she laughed and looked at Nikki.

"Maybe that's exactly who he is hon; maybe *he's* your Prince Charming." Nikki continued to wipe down the bar. "Is that you buddy? Are you Prince Charming?"

"Well, maybe I am, and maybe I'm the Big Bad Wolf. Isn't half the fun not knowing for sure?" He sat up straight and rotated his bar stool to face Jodie. Jodie laughed and squinted at him as she leaned closer. She didn't have her contacts in or her

29

glasses on, and she didn't want to put them on in front of this potentially handsome and charming stranger, but she couldn't really see him that well.

"Let me see your teeth there handsome," Jodie said as she sat up straight. He smiled a broad smile and showed his teeth with a growl. "Nope, he's Prince Charming. Those teeth are too nice and there's no strands of Little Red Riding's hood in there." Jodie laughed and snorted. Nikki started laughing when she heard Jodie snort; Prince Charming started laughing too. He swung his chair back around, facing the bar.

"Okay my good bar waitress, I would like one of your finest beers."

"All right, Bud Light it is." Nikki replied as she grabbed the bottle from the cooler below the bar and twisted off the top, tossing it into the trash can behind her without looking as she handed him the beer.

"What is this? Do you not have anything a little more flavorful?"

"Sure. Do you know what you'd like? Here's our beer menu." Nikki handed him a laminated piece of paper with a list of a dozen beers on it.

"Well, what do you recommend?" he asked. Nikki pulled another Bud Light out of the cooler, twisted off the top, threw it in the trash and stacked it next to the other untouched Bud Light on the bar in front of him. Jodie laughed.

"I'll take those if you're not going to drink them," she said, grabbing both bottles and sliding them in front of her.

"But of course. You're welcome gorgeous. I will have one of your Saranac Adirondack Lagers, if you don't mind." He grabbed a bar napkin and used it to clean a spot in front of him.

"Okay then, coming right up." Nikki retrieved the requested beer out of the cooler, opened it with a bottle opener and paused. "Glass?"

"Yes thank you," he replied. She poured the beer into the glass, pausing twice to let the foam settle.

"Here you go hotshot, sorry, Prince Charming." Nikki pushed the beer toward him. It was at that point that she recognized the man, she had never seen him without his beard before and he's all be eliminated his accent. Chills went up her spine and she froze. This man was responsible for the horror and pain she endured over the last decade working as a prostitute in a Russian brothel.

"Thank you my dear." He reached for the beer, briefly grabbing Nikki's hand. She looked up at him and paused for a split second, then quickly pulled her hand back, glancing at Jodie. Jodie was in mid sip and froze when he grabbed Nikki's hand.

"Oh boy," Jodie said under her breath and looked at Nikki, then down at the bar. She grabbed the two bottles of Bud Light and somewhat clumsily got to her feet. "Ok, I'm going to go shoot some pool. You kids have fun."

"Where are you going gor - " Prince Charming tried to inject.

"Save it, Slick," Nikki said to him, hiding her knowledge of who he was.

"I'll see you in a few, doll," Jodie said to Nikki and winked at her.

"Okay kid, see you in a few." Nikki stared daggers at the man who just hurt her best friend and played along. It was obvious that Yusef did not recognize Nikki. "What'd you do that for. you dick?"

"What...?" He shrugged his shoulders.

"You flirted with Jodie and then you make some lame ass move on me?"

"It means nothing, none of it. I was just having fun...jeezzz...I was just having some fun." He started to stand up.

"Okay, okay, sit down there Romeo, drink your beer, no big deal, just sit down and drink your beer. Oh, you owe for those two Bud Lights too"

"Gotcha Princess, gotcha. I got the beers, no problem." He settled back onto his bar stool and took a sip of his beer, then let out an audible "mm-ahh..." of satisfaction. Nikki wrapped a hand around the short baseball bat they kept behind the bar for unruly customers and squeezed it until her fingernails turned white.

The door pushed open again with the accompanying

burst of sunlight and everyone squinted. Donovan walked in with two of his fellow Airmen. They maneuvered over to the pool table and he sauntered up, sitting at the bar next to Yusef. Just as he did, Nikki was reengaging with him. She let go of the bat and continued drying beer mugs.

"Hey, what's your name by the way?" She pressed the point to get a reaction and to make sure he didn't know who she was. "You just bought more beers in the last five minutes then these three guys have in the last hour." She glared at the three figures stooped over the bar. They looked up, paused and then looked back down at the bar cradling their beers. The old men weren't together; they were just in synch.

"My name is..." He paused for a second.

"It's not a trick question. Forget it, Slick. Just being friendly." Nikki went back to wiping down the bar, something she did a lot; it didn't need it and was more of a habit than anything else. She picked up one of the empties. She wanted to hit him in the head with the bottle.

"You mean working your tip!" Donovan said as he tapped the fistful of money he had in his hand on the bar.

"What do you know about it wise guy? You just walked through the door about fifteen seconds ago," Nikki said curtly to Donovan.

"Yeah Sport, none of your business," Yusef said in quick succession.

"Sport? Where are you from, buddy?" Donovan looked at him, tilting his head to one side like the RCA dog.

"He's from Canada," Nikki said.

"Yeah, and I'm from Zimbabwe," Donovan retorted.

"Okay, okay, no big deal people. How 'bout I get your attention focused on something more important? How 'bout I buy the house a round?" Yusef said with a big smile on his face.

"Well now I don't care where you're from. Hey fellas, come on over here. This fine gentleman is buying the house a round!" Donovan shouted over to the pool table.

An hour or so went by and everyone seemed to be having a good time. Jodie was shooting pool with the Airmen and Donovan was ferrying drinks back and forth. Nikki was working the bar expertly and at the same time chatting frequently with Yusef, who hadn't moved, enjoying the ability to tease and taunt him with anonymity, or so she thought. The door swung open again and a tall man with a baseball hat came in through the still blinding light. The sun was starting to go down and now it actually shone through the open door. He approached the bar and sat. Donovan had come back to the bar for another round but looked back over at his guys to see they both still had full beers so he sat to the right of the new arrival.

"Hey Sir, how's it going?" Donovan asked him.

"Don't call me Sir; I work for a living," the man said without looking up from the bar. "Hon, can I have a shot of Jim Beam and a Miller Lite?"

"Sorry about that, looks like we're all kinda sensitive about names today." Donovan stuck his hand out toward his new bar mate. The man turned toward Donovan, looked him over for about five seconds, then took his hand. As he turned to greet him, Donovan noticed his hat. It was a VFW hat with several pins on it. The two he noticed were a Purple Heart and the 101st Division Patch.

"You in the Army? Or, were you in the Army?" Donovan stammered, half nervousness, half alcohol.

"I'm in but getting ready to get out."

"Oh, quitting? Just kidding... no, wait. Why are you getting out?" Donovan stumbled to get the words right.

"Easy kid, I'm retiring. Coming up on thirty years."

"Thirty years! Holy shit that's almost those two kids at the pool tables' ages added together."

"Not quite, but yeah, it's a long time."

Yusef was listening to the conversation, intermittently sipping his beer.

"Shit yeah, it's a long time. Let me buy you a beer." Donovan reached for his wallet.

"No, no, that's ok, your awe and admiration is good enough." He stopped Donovan's hand from coming out of his pocket with his wallet. Nikki laughed as she dried a glass.

"That's quite a commitment, soldier. Thank you for your tremendous service." Yusef hoisted his glass in a toast. The old

33

soldier lifted his glass slightly off the bar.

"Thanks."

"Hey, hey where did you get the Purple Heart?" Donovan asked.

"That's not for polite conversation," he responded.

"Well, no offense." Donovan rotated his bar stool to the old soldier. "But then why do you have it on your dang hat? If you don't mind me asking? Is it so you don't forget?"

"No...no..." he said hesitatingly. "I've got all that tucked away *inside* the hat." He tapped the side of his head. "I wear it on the *outside* so that other people will remember, that there are Americans who leave everything behind and go kill people for our country and sometimes they get hurt doing it." He took a sip of beer.

"So, where did you get it?" Donovan missed the significance of the exchange.

"Viet Nam," he said, staring into his beer glass.

"Oh." Donovan paused. "Is that when you were in the 101st?"

"Yeah. Now I think we've gone down this road enough, okay? How's about I buy you and this fella here a drink?"

"Okay, okay, but two conditions," Donovan asserted as he raised a finger skyward, hesitated for a couple seconds, then raised a second finger.

"Okay, never had conditions on buying a *dude* a beer before."

"Okay, okay... this guy," he pointed to Yusef, "has to tell you his name and you have to tell us your name, otherwise no deal." He crossed his arms on the bar.

"Okay, no deal."

"Wait, c'mon, just agree," Donovan pleaded.

"Okay, my name is Shawn Wallace, I'm a Sergeant Major here at the 10th Mountain," he said, extending his hand again to Donovan. They shook. Then he turned to the stranger to his right. "Okay, I've heard folks calling you Prince Charming but what's your name?"

Nikki was still drying that same glass, now suddenly more interested in the conversation.

34

"My name is... uh..." he hesitated.

"It's not a trick question," the Sergeant Major interjected.

"That's what I said the first time around," added Nikki.

"Okay, I'm sorry, my name is Bud...Buddy Lightner." he said and waited for response. Donovan, Nikki and the Sergeant Major all burst out laughing.

"Holy shit dude, why don't you call yourself, 'Door Jamb Shotglass' or 'Squeaky Barstoolenstien' or 'Beam, James Beam," the Sergeant Major said through laughter. They all continued to laugh for a good minute. Now Yusef was laughing too. "Okay man, here's the deal, we'll give you one more chance, I don't care if it's a made up name or not, but it better be good. If not, I'm picking it, and I've got a talent for picking humiliating nicknames.

"All right, okay, I'm sorry. My name is Yusef."

"Okay Yusef, why was that so hard? We're all glad to meet you I'm sure, right everybody?" he asked the small crowd around the bar. There were a few muffled, "Yeah, yeahs...pleasure to meet you's..." At that point Yusef grabbed his beer, got up and headed over to the pool table. He walked up and started talking to Jodie. She was shooting pool, but she started to pay more and more attention to Yusef.

Nikki felt sick that Yusef was there. She didn't know what he did after he got her across the Uzbekistan border and she didn't know why he was here.

"Interesting cat, huh Sergeant Major?" Donovan took a drink.

"Yes he is. And don't call me Sergeant Major in here, unless you're in the service...wait, you're not an officer are you?"

"Why yes, yes I am. Major Pat Donovan; nice to meet you Sergeant Major." He stuck out his hand to shake again. Wallace got to his feet, shook Donovan's hand and was reaching for his wallet. "Whoa, whoa... Sergeant Major, don't leave on account of me. This is probably your local watering hole. Stay, stay. C'mon, I'll buy you another beer and I'll leave you alone. Okay?"

"Okay, sure Sir, thanks, but I can buy my own beer. What unit are you in, the 10th?" he asked Donovan.

"I'm an ALO aligned with 2nd Brigade."

"An ALO! Well, then Hell yes you can buy me a beer Air Force! Goddamn, I should charge you just for sitting next to me. Air Force? Shiiittt..." He shook his head and sat down. "Look Major, after today, I don't know you, okay? I mean we don't run skipping toward each other on the parade field on Monday morning, right? This is just one of those accidental, co-occupancy situations. We just happen to be sitting next to each other at this bar." He squared his barstool off with Donovan's and made several very deliberate hand gestures.

"Okay, all right, geez. Take it easy Sergeant Major, holy shit. Relax. For shit sake, you're quite the Air Force-phobe. I'm sure you'll accept the flight of A-10s we'll roll in to save your ass, but you just don't want to be seen in a local bar with us." Donovan rotated his barstool back square with the bar and rested his elbows on the lip, shaking his head.

"Exactly! That's exactly it! No offense." Wallace slapped Donovan on the back.

"Who would take offense to that?" Donovan started laughing.

"What did you fly before they grounded you?" Wallace asked Donovan.

"They didn't ground me, I'm on ground duty. B-52s."

"B-52s! We still got those? Shit, we had them in Nam. The only thing they could hit was the ground!" Wallace chuckled.

"So how the Hell did you end up here flyboy?"

"Well, since you don't look like you're going anywhere and I just bought you a beer, I'll tell you."

"Sure, go right ahead. If I finish this beer and your story is boring, I hope you don't mind if I get up and leave."

"No not at all, I'd expect nothing less." Donovan shifted on the bar stool and turned it slightly toward Wallace and took a sip of his beer. "So, believe it or not, I was pretty good at what I did as a SAC bombardier. My leadership appreciated my skills and I progressed fairly well in the different duty positions in the bomb squadron."

"This better start picking up, I'm almost done with my

beer and you're boring the shit out of me." Wallace made an exaggerated yawning gesture.

"Anyway," Donovan continued. "One of the bennies of being squared away, at least at the 325th Bomb Squadron was I got to fly the airshow every year."

"What the Hell does a bombardier do during an airshow?" Wallace asked between swigs of beer. He looked over at Donovan and pointed to an imaginary line on his beer bottle showing how much was left.

"Actually, not a whole heck of a lot; mainly safety of flight stuff like airspeed, altitude, stuff like that. Again, anyway, so I was on the Standardization and Evaluation, Stan-Eval crew, the guys that give check rides and the A/C, sorry, the aircraft commander was a great guy, who did nothing his whole career but fly. He had something like 5000 hours, that's a lot, in the jet and he had a great reputation as the best flyer in the unit, if not in the Air Force, as far as BUFF pilots go."

"What's that stand for again…Oh yeah, Big Ugly Fat Fellow, or Friend or something like that right?" Wallace asked.

"Something like that. So anyway…" Donovan took a drink and motioned to Nikki to bring two more. "…Bud, that was his name flew all the air shows and anytime they wanted a B-52 flyby, he was at the yoke. After a couple of incidents," Donovan made air-quotes, "A couple of times where Bud really pushed the limit, flew real low, stuff like that, he started getting a few folks very concerned about safety. The squadron commander, Lieutenant Colonel Mark McGeehan, was a great guy and we became great friends. He figured as the squadron commander, he had to do something. On one particular mission at the Yakima bombing range Bud brought the 186,000-pound B-52 down to an altitude less than 50 feet; some said later it was ten. The copilot just about wrestled with Bud to take control of the aircraft since he thought they were going to hit a ridgeline they were approaching. The co finally announced over the intercom that he was getting airsick so everyone could hear it, standard procedure at that point is to climb up out of low-level flight. Bud pulled up, they cleared the ridgeline by like 50 feet. The co said Bud called him a pussy.

"Big plane like that, going that fast, that low, shit I'd be a pussy too," Wallace offered.

"Well, the co comes back to the squadron and tells McGeehan, McGeehan goes to the Bomb Wing leadership and tells them to ground Bud. So, get this, they think Bud's flying is good for 'business,' you know, sells extra hotdogs at the airshow or something, so they say something like, 'Thanks for your interest in national defense, but he's gonna keep flying.' Or something like that.

"So what's McGeehan do?" Wallace asks, now seemingly interested.

"Well, he tells them, 'Ok, then I'm the only one that's gonna fly with him.'

'HooAh. Good for him.'

"Yeah well, so he does. He doesn't let any copilot in the squadron fly with Bud. Anytime Bud is flying McGeehan is sitting next to him. So, the final airshow is coming up. SAC decided to shut down the squadron and they were going to move the BUFFs to other bases, so this is it, the big finale for a unit that's been at that base for like 50 years. Oh, this is 1994 by the way, forgot to mention that.

"So what's McGeehan doing now?"

"Hang on, that's the story, that's the worst part of it."

"Wait a second, I think I heard about this…"

"Not from somebody that was there. Just hang on Sergeant Major, let me tell it right, and you are getting the Readers Digest version."

"Ok, go ahead."

"So, I just gotta say, I really can't tell you how great a guy McGeehan was, I mean the best, athlete, handsome, great sense of humor, great family, beautiful wife and great kids… he was awesome. And, he helped me out. He was an academy grad, '78, and helped me get a job at the Air Force Academy. So, a week before the airshow I gotta leave for my assignment. I ask him if he can help get my orders slipped so I can fly and he tells me no. To this day I think it was partly to keep from getting in the jet with Bud, especially in an airshow, one more time. Went on a TDY once together up to Alaska. He gave me a ton of responsibility and whatever I did; no matter how hard I worked it was so I didn't disappoint him. Now, I flew with Bud dozens and dozens of times, we were on the same crew. I liked him and I have to admit, I thought it was a blast when he pushed that plane to the limit. There were times I should have piped up about how we flew, but I didn't. I got complacent, I didn't even put my chute on during low levels anymore, figured I'd never have time to get out." Donovan wiped the bottle of his fresh beer down with a bar napkin and pauses for a few seconds.

"You ok there Major?" Wallace asked.

"Sure, anyway, get this, the Monday before the airshow a disgruntled Airman comes back onto base and shoots 26 people, five died. That Friday, four days later, they're running a practice flight for the airshow, Bud's flying, McGeehan's in the copilots seat and another friend of mine, I guess I'd say he took my place on that flight, Ken was the navigator and one of the Wing Colonels was in the pilot jump seat. That Friday, they all die in a ball of fire just off the side of the Fairchild runway." Donovan pauses, has a long draw off of his beer and sits still for a few seconds.

"Wow, that's horrible, sorry Major." Wallace takes a drink.

"Yeah, for most of those guys it was going to be their last flight, I think Bud was going to retire. All the families were there with champagne and picnic lunches. The wives and kids saw their husbands and fathers die in an instant. So, anyway, I was an ADO, assistant director of operations, so I got caught up in the frag pattern a bit. My Air Force career isn't over, but I'm not going to have to buy new rank anytime soon, or ever."

Jodie sat on a stool in the corner by the pool table; Yusef was standing between her legs, nuzzled up close. They both still had their pool cues in their right hands. Jodie was smiling and giggling and Yusef's eyes were riveted on hers. Nikki watched what was going on with Yusef and Jodie but didn't know what to do. She didn't know who he was now; it had been years. But why was he here? She started to feel foolish thinking that he wouldn't know her, that he wasn't here for her.

"So then I'm going to see you tomorrow right?" Yusef

brushed strands of Jodie's hair out of her eyes.

"Why sure tall, drunk and fuzzily handsome, but what about tonight? You ain't going anywhere are you?" Jodie reached up and adjusted Yusef's collar.

"Ah, gorgeous, now that you've agreed to help me out with my little project, I should really go get things arranged, so I have to leave early in the morning. When you come back from your task we will go out dining and dancing in Canada, just like we talked about. You should go too. I'm going to have to leave very early in the morning to make it to Manhattan by 8 o'clock. I'm going to drive there, just to see how long it takes and maybe see some sites."

"You're talking AM!?" Jodie stood up on the cross rungs of the bar stool.

"Yes silly, but when you go I'll have all the information you need so it should be fun. Why don't you take your friend the barmaid with you?"

"Well I will, but I wouldn't let her hear you calling her a barmaid. So, what's any of that got to do with tonight? I'm raring to go. The night is young - whoohoo...!!" she shouted, again standing up on the rungs of the barstool. Yusef grabbed her around the waist and guided her back down.

"Okay, let's go. We can go have a different kind of fun." He wrapped one arm around her waist and lifted her up off the bar stool and headed toward the door.

Jodie started laughing, spilling her beer on the floor and then straining back to see Nikki and waved. "Good sister night, I'll call you tomorrow."

"No, Jodie, wait, wait!" Nikki moved from around and bar and ran after Yusef and Jodie. "Jodie, you have to stay with me and help me close, remember?"

"Come on sister, you don't need me for that," Jodie leaned in to whisper to Nikki, but her voice was still loud, "Hey, are you kidding, this guy's great and, well, I'm due, aren't I?"

"No, not this guy, not now, not tonight, actually not ever, not this guy." Nikki grabbed Jodie by the arm.

"Hey, fuck off, what are you jealous?" Jodie pulled her arm away from Nikki's grasp.

"No Jodie, please, just stay here with me."

"Okay, okay, geez, I don't know what your problem is, alright I'll stay." Jodie looked back at Yusef and shrugged her shoulders. Yusef looked back and waited until Nikki turned to get back behind the bar. When he saw she wasn't looking, he motioned for Jodie to meet him around the back of the bar with an arm wave and mouthing the words. Jodie sat down at the bar and ordered a drink. After a few minutes, Nikki went in the back to get more beer. When she came back Jodie was gone.

"So Sergeant Major Wallace, 10th Mountain Division, look we've been talking for, like what, hours, right? Give me something, some pearl of wisdom," Donovan beseeched.

"What kinda wisdom you looking for kid... I mean Sir?"

"Well, you've been in combat, been wounded, the kind of wisdom that comes from going through that." Donovan pushed a beer toward Wallace.

"Well, okay, I don't have any wisdom, just one piece of advice. I have more than one, but I'm only gonna share one here, tonight. I've been faced with this situation a few times in my long career, and I'm gonna say something to you but you really have to make up your own mind about all this," the Sergeant Major went on, twirling his empty beer glass on the bar. "When you get in the shit and you're going to have to make a choice between killing non-Americans or getting Americans killed – kill the non-Americans. That's your job." He let go of his glass and turned and faced Donovan. "You're not out there to be fair. There ain't nothing fair about war. You're out there to get it done and get as many of our guys home as you can. There's going to be plenty of time to debate and mull over moral dilemmas but not when the bullets are flying. You understand what I'm saying?" he paused. "Do you read me Major?"

"Yeah, I read you Sergeant Major." Donovan took a few gulps of his beer.

"Okay then, my work is done here. You got the tab, right Major? Kind of a fee for service deal, right?" He got up and headed for the door.

"Sure, sure Sergeant Major. I'll see you on the parade field," Donovan yelled at him as he opened the door. The

Sergeant Major gave Donovan the finger over his shoulder as he passed through the door.

Donovan sat quietly at the bar; he became pensive after the conversation with Sergeant Major Wallace. He glanced up while taking a drink from his beer and caught Nikki out of the corner of his eye. He put down his beer and looked at her. He really hadn't noticed how beautiful she was. He also noticed she looked deep in thought or sad, starring at the floor slowly wiping down a beer mug. Nikki must have felt Donovan's eyes on her, she looked up and over at him, their eyes met. Donovan got down off of his bar stool and positioned himself across from Nikki.

"Hi, Pat Donovan." He stuck out his hand.

"I know; we've already met." Nikki grasped his hand.

****

Nikki and Donovan struck up a romance the night they met in Nikki's bar. They went out a couple times to the few restaurants in Watertown and the surrounding areas. They drove south to Syracuse and had a fun night of eating and drinking at the Dinosaur Bar-B-Cue. They had a great meal and a few drinks, it was loud, so they leaned in to talk to each other over and over. On one of the lean-ins, Nikki kissed Donovan on the neck. He put both his hands on her shoulders, gently moved her upright then gave her a long deep kiss. They quickly got serious. Nikki loved the stability Donovan seemed to have, she needed something to hang on to and he loved her vulnerability, her accent and that she was mysterious. In just a few short weeks Nikki moved in with Donovan and he started to think about her all the time. Donovan realized there was a lot Nikki didn't tell him about her past, how she ended up in Watertown, really anything. She never talked about anything except what was happening right now or in the near future. To him, she always seemed to be worried. He tried to make her understand he wasn't going anywhere, at least that's what he thought.

CHAPTER THREE

WHAT THE HELL JUST HAPPENED

After checking in with the unit admin troop Donovan knocked on the commander's doorframe.

"Enter," came the reply from inside the office. Donovan opened the door and stepped up to the front of the commander's desk. Before he got a few steps inside the door Lieutenant Colonel Coltrain came out from behind the desk and stuck his hand out to greet Donovan. "Dude! How's it going buddy?"

"Good sir, how you doing?"

"Oh, I'm doing. Sit down." Coltrain pointed to a red pleather couch next to his desk and went back and sat in his desk chair. "So, how's the training going?"

"Good sir, no issues, lot of fun."

"No shit right, best gig in the Air Force."

"Yep, not bad, and the guys are great."

"Oh yeah, top notch. Hey, I wanted to tell you there's not a whole lot I can do for you, being passed over a couple of times and all. But, if there is anything I can do, I'll do it."

"Yes sir, thanks."

"Well, first thing I'm going to do is make you the Director of Support. Can't make you the DO, but that'll be something anyway."

"Yes sir, thanks, that's great. What is that?"

"Get with Sergeant Elder after the staff meeting and he'll let you know what they do over there. You know, take care of the vehicles and maintenance equipment and all that."

"Ok sir, sounds great." Donovan put his hands on his knees and leaned forward, but paused to make sure that's all the boss wanted to talk about. Coltrain looked up and caught the posture cue.

"See ya!" Donovan got up and turned to salute Coltrain, he was looking down at some notes but caught site of the frozen figure standing at attention in front of him, looked up, "Thanks Dude, see you in the staff meeting." Coltrain gave a relaxed salute, still with his pencil in his hand. Donovan dropped his and about faced and walked out the door.

The 20th Air Support Operations Squadron's weekly staff meeting was just getting started. It was 11 September 2001.

"Okay, next slide," directed Coltrain, advancing the slide show that highlighted his unit's issues and activities. Coltrain had taken over a few weeks earlier from his predecessor, who was unceremoniously canned for what the Air Force leadership termed, "A loss of confidence in his leadership." "Stacks" as he was known by his Air Force call sign, given for his love of gambling, a combat veteran of Desert Storm, was about average height, had the lean physique of a long distance runner, but could also knock out seventy-five pushups for his fitness test. His hairline had started receding, probably the day he was born, and he occasionally sported an out-of-regulation mustache to tip the hair-skin balance of power on his head. He was old school. He still chewed tobacco, drank, cussed and called, "Shot out" when he farted – a reference to the phrase artillerymen use to announce a round has been fired and is in the air. He didn't have the pedigree to make General Officer, but earned his rank through hard work and good old fashion leadership. He liked being an operator and it didn't bother him in the least that he wouldn't end up a General. He loved his current gig. During Desert Storm he was on the ground with the 1st Armored Division as an ALO. He rode into Iraq inside a "trac" – an M-113 armored personnel carrier, versus flying in in his F-111, OV-10 or F-16; he'd flown all three. That experience gave him instant credibility with the Army for the job he was in now. He wore the 1st Armored Division combat patch on his right shoulder signifying combat time with that unit. This was like a badge of honor in an Army Tactical Operations Center, a TOC. The 20th supported the Army's 10th Mountain Division garrisoned at Fort Drum, near Watertown in upstate New York. The Division had a long and storied history and a reputation for always being in the fight. Stacks was "dual-hatted" as both the Division ALO, the senior Air Force representative to an Army Division, and as the squadron commander. The squadron consisted primarily of Enlisted Terminal Attack Controllers,

ETACs, about a dozen ALOs and about twenty combat weather personnel. Since World War II, the Air Force had aligned air support units with Army maneuver units; this relationship created interesting situations for the Airmen who served in them – one foot in the Air Force, the other in the Army. The "20th" had about 75 "type-A" personalities in the ETACs whose job it was to call in close air support while standing shoulder to shoulder with the 10th's light infantry soldiers.

"Ok, next," Stacks directed as he briefly reviewed each slide; he wasn't big on meetings. Each squadron section was briefing their particular information to Coltrain. "Okay, next."

As the next slide came up Sergeant Writtenhouse opened the door to the briefing room, approached Stacks and knelt down beside his chair at the head of the table. The briefing room was long and thin, barely wide enough to fit in the twelve-foot long conference table. It was visually disjointed; there were two structural support pillars in the middle of the room with the conference table pushed up against them. Those who sat on the wrong sides of those pillars were constantly leaning forwards and backwards to keep their eyes on the boss or whoever else was talking. During a meeting if you looked down the length of the table those maneuvering heads made it look like a big machine with pumping pistons on both sides, slowly going in and out. The whole building was a challenge. It was a World War II era converted barracks. The plumbing didn't work very well and the heat wasn't enough to warm it in the frigid Upstate New York winters and the Army didn't allow air conditioners so it was sweltering in the two or three weeks it actually got hot in the summer. Sitting next to Stacks to his left was his DO, Lieutenant Colonel Jeff "Sandman" Sanders. Sandman had gotten to the 20th a few weeks before, but had already established himself with the men and women of the unit. As the DO, in cases of discipline, he was the "bad cop," dropping the hammer as appropriate while the boss, for the most part, held on to the "good cop" role, recognizing the positive accomplishments of the Airmen. That wasn't always true; Stacks would unleash his dark side when necessary but hadn't had to since taking command. Sandman was firm but fair and the guys appreciated that. He managed the nuts and bolts of the squadron so he worked a balance between diplomat and police chief. Sandman was about six feet tall, broad shouldered, and was also losing the hairline war with his head. The guys liked him and respected his role as the hammer, never really taking it personally when they had to take their medicine. Across from Sandman was Donovan. Donovan, as the ranking Major, earned a seat at the head of the table. As Stacks had explained to Donovan before the meeting, he had worked out an organizational adjustment to put Donovan in a job worthy of his rank and experience. Something he did because as Donovan's commander he knew it was his job to assist all his subordinates in their careers and because he liked Donovan right from the start. The help was something Donovan appreciated but knew was all but futile. At this point he'd been passed over for promotion to Lieutenant Colonel twice. Donovan was now a senior Major and wasn't going to be heading over to the Clothing Sales store to buy new sets of rank anytime soon, not to mention most of his "mentors" were either dead or had their careers derailed because of the Fairchild crash. Major Hank Johanson sat to Donovan's right at the conference table. He'd been in the unit for a few months longer than Donovan. He was the unit training officer.

As the men toward the far end of the table maneuvered to see why Sergeant Writtenhouse came in, Stacks kept his eyes on the screen at the end of the room, but those with a clear view saw his gaze move from the slides to some non-specific place in the distance. His usual smile straightened out.

"Sandman, you got it, I'll be right back." Stacks got up and left the conference room with Sergeant Writtenhouse.

"Okay, next slide," Sandman said as his eyes followed Stacks to the door. So did everyone else's. Stacks shut the door behind him and went toward the stairwell at the front of the building. Writtenhouse had told Stacks it was urgent and there was something on the news that he needed to see immediately. He strode over to where about a dozen Airman and NCOs were huddled around the TV.

About five minutes later Stacks opened the door to the briefing room and sat back down in his seat at the head of the table.

"An airplane just hit the World Trade Center," he said.

Everyone around the table looked around the room at each other. Nobody said anything until Sandman asked, "A private plane?"

"No" Stacks said and paused. "An airliner."

"Holy shit!" everyone seemed to say at the same time. Stacks terminated the briefing after the next slide, which happened to be the last.

"Okay, let's call knock-it-off. Thanks everybody," he stated as he stood up. The room came to attention.

"Carry on." Stacks headed out the door without looking back. Donovan went down the hall, down the stairs to the B-flight section and walked up to the TV.

"Sir, have you seen this?" said Sergeant Holliday, the senior NCO for the flight.

"No, I just got out of the staff meeting" Donovan replied. All stared at the screen.

"Is this live?" Donovan tried to figure out what he was looking at. He'd been to Manhattan dozens of times; "Is that the World Trade Center?" he asked knowing the answer.

"Yes sir" replied Sergeant Holliday. Just then a second aircraft came from the left of the screen and hit the second tower.

"Holy fucking shit, was that a replay?" Airman Moran, one of the younger Airmen was on one knee to the left of the screen trying to get a better look, blurted out, followed immediately by, "Sorry sir."

"Don't worry about it Moran," Donovan shot back without taking his eyes off the screen.

"No that was no fucking replay," Sergeant Holliday answered. Now they all watched as the buildings burned.

***** A few weeks before *****
(The morning after the night at the bar)

"All right, all right...what the fuck? I'm coming! I'm coming! Stop banging on my fucking door!!" Nikki climbed out

47

of the small bed in her apartment, stumbled and fumbled for her robe, put her socks on and moved to the door. "What the fuck is your problem?" she said as she flung the door open. It was Jodie and Yusef in the same clothes from the night before.

"Hi soul sister! Rise and shine!!" Jodie yelled, trying to annoy Nikki even further. Yusef walked in on Jodie's arm with a broad grin on his face.

"What are you two doing here? What the fuck time is it? Why did you leave me last night Jodie?"

"It's time for breakfast, that's what time it is." Jodie said as she plopped down in Nikki's only easy chair. Yusef stood for a couple of seconds, then dropped in place and sat on the floor with his legs crossed.

"Why are you here?" Nikki ran her fingers through her hair.

"Yusef made me promise him something in return for something he promised me last night, so here we are."

"What do you mean, here 'we' are. Why are 'we' here?" Nikki drew an imaginary circle around Jodie and Yusef with her fingers.

"I dunno, he just said he wanted to come here this morning and talk to both of us. Beats the shit out of me, he wouldn't say a word." Jodie put her head back on the back of the chair.

"What the fuck Yusef, did you tell her who you are? What the fuck do you want? I don't even know you," she said as she rubbed her forehead, still hoping there was a chance him being there was all a wild coincidence.

"Oh, but you do Nika." he said as he stood up, calling Nikki by her given name.

"What did you call me?" she said. She was visibly shaken. She slowly put her hands on her hips and waited for his response. He righted himself, then rolled his neck around his shoulders and took two big steps toward Nikki.

"You know I know who you are. I know where you are from. And I know your family." Yusef, with a very thick five o'clock shadow and bloodshot eyes ran both hands through his black hair.

"What are you talking about? What family?" Nikki was shaking.

"Oh come now my dear, I am very good friends with your brother Uktam and your little sister and your momma. They are still in Uzbekistan and you are here in wonderful Uptown New York, and I know you remember me so let's stop the silly game, okay?"

"Upstate," Jodie corrected, then, "What do you mean remember?"

"Shut up Jodie!" Nikki commanded. Jodie raised both hands in surrender.

"Yeah Yusef, this is starting to freak me out. What is all this about? Who are you?" Jodie asked. She shook her head, rubbed her eyes and sat upright in the chair, just then starting to come out of the haze of last night.

"I am no one. I just need some help." He turned directly to Jodie. "Why don't you go get us some donuts and coffee, or bagels or something? I want to talk to my countrywoman."

"No fucking way. I'm not going anywhere" Jodie stood up, now looking very serious and a little scared.

"It's okay honey, go ahead, but don't be gone more than 30 minutes."

"Holy shit Nikki, I've got chills running down my spine. What's going on? I'm not leaving you with him. Oh no, I think I'm going to puke."

"Well you can do that on the way to the donuts my dear," Yusef stated, not taking his eyes off of Nikki.

"Are you sure Nikki? I can go call the cops as easy as get donuts..."

"You don't..." Yusef started.

"No...no, it's okay Jodie, go ahead. But like I said, don't be more than 30 minutes. It's okay," she said waving her off, not taking her eyes off of Yusef. Reluctantly, Jodie left. When Nikki heard the door close she sat in the easy chair. Yusef stepped over to the small table in the corner and grabbed one of the metal folding chairs. He swung it around and sat in it backwards facing Nikki. She started, "So talk."

"Well, there is nothing to worry about. Your family is

very well. As well as they can be back there, but they are fine," he began. "I just need your help. I asked the lovely Jodie and she agreed, but I would feel much better if you were involved, because I know you'll do what I say. You see, this is a very simple thing but I can't do it myself. I got close to Jodie to maybe, possibly, use your friendship with her as very gentle leverage if I needed to, but I don't think I need to." He paused and pulled a cigarette and lighter out of his pocket. He gestured toward Nikki; she declined.

"You can't smoke that in here," she said while barely moving. He didn't hesitate, lit the cigarette and smoked. Nikki got up and opened the window, then pointed at the ceiling toward a smoke alarm and sat back down without speaking.

"You and Jodie will take a ride to Manhattan, New York City, and be someplace at a certain time and call me on the telephone. She has all the details."

"What for?" she asked.

"It is not of your concern. It could be of a concern to your little brother or mother, but certainly not to you. Once this is complete, I will have other things for you to do; little things, minor things, things that no one will notice. Do you remember the young, handsome gentleman at your bar the other night, Donovan I believe his name was?" He took a long draw on his cigarette. Tears ran down Nikki's cheeks. She didn't make a sound.

1100pm, 10 September 2001, Donovan's House, Evans Mills, New York

"What are you upset about?" Donovan asked Nikki.

"I'm not upset, just leave me alone. I just need to go to bed, I've got to get up really early tomorrow."

"Why do you have to leave for New York at O'dark thirty?" Donovan paced the floor. "I don't get it. If you guys are going shopping what difference does it make what time you get there?"

"It's more than that, it's, it's nothing, just let it go. I have to go with Jodie, it's Jodie's thing; I just have to go with her.

Please just let it go."

"Okay, I'm just trying to understand why you're so short lately." Donovan moved toward Nikki.

"I've always been this height, and I'm not short." Nikki said without thinking.

"Okay, there's my girl. I'm just worried about you and I guess I'm just worried that something's bothering you that you're not telling me about."

"Just let me do this thing and I'll be fine. I need to go to sleep, okay? Please?" Nikki plopped down and sat on the floor. Donovan put out his hands, she reached for his, he pulled her up and gave her a hug, she didn't respond. Nikki walked over and climbed into their bed, fully clothed and pulled the covers up over her head.

"Okay, go ahead, I'll see you tomorrow night." Donovan shut off the light, went downstairs, grabbed a beer from the fridge, sat on the couch, turned on the TV and started flipping channels.

11 September 2001, Fort Drum, New York

Donovan hadn't heard from Nikki since she left early in the morning for Manhattan. The thought crossed his mind that she would have made it to the city by now. He felt even more anxious to make contact since they'd had that fight the night before. She was upset about something and it turned into a nonsensical argument over nothing. He didn't understand what they were fighting about; it seemed that ever since that night at the bar everything was making Nikki mad. He wanted to call and at least make sure she knew what was going on and maybe to say he was sorry. He quickly walked up the steps to the office he shared with Johanson; he wasn't there. Donovan picked up the phone and got an outside line and dialed Nikki's cell phone. It rang busy. He tried again; same thing. He put down the phone, paused a second standing motionless at the desk, looking blankly out the window; "She's okay, right... yeah, she's got to be okay." He went back down the two sets of stairs to the flight room to get the latest. As he approached the TV he noticed the picture had changed, it. The view had been over the towers burning and now it was of something else. The screen was filled with smoke.

"One of the towers fell down," Sergeant Holliday said when he noticed Major Donovan in his peripheral vision, never taking his eyes off the screen.

"No way, there's no way that tower would fall down," Donovan asserted. "No Way."

"Sir it's down, we just saw it." Holliday went down on one knee, still staring at the screen.

"It was on fire, right?" Donovan asked.

"Sir, we just saw it fall." Holliday looked right at the Major, the volume of his voice increasing, the tone more severe.

11 September 2001, Manhattan, New York

Nikki and Jodie pulled into a parking garage off of West Broadway; it was 8:35 am. They were to go to the observation deck of the World Trade Center and call Yusef. They got out of the car and started down the ramp of the parking garage. They got about fifty yards. They were both nervous and neither one of them knew what they were really doing there.

"Jodie, hon, I can't make this walk in these shoes. We've got to go back and get my sneakers. Do you need to get your other shoes?" Nikki asked Jodie.

"No doll, I've got these on." She pointed to her hiking boots. "I'm ready to walk! Hey, as fucked up as this situation might be, I've never been to N.Y.C. before and I have to tell you, I'm a bit excited"

"Okay, you want to wait for me here or go ahead?"

"I'll wait for you. I'll just hang right here; I can see the car from here. I'll keep an eye on you."

8:36: "Okay, I'll be right back." Nikki started walking back up the ramp and was having a tough time. She stopped and turned back toward Jodie. "Go ahead. I'll be there in a couple of minutes. I'll see you in the North Tower lobby. You know where I'm talking about?"

8:37: "Sure, I've got the map, I'll see you in about twenty!"

"Okay, sorry about all this...errr...I've got to stop trying

52

to wear fashion shoes!"

8:38: "Amen sister, just get a pair of these on and nothing will stop you," Jodie said over her shoulder. Nikki made it to her car, sat in the driver's seat and retrieved her shoes from the back seat. She decided to give Yusef a call. It was a little early but she wanted to make sure she could complete her task to his satisfaction. She dialed the number he gave her. It rang and rang; he didn't pick up and it didn't go over to voicemail. She kept trying. After the fifth try she decided she should call Jodie. She dialed her number and after two rings Jodie picked up.

8:45: "Where are you, girl?"

"I'm really sorry honey, I'm still in the car. I changed my shoes then I tried to call Yusef," Nikki said, then immediately regretted it.

"Why are you calling that bastard when we're on our N-Y-C adventure? Come on, get up here!"

"Where are you?" Nikki checked her eyeliner in the rearview mirror.

"I'm up top on the observation deck. Come on, it's 8:45 and there's so much to see."

8:46: "Okay, okay, I'm really sorry hon, I'll be..." Nikki was startled by a strong vibration and a muffled, drawn out boom. "Did you feel that? Jodie, Jodie..."

"Holy shit, the whole building just shook. Nikki I'm scared, where are you!!" Jodie asked, her voice rising.

"I'm on my way, I'll be with you in a few minutes, okay? You gonna be okay Jodie?" she said while moving her finger closer to the hang up button on her phone. "Maybe it was an earthquake. I felt it too."

"I'm okay, yeah, okay that's probably it. There's been lots of those, right? I mean this building ain't going anywhere right?"

"No way. Those two towers are monsters. I'll be up in a couple of minutes and we'll get on with our adventure!!" Nikki said excitedly. She hung up the phone and just then noticed the sound of sirens.

CHAPTER FOUR

PERSPECTIVES

11 September 2001, Tashkent, Uzbekistan

Uktam Kassymbek was returning from the market located just down the street from his apartment when he saw a small crowd gathering outside of a store front. He approached and strained to see what everyone was looking at, stretching himself out, leaning forward, standing on his toes. He maneuvered his head back and forth until he got a view of the small TV screen. It showed a tall skyscraper burning and the newscaster was saying that an airplane had hit a building in New York City. As all were leaning, listening, elbowing for a better view, a second airplane flew into the building right next to the one on fire. There was a collective groan. Two women brought their hands to their mouths; a man ran his hands through his hair, others stood silent. A tall man in back stood motionless with his hands in his pockets, expressing no reaction. Uktam didn't really grasp what was happening. He turned to an older man standing to his left.

"What's going on, sir?" he asked.

"Can't you see? The Americans are being attacked," the old man replied.

"Who said anything about an attack?" injected the man with his hands in his pockets.

"Are you blind?" said the old man. "Two planes don't hit skyscrapers like that unless someone wants that to happen."

"But who's attacking them?" the man with his hands in his pockets asked.

"I don't know. How would I know?" shot back the old man.

Uktam backed out of the crowd and hurried home. He thought of his sister, Nika; he was worried about her. He didn't know where she was, just that she was in America. When he got home his mother and sister, Ulyana, were there, but his younger brother, Aaqib, was still at school. The images of the planes striking the buildings and them burning stuck in Uktam's head. He couldn't help thinking of all the people who must have been trapped inside.

"Mother, there was something I saw on the way home."

"Yes son, what was it?"

"It was on the television in the window of the big store in town."

"Yes?"

"Two large airplanes, everyone said they were airliners, smashed into two tall buildings in America, in New York."

"My goodness, how horrible an accident."

"Yes mother, but the men said they thought that America was being attacked."

"By whom?"

"Nobody would say. What do you think?"

"I don't know, son. I don't want to think about it. There is so much going on in the world that doesn't concern us, but then it does concern us. Don't forget, just two years ago we had the bombings here in Tashkent. These are the times I miss your father and worry about your sister Nika. I wish your father would come home. I wish Nika would come home."

"Me too, Mother."

"Well, did you get the meat from the market?"

"Ahhhh!! No, I forgot!"

"Okay, well run on back and go get it. Do you still have the money I gave you this morning?"

"Yes, I'll get it right away."

Uktam darted out the door and ran back toward the market. He would have to pass by the store with the TV in the window again. He wanted to see what was happening. As he turned the corner, he saw that the crowd in front of the store was bigger and that there was someone standing up on a chair in front of the window where the TV was. He slowed to a quick walk when he got close to the outer ring of people gathered around the store. They spilled out into the street. He strained again to look but couldn't see anything except heads. He pushed his way a little closer and stepped up onto a cement curb. He could now see the storefront and the man on the chair. He was tall and thin, had black hair and black facial hair with a few specks of grey. He wore dark green pants, a white shirt, a brown sweater and boots. On his head he wore a tubeteika, a traditional cap.

"Brothers, brothers, listen to me. We need to stay united and remember our teachings. As the world may be preparing for war, we must be a voice for peace." Just then Uktam's best friend Babur, who stood out because of his red hair, tugged on his shirttail.

"Uktam! What are you doing up there?"

"Babur, hello. I'm trying to see what's going on. Have you been listening?"

"Yes, for a short while."

"What does he mean about the world preparing for war?"

"Well, I assume he means that since America was attacked they will attack everyone or everyone will attack them. I don't know."

"Why does everyone keep saying it was an attack?"

"Well Uktam my friend, if two airliners crash into two buildings next to each other, within minutes of each other, that doesn't sound like an accident. Does it?"

"I guess not."

11 September 2001, Fort Drum, New York

Fort Drum locked down. No one could enter or leave the post. Stacks had gotten the word from Army leadership and he passed the message through the flight commanders. Post phone lines were constantly busy. One of the Sergeants said he thought the post shut the communications off but cell phones still worked. Donovan kept trying to get ahold of Nikki; still no luck. He called his parents and they talked only for a few minutes. He wanted to make sure his folks were okay but he also wanted to get back to his comrades. He kept checking his phone, hoping he'd hear from Nikki soon. That call came around 2:30.

"Pat, are you okay?"

"Me, yeah I'm fine, I'm locked down inside a fort with an Army Division. I think I'll be okay – how about you? You okay?"

"No, I'm not, no I'm not."

"What happened, what's wrong? Did you make it into the city?"

"Yes, but I was fucking around with my shoes and me and Jodie got separated. Pat, I lost her. I can't find her. I don't know where she is but she was up in the tower on the observation deck...waiting...she was waiting for me!" She started sobbing.

"Oh my God. Holy shit, Nikki I'm so sorry. She'll be okay. She'll be okay," Donovan said, not sounding at all believable. He didn't think she'd be okay.

"What the hell is going on?" She asked through her tears.

"I don't know but it sure looks like it was deliberate. I didn't believe it, even when I was watching it, but there's no way that was all an accident. What do we do about Jodie?"

"You said you're locked down? What's that mean?" Nikki asked with noticeable concern in her voice. "I don't know what to do. What should we do? I'm scared Pat, I'm terrified. She's my...she's my...my only, my best friend." She started sobbing more intensely.

"Oh Nikki, God, I wish I could do something. I can't leave. Nobody can come on or off the post."

"For how long?"

"I don't know. It's been about three hours so far. So if we're going to stay locked down, you need to get home. Staying there won't help find Jodie."

"Oh my God, I can't leave her there. What if she got out and is wandering the streets? I'm scared. I can't leave my friend."

"Yeah, I know. This is fucked up but there's nothing you can do. Right? I mean what can you do? Nothing. Please come back here, leave your phone on and make sure it's charged. She'll turn up. She'll be okay."

"Do you promise? Promise me she'll be okay!" Nikki pleaded.

"Okay Nikki, I promise she'll be okay. Now come home. I love you," he said as he ran his hand over his face and through his hair. She hung up without a word. Donovan went back into the building and up to the second floor to his office. Johanson was there on the phone. He hung up after a few minutes. He and Donovan talked about what had happened but it was all guesses and opinions. At around 5:00pm Stacks passed the word to the squadron that they were released.

October 2001

The air attacks on Taliban forces in Afghanistan had begun. A few weeks later Colonel Mack "LO" Laredo, the 18th Air Support Operations Group commander, visited Fort Drum and the 20th as part of a whirlwind tour of his subordinate units. He wanted to see all his Airmen face-to-face. He knew he was going to be sending some or all of them into harm's way and he wanted to make a personal connection. The Colonel drove up from Pope Air Force Base, North Carolina and he was going on to Ft. Campbell, Kentucky and to as many of his units as he could get to, hopefully all of them, before hopping on a plane himself. Colonel Laredo was a career Combat Control Team officer and was recently put in charge of the 18 ASOG. Usually, ASOGs were run by fighter pilots and now they've got an officer with a different, although significant, background. The Colonel had jumped into Panama and later Kuwait during the Gulf War, but he was also one of the Air Force's chosen officers being groomed for bigger and better things and ultimately to be made a General. Donovan walked through the door of the auxiliary building the unit had for briefings and miscellaneous events – SMSgt Sampson called the room to attention. The Colonel walked to the middle of the front of the room; Stacks followed him in and took his seat up front. This was the first time Donovan saw his Group Commander and sized him up. At this point Donovan wasn't a spring chicken; he'd been in for seventeen years so he'd seen a lot of Air Force "leaders." He could tell right off the bat that Colonel Laredo was different.

"It's great to be here at Fort Drum with you great men

and women of the 20th ASOS. I'm going to try and make it to all of my units as quickly as possible. I think we all may be in for some trying times ahead. I hope you're ready to go, because if I need you, I'm going to send you and I think I'm going to need you all."

It felt to Donovan like the Colonel was talking directly to each of the 50 plus Airmen in that room. He was genuine. Donovan listened to what he was saying, took it all in, but really spent most of the time taking in the Colonel. He was impressed. Laredo continued.

"Any significant fight we'll face in the near future will involve our ASOSs and you air-to-ground Airmen. As you all well know, where the Army goes, you go." He also mentioned a concept he had in mind for enhancing the organizational structure of the TACP community.

"If we end up deploying to austere locations we're going to need a cross-functional capability to set up airfields, guard them, get supplies in and operate in support of the Army in forward locations." These words caught Donovan's attention. Donovan had worked on a related concept during his previous assignment at ACC in Virginia. Stacks knew that and had pre-briefed Laredo. Although the Colonel looked like he was in a hurry, Donovan approached him after he'd finished speaking. The room had been called to attention and the Colonel had put them at ease. He was surrounded by several of the squadron members, some just wanting to meet and shake his hand. Donovan waited for an opportunity; when he saw a window he took it. Donovan brought up the proposal the Colonel mentioned in the brief, and related how he'd actually worked on a key element of the concept while assigned to ACC. That piqued the Colonel's interest. They talked briefly about the concept. As Donovan suspected, the Colonel didn't have much time since he had to get to Ft Campbell, so nothing more was said about it, for the time being.

CHAPTER FIVE

LIFE GOES ON

Jodie never showed up. Nikki found out a few weeks after 911 that she had been killed. Everyone knew deep down but they all held out hope until the official word came from the NYC police. Nikki got the news passed to her from one of Jodie's relatives. She had no close family; Nikki was really it. Nikki was both deeply sad and racked with guilt. Every morning the first conscious thoughts she had were the image of Jodie's face and the replaying of the events of that morning, how she'd encouraged her best friend to go on without her while she changed her shoes. She started crying whenever she thought about the shoes. She'd refused to wear anything but work boots, the ones like Jodie always wore, since that day. The events and Nikki's grief pulled her and Donovan closer together. She found genuine comfort in him and he was genuinely falling deeply in love with her. This was fine with Yusef. Although not part of his original plan, having someone he had a handle on close to a military member might pay off for him in the future. Yusef went into Nikki's bar almost every day, and almost every day he'd mention Nikki's mother or her brothers Uktam and Aaqib, or her sister, Ulyana, always to make sure she still believed that he could reach out and affect their lives if she didn't do what she was told.

Donovan only knew how he felt about Nikki. Once he got the word he was going to deploy, he shifted his focus to getting ready to go. As his departure date got closer he started to think about a worst-case scenario: he deploys and doesn't come back. He loved Nikki and knew she had nothing. He wanted to take care of her, even if it was still very early in their relationship. This was all getting overwhelming and both he and Nikki were dealing with a level of emotion they'd never experienced before. This was war and Donovan was going to be at the pointy end of the spear. Nikki lost the only person she cared about outside of her family. She was feeling things about a man she'd never felt before and may never see again. Now she actually cared about what happened to a man named Pat Donovan.

From when Donovan found out he was going until his departure date was only eight days. Some of that would be consumed with planning, drawing gear, packing, processing, everything that went into deploying. It was clear to him that he only had one choice. After a brief explanation and a short discussion with Nikki, they decided to get married. He called his folks and his brother and sister. They decided together to invite a few local friends. When he got back, they'd do it all over right: wedding, reception, honeymoon. They set the date for the 17th of November; he'd be leaving on the 22nd. The 17th was a Saturday. His family would drive up to Watertown from New Jersey on Friday and they'd stay for the wedding and leave on Sunday. Donovan's mom and dad, his brother and his wife and four kids and his sister and her husband and their two kids would be there. Two of Donovan's friends from the 20th and their families would participate, the Johansons, Tammy and John, who'd host the wedding and reception at their home and the Roses. Major Dee Rose was a good friend. She was, 5'5"with blonde hair. She'd just showed up at the 20th a few months earlier also. She was an F-15E back-seater, married to a great guy, Paul, who was about a half a foot taller than his wife and had a happy-go-lucky personality. They had a baby on the way, which was in part why Donovan was deploying instead. That was great news for her, good news for Donovan. Since Rose couldn't deploy, he moved over and filled the 2nd Brigade ALO position. He was thrilled. Johanson was a bomber guy; he'd been at the squadron just a few months longer than Dee. He was about 5'11", brown hair and a great sense of humor; he was married to Tammy and they had two young kids. Nikki and Tammy became fast friends. John and Tammy opened their house to the soon to be Donovans and their family. It was a gesture neither would ever forget.

Donovan came home from the squadron early on Friday afternoon. He did a few things around the house to get it ready for his family's arrival. One of those was to plant a cherry tree he and Nikki had picked out earlier in the week. Donovan had bought a nice, modest house on five acres in Evans Mills, north of Watertown and just a few miles west of Fort Drum. It was about two thousand square feet, two stories. It was a kind of a modular home, prefabricated. The big selling point to Donovan was the land. The back of the five acres rested up against the Indian River and there was a small creek running down to it from the east part of the property. Nikki and Donovan now had a two dogs and a cat. Buck quickly became good friends with Nikki's cat, Stinky. Steve was completely indifferent to the cat. Nothing Stinky did captured or diverted Steve's attention. It was also obvious that Buck wanted more to do with Stinky than Stinky did with Buck, but all in all they all got along just fine. On one side of the property was a slight gully that seemed to always be wet. That's where Donovan was going to plant the cherry tree. He put the tree, the root ball still wrapped in burlap, in a wheelbarrow, grabbed a shovel and started for the gully. As he got to the task he looked down at the tree. He wondered if it would live and if it did how big it would get. As he rolled the tree away from the house he started to realize he was really wondering if he'd live, if he'd ever see it grow.

Nikki worked with Tammy on setting up for the reception at the Johanson's house and had just gotten back. Donovan was putting the tools back in the garage and met Nikki at her car door.

"Hi honey. How was everything?"

"Okay, I guess... no everything is fine... great," she said. He could tell she was thinking about a lot of things. "Hey, shouldn't you be getting stuff ready for your folks?"

"Yeah, I'm working on it. Not much to do. I made a commissary and a Class VI run. The food is in the fridge and the beer is getting cold. You doing all right?"

Nikki looked up at him and then put her arms around him and laid her head on his shoulder. "Yeah, I'm fine. I'm fine."

"Okay babe, you've only got one more day before you're Mrs. Donovan so you better enjoy it. Then it's work, work, work, lift that barge, tote that bale..."

"That's hilarious. I hope your sense of humor gets better

with age." They walked to the front door, arm in arm. "I'm going to go take a shower." She kissed him and went upstairs. As she got to the top of the stairs, her cell phone started ringing. She pulled it out of her sweater pocket. "Hello?"

"Congratulations Nika!" the voice on the other end said with enthusiasm. It was Yusef.

"What do you want? Can you not leave me alone today?" she said in a forceful whisper.

"Of course I will, of course. I am just so thrilled that you and our boy Donovan are getting married. I went to the bar and they told me you had the next two days off for your wedding. I said, 'Wedding, what wedding?' and they told me all the good news. Donovan is deploying, you're getting married, all good news," Yusef said in an upbeat tone.

"What do you want?" Nikki was angry.

"Where is our boy going? With which units? When are they leaving? You know, that kind of simple information, that's all."

"I can't get that kind of information."

"Oh you can, and you will. Have a wonderful wedding darling. I wish you all the happiness in the world. Too bad your family can't be with you. Do they even know? I bet they don't. Might break a mama's heart to hear her daughter's getting married from a stranger. Oh well, good luck, hope everything goes well and I will hear from you no later than Thursday, okay? Okay." Yusef hung up without waiting for a response. Nikki folded up her phone and put it back in her pocket.

After Donovan and Nikki got cleaned up they met downstairs. They carried a cooler out onto the porch, grabbed a couple of beers and sat in two rocking chairs with Buck, Steve and Stinky at their feet and waited for Donovan's folks to arrive. It was about 6:30 when the three cars turned into the 300-foot long driveway. Donovan's parents led the way; they pulled up next to the porch, on the grass, just off the driveway. Donovan's dad was the first to get out.

"Where's the beer?"

"Beer's in the cooler, hi to you too." Donovan's mom got out the passenger side of their car and met him halfway up the stairs in a big hug. She then opened her arms to Nikki and gave her a long, warm hug; this was their first meeting. Donovan's brother John, his wife Eve and their kids, Christen, Johnny, Joshua and Jake got out of the second car.

"Hey Uncle Pat, this place is awesome," said Johnny.

"I know, isn't it? We'll do some fun stuff while you guys are here."

"Hey Pat, how's it going?" asked John.

"I'm good, how 'bout you?"

"Good, good. So, you ready for all this?"

"Yep, I'm ready."

Dawn and her family pulled in and got out of their van.

"Hey Dude, nice digs," Dawn stated with enthusiasm.

"Thanks, thanks, yeah, I like the elbow room. We actually shoot trap in the front yard with our neighbors; it's a blast." Buddy, Dawn's husband and the kids took turns exchanging hellos and hugs, and they all gave Nikki a warm first welcome. They took a tour of the property, inside and out. Eventually everyone settled in while Donovan barbecued chicken, hamburgers and hotdogs. Everyone had plenty to eat and drink and then they all started to feel the effects of the drive and all the excitement. One by one they all went to bed. Nikki and Donovan spent a few minutes sitting on the back step, catching their breath.

"It was sure nice of everybody to come in for the wedding. I wish my family could have made it." Nikki rested her head on Donovan's shoulder.

"I know hon, me too." He kissed her head, "Okay hon, I've got to go to bed."

"Okay babe, I'll be up in a second." Nikki gave him a kiss and patted him on the back as she used his shoulder to help her stand up. "Darling, I heard you telling your brother you were going to Kuwait? Is that right?" Nikki asked.

"Yeah, that's where the headquarters is," he replied.

"So who all is going besides you? You're not going by yourself are you?"

"A few guys from around the Group. It's all a rush job, cobbling together an input to the Army HQ. I really don't know." Donovan said, then took a drink of his beer.

"So you're all leaving next week, when?" She risked asking a third question.

"Hey Mata Hari, what's with all the logistics questions?" He threw in a chuckle to keep it light.

"Oh, no, never mind, just wondering. I'm worried. I'm worried and I would be more worried if you were going over there by yourself. And I just wanted to know what to expect."

"Well, I want to know what to expect to, but I don't. It'll all be okay. I think. Yeah, well, I have no idea what to tell you. I don't know what to expect, so I don't know what to tell you. I'm sorry, but I really don't," he said, exasperated.

"It's okay darling. Maybe you won't have to go at all."

"No, I don't think that's an option. It's on, we're bombing right now and we've got to get over there and clean up. We're going." Donovan took a swig of his beer and looked out down toward the river. It was quiet except for the frogs. Nikki continued in through the back door and went up to sleep. Buck and Steve were lying at Donovan's feet. Buck just lifted his head up when Nikki left and then put it back down, resting on his outstretched paws. Steve didn't move.

The next day, the wedding day went by in a flash for Nikki and Pat Donovan. First thing in the morning they focused on getting everyone breakfast. No small chore, but one Nikki loved. She'd been cooking for herself and Stinky but she loved cooking for other people, the more the better. She used to help her mother cook back home and eventually took on the task altogether, so cooking for a big family made her feel a little less homesick. Donovan took the kids out into the backyard and started up the AirHog toy airplanes he'd gotten for them. It was quite an airshow that went on until all the wings or tails were broken. Buck helped with that part when he tried to retrieve the biggest of the planes. He did a great job of carrying it gently in his mouth. He put it down at Donovan's feet where he was used to dropping the ducks he'd retrieved for him on their hunting trips. Steve watched from a distance. Donovan didn't notice it while he was still flying one of the other ones and stepped on it. Before they knew it, it was time to shift gears and start getting ready for the ceremony. The Watertown Justice of the Peace, a local judge, would marry them. Neither knew or had met him before, but he was the only one available. Nikki went up to their bedroom and started her process. Dawn helped Nikki and when she was ready, Nikki put aside any superstitions and asked for Donovan. He went up to their bedroom and knocked on the door.

"Come in." Nikki said, almost giggling. Donovan opened the door and saw her in her wedding dress; she was stunning, her blonde-brown hair was down around her shoulders and her lean body fit perfectly into the white dress, and her smile was bright and wide.

"You're beautiful. I've never seen anyone more beautiful." Donovan choked up.

"Really, thank you darling."

"Are you ready for this?"

"Yes I am."

"Me too. I love you."

"I love you too."

The wedding took place in the judge's backyard and went off without a hitch. It was cold, but nobody seemed to notice it. The ceremony was short. The judge sat on a chair; he seemed to have trouble standing up for very long. The vows were exchanged and Nikki and Donovan kissed for the first time as man and wife. The reception was at the Johanson's a beautiful old home in downtown Watertown. Dee took dozens of photos. They all had a great time. They eventually headed back out to Donovan and Nikki's house, got more comfortable and had some more toasts and drinks. A few of the kids went to bed. No one had known beforehand, but it turned out that that night was the height of the Leonids Meteor shower; it was spectacular. The dark sky was filled with meteors, hundreds of streaks of light running across it. The "shooting stars" were constant. Donovan went in and woke up all the kids and got them to bring their blankets and pillows outside and lay them out on the concrete patio. Everyone was in awe. Nikki and Donovan, silently, thinking to themselves, separately, hoped that this was a positive sign for their future together.

CHAPTER SIX

THE GLOBAL WAR ON TERROR

26 November 2001, Fort Drum, New York

It was the Monday after the Thanksgiving weekend. Donovan had just finished about two weeks of planning with the Army in preparation for the Division's participation in Operation Enduring Freedom, with the brief interruption of his wedding. The squadron got spun up for the OPG, the Operations Planning Group on Wednesday, 21 November for a Division tasking. The OPG was a group consisting of members of the Division staff and supporting elements that came together to conduct broad-scope mission planning. The group looked at big-picture items, assigned research tasks and put together an overview brief for the Division leadership. The OPG plan was to gather information from all its members by 1300; they made that decision at around 1100. Donovan pow-wow'ed with the FSE, the Fire Support Element, the soldiers that coordinated and operated the Division's guns, artillery, rockets, mortars and worked with the ALO to integrate air support. They informed him that he'd have to pitch the Air Force position, specifically how many passengers and how many vehicles. The ASOS's specific audience with the General would be at 1300. Donovan got back to the squadron, which was just wrapping up "Safety Day" training and ran into Sandman, acting Commander since Coltrain's recent departure. Donovan told him they needed to convene their working group at 1130. Colonel Laredo had pulled Stacks from command of the 20th to send him forward to run the air support for Task Force Dagger. Task Force Dagger was the name of the CJSOTF, the Combined Joint Special Operations Task Force running special operations in Afghanistan; Colonel Longstreet was its commander. Laredo argued long and hard to convince Longstreet that putting a guy like Stacks, actually putting Stacks specifically in that capacity, in that spot, at that time was exactly the right thing to do to ensure the most effective and well integrated close air support for

Longstreet's special forces soldiers. Laredo eventually succeeded. The unit hadn't heard any updates from Stacks since he left a few weeks earlier because his departure had been quick. He pulled Sandman into his office and had a long conversation as part of the handoff of command. Stacks liked and trusted Sandman and had complete confidence in his ability to run the unit and prepare it for the inevitable follow on missions they all knew were coming. Stacks left in early November. Donovan wished Stacks could have been at his wedding, but duty called. Prior to leaving, Stacks called in Donovan to give him his personal rundown of the situation. He wasn't exactly sure what was waiting for him, but he knew he was going to Uzbekistan to link up with the Army and Air Force Special Operations Forces.

"Dude, I'm outa here, Sandman's got the stick." Stacks was gathering things from around his office, pens, pads, a stapler.

"Sir, I wish I was going with you."

"Dude, be careful what you wish for." Stacks glanced up to make eye contact with Donovan.

Donovan was excited. He'd gone through at least three different scenarios, worked out over the past two weeks and in every one of them he was the primary and would lead each contingent, regardless of the Army course of action chosen. He outlined what transpired during the 1100 OPG meeting to everyone and assigned taskings; there weren't many since they'd already run the drill for a couple of the other scenarios. Sandman made the decision on the make-up of the deploying team with inputs from key leadership. After about 20 minutes Donovan wrapped up the meeting. He got on the phone while still in the briefing room with Chief Warrant Officer, "Mister" Rios, who took the names of personnel, types and numbers of radios and number and specs on the Air Force systems. The standard TACP was outfitted with the typical High Mobility Multi-Wheeled Vehicle, HMMWV otherwise known as "Humvee" with a few modifications. The Air Force version had a metal rack system, known as a pallet in the middle of the vehicle between the driver and the passenger. It also took up the space of the left rear seat. The pallet held a suite of radios that covered several spectrums in order to ensure long haul and tactical communications on the move. The Humvee was an upgrade to the previous Mark 108 "Jeep" variant that was in use since the Korean War. Some of the vehicles the 20th had were early 80's models.

Donovan asked Sampson to come along with him for the meet with the General. As he was the squadron Superintendent, he was the most experienced operator in the unit. The two agreed to meet at the Division Headquarters at 1300. When they showed up it didn't appear that anything was happening. They waited and eventually spotted Major Lance Baker and Mr. Rios. Lance Baker was high energy, nice guy, from New York, New York. He and Donovan had hit it off despite both primarily looking out for the best interest of their services, which didn't always have them on the same side of an argument. Baker was about 5'8" black hair, olive tone to his face and always seemed to be moving at just short of a double-time pace. Mr. Rios was another nice guy, very friendly and knew his business. He operated a notch or two lower on the intensity-dial than Baker. He was easy to talk to and any time Donovan got the chance, he tried to strengthen their relationship. He knew the Army officers were in charge but you had to work with the Warrants and the NCOs or you'd never get anything done.

"Hey Pat, or what's your call sign, Dude? Dude, the meeting has shifted to 1535. You're going to have to pitch your position to General Gordon." Baker informed the Airmen.

"Ok Lou, got it, no problem." Donovan and Sampson decided they'd meet back over at the "Eagle's Nest," the Division Headquarters conference room, at 1500.

Donovan ran back to talk to Sandman and let him know what the plan was, to stick to the recommendation of a six and two, personnel and vehicles, and use four and two as a fallback.

They later met back up with Major Baker, Mr. Rios and another Major, who appeared to be running the Fire Support efforts. He approached Donovan and told him they figured the Air Force position should be three and one.

"Yeah, right"! Donovan laughed. "That's not an option."

The soldiers seemed to be really nervous about briefing the General. A couple of days before Donovan had seen the G2, Intel brief to the Commanding General, Major General Hacker; it was a fiasco. Major Greene was the briefer; Donovan knew him, he thought he was a pushy and arrogant guy.

"Sir, on this first chart you can…you can, sir you can see our objections, I mean our objectives outlined here and… here." Major Greene started to come apart like a wet napkin. Donovan didn't like the guy, but as he looked quickly around the room he could see the entire staff visibly cringing. It was like catching a rat in a trap, you don't particularly care for the rat, but with his head squished under the arm of the trap, you feel a little sorry for it. What made it ten times worse, he was using a laser-pointer to walk the CG through the briefing. He was shaking so bad, the laser dot was dancing around the map like a spot of grease on a hot frying pan. Eventually Colonel Moriarity, the Division Chief of Staff, intervened.

"Major Greene, feel free to walk up and put your finger on the spot you're talking about, you're making me sick with that pointer"! Everyone visibly winced from the pain of watching the Major disintegrate.

One of the orderlies gestured to Donovan's group; the General was ready. As they walked into the room, the General quickly dispensed with all the normal formalities and waved his hand, motioning for everyone to sit down, cutting off Major Baker midsentence as he tried to introduce the team. Major Baker presented his case, four fire support troops, although there was no plan to deploy artillery. That fact alone wasn't a reason not to bring fire supporters. Any type of fires, delivered by any type of platform, from any service had to be integrated into the plan – which was their job.

"Okay, I see that," the General said. Major Baker then turned it over to Donovan.

"General, we work in three man teams, an ALO, ETAC and a One-Charlie-Four, which is our non-ETAC qualified enlisted apprentice, and we match those personnel to a system, our combat vehicle," Donovan said and also pointed out in order to run a 24-hour operation they'd need two full teams.

"Okay, let me tell you what I'm trying to do here; we need to keep the numbers down. We've got a host nation cap." The General looked Donovan in the eye.

"General, we could knock off one of the ALO's and one of the ETACs could split shifts with me." He turned and looked at Sampson, who was sitting behind him, to give him a chance to chime in.

"We could also lose one of the 1C4s," Sampson said. Now they were at the minimum they agreed to in their planning meeting.

"What do I lose if we go down to four?" the General asked.

"General," Donovan shifted in his seat. "We'd lose the ability to send a system forward, we'd lose the ability to support 24 hour operations, and we'd lose the ability to protect the division's HQ with Close Air Support with a second full system."

"Okay, I realize you won't be able to support 24 hour ops but I don't see needing CAS; if we did we'd have all the help we could get." The General turned to Colonel Kelly, the assistant deputy commander for support. "Jim, what do you think?"

"Sir," he replied. "I think that's the right mix".

Prior to his pitch, Major Baker had brought up the point to Donovan that Lieutenant Colonel Coltrain was already in theater. "I think the General would want to know that." Donovan told him that they'd previously briefed the Chief of Staff. It was obvious to him that Baker wanted to bring that up in order to reduce the Air Force numbers. If Coltrain was already there, that would be one less Air Force body the Army would need to take; at least that was his rationale.

As Baker sensed the meeting was coming to an end he stated, "Sir, it's also important to note Lieutenant Colonel Bohain is already in theater."

"Coltrain – we know," the General and Colonel Kelly almost simultaneously said, "He's been doing great work!"

"Nice move," Donovan thought to himself; he'd told him not to bring that up. Plus, Stacks was supporting a Special

Ops Task Force and wouldn't be pulled from that to support the Division.

At the conclusion of the pitch Major Baker stated, "Sir, I view our efforts, FSE and TACP as a truly joint effort."

"Oh, yes, absolutely," replied both the General and Colonel Kelly. The briefers got up and walked out.

"That was really a good presentation and you made some great points to justify these numbers," the Major running the FSE said.

Sampson and Donovan went back to the squadron. They told Sandman what had transpired and that the Division wasn't planning on working the next day, but would reconvene the OPG for Friday morning at 0900. Donovan talked it over with Major Johanson. Johanson agreed to cover the Friday OPG while Donovan and Nikki drove back from New Jersey. They were planning to go home to his folk's house for the four-day weekend until the meeting popped up.

It was close to five o'clock so Donovan called Nikki to talk about whether they should go or not.

"Hi hon, what do you think about heading over to Jersey?"

"Hi darling, I know we've been bouncing back and forth on this over the last couple of weeks, but I think we should go. I really think we should go," Nikki sounded adamant.

"Yeah, I think so too. I know there's a lot of what-ifs and all, but if I'm gonna go, I'm sure it's gonna be quick. Ok, let's go." He drove straight home after he hung up. As soon as he got home they started running around getting ready. "I'll put Buck and Steve in the car. Make sure Stinky's good to go and maybe grab some snacks for the road." Within a few minutes they were in the car ready to go, Donovan was driving.

"Darling, can you give me any of the details about where you think you might be going or what you might be doing?"

"I could tell you, but I'd have to kill you," he quipped; he could tell she was frustrated. "I really don't know anything definite at this point, and I really couldn't tell you anyway. Just know that I'll be fine and I'll stay in touch as much as I can."

"I know, it's just that I think if I know where you're at

and who's with you, it would make me feel better, looking at a map or knowing you're with your friends, I don't know." She looked down at her lap.

They got into South Plainfield around 11:00 pm and headed straight over to Donovan's sister Dawn's. They left the dogs over at her house. Buddy, Ryan and Sean were all asleep. Buddy had been having back problems so he was out with the help of some muscle relaxers. Donovan thought it was nice to be able to spend time with just Dawn. Plus, they always liked to make sure the dogs were settled down before they left. Once they visited for a while they headed over to his folk's. He thought to himself, "It's always good to come home." He and Nikki parked the car in the driveway and walked to the front door. They didn't make it to the top of the steps before his mom was standing in the doorway, his dad holding the screen door for her. He thought his dad looked good, especially since he'd just had an angioplasty done. Donovan was hoping he would really start to feel the benefits in a few weeks. His mom looked great as always. They stayed up until early in the morning visiting, talking, eating and drinking.

The next day the whole family got together. They all had a good time. Everybody talked to everybody, not really saying anything, just being with each other. But mostly, no one talked about what was coming up. Donovan felt the unexpressed emotions floating around the room, in the conversations, and in the rare touches. The Donovans weren't a touchy-feely family. They loved each other but didn't make a habit of showing or saying it. Donovan got to spend some time talking with his brother John over the phone. He was about an hour away and had to work weekends so he couldn't haul his family to their folks' for the quick visit. Unlike everyone else, John did mainly talk about what was going on, about the war and what Donovan was expecting to do in it.

"So hey Pat, what do you think is gonna happen? Are you going over there or not?" John asked his brother.

"Well, I guess we'll find out within a couple of days." Donovan didn't know what else to say.

"If you do go over there, get some, we need some

payback. But don't go getting yourself killed, that would really upset mom and dad."

"Ha, yeah, you'd be cool with it though right?" he joked.

"Oh sure, that's your job isn't, do or die? But update your will and remember what a great brother I am when you do, okay?" They talked for another few minutes and they each told the other they loved them, something they didn't normally do. Donovan also talked with Buddy about his job, about how he was doing. He always wished things were better for Buddy. He worked long hours, had lots of frustration, but he handled it well and always kept a good attitude. He was a good guy and he and Dawn were happy.

The next morning Donovan woke up thinking about the planning and the mission and whether or not he was deploying; he was getting pretty frustrated at this point. They were ready to go, got all spun up and then nothing. He and Nikki had planned to go back first thing in the morning. Johanson was going to call him and let him know what happened that morning, if they'd held a meeting, or whatever happened. Donovan was anxious to get back but whenever they visited his folks, on the day they left they would go to Sherban's, the local diner for breakfast. He had been going to Sherban's since as long as he could remember. In high school, when he and his friends went out drinking, they'd go to Sherban's for breakfast – no matter what time it was. And, no matter what time it was, always had the cucumber salad, with breakfast lunch or dinner, middle of the night, middle of the day – it was the staple.

They got up the next morning, got ready, packed the car and started down the walkway from Donovan's folk's house toward their car. His dad stopped him halfway down the steps. He wanted to say something to his son but didn't want to do it in Sherban's parking lot.

"Listen Pat, don't ever give up. I mean it, don't ever quit, don't give up," his dad told him as his mom stood by his side.

"Okay Dad, will do... or won't do. I understand. I won't give up," Donovan told them both. They got in their respective cars and drove to Sherban's. Donovan's folks met them there. He had the cucumber salad. When they were done, they drove over and picked up Buck and Steve, said goodbye to Dawn, Bud, Ryan and Sean and then headed to Ft. Drum. They got back around 1300 Friday afternoon; Johanson called around 1500. He said he showed up for the OPG at 0900 and there was no one there, and no one knew what he was talking about. So, Donovan and Nikki settled in; they were tired and enjoyed a leisurely rest of the weekend.

Monday morning rolled around; Donovan and Nikki got up at around 0500. They had coffee and got a pretty leisurely start to the day. He left for Physical Training at 0620. He got to the Pines Plains Gym at 0645. He couldn't tell if he was early or they'd switched back to the PT meeting spot at the MaGrath Gym. He was still having trouble finding his way around the Post. At that point he figured "Fuck it!" he'd just go for a run. He went out and did the "River Run." Afterwards, sweaty, he realized he had forgotten his gym bag with his change of clothes. He went home, took a shower, got changed and came back. He phoned Sandman and got Sergeant Writtenhouse. She told him Lieutenant Colonel Sanders had gone to the Chief of Staff's meeting. It was now about 1030. Sandman got back and called a meeting for 1130. Everyone milled around gabbing until he came into the room.

"Room tench-hut!" Sergeant Writtenhouse called the room to attention; everyone shot to their feet.

"Everyone at ease please, take your seats." It was obvious Sandman wasn't totally comfortable with the room coming to attention for him yet. "Ok, here's the latest. The Division planning we've done, that plan is a go. We're going to need a TACP element, we'll have the timelines and equipment requirements generated after this meeting." He then looked down toward the end of the table at Major Johanson and said, "John, you'll be the ALO;" he pointed at Donovan, he didn't look up... just pointed and said, "The Group has other plans for you..." Donovan didn't know what to make of that statement, but he figured he was in somebody's plans.

CHAPTER SEVEN

LOOSE ENDS

Donovan knew that he was going to leave Nikki with a lot of responsibilities she wasn't accustomed to dealing with. He was worried about her because he wouldn't be able to talk to her very often and his family was almost six hours away. When he was told he was going to deploy, he was thrilled and ready to get into the action. He felt he had to explain his mixed emotions to his new bride. They really had just started to get to know each other, he didn't really actually know what made Nikki tick, and she'd been so easily upset lately he wasn't sure how she'd deal with him being gone. She had been standing out on the back deck of their house, starring down toward the river. He went out to join her.

"Nikki, I want to tell you that I don't want to leave you. I don't want to be away from you. I love you." She looked over at him and smiled slightly.

"I know darling, but here comes the big but right?"

"Hey, I never said that about you," he tried in vain to be funny, "But...I have to go. I have no choice, and I want to go, I have to go. This is history babe, do you understand."

"Yes." She turned and looked back down toward the river. He moved around behind her and put both arms around her and rested his head against hers.

Consumed with all that was going on, he'd forgotten about Steve, who had gotten even worse in just the last few weeks. He'd gotten Steve as a puppy, his first dog. Steve taught Buck the ropes of being Donovan's dog, taught him how to hunt, how to behave in the house and how to have fun. The three were inseparable. He had really started to slow down over the last year and was starting to have trouble moving from laying down to standing up. He could no longer hop up on Donovan's bed. When Steve was feeling particularly bad, Donovan would sleep on the floor with him while Buck would still sleep on the bed. Steve was now starting to have trouble with incontinence. Facing the deployment and not knowing when, or if, he'd return

Donovan thought about what he should do for him now. He didn't want to leave a tough decision like that on Nikki's plate and knew in the back of his mind that when he left he would never see his old dog alive again. His dad told him a story once about his dog when he was growing up. He told him that his father, Donovan's grandfather, didn't take their dog to the vet when the time came, that he took care of what had to be done himself because of how much he loved the family dog, Red. He said his father took Red for a long walk, from which Red never returned, not under his own power. Donovan came to the conclusion, spurred on by the realization that he was going to war, that he would have to, that he should, do the same for Steve. After the date for departure was set, he made his decision. He would take him to the forest north of Fort Drum where he'd taken Buck and Steve for walks; it was a place they all loved.

He was running out of time so he got Johanson to cover for him for an afternoon planning meeting. He had to make the drive to the woods with Steve or it would have to fall to someone else to take care of while he was gone, and he didn't want that. He went home and packed his truck. He had an M1 Garand his Uncle Pat had brought back from World War Two and given him on his sixteenth birthday that he kept under the bed. After his final preparations he walked back to his bedroom, kneeled down next to his bed, reached underneath and pulled out the M1. When he turned around and started to stand, he saw that Steve was watching him. Steve saw the gun and his big heavy tail started smacking the floor; he knew that meant a drive to the woods and some quality time with his master. Donovan paused on one knee, tears running down his cheeks; he sniffed, put his hand on Steve's side then stood up and walked out the bedroom door. The dog struggled to stand and lumbered after him.

Donovan let the screen slam shut as he exited the house. Steve stood behind it and watched his master. After putting the rifle on the rack in his pickup, Donovan went back and opened the door for Steve; he went down the three steps, almost stumbling. He turned right and peed on the closest bush next to the house. Donovan got him into the truck and started the drive to the woods. That night he'd slept on the floor with his arm draped over his buddy, who snored peacefully. Donovan didn't sleep much, not because of the snoring but because of what he knew he had to do. As he was thinking about how he would actually do it Steve howled in pain. Donovan stroked his canine friend's face. Steve struggled to lift his head, looked into Donovan's eyes, really looked at him, closed his eyes, put his head back down and let out a long heavy sigh.

For a minute, he thought Steve was dying but he wasn't. The vet told Donovan during their last visit that he thought he had cancer and his level of pain would increase and he recommended that he be put down right then and there. Donovan understood what the vet was saying and appreciated it, but he wasn't willing to make that decision at that time. Now he talked to Steve the whole way, only pausing every few minutes for a sip of coffee. Steve sat up and had his head out the window for most of the trip. When Donovan didn't have his coffee cup in his free hand, he stroked Steve's head when it wasn't out the window, or rested it on the old dog's back. They pulled into the parking area just over an hour after leaving the house. Donovan got out, stretched for a second then went around to the other side of the truck to help Steve out and opened the door. In the past the younger, pain free dog would have bounded out and started exploring the area immediately. Today he just sat there with his tongue hanging out, bobbing up and down with each pant. He looked at Donovan and as much as a dog could, he smiled. Donovan went to put his arms around Steve but at the same time the dog made a move to step down and he couldn't get a grip soon enough. Steve fell as he tried to grab him, which turned the dog sideways. He hit on his side and his head smacked the ground with the thump of a watermelon, knocking him unconscious. A puddle of urine formed around his back legs.

"Goddamn it! Fuck! Steve! Sorry boy! Sorry! Steve! Steve!" Donovan was down by Steve's side. "Sorry boy! I'm so sorry!" he repeated as he stroked his head.

Steve's eyes opened. He didn't lift his head, but his eyes moved in Donovan's direction and his tail started thumping the dirt, splashing in the pool of urine.

"There's my boy! Hi Steve, where you been?"

Steve's tail beat faster. Donovan held him down by the shoulder to make sure he was fully conscious. Just then, he thought to himself, "Shit," realizing that had Steve not regained consciousness, he would not be faced with what he had to do. The dazed dog got up and moved very slowly away from the truck.

"Hold up Steve," Donovan called after him. Steve stopped and sat. Donovan reached underneath the front seat of the truck and grabbed an old tennis ball and put it in his right rear pocket. He then reached into the cooler he had behind the seat and pulled out a plastic bag and stuffed it into his left coat pocket; he'd brought a beautiful T-bone steak for Steve. He knew he had to get on with it.

They went for a short walk and circled back to the truck because he wanted to make sure no one was around. He grabbed the rifle out of the truck and the two walked very slowly back into the woods. Donovan found a fallen tree and took a seat on the trunk. Steve came up and put his head under Donovan's hand, wanting a pet and he got one. After a couple of minutes sitting quietly together, he reached into his left coat pocket and pulled out the steak and unwrapped it. Steve's ears went up slightly with the crinkle of the plastic wrap and his head tilted a little to the left. The old dog sat alert with anticipation. Once the steak was unwrapped, Donovan handed it to him. Steve slowly opened his mouth and gently took the steak between his worn and yellow teeth, his tail wagging. He lay down in front of his master and worked on the steak for about twenty minutes, then spent about another twenty on the bone. Donovan waited until it was gone.

The old dog laid his head between his front paws and burped. It was time for a nap. When he awoke about 30 minutes later it was to the sound of a round being chambered into the M1. Donovan stood up. As he did, Steve pushed himself up paw by paw with his front legs to a sitting position; his tail was wagging, carving a semi-circle into the dirt. He was at the ready for whatever his human friend had planned. Donovan reached into his back pocket and pulled out the tennis ball. Steve stood up on all fours. Donovan had made sure no one was around and that the direction he would be shooting was clear. He reached back and tossed the ball away from the downed tree, downhill about fifty feet. Steve walked briskly – that's all he could manage –

to retrieve the ball. Donovan raised the rifle to his shoulder, waiting until Steve grabbed the ball – he always raised his head after a retrieve to see where his master was and would then bring him back the prize. Steve approached the ball, lowered his head to pick it up. Donovan shut his left eye and aimed at a spot he estimated Steve's neck would be when he raised his head. Steve got the ball, raised his head. He started to turn to search for his best friend. Donovan slowly squeezed, gradually putting more and more pressure on the trigger; it fired. He missed his target. The bullet hit Steve in the shoulder and he yelped. Even from that distance, Donovan could see he'd torn a large gash along Steve's shoulder and chest but didn't hit any vital organs or arteries.

"Oh my dear God." Donovan said softly to himself. "What the fuck am I doing?"

Steve saw Donovan standing at the top of the hill; scared, he wanted to be safe with his master, the boy he grew up with, the man that had tended to him in his old age. He hadn't gone to the ground when he was hit. He turned by hopping on his good front leg and faced back up hill, struggling on three legs. Donovan didn't know what to do but now he had to finish what he started. He fell to his knees crying. The rifle was still in his right hand, a fresh round cycled into the chamber. It was ready for another shot but he wasn't. He got back to one knee, raised the rifle to his waist but couldn't lift it any higher. It felt heavy as a telephone pole and he could not raise the weapon to draw a bead on Steve as he tried so hard to make it to Donovan so he could make everything all right. He dropped the rifle, ran toward Steve, put his arms around him and lifted him. Steve howled in pain. He carried him to the top of the hill and laid him on his side, wounded side facing up. He didn't know what he was going to do next. He knelt next to his best friend as he lay there panting. Steve looked up into his eyes; they were telling him something and he wished he knew what it was. He couldn't let him bleed out and he wasn't bleeding as much as he initially thought.

Donovan leaned over, put both his hands around Steve's snout and kissed his nose. He slowly picked up the rifle and stood up over him. "Goodbye Steve. I love you." In a flash it was over – for Steve.

CHAPTER EIGHT

DUDE, WE'RE GOING TO WAR

27 November 2001, Syracuse International Airport, New York

Donovan and Nikki drove to the airport the Tuesday morning after Thanksgiving. They left at 0515. After they'd driven for a while, they talked about what lay ahead for the both of them. He was broken hearted and disappointed about being pulled from the 10th Mountain deployment and about Steve.

"Hon, when I get to the Group I'm going to talk to Colonel Laredo about this situation. I didn't join the military to make freak'in slides in the middle of a war."

"I don't understand why you would want to go where it is dangerous, be happy making slides." Nikki appealed.

"I couldn't stand it if I got left behind, I don't know how to explain it to you, but, well, I just feel the way I feel. And look, you'll be taken care of…"

"What do you mean, taken care of? What are you saying?"

"I'm not saying anything, I'm just telling you now that we're married if something happens, it won't, but if something happens, you'll be taken care of."

"I still don't know what you mean, like insurance? I don't want insurance, I don't want money, I just want you and our life, that's it, so don't do anything that will put that at risk." She started to tear up.

"Well, I won't do anything stupid, I'll be careful, but you know, it is a war." He wanted to end the conversation.

Nikki pulled the car up to the curb, as close as she could get to the terminal. A skycap came over to help them with their bags and Donovan told him he had a weapon in his baggage. The skycap told him he couldn't help them at the curb; they would have to go inside to the counter. He helped Donovan carry his bags, four large "A-Bags," to the line. Donovan started the long serpentine through the line as Nikki parked the car. Nikki joined up with him near the end of the line. The airline rep behind the counter was short and stocky, but had a bright round face with a big smile across it; she noticed the A-bags.

"Hi there soldier, you going somewhere interesting?"

"Hi, actually I'm an Airman, and I hope so."

"I have a son and a daughter in the Army," she beamed.

"Well ma'am, you should be very proud. I hope they're somewhere safe."

"My son is at Fort Bragg and my Daughter is at Fort Carson and my husband is up there at Fort Drum."

"Me too. Thanks to them for their service and to you both for raising patriotic kids that volunteered to serve." Donovan loaded the bags one after the other on the scale.

"Well, they had no choice, we've had many generations of soldiers in the family, I'm sure my grandkids will serve too."

"Well, hooah." Donovan knew she'd appreciate that; she smiled.

After checking his bags he and Nikki went to the security checkpoint. There was a sign there that said, "Only Ticketed Passengers." They were early so they had time to sit together outside the checkpoint. The two sat next to each other on a small bench holding hands with their heads hung. At that point if given the choice Donovan thought to himself that he wouldn't go. Leaving his wife to go work at the Group on a slide presentation while his comrades were going to war wasn't worth it. They were both upset. When the time came they hugged; Donovan grabbed his bags and started for the checkpoint. The frail and skinny security guard asked Donovan for his ID. He looked it over, looked at Donovan and then looked past Donovan at Nikki.

"Come here young lady," the guard said with a cigarette voice and waved her over for a last goodbye.

"Sir, thanks very much for that, I really appreciate that." He shook the guard's hand, the guard nodded back, he got a little choked up. Nikki and Donovan said goodbye.

"I'm ready for you to be gone now. But don't ask for more time and more time…" Nikki said as a tear ran down her cheek.

"Okay," Donovan agreed as he pulled her close and

hugged her one last time.

Airport security was doing random checks; as he approached the gate, they picked Donovan. He had to step to the side and the agents were going to go through his carry-on bags. The lead agent, an older man with gleaming white dentures, asked if he was on orders and he said yes. The agent gestured for his bags, quickly handed them back to him and let him get on the plane.

His flight arrived at the Fayetteville Airport late in the afternoon. He got off the plane, headed down to baggage claim and waited for his gear to show up. As he waited, he went over to the rental car counter and picked up a car. Eventually his bags showed up; he loaded up a cart and pushed it to the rental car. Pope Air Force Base was adjacent to and primarily supported Fort Bragg. He had never been there, although he often thought about it as the place his biological father died. He took the All American Expressway to Bragg Boulevard onto Fort Bragg, which, as the sign at the front gate stated, was "The Home of the Airborne and Special Ops." Once through the gate he used a map and got onto Pope eventually finding the 18 ASOG building. It was surrounded by what looked like tank-traps, I-beams welded together in a crisscross pattern. Sandbags were piled up around the windows and stanchions were positioned around the perimeter to push parking beyond 50 feet from the building. He parked and walked up to the front door, showed his ID to the guard and entered the building. He looked up and down the hall: empty. He saw a directory and got the room number of the ASOG command office on the second floor. He went up the stairs; the office was the first one on the right. Seated in front of the door was a Senior Airman who came to his feet as Donovan approached. He was still in civilian clothes.

"Hi sir, are you Major Donovan?" the lean and well-manicured Airman asked. "I'm Senior Airman Driscoll."

"Hey Airman Driscoll, yes, I'm Major Donovan." He extended his hand.

"Hey sir, Colonel Lipscomb is waiting to see you." The Airman pointed to his left. The door read, 'Deputy Group Commander.'

Lipscomb heard him speaking with the Airman,

"Donovan, get in here," the Colonel directed.

"Hi sir, Major Donovan," he ID'ed himself as he stuck out his hand; the Colonel's grip was cold but firm, he was short and sinewy with wavy black hair and a prominent nose upon which a pair of black-rimmed BCGs, birth control glasses as Donovan learned they were called in Officer Training School, were resting.

"Hey Donovan, welcome. Thanks for getting down here so fast. Have a seat." The Colonel went back to his paperwork as he detailed the schedule and gave him a rundown of what to expect. He told Donovan he'd be heading out via vehicle convoy to Robins Air Force Base, Georgia to catch airlift over to Kuwait. He also told him he was going along primarily to work on Colonel Laredo's project that they'd briefly discussed up at Fort Drum. Donovan's heart sank and he figured now was not the time to hold anything back.

"Sir, any chance I can meet with Colonel Laredo for a few minutes before we depart. Is he traveling with us?"

"First off, he's not going with the rest of you at this time. He's got other obligations but will meet you all in Kuwait. Second, sure you can meet with him, maybe tomorrow, but keep it brief. He's got a lot going on right now, got it?"

"Yes sir got it."

"Okay, I'll have Senior Airman Driscoll get your contact info and he can let you know when you can meet with the boss." The Colonel had been signing forms since Donovan started talking but now looked up over the top of his glasses. "Anything else?"

"No sir thanks." He started to raise his arm to salute, but the Colonel put his eyes back on his paperwork and gave him a quick, "You're dismissed."

Donovan left the Colonel's office, shut the door and approached Airman Driscoll.

"Airman Driscoll, the Colonel directed me to pass you my contact info and to have you set up an appointment with Colonel Laredo, 15 minutes, for tomorrow. Once you get that ironed out, give me a shout or I'll see you first thing in the morning and you can give me the details then."

"Sir, I'm just filling in for the secretary. She's out sick today but will be in tomorrow. I'll pass all this on to her."

"Okay, great. Thanks. Hey, do you have a commercial phone I can call out on?"

"Sure sir, right back there, help yourself." The Airman pointed over his right shoulder at a partitioned area with a small grey metal desk. It had a manila-colored phone on it. That was it.

"Thanks a lot." Donovan made calls to his brother and sister and to his mom and dad, figuring he wouldn't have the opportunity for a while. He just let them know he was getting ready to launch out of the country and that he loved them. He would call Nikki tomorrow.

He figured there was nothing else he could do and he'd show up early tomorrow to start meeting people and find out when he'd see Colonel Laredo. He left the building and headed to his off-base billeting, the Gateway Inn and Suites on South Bragg Boulevard, right outside the Butner gate. He stopped at El Tucán, a Mexican restaurant near the hotel to get some takeout and a gas station across the street to get some beer. His plan was to eat and drink and watch TV in his room until he got tired. He finished eight of the twelve Pabst Blue Ribbons and ate two fish tacos and some chips and salsa. He never really settled on any channel but watched five or ten minutes of a show and then switched channels over and over for about three hours before he went to sleep.

He showed up at the Group at 0730 the next morning. He was none the worse for wear but was conscious of the fact that he was processing beer and fish tacos. He parked and walked up to the second floor where he opened the Group door and saw the secretary was back in place. She looked up and smiled when he approached. He was now wearing his DCUs, the Desert Combat Uniform. She saw his name and rank and greeted him first.

"Good morning Major Donovan, how are you? Welcome to the 18 ASOG," she said with a jovial tone.

"Why thank you very much. I don't believe we've met; Pat." He extended his hand and the secretary shook it in a ladylike fashion.

"Hi sir, I'm Maria, pleasure to meet you." She was very attractive, a medium-sized woman with a neatly coifed Afro. She was wearing a stark white dress and had a hearing aid in her left ear and a thin gold headband across her forehead.

"Likewise, my pleasure. Have you been at the Group for a while?"

"Yes sir, a couple of years. You're here to see the boss right?"

"Yep, amongst other things, but yes. Do I have a time yet?"

"Yes sir, he can see you right now. Just knock and go right in."

"Oh, okay great." He was surprised he'd get to see the boss right off, but he was ready. Colonel Laredo's office was just past Colonel Lipscomb's. He approached the door and knocked.

"Enter," came the reply.

"Major Donovan reporting as ordered sir." He held his salute. The Colonel stood up and returned the salute and extended his hand.

"Hey Pat, nice to see you! How was the trip down? Come here, sit down." Laredo directed him to a set of two chairs to the side of his desk. They sat, Donovan waiting until the Colonel sat first. Donovan looked around the room. There were various awards and mementos from Laredo's career, a lot of them had some type of paratrooper figurine or free fall wings, or jump paraphernalia associate with them. His desk was clean except for an inbox just about to overflow with personnel file folders.

"Nice to see you too sir, the trip was fine. It's great to be here."

"That's good, great to have you. You ready to go?"

"Yes sir."

"That's great. I want you to help me flesh out the Contingency Response Group concept. I was really happy to hear you played a part in setting that up for Air Combat Command. I've got an idea to roll up several different types of units into one unit, to be able to put expeditionary airpower where we need it in support of any warfighter, but all under one

Air Force Commander. I think ACC would support that concept."

"Oh, yes sir, great idea. I've got some thoughts on that having worked with all the functional experts in setting up the ACC CRG."

"Great, great, that's why I want you along."

"Well, sir, that's what I'm here to talk to you about."

"Okay, shoot. What's up?" Laredo swiveled his chair to directly face Donovan and put both elbows on his knees. Donovan thought to himself that he didn't know the Colonel, so didn't know if he was full of shit or not, but he sure looked like somebody who was interested in what he had to say.

"Well sir, I'll just be blunt. I didn't want to spend the war making slides. All due respect to the concept and I really do appreciate the opportunity to work on this and help develop this necessary capability but you gotta get me into the fight."

"Oh, okay, I got it. Uh, sure, we'll see what we can do. No, I'll get you in. I have a feeling we're all going to get our opportunities. But I appreciate that, glad to hear it. Are you ready for that?"

"Oh yes sir. I'm a full up round. I'm current and qualified and I am ready to go." He tried to contain his enthusiasm but noticed he'd moved to the edge of his seat, and actually noticed the Colonel had crept up on the edge of his.

"Well, all right then. I'm not going with you guys; I'll meet you in Kuwait. So, spend the next day or two before you leave getting spun up on whatever it is you can get spun up on. I just ask though that on the long flights over into theater, put some brain bytes on this concept, maybe some notes that we can turn into some slides. This is vital for the future of the TACP mission area and our Air Force."

"Yes sir, will do." He rose with the Colonel as he stood and extended his hand. They shook and he rendered a salute. The Colonel returned it and walked back around his desk. As Donovan turned and headed for the door, he winced to himself, thinking that that exchange could have easily come off as extremely selfish to the Colonel. He thought about it for a few seconds, but then thought again that although he didn't know the Colonel very well, he knew he was a warfighter. He let his mind settle on that fact and figured the short conversation with the Colonel was genuine and what was said was meant and he put it quickly out of his mind.

For the next couple of days, he met and worked with some of the key players on the 18 ASOG staff. The first he met was Joe Kisela, a retired Chief Master Sergeant and a legend in the Air Force Weather community. Joe was taller than average, svelte, with black hair, very focused. Donovan quickly picked up on how smart Joe was and how important he was to operations. He managed the deployments of all those Airmen tasked to head downrange. Plus, with his experience as a Chief, he was a great one to bounce questions and ideas off of. Donovan got his orders and movement information from Joe. Next he met Lieutenant Colonel Masotti, who would take over the Deputy Group Commander position when Colonel Laredo went downrange as Colonel Lipscomb stepped up as the acting Group Commander. John had retired but was recalled to active duty after 911. He was a former B-52 radar so he and Donovan had an instant connection. Masotti looked like what Donovan remembered B-52 radar navigators were supposed to look like, grizzled, weather beaten, but like a mafia capo, he put out the vibes that he was in charge. He also met Technical Sergeant Rob Gutierrez who, Donovan soon learned, was definitely a guy to get in good with. He also soon discovered that Gutierrez was a camouflagd intellectual. He knew his shit, but he knew enough about everybody else's shit to be one of the Group's MVPs. They got along as it was but Gutierrez was the money guy and he had control over all the latest and greatest gear. After they chatted a few times, Gutierrez pulled Donovan into his storage room and loaded him up with flashlights, knives, camelbacks, compasses, all authorized, but he made sure Donovan got all the new stuff versus the recycled gear. He also gave him a green hardcover standard-issue notebook, 4 x 6 inches, with lined white pages.

After two days at the Group it was time for Donovan and the team to move to Robins to depart for Kuwait, it was about six and a half hours from Pope. Kuwait was the center of operations for Southwest Asia. There were several headquarters there and it was a huge logistics staging area. That afternoon they loaded up their gear; there was tons of it. Six of them would be going on the first wave. The troop commander was Lieutenant Colonel "Kermit" Brundidge. He was kind of a mousey guy but salt of the earth, very nice, never a harsh word to or about anyone, very religious. Donovan always wondered how he ended up in the military. He was an ex-bomber guy too. So he and Donovan had the obligatory exchange, "I was here...oh yeah, I was there...do you know Joe Blow...yeah, how about Jack Sprat...alert... 30 hour missions..." Also along with them was Lieutenant Colonel "R. Lee" Nickerson. He came up from the 19th ASOS, Fort Campbell, KY. He was a "seasoned" vet and had had a couple of tours in the TACP business. Another good guy, seemed like a bit of shyster to Donovan, always appeared to be making a deal, sometimes sounded like a used car salesman when just chit chatting. "Hey, whatta I gotta do to get you to get me a cup of coffee today?" When talking to him a few times Donovan caught him shifting from looking him in the eye to looking at his uniform to make sure he wasn't wearing a teal leisure suit.

The trip was long and they were all tired. They got there in the early hours of the morning and had to go through the processing line in order to get on the aircraft manifest and to ensure everyone had everything they needed; shot records, ID cards, orders, etc. Finally ready, they climbed the stairs to the L-1011 and Donovan could see there was a flight attendant at the door. He thought to himself, *What the...?* The presence of a flight attendant didn't come into his head when he was thinking about the flight over. The long line of soldiers and Airman stretched back to the row of four buses parked about a hundred feet from the plane. Once he got on he noticed there was an entire civilian flight crew all with smiling faces, those boarding were in uniform and carrying their weapons. He picked a seat and settled in, stuffing his weapon under the seat in front of him and putting his backpack in the overhead. The rest of the team all congregated in about the same area. Once they all got seated they couldn't help but look at each other and smile. This is not what any of them had envisioned during their planning sessions. The flight crew were extremely friendly. Donovan realized this had to be one of the first flights heading into theater and possibly the first one this crew has serviced, so they seemed genuinely appreciative of the fact that they all were going over to get some pay back for 9/11. After about thirty minutes, they buttoned up the hatches and were ready to go. The captain came over the PA system,

"This is Captain Darin Helgeson. On behalf of myself and my two copilots, Rene Gonzales and Kelly Kane, my flight engineer, Pete Volz and the rest of our crew and the United States of America, welcome aboard and thank you for what you're about to do." The plane erupted in cheers. It took about three minutes for the cheering to subside. Once it did, the Captain came back on the PA,

"If there's anything I or my crew can do to make your flight more comfortable, let us know. For now, sit back relax and the first drink is on me." Again the plane erupted in cheers. The aircraft taxied and held short of the runway for a few minutes. Having flown hundreds of missions Donovan felt he made a connection with the aircraft and like its cargo, he thought the plane felt, ready, and anxious to cross the line of departure. Once they rolled down that runway they were going to war. The aircraft moved into position on the runway and applied its brakes. The pilots pushed up the throttles and the plane shook in place. Then the brakes were released. Donovan thought to himself at that moment, "There's no place on earth I'd rather be." They barreled down the runway, took off and began the flight.

Their first leg was to a refueling stop at Gander, Newfoundland. Everyone was allowed to deplane and mill around the small terminal area. Donovan and a few of his traveling companions had a beer. They topped off the tanks and took off within an hour. He wrote the following in his notebook:

We just left Gander, Newfoundland about 30 minutes ago, we're probably 200 miles over the Atlantic at 35,000 feet, it's dark out and I'm wearing sunglasses... I've got Brick House coming loud

*and clear over the airline headset. I'm eating a nice hot chicken
entrée. I've got the whole row of seats to myself, my closest neighbors
are two recently emptied mini-bottles of Scotch, and I've got my
weapon at my feet. I'm accompanied by about 100 other desert-clad
troops, 3rd Army, Airborne and engineers. How can you beat a
military that deploys like that? A couple of hops from home, and
into the war zone. Everyone is anxious to get in it.*

After many hours, sleeping, eating, reading, sleeping,
Donovan pulled out his notebook again:

*0225 EST: We're about 30 minutes out of Kuwait City.
Washed my hands and face. Our baggage left on a separate
airplane, C-17. No idea when me and my bags will meet again.
0300 EST: Turns out our bags were on the plane. We saw some
Army dudes unloading them and spotted some of ours. Good news!
We boarded three buses and headed to Camp Doha. We were
greeted at the plane by MPs from the 10th Mtn Division. One of
them jumped on board as our guard. I struck up a conversation
with him and asked how he was doing. He said he was fine.
They'd done a 15-mile ruck that morning. He said the Dallas
Cowboy cheerleaders have been at the camp over the last week. He
said they'd be at the gym tonight. He also said David Letterman
will be out here on 21 Dec 01. Gotta catch that one if I'm still
here; like Dave.*

*Bus ride is slow and we're riding with the curtains drawn for
security reasons. The driver cycled through some radio stations and
settled on a religious channel. Chants. I like it; it's very calming.*

They were now in Southwest Asia.

CHAPTER NINE

THE DESERT

The bus carrying the recent arrivals to the war brought them through the security gates onto Camp Doha, Kuwait. Donovan and his team dropped off their gear at the 332 EASOS, located in a sectioned off part of a warehouse on the Camp. The facility was originally built as an industrial and warehousing complex twelve miles as the crow flies from Kuwait City. The US Army kept a Brigade's worth of soldiers, approximately 3000 troops, equipment, some armor, aviation and support units as a rapid response force to counter any move Saddam Hussein might make back toward Kuwait. The 332nd kept a small contingent of TACP and ran a small ASOC slice, the Air Force's Air Support Operations Center, to control any air support needed as part of a counter attack. The ASOC was plugged in with the Army maneuver units and coordinated and integrated Air Force support and was a key element in the Joint command and control of combat forces.

Camp Doha stank. There was a desalination plant nearby and it wafted fumes over the camp 24/7. The smell was hard to describe, kind of like rotten eggs, burnt hair and gas, but for all those who would serve there it just smelled like Camp Doha. The plant had two huge red and white horizontally striped smoke stacks. They had the nickname "The SCUD Goal post" because they were in the direction of Iraq and the joke was that a good SCUD shot from Iraq would come from between the two stacks. The camp was energized by what seemed like hundreds of generators; it was never quiet. There was a constant drone, day and night, around the clock. It was like the ever-beating ocean waves against the shore at a beach house, you got used to it and eventually didn't notice it anymore. The generators were equally relentless except deafening and completely annoying. The 332nd's part of the warehouse was a vehicle bay, equipment storage area, a couple of offices and some limited bed space. It was always dark inside, at least since the war started. People slept all hours due to the shifts they had to cover.

93

All new arrivals had to show up for a mass briefing at 1300. The brief covered everything the newbies had to know and introduced some of the Airmen who had never worked with the Army before to Army 101. Each specialty area gave their portion of the brief. It went on and on; everybody kept nodding off. Eventually, Lieutenant Colonel Brundidge, the senior ranking Airman on the flight from Robins, pulled all of his guys out. He figured the TACP Airmen didn't need the Army intro basics. They all went back to a billeting area near the 332nd building and searched out their bunks. Camp Doha was growing rapidly. There were over 6000 people in the normally 1200-person camp. The bunks were in an open-bay and there were lockers, but not one per bunk. It was like a game of musical chairs. If you searched too long or were too picky about which bunk you got, you might lose out on getting a locker. Some of the earlier arrivals had commandeered several lockers and positioned them to make a closed-in apartment; ingenious, but selfish. Several of Donovan's team didn't get a locker and several others didn't get a bunk. After getting the unlucky ones settled in various places, they headed off to chow. The dining facility "D-FAC" was very nice, and huge. There was a wide variety of food, although most of it wasn't "healthy heart." They served the typical American fare, hamburgers, macaroni and cheese, chicken, rice and plenty of desserts. The local workers could dish it up; they could serve 5000 – 6000 people in an hour and a half. They all realized after their first meal that they weren't going to be able to eat three meals a day unless they went to the gym three times a day. The gym was also great and it became a sanctuary, it was always packed. It had its own bathroom – only the chow hall and the gym had those – plus it had showers and it was huge. It was a topnotch gym.

The next day the team arrived from Pope and had to drive to Al Jaber to in-process through the Air Force PERSCO function, which meant Personnel Support for Contingency Operations. This was a deployed unit focused on the accounting and admin tracking of all the deploying Airmen. It was an ordeal to go through the security gates and checkpoints when leaving and returning to the camps. The guards had to search the vehicle throughout and underneath. The Airmen waited off to the side where they got a view of the aircraft bunkers that the Coalition hit during Desert Storm. With the in-processing accomplished they stopped to take a closer look at one of the aircraft hangars. The French built the hangars for the Iraqis and claimed they were bombproof, but Donovan thought it was obvious the Iraqis should have asked for their money back. The roofs of all the hangars had one or two holes the size of 2000-pound bombs through them. Each hole had a tangled web of rebar surrounding it, pulled out and down from the force of the penetrating bomb. The insides of the hangars were a shambles except where they'd been cleared out to be used for cover from the sun for the US fighters now operating out of Jaber. They walked around a few of the other hangars and took a lot of "hero shot" photographs. After they got back to Doha, the normal work schedule began.

Donovan worked in the Joint Operations Center, the JOC. The organization was similar to the Army TOC concept but involved members or multiple services, thus Joint. In the middle of his shift he was told by one of the NCOs working the JOC floor that Lieutenant Colonel Nickerson needed to talk to him. He found Nickerson at his desk in the ACCE section of the JOC.

"Hey R. Lee, what's up?"

"Hey Dude, just got a call from Colonel Lipscomb. He wants you to call him at the Group at Pope. Here's the number."

"Thanks. Any idea what it's about?"

"Nope, he wouldn't say."

"Okay, I'll call right now."

"He said to give him 15 minutes. That was about 10 minutes ago, so wait five."

"Rog." Donovan walked over to the maps on the wall and started looking them over. After what he thought was about five minutes he sat down at one of the metal desks and picked up the receiver on one of the secure black phones, dialing the number to the 18 ASOG. After three rings Colonel Lipscomb picked up.

"18 ASOG, Colonel Lipscomb, unsecure line."

"Hi sir. Major Donovan."

"Hey Dude, standby while I get my key, can you go secure?" Lipscomb asked, checking to see if Donovan was on a phone that was capable of encrypting the conversation.

"Yes sir."

"Okay I'll initiate." Lipscomb hit the "secure" button on his phone and it initiated the encryption mode, synching up both phones so that they could understand each other but anyone trying to "tap" the phones wouldn't be able to. Once Lipscomb hit the button a series of beeps and squeaks went over the line until on the face plate of the phone, in digital letters, the word SECURE emerged.

"Okay, can you hear me?" Lipscomb asked.

"Yes, sir, five by five."

"Ok, Dude, here's the deal. Colonel Laredo needs you to make your way to Camp Rhino and meet up with the Marines there. There was a friendly fire incident around Kandahar involving our TACP, Army Special Forces and the Northern Alliance. The aircraft was a B-52 dropping a JDAM. Killed three US and five Afghanis. The boss figured your expertise would be a valuable asset to the Marines. Copy?"

"Yes sir, copy."

"Okay, that's it, that's all I've got. Any questions?"

"Yes sir, is this an ASAP mission? Any point of contact on the ground -"

"Dude, I just told you, that's all I've got so you've got it from here. Good luck."

"Roger sir, out here." Donovan hung up. He had no real idea what his mission was, who to link up with – nothing.

"Sir," one of the ACCE Airmen called for Donovan.

"Yeah?"

"Lieutenant Colonel LeBlonde just called from the squadron and wants to see you."

"Now?"

"Yes sir, ASAP."

"Okay, thanks." He had already pulled a twelve-hour shift so he was beat. He grabbed his notebook, signed out with the shift NCO and headed over to the squadron.

It was late afternoon. When he pushed open the outer door to the JOC he felt the dramatic temperature and humidity change immediately and he reacted to the bright sunshine by shielding his eyes as he put his cover on. He would remember to do that before he opened the door next time. The smell and humidity enveloped him, but it only took a few seconds for his senses to adjust to the outside world versus the inside world of the air conditioned JOC. Before he could tell he didn't notice either anymore. The distance between the JOC and the squadron was only a few hundred yards; he arrived at the squadron building within a few minutes and pushed opened the door, which didn't latch but always stuck. It made a loud creaking, metallic scratching noise that woke up all the light sleepers. It was dark except for the lighted commander's office in the far corner. Between the door and the office, like elsewhere throughout the camp, lockers were arranged to create a makeshift sleeping area for cots and bunks to try and provide privacy and cover for all the shift working squadron members and the numerous Air Force transients that were passing through Camp Doha en route to numerous locations downrange. Donovan made his way as quietly as possible through the maze until he could see the light of the office directly. He side stepped the pool table and stopped in front of the door. He stood there for a second, knowing that when he stepped through it he'd know what he didn't know before and that whatever that knowledge was would be significant. He was excited, but also nervous. He grabbed the doorknob with his right hand and knocked once with his left.

"Enter," came the reply from within. As the door swung open Donovan saw Lieutenant Colonel LeBlonde and Lieutenant Colonel Hoge seated in two steal chairs in front of a large wooden desk. A third individual, a Senior Master Sergeant, whom Donovan hadn't met, he assumed was LeBlonde's superintendent Bruce Voight. Behind the wooden desk was Colonel Laredo. The Colonel smiled when he saw Donovan.

"Dude!" the Colonel called out as he stuck out his hand. Donovan saluted and the two Lieutenant Colonels and the Senior stood up when Colonel Laredo stood up and reached forward across the desk to shake Donovan's hand, returning his salute halfway through the reach.

"Hi Sir!" Donovan said with a smile, "Good to see you."

"Good to see you too. You ready to go?"

"Yes sir," he replied without hesitation, but knowing he in fact wasn't ready to go.

"Good. Blondie and Andy will make sure you're squared away. I gotta head over to a VTC. Good luck."

"Thanks sir." They all came to attention when the Colonel walked out the door. As he crossed the threshold he instructed them to, "Carry on." They relaxed in place and then looked at each other without saying a word. Then Blondie LeBlonde broke the silence, "Dude, this is Bruce. I'm not sure if you guys have ever met," he said as he turned toward Voight.

"Nope, nice to meet you, heard a lot about you," Donovan replied.

"All lies," Bruce said with a big smile. Voight was tall, had black mussed up hair a square jaw and a chipped front tooth. He looked to Donovan to be a strong and powerful man. Blondie LeBlonde was a legendary ALO, Donovan knew him from his Academy assignment. Blondie left the Academy and went to Alaska to be a jump ALO. Donovan remembered how cool he thought that was when he made the decision to become an ALO. To Donovan, Blondie looked like the officer version of Voight. Andy Hoge was also a renowned ALO. He was a jump ALO with the 82d, he was hard as nails and Donovan immediately thought of him as the older, but not lesser version of the other two.

"Hey Pat!" Andy Hoge burst in and grabbed Donovan's hand, strongly shaking it.

"Hey sir, nice to meet you," he replied. Hoge was now the deployed DO for the ACCE there at Kuwait.

"You got your stuff squared away?" Andy asked.

"Nope, not yet."

"Let's run through what you need real quick and then you need to get some sleep. Do you have your transpo arranged yet?

"Nope, I just found out from Colonel Lipscomb where I

was going. I'm still not sure what I'm supposed to be doing. Did the boss fill you in?"

"Nope, you'll just have to figure it out as you go," LeBlonde said with a laugh. "We'll get someone working on transportation."

"Great." Donovan said as he turned toward the door. The three stepped out into the bay toward Donovan's bunk.

"Hey Dude, get your stuff and bring it over to the vehicle bay so we can lay it out."

"Okay." He went over to his bunk, grabbed his ruck, slung it over his shoulder and grabbed his two A-bags. He also rolled up his poncho liner from off the top of his bunk and tucked it under his arm. Once he got over to the vehicle bay where LeBlonde and Hoge were standing, he dropped the bags and swung the ruck around from his shoulder and dropped it on the concrete floor of the bay. He spread out his poncho liner on the floor and dumped the first A-bag out on it. It took about ten shakes to empty all the tightly packed contents out on the liner. It looked like the beginning of a very expensive garage sale.

"Good grief," Hoge said, chuckling.

"I know," replied Donovan as he went down on one knee and started spreading out all the equipment.

"Okay," started LeBlonde, "You don't need this… you don't need that… this is dead weight… you gotta have this… don't take this…" He went through the gear like he was at that garage sale. "I have no idea why they gave you this…" He continued for about 10 minutes with Hoge helping and adding his professional opinion on each piece of equipment. Hoge took Donovan's gas mask and tossed it in the not-going pile.

"You sure about that?" he asked Hoge.

"Yep, if you need that we're all in a whole lot more trouble than we think."

"Yeah, I think I'll take that along I figure it's one of those things that it's better to have and not need than to need and not have."

"Okay, you've gotta carry it" Hoge replied.

"What, the gas mask?" LeBlonde broke in while still focusing on Donovan's TAC kit. The TAC kit was what FACs,

Forward Air Controllers, used to do their airstrike planning.

"Yeah," Hoge answered in an incredulous tone.

"Oh hell yes; take that. That's one I won't leave home without," LeBlonde shot back. Other than the gasmask, Donovan took the advice of the two senior officers on what to pack out.

"You gents know anything more about the friendly fire incident?"

"Not much. Two of our guys from Campbell were involved; one was wounded. We don't know any of the particulars yet," LeBlonde told him.

"Man, that sucks."

"No shit," chimed in Hoge.

"Okay that whittles you down to a manageable size." Hoge pulled the rucksack upright and slapped it with his open hand. It sounded like he smacked the side of a 300 pound tuna.

"Still way too much if you ask me," LeBlonde injected.

"Yeah, that's a lot of gear and I don't even have a radio or batteries yet."

"And you ain't getting them either," responded Hoge. "Gotta keep them for the ETACs."

"Understand, but going forward without a radio seems kinda dumb. What am I supposed to use if I get in the shit, harsh language?" Donovan was irritated.

"You can try that but you might want to use your weapon," LeBlonde quipped back.

"I would if I had one."

"What?"

"Yeah, I got my M-9, that's it."

"What the fuck? Whose brilliant idea was that?"

"The squadron's."

"The 20th?"

"Yeah, the supe made sure that the officers only got 9's and the enlisted got the GAUs or the M-16s." Donovan was starting to get a bad feeling about his situation. He recalled what Stacks told him when he complained to him about getting pulled off the 10th Mountain mission to go to Kuwait: *Be careful what you wish for, you might get it.*

"That's the stupidest fucking thing I ever heard, was that Sampson?"

"Yep."

"Okay, we'll see if we can get you a long gun, get your transportation finalized and see if we can get any more info out of the boss." LeBlonde shook his head in disappointment.

"Great, thanks." Donovan rolled up all the stuff that wasn't going with him in the poncho liner, grabbed his ruck and the two A-bags and hauled it all back to his area. He had another empty A-bag folded up underneath his bunk, he pulled it out and put all the excess gear inside then stuffed it underneath the bunk. He pushed the two A-bags up against the side of the bunk and dropped the heavy ruck on top of them. He sat down on the edge of the bunk with his elbows on his knees and his hands clasped. He tried to figure out what to do next but right then his physical exhaustion and lack of sleep caught up with him. He leaned back, unlaced his boots and lay down. He put his head on his rolled up jacket and thought about the fact that he had not reminded his bosses that he hadn't flown the B-52 in over seven years. And in the age of the GPS-guided smart bomb, he told people, he flew in a time ...*when the bombs were dumb and the crews were smart.* He wasn't current in the BUFF but he was getting sent to the only conventional outpost in Afghanistan, Camp Rhino, to help the Marines as the Air Force's B-52 expert, he only had a pistol, and no radio.

After what seemed to him to be about 15 seconds... "Major Donovan?"

"Yeah?" Donovan replied with his eyes still shut.

"Sir, we got your travel information," stated Staff Sergeant Johnson in a loud whisper.

"Okay, what you got?"

"Sir, we're going to drive you to Al Jaber, then you're gonna catch a C-130 to Oman and then you're going to have to figure out the rest."

"Okay, so driving to Al Jaber, then 130 to Oman and then hitch a ride, got it. Thanks, what time?"

"In about an hour sir," Johnson said as he walked away.

"Awesome." Donovan threw his feet, boots still on,

over the side of the bunk and let their weight carry them to the floor, he used the momentum to help right himself. He figured on one last shower, not knowing when he'd get another. He slogged down to the shower trailers, took a hot one and was back on his bunk within 15 minutes.

Just as he was lacing up his second boot he heard the squeak and slam of the entry door to the squadron. A couple seconds later Staff Sergeant Johnson was standing over him. "You ready to go sir?"

"Yep."

"Where's your gear sir?"

"It's right here," Donovan said as he slapped the top of his ruck. "If you pull your vehicle up to the door I'll load it in."

"That's okay sir, we got it."

"All right, I'll be right out." He got up and headed back over to the commander's office. The lights were still on. He knocked on the door but there was no answer so he turned around and headed for the exit. *Okay,* he thought, *off we go.* He left the squadron and the door slammed behind him. It was dark now. The "Doha smell" was particularly strong. The passenger side door was open, so he stepped in and shut the door. He saw Johnson in the back and he looked over at the driver; he'd not seen him before.

"Major Donovan," he said as he stuck his hand out toward the Airman behind the wheel.

"Nice to meet you, sir. Airman Reed."

"Where you from?"

"Albany, Illinois"

"Never heard of it"

"It's just a small town."

"I'm just kidding," Donovan laughed and put his hand on Reed's shoulder. "Didn't you ever see *The Dirty Dozen?*"

"No sir."

"I'm sorry, it's a movie where a guy, Donald Sutherland, you know who he is?"

"No sir."

"Well, he's an actor who plays this soldier who's impersonating a general, he does an inspection, asks one of the soldiers in formation where he's from, the guy tells him and he says, 'Never heard of it...' anyway, so a small town huh?"

"Yes sir...we better get going sir."

"Okay, let's go. How you doing Johnson?"

"Good sir."

"Where you from?"

"New York, New York!"

"Never heard of it..."

"Funny sir."

"Wow, tough crowd," Donovan responded. "Okay, so let's get going, Reed. Let's get me to Afghanistan"

"Yes sir." Reed put the Pathfinder in gear and turned left up the alley to one of the main roads on Camp Doha. They went around the PX, past the running track and toward the gate. They stopped to be checked by the guards and after about fifteen minutes headed out the gate. They drove along the Doha Spur to Sixth Ring Road toward Ali Al Salem. Donovan nodded off a few times, head bobbing, catching himself as his head dropped toward his chest. In between they chatted about each other's lives before the Air Force and he took the opportunity as he always did to mentor the young men on their career paths and what they should be doing to advance if they planned to stay in. It was dark but the moon was out. At one stretch on the Ring Road they all spotted a dark mass on the right side of the road. They couldn't tell what it was.

"Slow down Reed."

"You sure sir?"

"Yeah, if you've got the room, move over to the left, keep it about 25 miles per hour."

"What's that in kilometers sir? This gauge only reads klicks."

"Ah, about 40."

"Roger sir."

"What the fuck is that? Is that a dog on top?" Johnson said from the backseat.

"Wow, that's something you won't see back home." Donovan added as they drove by the carcass of a camel with a small dog perched on its hip tugging as hard as it could on the camel's rectum.

Then Reed said, "Man, that little dog is tearing that camel a new asshole!" They all laughed, hard. Donovan looked over at Reed and he could tell the young Airman was thrilled at having come up with the joke that made them all laugh and broke the tension a little. He figured Reed would be telling that story until he was an old man.

It took them about 45 minutes to get to the checkpoint before the base gate and another 30 to get through the main gate. Once they got through the gate they headed to the passenger terminal.

"Sir, we're going to swing by Security Forces and get you a weapon. Lieutenant Colonel LeBlonde arranged it," Johnson told the Major who was jotting notes down in his green notebook.

"What was that Johnson? Sorry I wasn't listening."

"Weapon sir, we're picking one up for you from Security Forces. Lieutenant Colonel LeBlonde worked a deal."

"Okay, great. Reed you know how to get there?"

"Yes sir, we make a BX run here once a week and it's small so we look around, see if we know anybody."

"Okay, how much time we got till the flight?"

"About four hours." Johnson replied. He helped Reed navigate his way to the Security Forces squadron and they pulled up to the barriers around the building and got out. As the three entered the building Donovan approached the Watch NCO.

"Morning Sergeant." He tried to read the sergeant's nametag but it was partially obscured by a fold in his shirt.

"Schwartz. I'll take your word for it sir, good morning. What can I do for you?"

"Hey Sergeant Schwartz, Major Donovan. I'm on my way downrange…"

"Yes sir, I'm tracking. We're going to loan you a weapon right?" Schwartz had short, bright-red hair and a plaster white face covered in freckles.

"You got it," he replied with a smile.

"Sorry state of affairs when the Air Force has to send guys downrange with hand-me-down weapons."

"No shit," Donovan said.

"Okay sir, standby one; let me get somebody to cover the desk then you can follow me to the armory. You guys can wait out here," Schwartz told the other two. Schwartz picked up a black phone, which was a hotline to the squadron's back offices. After a short discussion and a minor argument, he hung up. A few minutes later an NCO looking like he'd just woken up walked through the door the three had entered earlier.

"Okay man, I got it," the sleepy NCO asserted.

"You sure?" Schwartz asked using a whiny tone.

"Fuck you Jack, I haven't slept in two days. Do what you gotta do and get your ass back and pull your shift."

"Okay, fuckstick, I'll be right back," Schwartz replied.

"Where you from Sergeant Schwartz?" asked Donovan, using the standard icebreaker as they walked through the building toward the armory.

"I'm not from anywhere sir, I'm an Army brat."

"Oh yeah? Where were you stationed growing up?"

"Well... I was at Lewis, Campbell, Drum..."

Donovan interrupted, "No kidding, that's where I'm stationed."

"Drum, whadya doing there?"

"I'm an ALO with the 10th Mountain."

"No shit, my dad was in the 10th Mountain."

"Awesome, what's he doing now?"

"He's dead sir."

"Oh, sorry about that Schwartz."

"It's ok sir, he died in Somalia – not part of the whole Blackhawk Down deal, killed in a training accident."

"Sorry man" Donovan added sympathetically.

"Okay sir, here we are." The armory had a cage protecting the vault door. There was a small grey metal desk inside where a young Airman sat cleaning a disassembled M-16. The cage door had an eight-inch by two-foot slot. Sergeant Schwartz approached the slot. The Airman noticed the two and got up and moved quickly to the slot before the sergeant reached it. "Evening sergeant."

"Evening, morning, whatever you say. How you doing?"

"Good sarge, just doing inventory and cleaning my weapon. What do you need?"

"The last watch NCO should have set aside a weapon for the Major here."

"Okay, right there was a note." He turned and went back to the desk, rummaging around for a few seconds. "Here it is, got it," he read it quickly, "Ok, GAU-5, 86-344568. I'll be right back." Schwartz turned back toward Donovan.

"GAU-5, you know sir they're retiring those. So, where you going?"

"Well you know sergeant, I could tell you but then I'd have to kill you."

"Okay sir, got it. Good luck."

The Airman came back with a rifle, holding it with the muzzle down toward the floor. He approached the slot and reread the serial number out loud, "86-344568," and passed the weapon through the slot to Sergeant Schwartz. Once Schwartz had the weapon the Airman took the two steps back to the desk and grabbed a brown clipboard with a pen tied by green 550 cord hanging from it. "Okay sarge, sign here."

"Not me." He turned and motioned toward Donovan. "Sir your weapon, your signature."

He took the clipboard, verified the weapon serial number as Schwartz positioned it so he could read it, then signed and passed the clipboard back through the slot.

"Thanks Airman," Donovan said. He held the weapon in both hands and rotated it like a rotisserie, looking it over. It looked old. It felt old. He shook it, it rattled. It sounded like a cheap car jack.

"Thanks bud. Keep up the good work. Don't clean that weapon too much, you'll wear it out," Schwartz joked with the Airman.

"Okay sarge, have a good night-slash-morning." Schwartz stepped in front of Donavan and led him back to the watch desk and his two escorts. The two Airmen came to their feet as he and Schwartz approached.

"Okay gents, let's get to the pax terminal. Sergeant Schwartz, thanks very much for your help and thanks for the loan of the weapon."

"Don't mention it sir, good luck." He leaned to the side, around Donovan as he was still shaking his hand. "Nice meeting you guys too, take it easy." They returned the pleasantries.

Reed held the door open and Donovan, weapon in hand, and Johnson headed back to the vehicle. They got in and drove the short distance to the pax terminal where they unloaded Donovan's gear, hauling it into the terminal and up to the processing point.

Donovan turned to Johnson. "Hey, you guys can head back. It's still three hours to take off and I'm going; flight delayed, cancelled, whatever, I'm here till I'm gone so you guys get back and get some rest."

"Okay sir, you sure?"

"Yep, no problem, I'm good."

"Okay sir, good luck." Johnson shook his hand, Reed did also, then they simultaneously came to attention and saluted him. He straightened and returned the salute,

"Thanks guys. I'll see you around."

The Airmen dropped their salutes, turned around and headed out the terminal door. Donovan turned around and moved back to his gear, which was piled up against the counter at the processing point. He looked at it; now without the two Airmen helping him he thought, *Man, that's a lot of shit.*

"Hey sir, where you headed?" asked the NCO working the processing point. The muscular NCO had his uniform shirt slung over the back of his chair. His tee shirt revealed two large tattoos running the length of the inside of each arm. The one on his right arm was an elongated crucifix with a scroll across the top with I.N.R.I. inscribed on it and the one on the left arm was a long stem rose with "LoVe" written at the base of it.

"I'm heading to Seeb, Oman. Supposed to be out in at about three hours."

The NCO pointed to a door to the left of the terminal, "Okay, sir, move your stuff outside that door; there's a pallet out there with Seeb written on it. Just drop your stuff on there and we'll secure it"

"Okay."

"Sir, there's some water in the coolers in the back of the terminal you can have, we just ask that if you take one out, get a warm one from the boxes next to the coolers and replace it. Other than that, take a seat and we'll call 'Reach 34' when we're ready to load pax."

"Okay, thanks." He grabbed two of his A-bags and walked toward the door the NCO had pointed at. He maneuvered around the rows of chairs and then pushed the door open with a firm kick across the cross bar, and then stepped out to hold the door open until he got through. Once he got on the other side, he glanced around for the pallet and saw it about twenty feet away – there was nothing on it. He stepped up on the pallet, which was positioned on several four-by-fours and dropped his bags, side by side in the middle. Two more trips and all his gear was outside. He went back into the terminal, grabbed two water bottles and replaced them with two warm ones and sat in the seat closest to the door he just used. This was just one of the many routines that he would discover traveling around the theater. He sat and looked around the terminal; there were a total of six people, including the Airmen working the terminal. Once he sat down, the fatigue again washed over him. He pulled his patrol cap out of his cargo pocket and put it on, tugging the bill down over his eyes as he slumped down in his seat. He'd kept his helmet, weapon and ruck with him. He put his helmet on the floor in front of him and put his crossed feet up on it. He shifter his shoulders and legs around until he got comfortable and fell asleep.

"Reach 34 flight personnel move to the loading area – Reach 34 flight personnel move to the loading area," boomed the terminal intercom. "Reach 34 flight is ready for loading."

When Donovan woke up to the sound of the garbled PA system, he pulled his cap up and squinted, looking around the terminal. There were now about twenty-five people, all Army standing up and gathering their things.

Holy shit, he said to himself. *Look at all these fucking people.* He got to his feet and moved to the loading area. The passengers sat in the loading area for another ninety minutes. The Airmen in the terminal marshaled all the pax for Reach 34 outside where

Donovan had loaded the pallet. It was gone. The NCO without his blouse on ran through the manifest, name by name until all assigned to the flight answered up and were confirmed. The ground crew passed out earplugs and led the group out a gate onto the flight line. They all walked in single file a hundred yards to the aircraft. The aircraft was facing away from the terminal and the rear ramp was open, resting on the tarmac. The NCO had a set of red ear protectors on, held his clipboard in his left hand and took a beeline to the ramp of the aircraft. Once he reached the left edge of the ramp, he turned around and started waving the passengers forward, like a traffic cop. He touched each passenger on the shoulder as they walked by, counting. Once he hit fifteen, he stuck his left arm out and directed the remaining passengers to the right side of the aircraft. In about fifteen minutes, the aircraft was loaded and ready for takeoff. Donovan buckled in, listened to the garbled intercom transmissions on flight safety, then leaned back.

He was seated a few passengers from the last seat on the left side of the aircraft; next to him on one side was a Sergeant Major and on the other was an Army private. They both had Third Army patches on and the private looked to Donovan to be twenty at the most, was frail and was white as a sheet. "Hey soldier, how you doing?"

"I hate to fly sir, that's why I joined the Army."

"How do you feel about boats?"

"I hate the water too sir. I can't swim."

"Well, you'll be okay. Hey, how did you figure you'd get anywhere in the Army – you can't drive to the remote corners of the world."

"I know sir, I didn't think I'd be deploying so soon. I thought I might have a chance to deal with it. Not so much. I think I'm going to be sick."

"Well at least wait until you get airborne. If you get sick on the ground they might kick you off the flight."

"Really sir?" the young soldier asked, then turned away from him and without missing a beat, stuck his finger down his throat and started gagging. Donovan reached to grab his arm but it was too late, halfway to the soldier's arm he saw that the young man was going to be successful and rapidly transitioned from trying to stop him to trying not to get puked on. The soldier threw up.

"Whoa!! What'd you do that for?"

"You said they'd kick me off the flight," the young soldier said with a string of spittle hanging from his bottom lip.

"Okay, technique only, but you know they have puke bags?" He leaned forward, reached behind the soldier's head and pulled out one of the brown envelopes containing a white plastic airsickness bag that was stuffed behind the webbing of every seat position and handed it to the private. By now the loadmaster, the biggest guy Donovan had ever seen shoehorned into a flightsuit, had seen the puke on the floor in front of the private and came over to the private, moving with a purpose.

"HEY! What the fuck's your problem Army? Jesus, we're not even taxiing yet. Holy shit, you've got a goddamn puke bag in your fucking hand and you want to puke all over my airplane!?"

"Sorry Air Force, can I just get off?"

"Fuck no. Clean that shit up, now!"

"How am I supposed to do that? Don't you guys have flight attendants or something?"

"Flight attendants? FLIGHT ATTENDANTS? This ain't United Fucking Airlines. Jesus Christ, since when did they let retards in the fucking Army? I don't give a shit if you have to use your fucking T-shirt, just clean you're nasty ass puke up off my airplane!"

"Then can I get off?"

"Fuck no, that ain't my call. You're on this aircraft for a reason, whatever it is; puking doesn't remove the requirement. So shut the fuck up, clean up your bile and get back in your seat. You've got three goddamn minutes!"

Donovan pulled a flattened out roll of toilet paper out of his cargo pocket, unrolled a few turns and handed it to the private. He unrolled more and put the rest back in his pocket, leaning over to help the private. Before he got a few inches the Sergeant Major seated on his other side grabbed him by the shoulder.

"Negative sir, he can take care of that himself. We don't need no Air Force officer mopping up one of my Army private's messes, hooah?"

"Okay, Sergeant Major, copy." Donovan handed the private the toilet paper and leaned back in his seat.

"Hooah," stated the Sergeant Major.

The C-130 took off on time. The trip to Seeb, Oman was uneventful. Donovan got off, got his gear and set it all off to the side of the terminal at Seeb. He talked to the movement NCOs and got manifested for the next flight into Camp Rhino. There were no routine flights, this one was scheduled to take some international special forces in with their gear. It was an MC-130 and he was lucky to get on it. The MC-130 was the Special Ops version of the C-130 and was a much more capable aircraft than the "slick" C-130. Armored and equipped with robust infrared and electronic counter measures, it was designed to infiltrate defended enemy territory at night, usually at low altitude. He went through basically the same process he did on the flight from Ali Al Salem to Seeb for this one and sat in an assembly area waiting for a manifest call. He had a couple of hours so he found an office in the back area and called back to Kuwait to give his headquarters an update. He got a hold of R. Lee and told him he'd made it to Seeb and was scheduled for the next run to Rhino. R. Lee had no updates. He pulled out his green notebook and jotted down some notes, flight information, names, locations; he wrote a few lines about his trip so far, then closed the notebook and stuffed it back in his pocket; he thought maybe one day he'd write a book about all of this. He grabbed his ruck and threw it on his back, grabbed his helmet bag, stuffed it into one of his two A-bags and dragged them to the waiting area. He pushed them off to the side near the front row of metal chairs lined up in two columns that went back fifty rows. Slumping into one of the chairs, he leaned his head back and began the three plus hour wait till his flight took off. The whole terminal was made out of plywood, except for the metal chairs. After a minute or two he figured he'd have a better chance of getting some sleep if he transitioned to the side of the terminal and stretched out on the floor using his ruck as a pillow. He tried to get what little sleep he could in this new position.

"Sir...sir?" the Airman working the desk said, initially soft, then increasing the volume when he didn't get a response, "Sir... Major Donovan?"

"Yeah, that's me. What's up?"

"Sir, you've got a call up at the desk."

"Okay, thanks," he replied without lifting his head up off his ruck. He stayed still for a minute, then slowly got to his feet. He tipped his hat back on his head so he could see and walked up to the counter. Another Airman, not the one who woke him, was working the desk. "Major Donovan," he said to the Airman whose face was buried in a computer screen.

"Sir?"

"Yeah, your buddy just told me I had a call?"

"Oh, sorry sir; yep, come on around behind the counter."

"Okay, thanks." He made his way around the counter, picked up the receiver and pushed the button next to the blinking light.

"Donovan."

"Dude, Stacks, how's it going buddy?"

"Sir! How's it going? Great to hear from you, what's going on?"

"Dude, can't talk but I wanted to pass you a couple of names of our guys at Rhino – Mike Stanke and Bob Buress. They're two ETACs, they'll be there hopefully when you get there. We're trying to get them out of there and linked back up with our SOF guys, so not sure where they'll be, but track 'em down."

"Thanks sir, I'll track them down. You got any idea who I'm supposed to link up with on the Marine side?"

"Nope, no idea."

"Okay, I'll figure it out."

"Giddy up!"

"Roger, I'll try and make contact when I get down there."

"Dude, good luck! If you need to, use my call sign,

SOLAR Zero Six and add 'Alpha' to it, so you'll be SOLAR Zero Six Alpha. See ya."

"Thanks boss. See ya!" Donovan put down the phone and moved around the counter and went back to his gear, sat down, and leaned back against his ruck. For the first time, probably brought on by the conversation with Stacks, he thought about what he was involved in. It was the first time he thought of the enormity of it. He was part of the 9/11 response. He was going to war. But just then it occurred to him that he never thought he'd be going to war by himself. All of the thoughts that he ever had about going to war were that he'd go with his buddies, with his comrades, in a group. When he played war as a kid, that's what it was all about, being brave for your buddies, fighting together, savoring victories and consoling each other in defeats. He was heading in by himself and going to a place where he knew no one and no one knew him. He nodded off.

When the time came to board, all the passengers were instructed to grab their gear and haul it to the loading area. The flight would be an engine running offload, so the gear wouldn't be palletized; it'd be floor loaded and secured via cargo strap or loaded into the vehicles that were moving into Rhino. The manifest call came and the names of the scheduled passengers were read off. After each was confirmed, they hauled their gear out to the bus and loaded for movement to the MC-130. Each carried their own gear. Once out to the aircraft the crew chiefs and loadmasters assisted with the loading and positioned all the gear along the centerline of the aircraft, as much of it that was left around the two SOF vehicles that were positioned near the tailgate. Bumper to bumper they took up most of the floor space in the MC's cargo area. The gear was strapped down in the little remaining floor space in front of the vehicles. Donovan grabbed a seat toward the forward starboard side of the aircraft. He stuffed his helmet bag behind the seat webbing and re-secured his body armor and fastened his seatbelt. He looked to his left where two French Special Forces soldiers sat next to three US Green Berets. Across from him were two German Special forces soldiers and to their right were three Turkish Special Forces soldiers, to their right were two Australian Special Forces. The vehicles were US armored Humvees – heavy, loaded down with ammo, supplies and extra gear. All the passengers were focused. No one seemed to be looking at anyone else. Donovan thought to himself that this was one group of hard looking men. Everyone was staring straight ahead or at the floor. About thirty minutes went by before the loadmaster came up on the intercom.

"Gentlemen, we're prepping for takeoff. Secure all your personal gear and prepare to strap in for the duration of the flight. We'll take off and once we enter the box, we'll have to cut the lights and block out the portholes. If there's anything you'll need to get to you'll need to keep it within arm's reach. The duration of the flight is two hours. Again, once we're in the box, we'll assume a tactical profile, you'll need to stay strapped in until we land. We may have to maneuver and we'll try and keep you informed of the situation." The "Box" was the combat zone inside Afghanistan. Once that imaginary line was crossed, the aircraft configured for combat actions. The crew would arm their defensive countermeasures, secure the aircraft from white light, cover any windows in the cargo area and shut off all external light sources. The aircraft would get as stealthy as possible.

They taxied, did a rolling run up and once they straightened out on the runway the pilots pushed up the throttles. The aircraft lumbered down the centerline, slowly picking up speed. It was weighted down with armor, heavy vehicles, soldiers and supplies. It seemed to the passengers that the takeoff run was taking too long. They were right. Both pilots had their hands on the throttles pushing them forward hard against the stops, trying to get the maximum performance out of the aircraft's engines, it was like trying to get a dump truck airborne. As they got to about halfway down the runway they both pulled back on the yokes, as hard as they could, burying them back into their chests – the nose of the aircraft stayed on the ground. The airspeed indicator ticked a knot at a time 128 – 129 – 130 – not rotation speed yet – 131 – 132… The passengers in the back all had flown dozens if not hundreds of missions in the back of the Combat Talon; this one was different. Just about the time full fledge praying started the nose began to rise. After a few more seconds the gear started to shutter as the heavy weight aircraft started to lift off. After another few seconds, with only a little more than a hundred feet of runway left, they were airborne. The pilots pushed the yokes forward slightly to decrease the angle of attack and start gaining speed. Once they got a few more knots, they pulled back again. All the passengers in the back strained to lean sideways toward the nose of the climbing aircraft. After a couple of minutes of climb the aircraft leveled off and accelerated. The higher pitched roar of the engines now settled back to the drone of cruising speed as the pilots pulled back, adjusted and set the throttles.

The two crew chiefs and the loadmaster moved around the back of the aircraft, accomplishing checklists, double checking tie downs and prepping to cross into the box. The three crewmen pulled what looked like plastic manhole covers from behind the web seats and positioned them over the porthole windows that were visible. Some of them were hidden by the armor covering the middle section of the aircraft. This process took about thirty minutes. During their work, Donovan had pulled out his notebook:

Never thought I'd be going to war by myself. I'm not sure what's coming, but I thought I'd be with my guys, comrades to go through it with. I don't think war is something you should have to do by yourself – if you gotta go, you gotta go – but everything I ever read, all the history, all the war stories, all the movies, you had buddies or teammates, somebody. Your buddies or your men are who you fight for, who you're brave for, who you risk your life for.

He didn't know where to go with his thoughts. It wasn't going to change, at least on this mission. He looked around the aircraft. *Don't think I'm going to make any friends on this flight,* he thought. At that moment the white lights went out and red lights now dimly lit the cargo and passengers. The loadmaster's voice came over the scratchy intercom,

"Gentlemen, we're about 30 minutes from crossing into the box. We'll stay lights out for the duration. Ensure your seatbelts are tight and all your gear is secured. Don your helmets and body armor. We may have to maneuver. The crew will be on NVGs, do not use any white light until cleared to do so. We'll give you a ten-minute out call, then a crossing into the combat zone call. That is all."

The aircraft was cold. Donovan tore open his body armor, adjusted his fleece and reattached the Velcro front. He picked his helmet up from between his feet and put it on top of his head. The temperature had made the inner cushion pads of the helmet hard. He left the helmet sitting high up on top of his head until his body heat warmed the pads up enough to push it down into position. He had his ruck secured to the floor in front of him and kicked it a few times to make sure it stayed put. He pushed his helmet down; it was still tight, but the pads were soft enough for him to tighten his chinstrap. "Here we go," he said out loud to himself.

"Oui monsieur," came a reply to his left. One of the French Special Forces officers had heard him.

"Bon chance," Donovan offered back with his New Jersey accented high school French.

"Vous ausi."

He was happy the Frenchmen didn't continue the conversation further since he was about out of French phrases he could remember and knew he could barely order a croissant after the many years since high school.

"Ten minutes!" came the alert from the loadmaster over the intercom, echoed by the two crew chiefs that yelled it and simultaneously held up ten fingers. Ten minutes later: "We're in the box – use light discipline, remain seated, keep your helmets and body armor secured."

The aircraft had crossed over the border into Afghanistan. The two crew chiefs had positioned themselves at the right and left rear doors in wide straps that hung across the width of the doors like hammocks. They sat in these swings, looking out the windows spotting for Surface to Air Missiles, "SAMs" and Anti-Aircraft Artillery, "Triple A." The aircraft lumbered along. After what seemed like hours to the crew the aircraft reached the point it would start its descent to low altitude. The pilots pulled back the throttles and abruptly pushed the nose over. Everyone in the back became weightless, rising up off their seats against their lap belts. The noise level increased as the aircraft dived toward the ground picking up speed. Just a second or two after the pushover the pilots banked hard left and pushed the nose further over. Donovan had descended into low level in the B-52 hundreds of times, it was a portion of the mission he really enjoyed, this time, he wasn't so sure. His eyes darted around the aircraft. He was looking for anything that would give him more situational awareness; he needed to know what was going on. He saw the crew chief in the swing on the left side of the aircraft apparently yelling into his oxygen mask. He could see his jaw moving rapidly, then a bright flash visible even through the plastic porthole covers popped on the left side of the aircraft – *Fwoomp!* The aircraft banked back hard to the right and the nose started coming up, forcing everything and everybody toward the floor of the aircraft. The copilot spotted another SAM climbing up from just right of the nose. He took the aircraft, straightened the wings, then banked hard right, "Flares, flares!" he yelled into the intercom– *Fwoomp-crack!* The second SAM had popped well below the aircraft. The pilot took the aircraft back from the copilot. "I've got it."

"You've got it." As soon as the copilot replied he shot his eyes back to the window scanning for more SAM shots. The pilot saw the next one, it was coming up from their eight O'clock, he banked into it and lowered the nose, pulled back the throttles. It arched over the top of the aircraft, missing by sixty feet. The pilot had the airfield visible now, about five miles off the left wing and banked to line it up. He could see bright flashes all around the airfield. The field was under ground attack.

Donovan's mind raced after the second SAM. He thought for the first time that he might never see his wife again. *My poor wife. Poor Nikki… she'll be so sad… my poor dog, he'll never know… my mom and dad will be devastated…* The third SAM snapped him out of it but he still felt absolutely helpless sitting in the back of this heavy crate without being able to do anything. He trained for the first half of his career to operate in environments like this but as a crewmember, not a pink-bodied passenger. *Goddamn it!* he thought. The fourth shot appeared to break lock early and detonated well in front of the aircraft. The pilot saw the plume and smoke trail and it appeared to come from just outside the dirt strip of Camp Rhino. With the enemy in a position that close to the final approach, he knew they'd be sitting ducks. At that point, he'd had enough. The passengers in the back still had no clear idea of where they were or what was happening. They felt the aircraft pitch up and the engines push to their max capacity. There were more turns and evasive maneuvers, then steady level flight. They cruised in the red darkness for another 45 minutes before the white lights came on. None of the passengers were told of the mission change but it was obvious to all they weren't landing at Rhino.

As one of the crew chiefs moved to check a system near him, Donovan reached up and tapped him on the arm to get his attention and motioned him in closer; the crew chief leaned over. "What's up?"

"Heading back to Seeb sir, too hot."

"Okay, thanks."

When the lights came back on he noticed the Frenchman to his left had been shaping something out of a cardboard flap he'd pulled off of an MRE box that was strapped down in front of him. He put the finishing touches on it and then he handed it to his comrade to his left, He had formed a "medal" out of the cardboard and had written, "Pour le Merite": For Merit, on it, apparently for weathering the hail of surface to air missiles. The older Frenchman laughed out loud, the younger smiled awkwardly.

Donovan leaned back, tilted his head back against the webbing of his seat and thought to himself, *Shit, I've got to do this all over again.* Once they landed back at Seeb he went straight to the flight scheduler to check on the next flight. There was another going out that night; it was now 0300 in Seeb. He and the group of international Special Forces members were taken with their gear to a transient billeting area. By the time they all took their weapons to the armory and got settled the sun was starting to come up. They were dropped off in an area with rows of tents with between sixteen and twenty bunks in each. It was already hot. He knew with the sun and the heat and people coming and going in and out of the tents all day long he wasn't going to get much rest. He tried anyway. As he lay in his bunk he couldn't help think about how close he came to buying the farm and he hadn't even set foot in Afghanistan yet.

CHAPTER TEN

RHINO

Donovan woke up at about 1400, got dressed, got his gear together and looked for a ride to the pax terminal. Eventually he made it to the terminal and checked in with the Airman at the desk. He'd travel on another MC-130, this time hauling Australian medics and their vehicles. Same routine, same hauling gear, same waiting, same same same.

When he responded to the manifest call he saw right away the list would be short. He and only one other person lined up for the call. It was an Australian medic escorting two armored vehicles into Rhino to link up with the forward deployed Australian Special Forces. He figured with the time they had left to wait he might as well say hi.

"Hi, Major Pat Donovan, USAF. How you doing?"

"Right, great, Major Jackson Smythe, RAAF, medical officer, how goes it?" he replied with a big smile. Major Smythe was about 6'2" 190lbs, dark black hair, wearing dark green camouflage and tan boots. To Donovan, he looked like a thinner, stretched out version of Russell Crowe.

"Going good. We had a run at Rhino last night; didn't go so well."

"Oh yeah, how so?"

"We got within a few miles, but had four SAMs shot at us, a couple popped off pretty close. After a couple of attempts, the pilot had enough and came back here."

"Holy dooley, that must've been rough gettin' knocked back like that. Those pilot boys are true blue battlers."

"Yep," replied Donovan, not knowing exactly what Smythe had just said. Not just what the words meant, but understanding what he was actually saying. He thought to himself the last time he had that much trouble understanding somebody speaking English was in southern Louisiana. They chatted for the next couple of hours, mostly about beer.

Donovan and Smythe boarded the aircraft. It was packed to the gills. There were the two armored Australian Range

120

Rovers, a large pallet of bottled water and a large pallet loaded with wooden crates full of 80-millimeter mortar rounds. The two stowed their personal gear and strapped in for the flight. The aircraft took off on schedule, struggling to get airborne. The flight path was the same but this time much less exciting. He knew a lights out NVG landing on a dirt strip was exciting enough without getting shot at, so he was relieved when they touched down and the pilots reversed the props and stood on the brakes, taxiing to an engine running offload area. The ramp opened up to darkness. Several ground crewmen wearing NVGs on ATVs maneuvered to the back of the aircraft and helped with the unloading. He and Smythe were held back until the cargo was unloaded. They grabbed all their gear and waddled down the ramp. Donovan had his body armor, ruck, helmet, weapon and ammunition and a 50-60lbs A-bag in each hand. As he stepped off the ramp he lost his balance and started to tumble forward as his foot sank in the powder-soft sand. He reflexively moved it forward to counter his loss of balance. Now the other foot kicked forward and he dropped his bags to try and right himself. One of the ground crewmen, back on his ATV, watched him struggle through his goggles and the scarf covering his face; he shook his head in an exaggerated way disapprovingly at Donovan.

"Goddamn Mother Fucker!" Donovan shouted, muffled by the running engines, not at anybody, just at his frustration. "Goddamn it; fucking shit." He picked up his bags and kept moving out from behind the hail of rocks, dust and exhaust kicked up by the engines. Smythe had a much easier movement from the aircraft; all his gear was loaded in his vehicles. Once Donovan cleared the back of the aircraft he saw a lighted area in a single story building with dozens of antennae on top. He figured that would probably be the headquarters. He pushed through the plywood door and into an open area, a kind of lobby with two hallways running at 90 degrees. The hallways were worn tile, mostly covered by sand. There were bullet holes all along both lengths of the corridors and the place was full of Marines, all busy.

There was one Marine private behind a wooden desk at

the juncture of the two hallways. Donovan dropped his gear across from the desk and approached the private. "Private, where's the CO?" The private stood up and pointed over his left shoulder with the eraser of his pencil.

"Right over there, sir."

"Okay, thanks." He spotted the general reviewing papers on a clipboard with one of his Captains. As he approached, he saw the General's nametag; Morris. As he got closer the General caught him out of the corner of his eye, lowered his clipboard as he turned toward Donovan.

"Sir…" Donovan got no further. He had started bringing his hand up in a salute but never got past chest high.

"Who the fuck are you and what the fuck are you doing on my airfield?" the General challenged loudly with fire in his eyes and gritted teeth.

"Sir, I'm Major Donovan, I was ordered here…"

"Who ordered you here?" he accentuated each word.

"Sir, my commander, Colonel Laredo."

"Who the fuck is he?"

"Sir, he's the 18 ASOG commander. He sent me here on orders from the CFACC."

"What do you do?"

"TACP sir."

"We got those! Don't need no fucking Air Force to help us with Close Air Support. I don't need another goddamn shitter-and-eater out here!"

"Sir, I'm here because I'm a FAC and I'm a bomber guy – the fratricide…" Donovan knew he was in a verbal knife fight with the general and the general had the knife, and a hammer.

"Where's your gear?" the General said, cutting him off.

"Right over there, sir." Donovan pointed over his shoulder, not taking his eyes off Morris.

"Grab it."

"Bill." the General turned to his aide. "Grab some of the Major's shit. Let's go." The General grabbed his helmet; his aide grabbed one of Donovan's A-bags and the General grabbed the other. Morris was shorter than average, but was coming off to Donovan as a certified badass.

"Sir…" He was going to try again to convince the General he was under orders and couldn't leave without those orders changing.

"Stow it Major, let's move." The General, the Captain and the Major left the building and started walking with Donovan's gear. "I'm going to take you to the end of the runway to some of your Air Force CCT guys and they're going to put you on the next plane off my airfield. Copy?" He walked to Donovan's right, the Captain in trail. They kicked up a small cloud, visible in the moonlight, from the fine dust that covered the airstrip. The General moved with a purpose. "You got a weapon Major?"

Jesus Christ, I'm an ALO in the Air Force, not a Goddamn Girl Scout, he thought to himself, but he said, "Yes sir."

"Do you know how to use it?"

"Yes sir," he replied. He'd never fired a shot in anger, only punched holes in paper once a year, not counting the shooting he did with his dad and brother growing up. He'd shot a lot but not in combat, not at a human. *This is nuts, he thought, I've got a fire-breathing Marine one-star carrying my gear to kick me off his airfield.*

"Well, lock and load, you may need your weapon out here."

Donovan was getting increasingly pissed off at the Marine General's demeaning and condescending attitude towards him. "Yes sir." He pulled a magazine out of one of his front pouches and inserted it into the magazine well but it wouldn't secure to the weapon. He pulled it out, made sure it was lined up properly, slapped the bottom of the magazine, but it still wouldn't engage. "Goddamn it," he thought. *The General's been challenging my martial competence and I can't get the fucking piece of shit magazine to engage in this old ass rental rifle. Goddamn it!* He held the magazine in position. *For fuck sake – unfuckingbelievable!* he almost said out loud. They continued down the dark runway.

"Major, you get on the next fucking airplane out of here, you understand?" The trio was approaching the Combat Control Team position. The Captain jogged ahead with Donovan's A-bag and addressed what appeared to be the leader of the CCT element, Captain Flynn. He then came back, grabbed Donovan's other bag and ran back to the element and dropped it next to the other. The General turned around and started walking back to his HQ without another word. Donovan was still in shock. The leader of the CCT element approached Donovan.

"Hey sir, how you doing?"

"Not too fucking good, how about you?"

"Well sir, I'm Air Force but I'm part of this Task Force and I'm working for the General. He wants me to put you on the next flight out of here."

"Well Captain, I ain't going. I can't. I got orders from my chain of command to stay here and help. Until I get that retreat order from them, I'm staying."

"Well, you can stay out here with us until the next aircraft arrives or you can take your chances with the General. Or you can go talk to Colonel Tripper, the Air Component Rep to the Task Force."

"Bob Tripper?" Donovan asked.

"Yep. You know him?"

"I met him once, briefed him."

"He's back at the head shed."

"Okay, I'm going to haul my stuff back there and talk to him." He grabbed his ruck, his weapon and his bags and started walking to the HQ. One of the NCO's piped up,

"Sir, I can give you a ride up there."

"That'd be great thanks." They threw Donovan's gear in a small ATV, a "Gator" and started the drive up the runway back to the HQ building. Once there the NCO tossed Donovan's bags out of the Gator and took off back to his CCT brothers. Donovan moved his stuff back inside the building and looked for Colonel Tripper. He didn't know it, but Colonel Laredo and Colonel Tripper were peers and rivals, both CCT officers, always in competition. They had a cordial but very competitive relationship.

Once he checked that General Morris wasn't around he asked the private at the desk where to find the air component representative. The private pointed out a door opposite his desk. Donovan went through the door back outside and saw a small,

124

lighted area up against another building. There was a small table under the cover of a green tarp with three men sitting at it. He recognized Colonel Tripper and approached.

"Colonel Tripper, sir, I'm Major Donovan. We met at ACC a couple of years ago, I briefed you on the CRG concept."

"Okay" the Colonel responded, barely glancing at him. Tripper was tall and lean, had sharp pointed features, sunken cheeks and was grey around the temples. He looked hungry.

"Sir, I was wondering if you could help me out. Colonel Laredo…"

"Laredo, Mack Laredo?" the Colonel interrupted.

"Yes sir."

"Yeah, sent you here for what?"

"Sir, in response to the friendly fire incident to help the Marines out with some bomber expertise and lend a hand with CAS if necessary. I'm a TAC."

"Well, help you out with what?" the Colonel asked without looking up from the papers on the desk.

"Sir, General Morris just walked me to the end of the runway, actually carried some of my stuff, to kick me off his airfield. He left me with your guys and told them to get me on the next plane out of here."

"Well, sounds like you need to get on the next plane out of here," Tripper chuckled.

"Sir, I'm under orders. I'm not gonna just take off without clearing it with Colonel Laredo."

"I'll handle that."

"Sir, I'm not looking for that. I'm asking that you intervene with the General and get his okay for me to stay on."

"Oh, well, I'm rotating out of here tonight and Commodore Grant is coming in, but, I'll see what I can do."

He knew the Colonel would do nothing to help but he had nowhere else to go at this point. "Thanks sir."

Colonel Tripper got up slowly from the desk and went back inside the HQ building. In what seemed like a minute and a half he came back out.

"Major, I talked it over with the General. You're outta here. Head on back to the end of the runway and we'll get you out with me in a couple of hours."

"Okay sir, thanks for trying." He held back his anger and frustration. It was clear nothing was said to anyone. He figured he'd find the two ETACs supporting the task force before he got booted off the airfield. "Sir, you know where the two ETACs are from the 18 ASOG?"

"Nope."

"Okay sir. Thanks." Donovan hadn't been less thankful to anyone in a long time. He left his gear and tried to find a phone or a radio to get in touch with Colonel Laredo. He opened his green notebook and got the number for the ACE. There was one phone hooked up through a satellite that could link with the unclassified system, the Defense Switch Network worldwide military phone system. It was on the private's plywood desk. "Private, can I use that phone?"

"You can try, sir. Most times it doesn't work."

"Okay, I'll give it a shot." He dialed the numbers three times before he got a ring.

"A-C-E, Sergeant Foley, unsecured line."

"Sergeant Fole..." Donovan could tell the line disconnected, "Fuck!" He tried again, and again.

"A-C-E, Sergeant Foley, unsecured line."

"Sgt Foley, I need to talk with Colonel Laredo ASAP."

"Okay sir, he's right here. Hang on."

He heard the line break again. "Goddamn it!!" he shouted out loud. He tried again.

The Marine private turned to him. "Sir, that ain't your private phone."

"I got it private, give me two more minutes."

"Aye sir."

He had tried twice more while talking to the Marine. Finally, "A-C..."

"Foley!" Donovan interrupted, "Get Colonel Laredo!"

"Okay, can I ask who's calling?"

"Get the fucking Colonel! Now!"

"Colonel Laredo." The Colonel finally was on the line.

"Sir, Major Donovan."

"Pat! Where are you?"

"Sir, I'm at Rhino."

"Shit hot."

"Sir, I've got some problems." The phone went dead again. He tried again.

"Sir, that's it. I've got to keep that line available – do you read?" The private asserted.

"Okay, I got it." Donovan was frustrated, tired and angry. He figured if he found the two ETACs he might be able to make radio contact via SATCOM back to the ACE and to Colonel Laredo. *This is un-fucking-believable; you can't make this shit up,* he thought to himself. *What a goat rope, if I did put this in a book, nobody would believe it.* He didn't know his way around the camp, he didn't know anyone there, he had no points of contact, he wasn't sure of his mission, he was getting kicked off the airfield personally by the Task Force commander. "Son of a bitch!" He said out loud. He walked out the HQ plywood door and, for lack of a better plan, turned right. He walked along the low slung mud brick and plaster building, past a couple of doors and then saw one that was cracked open with dim light coming out from behind it. "Special Operations Command and Control Element" was magic-markered on the door. He stopped and pushed the door open to see a small room with three plywood easels with paper maps push-pinned to them and across the top of one read "ODB." In front of that easel, someone was standing with their back to the door. He stepped inside.

"Excuse me." The individual at the easel half turned and looked over his shoulder at him.

"Yeah?"

"I'm looking for two Air Force ETACs."

"Yeah, they're with us, what's up?" He turned further toward Donovan and he could tell now that he was an Army Special Forces Major. The Major was big and burly and his hair was about two or three times longer than the slackest Marine there at the base.

"Just trying to track them down. They work for our Group back home, just want to check on them, see if they need anything."

"Oh, okay…hey, how you doing, I'm Jim Kelly, 5th

Group."

"Hey Jim, Pat Donovan, how you doing?"

"Pretty good, what are you doing here, if you don't mind me asking?"

"Seems to be the question of the day. General Morris just asked me that, well not quite that nicely and then escorted me off his patch."

"No shit?"

"No shit. I've got orders just like everybody else but apparently nobody told the General about them. I'm an ALO and FAC with the 18 ASOG and got sent out here because of the frat. Sorry about your guys."

"Yeah, thanks," the Major responded as he looked back toward the map.

"I've been trying to get a hold of my boss. My immediate boss, my squadron commander, works for your boss, Colonel Longstreet up at Dagger.

"Oh, okay, yeah, Shack or Smack…?"

"Stacks."

"Yeah that's right, your guys told me about him. I think I might have met him. Hey, you can stay here with us. The next room is where we're bunking. You can stay with us until you get your situation figured out. Your guys are great. You say you're a FAC too?"

"Yep."

"Okay… okay, we might be able to put you to work."

"That'd be great. You mind if I move my stuff in next door?"

"No, no problem, there should be a couple of open cots. The shitters are out the door then two o'clock. No showers, MREs, you know the drill."

"Great, thanks, I really appreciate it. You don't have a phone or radio here do ya?"

"I've got a SAT phone. I hang on to it but you can use it to get a hold of home plate."

"Awesome, thanks."

"Yeah, there's an instruction card in the holder, you gotta dial a bunch of numbers, then you can get a DSN or commercial line. Not secure though."

"Anything would be great; thanks again. Okay, I'm going to move my stuff, then if I can try my higher with the SAT phone, that'd be awesome."

"Sure, knock yourself out."

Donovan retrieved his gear and took it to the room next door. He pushed the door open. There were two soldiers stretched out on their bunks; one was reading and the other was listening to music from a CD player. The room was four walls, a door and two windows with a concrete floor, and there was a big pile of sandbags against the back wall. Each of the sidewalls were lined with bunks.

"Hey gents. Pat Donovan, staying with you all for a while. I'm from the same unit as the Air Force ETACs."

"Hey, make yourself at home" replied the soldier reading the book. The other soldier just held up a hand in a greeting, still focused on listening to his music. Donovan threw his gear down in the corner and grabbed the bunk closest to the door on the left hand side of the building. He then stepped around his cot and went over to shake the hand of the soldier closest to him with the headphones on. He looked to be in his early 30's, sandy blond hair about 5'9," sporting a pretty deep red sunburn on his nose, cheeks and forehead. He had his DCU trousers on but had a dark blue New York Giants sweatshirt on. Donovan leaned over and extended his hand, the soldier caught him out of the corner of his eye, looked up, smiled and did the same. They shook.

"Hanley," he stated.

"Donovan. You a Giants fan?"

The soldier pointed to the logo on his sweatshirt and made a face that was meant to communicate, "Duh, are you blind?" Donovan stepped around Williams' bunk and extended his hand to the other soldier.

"How you doing? Donovan."

"Nice to meet you. Boone." Boone had a broad, full smile. He was 5'11", dark black complexion, very muscular. He was wearing his DCU trousers and a black long sleeve thermal shirt. Donovan went back to his bunk, arranged his bags and gear and threw his ruck up on the bunk. He stretched out and rested his head on his ruck, interlocked his fingers over his chest and shut his eyes. While still lying on his cot with his eyes closed, he asked Boone and Hanley, "Hey fellas, what's the deal around here? What's what, where's what?"

Boone replied, "Well sir, first things first, the shitter's over by the entrance to the compound, as you walk out the door to your two o'clock. You can smell it or follow the smoke. They're usually burning shit, seems like 24/7. There ain't no showers or anything like that and right now we're on MRE's – two a day."

"Good to know, thanks. I only brought a couple. Is there a supply point, how's that work?"

"Right now we're still pulling from our own supply but probably today or tomorrow we're going to have to shift over and start relying on the Marines. In the meantime, you can grab your two a day from our supply. You're not staying long are you?"

"Haven't got that all figured out yet but I might be helping you all out. I'm a forward air controller."

"Okay, good skill to have. We get the basics but could sure use a refresher if you get a chance."

"Absolutely," Donovan replied enthusiastically, seeing a possible opportunity to serve a purpose. "I'm going to try the same pitch with the Marines but right now, as far as they know, I got kicked off the airfield."

"Nice," replied Boone. Donovan fell asleep.

The next morning he woke up, still dressed. He grabbed his shaving kit, canteen cup and a bottle of water from his ruck and went outside to where the Humvees were parked. He rested his shaving kit on the hood of one and turned one of the mirrors outward towards him and started shaving out of his canteen cup. It was sunny and already getting warm at 0700. After he shaved he went back to his bunk, got his blouse on and headed back over to the SOCCE headquarters looking for Major Kelly. In between his billet and the SOCCE he ran into Commodore Grant. The Commodore was a Navy SEAL. He'd just taken over for Colonel Tripper the night before and would command what

Donovan just learned was Combined Joint Special Operations Task Force-South or Task Force K-bar. The Commodore was impressive. He looked strong, compact. He had no hair; Donovan couldn't tell if he was bald or shaved his head. He had a deep scar on his cheek. Donovan saw him just outside the hooches knocking out several pull ups on a makeshift pull up bar. When he was done Donovan introduced himself.

"Hi Sir, Major Pat Donovan," he said, sticking out his hand.

"Hey Major, heard about you," the Commodore replied. "I understood General Morris escorted you off the airfield last night."

"Well sir, he did, but I couldn't just leave. The Air Force has given me orders and well, sir, I was wondering if you could help me out."

"I work for the General. If he wants you out of here, I want you out of here."

"I understand sir. I think I can meet my commander's intent, leave shortly and maybe even help you out."

"How's that?" The Commodore looked at Donovan, one eye squinting against the sun, the other looking him over.

"Sir, I got sent out here to help with Close Air Support integration, mainly because of the fratricide. I'm a Forward Air Controller and a B-52 guy, I could brief up the Marine squad and platoon leaders and their FACs on the specifics of employing the B-52."

"Well, let me talk it over with the General."

"Thanks sir, that's all I'm asking and I'd appreciate it."

"Okay, we'll see. So, where you from Donovan?"

"Sir, I'm from New Jersey."

"Oh yeah? Too bad."

"How 'bout you, sir?"

"Rhode Island."

"Where do you live now sir?"

"California." The Commodore had taken a seat in a green folding chair next to the door of his hooch and started eating an orange. He instructed Donovan to sit down by pointing to another web chair; Donovan sat.

131

The two chatted for several more minutes. Donovan felt that they'd established a good rapport then he asked, "Sir, where'd you get that scar on your face?"

The Commodore looked over at him, smiling, shaking his head and laughing a bit. "You're not supposed to ask questions like that." He paused for a second or two, obviously thinking about whether or not to continue on that topic. "A guy stuck a knife in my face." He put another wedge of orange in his mouth.

Donovan figured it would probably be smart to go back to benign topics. It wasn't that he sensed the Commodore was sensitive about that subject, more like he didn't like talking about himself. Either way, the Commodore finished his orange, "Okay Major, I've got to get to work. Get out of here and we'll talk later."

"Okay, sir, thanks. Nice talking to you."

"Yeah." the Commodore went into his hooch. Donovan got up and continued on to the SOCCE. He pushed the plywood door open. There was already a lot of activity going on in the small headquarters. He found Major Kelly in the SOCCE sitting in the corner with two of his NCOs hovering over a map on the floor. The map had several dark marker lines on it indicating different paths and obstacles. Major Kelly looked up from the map, apparently looking for someone else and saw Donovan. Not remembering his name, he called him over,

"Hey Air Force, come here a sec," said Kelly, waving him in as he spoke. "I just got finished talking to the General. We're directed to conduct an SR mission to the northwest up to Lashkar Gah, and then head to the east along Highway 1 and link back up with the Marine assault force just north of Kandahar. I've got five of six required personnel for the team and I'm thinking it'd be great if you can ride with them as their FAC; we can use you if we need close air support and it'd get you out of line of sight of the General."

"Sure...of course," Donovan replied. "Who should I talk to about getting integrated with the team?"

"Hanley."

"Okay. Can you give me the timing?"

"Not a hundred percent sure yet but will be within the next 24 to 48 hours."

"Okay, great, got it," he looked over the map.

The next morning he got up and walked over again to the Humvees to shave. Kelly intercepted him.

"Hey Donovan, looks like overnight your Colonel talked to General Morris about the B-52s and JDAMs or something, so your good to stay here at Rhino."

"Great, that's great. Thanks for passing that on." He continued to the Humvee. As he got to the vehicle he noticed several Marines escorting a prisoner. The man was blindfolded and bound at the wrists and had shackles on his ankles. The Marines led him to a shipping container that was just outside of the hooches. The prisoner shuffled with difficulty, not able to take a full stride. Two Marines, one on each side held him almost up off the ground and walked him to the opening of the container and inside, out of sight, then the two Marines exited, shut the container door and left. Two other Marines took seats in folding chairs against the wall of the nearest hooch and watched.

Donovan tried to make contact with Colonel Laredo and Stacks throughout the day. He also helped with the planning of the SR mission he'd soon be part of. Each time he came and went from the area he looked at the shipping container. At one point a couple of Marines were tossing rocks on top of the container.

"Come on out Johnny," they said. "Come on out little Johnny Walker."

"The American Taliban," as he was called, John Walker Lindh, had been moved to Camp Rhino. He was removed from the container and taken into the room next to the one Donovan was staying in. He was in there all day. Although he had walked in he was taken out on a stretcher; back to the shipping container.

The planning for the SR mission was finalized and Donovan would go as their sixth man. They were going to take two Humvees; one would pull a trailer with additional gear and logistics equipment. Donovan would ride with Boone, who would man the Mk-19 grenade launcher and Hanley who would drive their vehicle. Saunders would be in the lead vehicle manning the 50 caliber machinegun with Hanson driving and Kirby in the passenger seat. They got their gear together and moved out in the late afternoon to get near the objective under the cover of darkness. They got a few miles clear of Camp Rhino and stopped to test their weapons. They radioed the Rhino ops center and got clearance. Boone fired several rounds from the Mk-19. It jammed twice. He worked on it until he could fire a short string of rounds without a jam. At this point, Donovan started to realize that this was all very real. All of his notions about going to war melted away as reality set in. Saunders fired the .50 with no issues. They contacted Rhino that they were complete and pressed on. They got stuck twice in the soft desert sand on the way to the village. It took about two hours to get out the second time; they had to unhook the trailer off the second Humvee and stuff a couple of cots under the wheels for traction, and then manhandled the trailer back on. The cots ended up being twisted piles of aluminum. They got the vehicles moving again. Good thing it was early December, not in the heat of an Afghan summer. They approached their waypoint on time and took up a position using the terrain to mask them from Lashkar Gah below. The team didn't know it yet, but they'd been spotted.

CHAPTER ELEVEN

LIBERATORS

The small formation approached the village in the mid afternoon. The sky was azure blue and the air was still. They came up from the southeast on the east side of the Helmand river; riding on the shielded side of the "military crest," the spot about three quarters of the way up toward the top of a hill which allowed personnel or vehicles to be shielded from the opposite side and to use the terrain to blend into, on the front side. If contact was made on the front side, a quick maneuver to the opposite side would shield from the enemy. The formation moved north toward the end of the ridge and stopped, surveyed for a crossing point and assessed the surrounding terrain, deciding to cross at what looked like a shallow ford and enter the village from the east. There wasn't a whole lot of observable activity as they crossed the river. Saunders, his cheek puffed up covering a wad of chewing tobacco and bubble gun, was in the turret of the lead vehicle on the .50 and Boone, wearing a brown dew rag and looking like a pirate, was in position in the turret of the second Humvee on the Mk-19. As they made landfall on the village side of the river Donovan saw a villager working in a field, hunched over raking shit from one of the elevated shit houses positioned at the end of the field for fertilization. The villager looked up, came upright, and leaned on the handle end of his hoe. He had on a brown "mushroom hat" and a dirty white long shirt – some called it a "man dress" – and a brown vest. His white beard went down to the middle of his chest. Donovan thought it was hard to try and guess what this guy was thinking. This village could have been out of the Middle Ages and there was no telling how exposed this guy had been to vehicles, technology, the Russians, the Taliban. Maybe he had a satellite TV and a pickup truck, but there was little doubt this was the first glance he was getting of US forces. The vehicles passed abeam a couple of mud huts, no doors, no covers on the doors or windows, dark inside. The team was tense. The road, more like a path, started to bend to the south so the view was obscured. Not a good situation so they paused while Hanson looked for a better route. They couldn't turn around easily; they were now bounded by a small two and a half to three-foot wall on both sides. They'd have to back out or press ahead, or if the shit hit the fan they would try to go through or over the wall. Just as Hanson got out of the vehicle to get a better look, he could barely fit between the half-opened door and the wall, two little boys came out from behind one of the mud huts; Donovan guessed they were around three or four years old. They had on little white prayer caps, vests, little versions of man dresses, one had sandals and the other was barefoot. They both had dirty faces complete with snot-encrusted upper lips. Both were chewing on their fingers, their eyes locked on the Americans. Sergeant Kirby opened the right front passenger door and also had trouble getting out due to the short wall. He moved out from behind and around the door, shut it and moved up toward Hanson who'd done the same. Donovan opened his door, same deal; squeezed out and left it slightly opened. He was glad to get out. He turned toward the kids, a little anxious to make some kind of contact with the people they were liberating. By the time he got turned back around there were three more kids standing there. The recent additions were a little older but looked like bigger versions of the first two. He reached into his right front pocket and pulled out a stick of "Charms." As soon as he moved all their eyes were on him, locked on, tracking. When the colorful wrapper of the Charms became visible all the little expressions lightened. Stern looks of curious concentration simultaneously morphed to looks of anticipation. Donovan's first thought was, *Shit, I don't have enough.*

He broke the package into five pieces and got a real kick out of handing those kids some candy. He smiled and they smiled back and giggled – Bingo – Contact! Donovan kept glancing up every couple of seconds to keep his situational awareness up. When he glanced up toward the lead vehicle he noticed Hanson looking back at him and he didn't look happy. Donovan looked back at the kids and it became obvious he was pissed about him passing out candy. By now there were nine of them; these new guys looked like they were probably teenagers and Donovan was out of candy.

Shit, he thought again. He tried to figure out what else he could give them or what else to do to keep everything friendly and positive. He knew he wasn't going to get many more of these opportunities. Two adult males approached the opposite side of the vehicle. The older, taller of the two was dressed the same as the man they saw in the field but had a thick black beard. The second man was younger, no beard, and a pillbox hat. Both had AK-47s draped over their shoulders. The older man had grey eyes, a dark grey mushroom hat and a dark green and silver scarf loosely draped around his neck. Donovan thought, *This guy looks mean.* His face was sunbaked, leathery, with deep vertical lines down his cheeks. He had deep crow's feet radiating from his eyes. His mustache separated a bit from his beard, looked groomed, the ends were distinct and looked like they were twisted together and brushed back. But he looked like he'd slit your throat as soon as look at you.

On an impulse Donovan pulled his right nomex glove off and stuck his hand out toward him, smiled and said, "Asalam alaikum."

He wasn't sure how his pronunciation was, not too good he was sure with his New Jersey accent, but the man grabbed Donovan's hand in a powerful grip and at the same time smiled a smile that transformed his whole face, his whole persona – he seemed to become a different person. He turned from what Donovan thought was the meanest looking guy he'd ever seen to what he thought anybody would consider a friendly looking guy you'd want to have a beer with. Donovan really enjoyed shaking his hand because it seemed to make all this more real. The kids were a start, making that contact, but shaking this man's hand and getting an emotional reaction – it was real. He hated to admit to himself that the second thought through his mind was, *Where was my hand sanitizer?* He remembered being briefed and reading in the Afghan Country Book during the pre-deployment briefs about the average lifespan of an Afghan male being 45 years and that approximately 70% of the population had tuberculosis. He wouldn't let that stop him, but he also didn't want to get TB and pay too high a price for the "hands across the water" moment. He shook the younger man's hand and got a similar reaction and then turned to the kids. Donovan unnoticeably hesitated, wondering if it would belittle the gesture to the men if he shook hands also with the kids. He figured since he singled out the oldest adult male first and shook his hand, he'd be okay going down the pecking order. He thought he got it about right. The youngest recoiled and slid behind what was probably his older brother and looked up for guidance. He seemed scared, but all in all it went well, it went great. As Donovan was going down the line he noticed two young girls had popped up further down the wall. They didn't have head coverings so he figured that must be mandatory at a certain age. They were beautiful little girls, bright eyes, one had green, one had blue; beautiful little faces. They reminded him of the *National Geographic* cover back in the '80s; he thought of the beautiful Afghan girl with the piercing eyes. He remembered seeing that picture and, like the rest of the world, was captivated by the mystery of the country she represented. He was really struck by how attractive the Afghans were. The men were rugged looking and handsome, even the old men who'd now also showed up, distinguished looking, tough. The girls were all very pretty, dirty, scuffed up a bit, but very pretty. He thought it was the combination of history, their reputation as warriors and this first face-to-face meeting that sparked admiration in him for them. This turned eventually into affection for the country and the people. Donovan liked Afghanistan and he liked the Afghanis. Those in the first wave, he thought, were initially motivated by the no-kidding thirst for revenge for 9/11. But now, not only did he want some payback, the American way, about 1000 to 1, but, he no-shit wanted to help the Afghan people. It might have been somebody else's bumper-sticker phrase or political tag line, but it's what he actually felt.

Now that he had created a maneuver problem, a logistics problem and a PR opportunity the team had to figure out their next move. Hanson had already decided, conversed with the village elder, and handed over two cases of MRE's to the locals. He approached Donovan, looking now pretty relaxed,

"How's it going Major? Make any pen pals?"

"No, but that old guy's my new AmWay distributor," Donovan replied with a laugh.

"You don't really sell that shit do you?"

"Fuck no." He winced. "I spent half my career breaking contact with guys trying to sign me up."

"Good, otherwise I'd have to shoot you and leave you back there in the desert," Hanson said as he laughed.

Donovan immediately regretted even referring to AmWay as a joke; he thought Hanson probably thought he did peddle the stuff and just made a joke of it to create some doubt.

"Okay everybody, huddle up," Hanson called out. "We're going to get through this village, exiting to the northeast, proceed to the bank of the river, go north to the outskirts of Lashkar Gah and continue our mission. We'll stop just short of the objective, rest a few hours and get moving again at 0400. We should be able to move faster along the harder ground near the river. Major, get up on the net and see what we've got for air tonight."

"Rog," Donovan replied.

They got back in the vehicles; waving to the villagers they just had the brief encounter with. They would most probably never see them again but this was the first contact for all of them, with their Allies, the liberated.

"Any questions?" he asked and waited a few seconds. "Nothing heard… okay, let's go."

They got a couple of hundred meters outside the village and took a security stop to check weapons, take a leak and double check their position and course. The vehicles stopped just below the crest of the small hill they were climbing. Donovan attempted to make contact on the radio.

"Hey Moon, set SOLAR up in the SATCOM would ya?" He asked. He would have done it himself but it was Moon's radio.

"Sure," he replied and set the SATCOM channel in the PRC-117 radio. "You're all set," he said as he passed Donovan the mic.

"SOLAR, SOLAR, this is SOLAR Zero Six-alpha – over," Donovan transmitted. He got no response, waited a couple of seconds and tried again. "SOLAR, SOLAR, this is SOLAR Zero Six-alpha - over."

"Last calling SOLAR, say again call sign – over," the response came back.

"SOLAR this is SOLAR Zero Six-alpha, how copy – over," he answered back. He was starting to get a bad feeling that his call sign info wasn't passed on as he'd coordinated with Stacks.

"Last calling SOLAR, I don't recognize your call sign, cease transmission and clear this net – over and out," the radio operator shot back.

Fuck! Donovan thought to himself. *I know the guy on the other end of that transmission.* He knew if he didn't get the hand off brief about the call sign he was right to cut him off, but… "Looks like we've got some admin issues with SOLAR," he said to Moon, who really seemed to care less, which was good for Donovan since he felt a little less incompetent for not being able to talk to his higher on the radio.

"You done?" Moon asked.

"Can you give me another minute or two?" Donovan asked, hoping to get this straightened out without looking too much more like an idiot. It'd be just as easy for Hanley to call via the command net, but he had to be able to talk to SOLAR to get air support, so he needed to work this out.

"Okay, I'm going to go take a shit; we'll switch back to the command net when I get back," Moon said.

"Yeah, after you use a big dose of hand sanitizer! Thanks," Donovan quipped. He tried again using his personal call sign. "SOLAR, SOLAR, this is Delta November for SOLAR Zero Six – over," he transmitted, hoping Stacks was on duty. He was and Donovan finally got the call sign issue resolved.

Donovan decided to take a piss and climbed to the top of the hill just a few meters west and abeam their vehicles. He got to the top and went into a stand of trees surrounded by low brush. He walked up to one of the trees and urinated on it. He heard some voices and looked around the tree and down the hill further west where he saw a group of men, about a dozen. They were all similarly dressed and he thought they must be from the village. They were circled around another man. The man in the center of the circle was bent over at the waist across an elevated branch of a fallen tree. His arms were pulled taut with rope, down toward and around the trunk and back around his ankles. His shirt was pulled up and back over his head. His lower body was naked and there was blood running down the insides of his legs. Donovan buttoned up his trousers and went back down the hill. Hanson was standing next to the lead vehicle talking with Boone.

"Hanson," Donovan said.

"Yes sir, what's up?"

"Hey, there's a bunch of Afghans on the other side of the hill. They look like they're from the village."

"Probably. What about 'em?"

"Looks like they've got a prisoner or whoever, and he's tied to a tree and he's injured." Donovan said, trying just to relay the facts.

"Yeah, the village elder told me they had some men out here dealing with a traitor."

"Traitor to what?"

"To the village. The village fought the Taliban and they decided together that they'd support us, the US, and fight with us to get rid of all Taliban."

"So what did that guy do?"

"I don't know man, uh sir, I just know what the elder told me and my Farsi isn't great. We need to keep pressing on our mission," Hanson said as he slapped his hat against his thigh.

"Shouldn't we do something?" Donovan asked.

"Like what? Yeah, I don't know… like what?" Hanson said, again slapping his hat back and forth across his thigh. "We can't take this prisoner and he's one of theirs. He's one of their own, it's their way."

"Fucked up," said Boone. "But that's the way it's got to be. We're not out here for police work. We've got a mission and we've got a timetable. Let's get going."

"Shit sir, look, this is how they've been doing things for a thousand years. We can't come in here with some moral

141

superiority and direct them to change and do things like we do them. You understand that right?" Hanson said, now becoming agitated. Donovan could tell he wanted to do something but he felt he couldn't.

"Well, I guess that's the thing," Saunders, who was up in the turret listening, now joined in. "This country, these people, let the terrorist fucks who killed our countrymen set up shop here. They took that risk so now they gotta get a dose of Uncle Sam's righteousness and make some adjustments. I don't feel bad about that one bit. We're not under the Prime Directive."

"Yeah, but these people didn't do that, it was the Taliban and we're kickin their asses for it," Hanson replied.

"Well, okay, but while we're having this intellectual chat that fucking guy down there is getting tortured," Donovan interjected. "I'm talking about that one guy. Right now. We should do something."

"Yes we should, but we won't. Saddle up and let's get going; we've got a mission," Hanson said.

They drove until they arrived at the planned waypoint overlooking Lashkar Gah just before sundown. Nobody talked. Donovan volunteered to pull the watch again so the others could get some rest. Throughout the night vehicles roamed the desert between them and Lashkar Gah. None got close enough to him to alarm the others, but they kept his attention all through the night. These weren't routine patrols; they knew what they were looking for. And they were getting close.

CHAPTER TWELVE

SEEING THE ELEPHANT

The two Humvees continued to drive up Highway 1 to link up with the Marines for the assault on Kandahar Airport. Everyone was kitted up, ready for combat. It was a gorgeous day; the sky was again azure, blue and clear, and the temperature had risen from the high thirties that night to near sixty. Donovan was alert, looking out the passenger side window of the lead Humvee. He was taking in Afghanistan and listening to the CD Nikki had given him before he left on his personal CD player he had strapped to his body armor. She'd put together a bunch of love songs on the CD, the ones they had planned on playing at their wedding. He had the volume way down. He thought about Nikki, he missed her and wondered how she was coping with being alone. Driving along, he was amazed at what he saw, and that he was in Afghanistan. Each time he saw a camel caravan or a mud hut or colorfully clad Afghan kids, he'd say to himself, *I can't believe I'm here.*

As they approached a small bridge they saw a stationary armored vehicle, a BMP-1 covered in heavily armed, black turban wearing men down in the dry creek bed. The team was traveling at about thirty-five miles per hour; Donovan stuck his head out the open window, eyes locked on the armored vehicle and the group. He saw one of them lift a fist and another wave hello. He strained to keep his eyes on the threat, then pulled his head back inside the vehicle. Just at that moment two Hi-Lux pickup trucks bristling with men, AK-47's and RPG's appeared to their front. They were driving ahead of and in the same direction as the Americans. Their brake lights lit up, the second one swerving hard to the left to avoid hitting the first. Hanson, driving the lead vehicle, took a hard right turn off the hard ball and descended down the opposite bank of the dry creek bed where the BMP had just fired up its engine, black smoke rising straight up from the two exhausts. Donovan's heart was pumping; he looked over at Hanley who was focused on driving and keeping the second Humvee upright. It was heavy and awkward towing the trailer. He chose a route to keep them between the Hi-Lux's and the BMP. There were six Americans and it looked to the team like there were about thirty Afghans. They still weren't sure if they were Taliban or Northern alliance, or local tribesmen. They weren't flying the green flag of the Northern Alliance and were wearing black Turbans, which Donovan had heard were worn by the Taliban, but nobody was shooting yet. Hanson accelerated down the terrain sloping away from the highway. A Humvee could go over sixty but he was barely able to hit forty-five with the load and the conditions. Donovan glanced at the speedometer then focused on clearing his side of the vehicle. Boone was maneuvering from the back seat into the Mk-19 turret. The lead vehicle started to pull away; they weren't towing a trailer. They were looking for a place to maneuver to, to provide covering fire for the slower vehicle. The Afghans were still within a few hundred meters.

Hanley turned and yelled at Donovan, "You grab the SAW and when we stop, dismount out your door and put the vehicle between you and the enemy as fast as you can!" He quickly drew a deep breath. "Lay down suppressing fire so Boone can fuck 'em up with the Mk-19!!"

Donovan's eyes were wide open and riveted on Hanley. "Roger!" He had only about thirty seconds of familiarization training on the Squad Automatic Weapon and he was worried if it got jammed, he'd take too long figuring out how to unjam it and cost somebody their life. Donovan put his GAU-5 on the floor at his feet and grabbed the SAW. Just then, he looked up and saw an RPG round leave a smoke trail from the BMP; it was heading for their Humvee. He had played football long enough to tell by the comparative speed and the trajectory that that RPG was going to hit right at his door.

"Brakes!!" He yelled. Hanley hit the brake pedal with both feet. The Humvee and trailer started to skid and then fishtail.

****

Uktam had only shot an RPG once during his training,

144

but he'd played soccer his whole life and he perfectly estimated the lead offset required to hit the American vehicle. The round hit just below the right front tire, shredding it and severely damaging the suspension. It skidded and started to jackknife, the trailer whipping behind. The American vehicle got up on two wheels but didn't flip. Uktam's group of fighters erupted in cheers and cries of "Allah Akbar!" Uktam lowered the RPG launcher and was transfixed with the result. The cheers continued until the leader of the group screamed at the group to get back on the BMP. The vehicle lurched forward; three fighters fell off and began to run alongside, then behind the vehicle. Uktam was hoisted by two of his comrades to a position on the front armor of the vehicle. They could see two Americans scrambling out of the vehicle. The second vehicle had passed the first and stopped, maneuvering back to the right, in the direction the stricken vehicle had turned. At the same time, the Hi-Lux's had swung their trucks around and headed back up the highway toward the point the Americans left the road. They were now racing toward the now stationary American vehicles at fifty miles per hour. The lead vehicle hit a depression and bounced two fighters out of the back of the pickup and both landed head first into the desert and into the path of the second vehicle. The second vehicle hit its brakes, skidded and started to fishtail to the left. It threw up a cloud of sand and bounced sideways to a halt. The driver hit the accelerator and turned hard to the left and back to the right; the vehicle leaned in both directions but didn't flip. They came to a stop again and the fighters in the bed of the pickup jumped out and raced toward their fallen comrades who'd been thrown from the vehicle.

****

As Donovan exited the Humvee he lost his balance, fell forward and caught the strap of the SAW around his foot. While stumbling, as he was flailing to regain his balance he hit the volume wheel on his CD player, turning it up to full volume. The song playing was by the Bee Gees, "How Deep is Your Love." He made it around to the opposite side of the vehicle but

145

instead of turning around facing the incoming BMP, he saw the lead Hi-Lux come to a stop just one hundred and fifty meters away. He raised the SAW and pulled the trigger. Nothing. He pulled the bolt back, cycled the action, raised the weapon – pop-pop-pop-pop-pop. He could barely hear the sound of the weapon reports,

"*How deep is your love, I really need to learn*" - pop-pop-pop-pop-pop- "*Cause were living in a world of fools, Breaking us down*"- pop-pop-pop-pop-pop...Donovan's fire was effectively hitting the enemy vehicle, empty shell casings were spraying a nearby rock and bouncing in every direction. He felt a feeling of slow motion for a few seconds, "*When you know down inside, that I really do, and it's me you need to show...*" He dropped two fighters as they exited the right side doors and he sprayed the engine compartment of the truck with bullets. He turned his fire to the stationary second vehicle and aimed for the area the enemy was trying to gather up their fallen comrades. He fired three bursts into the crowd of men. He couldn't tell how many, but they all went down in a red mist. He figured he'd suppressed the Hi-Lux elements for a few seconds and swung the weapon to his right and maneuvered around the front of the vehicle to assist with the incoming BMP. He stopped halfway to turn his CD player down, that particular song wasn't the best background music for a firefight. He took a knee behind the right front bumper, breathing heavily. The second Humvee had been providing suppressing and effective fire on the incoming BMP. Boone had reached out and touched the vehicle four times with the Mk-19, sweeping the top of fighters.

****

Uktam was knocked off, unhurt from the top of the vehicle with the first round; he'd been shielded by two comrades who'd absorbed the shrapnel.

The BMP turned to its right and headed back toward the dry creek as fast as it could go. Boone kept laying on the grenade rounds and thick black smoke started coming out from the back of the vehicle. He swung around and attacked the Hi-Lux's.

They were licking their wounds from Donovan's fire. Boone fired five rounds and scored two direct hits on each of the vehicles disabling both. The enemy was retreating. Two more trucks had come off the road and they were now focused on picking up survivors.

"Donovan, get on the radio and get us air!" Hanley shouted. Donovan got back in the vehicle and came up on the net.

"Any aircraft, any aircraft, this is Solar Zero Six Alpha." He kept trying. "Any aircraft, any aircraft, this is Solar Zero Six Alpha." He put the handset down and surveyed the area. The two trucks that had picked up the remnants from the burning Hi-Lux's were back on the road heading east. The BMP had limped back to the creek bed and turned north; it appeared they were breaking contact and either regrouping or retreating. They'd been hurt bad. It seemed the team was out of immediate danger. There were only two or three left from the group on the BMP and maybe one or two from the Hi-Lux's, but their position was known.

"Solar Zero Six Alpha, Solar Zero Six Alpha, this is Viper 33 flight, how do you read?"

"Viper 33 flight, this is Solar Zero Six Alpha, I've got you five by five," Donovan replied, happy to make contact with a pair of fighters, F-16s, he could tell from the "Viper" call sign.

"Viper 33, we're in contact with enemy elements to our east and our west, both within two klicks. We've engaged and they are retreating or regrouping. Say when ready for 9-line." Donovan was eager to pass the fighters the necessary information they'd need to launch an attack on the enemy forces.

"Solar Zero Six Alpha, send it."

"Viper 33, this is Solar Zero Six Alpha, Type 3 Control. Lines 1 through 3 N/A.

Target elevation: 2200 Feet

Target description: Egressing to the west, two trucks with approximately 10 to 20 armed enemy. Egressing to the east, one BMP-1 Armored Vehicle with unknown number of enemy.

Target location: First element east, northeast of friendly

position, second element west northwest of friendly position, traveling at approximately 30 mph.

Type mark: None

Friendly location: WGS84 31.69 64.68

Egress: Pilot's discretion

Remarks: No observed triple-A threats in the area. We were fired on by an RPG. BMP is the primary target. Request, if able split ops to keep one of your birds overhead while the other searches for the targets. Request read back, over."

"Solar Zero Six Alpha, Type 3 control, lines 1-3 N/A Target elevation: 2200 Feet

Target description: Egressing to the west, two stake bed trucks with approximately 10 to 20 armed enemy. Egressing to the east, one BMP-1 Armored Vehicle with unknown number of enemy.

Target location: First element east, northeast of friendly position, second element west northwest of friendly position, traveling at approximately 30 mph.

Type mark: None

Friendly location: WGS84 31.69 64.68

Egress: Pilot's discretion

Remarks: No observed triple-A threats but fired on by RPG. BMP is the primary target. On split ops, that's a negative. We'll stay together for mutual support; holler if you need us. Over."

"Viper 33, that's a charlie read back, copy on the split ops. Over." Donovan felt a lot better about the situation, especially since their vehicle had been hit and could be disabled.

****

Uktam lay on the ground until the incoming barrage of grenades ceased. The BMP continued to limp away trailing black smoke. He now got up and started to jog after it. He was losing ground but the terrain was flat and he could keep it in sight for a while he thought. He slowed to a walk, still taking it all in. He'd been a hero ten minutes ago, now most of those that cheered him were dead or dying and the rest were fleeing. He hadn't been hurt but his heart sank and he started to rethink all of his decisions since he stood at that storefront and watched the news about 9/11. He was worried about his brother and his mother; he missed home. He slowed to a walk but kept following the BMP as it moved on in the distance. What was he going to do now? He was on foot, most of his comrades were gone and he couldn't remember how to get back to where they'd slept that night in Lashkar Gah. He had no radio, no map, no idea what to do. He was staring at the ground as he walked and lifted his head to recheck the direction of the BMP –Flash! – just as he'd looked up at the BMP it disappeared into a cloud of fire and dirt. He ducked down. Pieces of the vehicle tumbled through the air streaming smoke – Whompf! The sound of the explosion had just reached him, followed a few seconds later by the shock wave. He fell to his knees, ears were ringing, and started to cry.

****

"Solar Zero Six Alpha, Viper 33 flight," the F-16 flight lead called for Donovan.

"Viper 33 flight, Solar Zero Six Alpha, go head," he answered. Having heard the report from now a few kilometers away, he figured the Vipers had gotten one of the targets.

"Scratch one armored vehicle!" the flight lead said with a higher tone to his voice.

"Shit hot, nice work Viper, appreciate the help," replied Donovan. Within the space of a few minutes he had directly killed at least a dozen people and directed an airstrike, which killed several more. He was glad things played out the way they did, there was no doubt of that, but the gravity and enormity of the events were now washing over him. He was right where he always wanted to be and was doing what he always thought he wanted to do, fight in combat for his country, but he wasn't feeling what he always thought he would feel. There was a heaviness to it. It started to overwhelm him and he started to choke, trying to stop himself. He took a couple of exaggeratedly deep breaths; in the middle of one he coughed, choked and felt his eyes welling up. "Fuck," he said out loud. "Fuck."

149

"Major!" Hanley yelled, "What the fuck was that explosion? How 'bout an update?"

"Yeah, sorry, that was a two-ship of F-16s, they got the BMP."

"Fuck yeah, that's what I'm talking about – fuck those cocksuckers! Yeah! Go Air Force!" Hanley was elated that threat was eliminated. That was something he hadn't expected. The fact the Taliban had some armor was highlighted in their spin up briefs, but he never thought they'd come across any. It was Russian made; it was just lucky they didn't employ it like the Russians would have. They could have torn them up, so he was damn happy it was burning in the distance. "Okay, what about those trucks?"

"Nothing yet, but they've got the 9-line. I made the BMP the primary, with that checked off, they'll be searching for those trucks," Donovan detailed.

"Okay, great. What's their loiter time? I'd like cover while we're sitting here dead in the water."

"ATO says their vul is 90 minutes."

"What's a 'vul'?"

"Vulnerability period, station time, how much time we've got them for."

"Okay, got it. What about when they check out? Got anything else?"

"Checking." Donovan got back on the radio. "Bossman, Bossman, Solar Zero Six Alpha. Bossman, Bossman, Solar Zero Six Alpha."

"Solar Zero Six Alpha, Bossman, go ahead." The AWACS acted as the airborne extension of the ground-based Air Operations Center and relayed orders, controlled the airborne flights of aircraft and prioritized resources, aerial refueling and radio usage.

"Bossman, Solar Zero Six Alpha, Viper 33 flight engaged enemy target for us. Looking to see what you've got on deck we could request to provide top cover as we relocate. Over"

"Solar Zero Six Alpha, we've got no available air for the next four hours, we've got a few higher priority missions, over."

"Copy Bossman. Break. We just rolled a pair of fighters

in on enemy armor; you got higher priority missions than that? Over." Donovan made sure the guy on the other end of that radio transmission knew he was pissed but staying professional.

"Solar Zero Six Alpha, standby one." There was silence for about 60 seconds. "Solar Zero Six Alpha, yes we do. Over."

"Bossman, roger that. Solar Zero Six Alpha, out." Donovan wasn't happy about the situation but he did realize they were a real small piece of all of what was going on right now. "Sergeant Hanley!" He yelled, but Hanley had moved to within six feet of him. "Shit, sorry about that."

"No problem, but keep your SA up a little higher than that okay?"

"Yep, got it. Okay, no air for the next four hours."

"Shit, okay. So, do we get air in four hours?"

"We gotta ask; it's a prioritization thing."

"Well, if we keep fixing the enemy for your fighters, I'd say killing them is a top priority, right?"

"Yeah, no doubt. There's a lot of other shit going on, so we better plan on pressing without air. If we get it, great, but I wouldn't count on it."

"Okay, understood. Let's get going. Hell, we'll be at the rendezvous point well before four hours. Shit, ain't no thing," Hanley raised a hand up to high-five Donovan, who didn't see it and left him hanging.

The second vehicle had joined back up with Hanson's. They did a quick assessment. The tire was shredded, the suspension would be good enough to get to Kandahar, but, driving as fast as they could, towing that trailer, it looked like they blew the head gasket. After about an hour, they hooked up the disabled vehicle and trailer to be towed by the second vehicle – they were all hoping whoever manufactured the Humvee's engines and transmissions knew what they were doing. Shortly after hooking up the vehicles they were back on the hardball and were heading to the rendezvous point 20 kilometers away. They drove for 90 minutes, only getting the daisy-chained vehicles up to about 25 miles per hour.

About one kilometer short of the rendezvous point, Hanson radioed their position and got clearance to advance toward the Marine force main body. These were Marines of the 15th and 26th Marine Expeditionary Units, MEU. Donovan had met some of the Marines and their commander at Camp Rhino. Once cleared the vehicles exited the hard ball and slogged through the deep sand to form up with the assault force. They stopped and all dismounted. Donovan got out of his vehicle, took off his helmet and let out a sigh. He looked at his watch; it was 14 December. Just to his right there was a group of Marines standing in a circle. He was close enough to hear the conversation and slowly walked up to them as they talked. The one doing all the talking was Captain Casey, a Marine aviator serving as an Air Officer, Donovan's Marine counterpart.

"We had a convoy of about 20 vehicles moving in our direction. I called Cobras and Harriers in on them and knocked the crap out of them; there was burning wreckage all over the highway," Casey went on, obviously excited and proud of what he'd done. Donovan waited for a break. Everyone was interested and glad Casey took care of the situation but they all had things to do to get ready for the assault on the airfield, so one by one they slipped away, some with an enthusiastic "Hoorah!" as they left to get back to their duties.

Donovan walked up to Casey. "Hey Captain, Pat Donovan. Great job."

"Hey thanks." Casey couldn't see what Donovan's rank was or even what service he was from because he was wearing a Cabella's tan fleece zip up jacket over his uniform blouse.

"I'm with the ODA that just came in and wanted to talk to you about air support. What have you got set up for tonight?"

"Uh, sorry, who are you again? I know Pat Donovan, but what are you? No offense, but this is a Marine op and you don't look like a Marine."

"Well, thanks for that. I'm Major Donovan. I'm providing FAC support to the ODA that's in support of TF-58. I'm just trying to synch planning for the assault. I don't want to put in airstrike requests if you've already done that or ask for air that we've already got, that's all, okay?"

"Yeah sir, sure, that's okay. Yeah, we've not got any particular requests put in, just going to rely on what's already planned."

"Okay Casey, okay. I'd say this is probably the biggest game in country tonight. I'd suggest we ask for dedicated air to cover us as we move on the airfield."

"What for?"

"What do you mean what for? You're the one standing here talking about knocking the crap out of a dozen -"

"It was actually more like 20!" Casey interrupted.

"Okay, 20 vehicles, and you're asking what for?"

"We've got shit loads of firepower with us, don't think we need the U-S-A-F."

"Right, so here's what I'm gonna do; this will be on my dime. I'll call for support to cover us until we've secured the airfield. It'll be transparent to anybody here on the ground but if we need it, it'll be there, okay?"

"Sure man, whatever." Casey said dismissively as he turned his back and started walking away.

Donovan called after him, "Captain Casey." Casey stopped and looked back over his shoulder. "That's sure man, whatever Sir, right?"

"Yes sir." He turned back around and kept walking. Donovan wasn't sure why Casey got so bent out of shape about requesting air support but that didn't matter to him at this point. Getting the air did. He went back to his vehicle. As he approached he saw that they were hooking it up to the back of one of the Marine LAVs, Light Armored Vehicles with a tow bar.

"What's up Hanley?"

"Hey sir, we figure this is the best way to get us into the convoy, as you know, the front end's shot and the head gasket is blown. We can't leave it out here. It'll be up on blocks by tomorrow morning. So we'll ride in, same crew positions, just up the ass of this LAV. What a way to go huh?"

"Yep, that's great, towed into combat."

The sun was going down. Donovan pulled out his camera and set it up on the trailer and set the auto timer. He wanted to get a picture of himself to capture this piece of history. He faced the setting sun and the camera got his picture, thumbs in his belt and squinting against the sun.

Everyone milled around, drank water, loaded ammo magazines, ate MRE's and waited. After a few hours engines started to fire up and Marines collected their gear and climbed into their vehicles. Hanley had gotten the radio call, "Okay men, let's saddle up!" The team entered their vehicles and readied their weapons.

Donovan lowered his goggles over his eyes. The sound of diesel engines revving up got louder and louder; the convoy started to move. One after another the vehicles powered forward. He couldn't see much; just out to the side and at the back hatch of the LAV. Eventually it was their turn to move out. The LAV lurched forward; there was a loud clank as the slack in the tow bar between the LAV and their Humvee was taken up. They started to move slowly. Hanley tried to hold the wheel straight; he was struggling and they were only going about five mph at that point but they slowly increased their speed. Donovan saw that Hanley was wrestling as hard as he could against the steering wheel before it became too much and he was either going to let go or the force was going to break both his arms. The wheel was wrenched out of his hands; he threw them up and out of the way of the spinning wheel. Donovan looked at the right front tire; it had turned all the way to the left and now was plowing against the desert sand creating a rooster tail up and to the right, sandblasting him and the side of the vehicle. It was rolling up over the top and coming down the turret; they were all coughing and choking.

"This is gonna suck," Donovan said out loud, knowing no one would hear him. Each pulled their neck garters over their mouths and noses. The convoy pressed ahead through the desert and after about 30 minutes they were back on the hardball. Hanley saw the steering wheel spinning again, and as it started to spin back in the other direction he grabbed for it. His timing happened to be perfect; he caught the wheel when the tires were dead center and he now had "control" of the steering. He looked to his right, even with his eyes and entire face covered up, Donovan could tell Hanley was proudly smiling as he nodded his head up and down. Donovan gave him a thumbs-up.

After another 20 minutes they were heading through the streets of Kandahar. Donovan thought that at any minute they'd start taking fire; he had his weapon lowered but ready. It was dark out but the streets were bustling, lined on both sides with Kandahar's citizens watching the impressive convoy navigate the city streets.

Donovan and the others now lowered their scarves and goggles. He locked eyes with the men on the streets as they passed. It was fascinating. He couldn't believe he was driving through the streets of Kandahar. After a few minutes they popped out on the other side of the city and rolled, unopposed, into the airport. One of TF Dagger's ODA's had done great work to secure the airfield, so the Marine convoy could move in without a shot. That ODA's call sign was Texas 17. Once they came to a halt, Donovan looked up and saw "Texas 17" spray-painted on the control tower of the airfield.

That night, the separate elements moved to their pre-assigned bed down locations and took up residence. Donovan's team set up in the terminal in one of the back offices. They unloaded their gear, set up cots and each built their personal nests. The Marines secured the perimeter and after Hanson checked that there were no planning meetings or duties required of his team, he told them all to get some rack time.

The next morning Donovan got up and looked around at the team's area. Half the team was asleep; the other half's bunks were empty. He grabbed his kit and a bottle of water and looked for someplace to knock the sleep off and most importantly to him at that moment, to empty his bowels. He left the terminal and saw small groups of Marines eating MREs, cleaning weapons, reading, writing, talking. He looked around to an area that looked almost like a junkyard. It was toward the city, opposite the flight line. As he walked toward it he noticed a truck mounted multiple-rocket-launcher; it was a fully loaded BM-21. He pulled his camera out and took a couple of pictures before walking into the junkyard-like area.

There were piles of Soviet aircraft parts, disabled vehicles, rusted containers, lots of junk. He found a spot to take care of his physiological issue, pulled out his hand sanitizer and rubbed his hands as he walked back to the terminal. As he was concentrating on his hands he stepped on something hard and stopped in his tracks. At that moment he realized how foolish he'd been. He looked down and was standing on a half-buried land mine. He didn't know it at the time, he wasn't well trained on Soviet era mines, but it was a TMRP-6 anti-tank mine.

"Shit!" he said out loud. He hadn't felt any movement, didn't hear any clicking or buzzing, so he hoped he hadn't activated it, he didn't think he activated it. He thought for a few seconds, then...he lifted his foot and walked away. The mine required over 250lbs to arm it, it was lucky for him that he hadn't been carrying his ruck at the time. As he walked toward the terminal he saw two Marines laden with a lot of gear.

"Hey fellas don't go over there." He turned and pointed to the spot he just left. "There's a mine right at the entrance to that junkyard looking area."

"Roger sir, that's what we're here for. We're the mine clearing team, we're gonna be working on this whole area."

"No shit, talk about timing... Hey, what's that one right there, it's sticking up a bit, tan color." The young Marine started walking in that direction, Donovan started to follow.

"Sir," the other Marine grabbed him by the shoulder and held him back. "Wait here, he's got it. Why don't you just move on and let us get after this?"

"Okay, sorry, sure thing. Be careful."

"Oh, trust me, I'm planning on getting home after this is all over. I'll be careful." Just then the other Marine turned back toward Donovan. "Yugoslavian anti-tank mine. You would have had to jump up and down on that one to make it go off."

"I'll take your word for it. Thanks guys. Good luck."

He got back to the billeting area and got dressed then stepped out into the terminal looking for some coffee. As he left through the main doors there was a group of three Marines and two SOF guys standing around a burlap sack. He walked up to join them.

"Hey gents, what's going on?"

"We're working out our retirement plans," said a tall, lanky Marine private.

"Oh yeah, well good for you. How's that gonna work?" Donovan asked.

"Well, we're going to split up what's in that sack."

"Okay, you mind if I take a look."

"Yeah, as long as a look is all you're taking."

Donovan half smiled and forced a chuckle. He grabbed the sack and opened it up. It was full of money, Afghanis, dozens of bundles wrapped in plastic and rubber bands.

"Wow, you guys should be set. By the looks of it there should be a total of about, just guestimating here, but I'd say you've got at least six dollars American."

"No shit!" said the lanky Marine, "That's it?"

"Yeah, maybe a little bit more but not much. Hey do you mind if I take a picture with it?" He pulled his camera out of his cargo pocket and handed it to the Marine. He took the photo and handed the camera back to Donovan.

Donovan went back inside to his cot; the rest of the team was assembled and Hanson was just about to brief. "Sir, glad you're here, we've got a mission."

"Great."

"Okay gents, we're to move through the city and check out what might be a chemical weapons plant, an old textile factory. We're going to go check it out then we're going to link up with ODA-574 at Mullah Omar's compound. So, get your gear and ammo. Major, make sure we've got air available. Any questions?" The room was silent. "Okay, we roll in twenty." Hanson held both hands up in the air and flashed ten twice, opening and closing his fingers.

They loaded up their vehicles. They'd gotten a loaner from the Marines, a thin-skinned HMMWV version with an open bed. Donovan hopped in the back with his weapon, an assault pack with a radio and batteries and a few bottles of water. As he climbed over the side rails he saw two individuals he hadn't seen before. One looked to be maybe in his late fifties or early sixties, white hair and heavy, and the other was much younger, also pudgy but tall. Neither one looked like they were in the military.

"Hey, Pat Donovan. How's it going?" He greeted both

with an outstretched hand. They all shook hands and looked each other over.

"Paul Boven and this is Jack Nicholson," the older one said.

"Hey Paul, Jack. What are you guys doing here?"

"We're with the NSA. We're going to lead the technical part of the SSE, do some testing; basically get the ground truth about this place."

"You all been on any other sensitive site exploitations?" he asked, spelling out the abbreviation so they knew he knew what they were talking about.

"A couple, but obviously none down here so we're pretty excited."

"Well, alright. I hope you don't find anything and we get in and out of there lickety-split. Hey Jack, how 'bout you?"

"Okay look, I was born when Jack Nicholson was getting famous, my mom loved him as an actor. He was her favorite so when I was born, with the last name of Nicholson, my mom thought she had to name me Jack," he explained, obviously sensitive and a little embarrassed.

"No, okay, well, thanks for that rundown but I was wondering what your role in the SSE would be," Donovan said, not letting him know what he responded to was exactly what he was going to ask him.

"Oh, shit, sorry. I'll do the physical testing and equipment analysis. I know the types, makes and models of industrial equipment that can be used to process hazardous chemicals and potentially be used to weaponize them. Sorry about that. I've been getting bombarded with that question ever since I got in country and it's getting old."

"No problem. I actually didn't pick up on that until you said something."

"Really?" Jack asked, surprised.

"No man, just fuckin with you. I was trying to think of a good Nicholson quote or something like that. Welcome aboard, maybe you'll become more famous than the other Jack and he'll be explaining, 'Yeah, no I'm the actor, not the war hero...'"

"Yeah, right," Jack said, starting to giggle and nervously

snort.

The vehicle started slowly moving forward. Picking up speed, a voice from inside the cab yelled out, "Y'all good?" and stuck a thumbs-up out the window. All responded with a thumbs up. The small convoy drove up the single paved road leading out of the airport. They left the airport and started to snake their way through the set up obstacles that lined that road. They were soon in downtown Kandahar. Donovan still couldn't believe they were just rolling through the city, that just a couple of days before was the religious center for the Taliban and under their complete control. They drove by shops, bazaars, thousands of Afghanis, all with their eyes riveted on the small two-vehicle convoy. Scooters and motorcycles, trucks and cars alternately pulled up behind and alongside to get a closer look. Donovan was sure all of them felt like at any minute they'd start taking fire, have a grenade tossed into their vehicle or be swarmed by a mob, but they just kept going, kept driving slowly through the streets, just eyes, looks and stares greeted them. Some kids waved. Donovan waved back but mainly everyone just sat there during the forty-minute ride.

They eventually pulled up in front of the target. It was a large building, for Afghanistan, that looked like it was built by the Soviets. Right in front of the building were several BM-21s and an older BM-14. There were additional US troops waiting at the large steel doors that secured the entrance. Two of the new arrivals split in opposite directions to join those already there as security. Donovan went with Paul and Jack and the rest of the team to the main doors. Quick greetings were exchanged and then four of the team formed a stack to breach the doors and clear the building. Donovan motioned to Paul and Jack to move back; they stood off to the side. Just as the four-man team looked like it was ready to make their move through the doors, they opened and two Afghan men pushed through, scarves covering their mouths. The team trained their weapons on them, but then quickly realized they were part of a group that was cooperating with the Americans. The small assault team relaxed and waved forward Paul, Jack and Donovan. They entered the building, weapons at the ready. The two Afghanis waited outside, lowering their scarves; the Americans started to move systematically through the dark building. They turned on the headlamps on their helmets and continued to search, having pulled their scarves up over their noses and mouths after seeing the men who came out of the building.

Donovan thought if this were a chem-plant run by the Taliban it probably wasn't held to any standards and their scarves wouldn't be doing them much good. He noticed as they all swept their headlamps back and forth that there was a cloud of suspended dust or fibers hanging in the air. *Oh shit,* he thought to himself. He scanned back and forth and spotted Paul and Jack on their knees with their kit open; they both pulled out their gas masks and put them on. "Fuck." He moved toward them. "Hey gents, what the fuck, do we need to be wearing pro gear?" he asked in a loud voice through his scarf.

"Nah, this is for the testing chemicals but you might want to back away," Paul yelled through his mask.

"Okay!" Donovan backed away and continued to look through the building. After about 30 minutes, someone he couldn't recognize with their face covered was moving rapidly throughout the building with a finger pointed up and swirling in the air.

"Let's go, we're pulling out, rally by the front door!"

Donovan gave a thumbs-up and was more than happy to get out of there. Once he cleared the door he moved another twenty or so feet before he stopped and pulled down his scarf and breathed the fresh air. He turned back around and saw the team assembled just outside the door and moved back to the group.

"Okay men, looks like this textile factory is being secretly used as a textile factory. Gentleman, anything?" Hanson looked toward Paul and Jack.

"No, nothing at this point," Paul responded.

"Let's wrap it up and get back in the vehicles." They all piled back into the Humvees and moved back through Kandahar, heading to Mullah Omar's compound. After thirty minutes of winding their way back through Kandahar the team arrived at the compound. There was a set of iron gates blocking

160

the entrance to the walled compound but the walls around the gates were blown down and now rubble. There were several Afghan militia guarding the gates and as the Americans approached they opened them, and the vehicles moved slowly through. To the left what once was a multi-story home or building was now a pile of rocks and debris. The walls were pockmarked from what looked like 20 or 40-millimeter rounds and it was obvious the building had been hit by 105s from a gunship and several JDAMs. As they proceeded they saw the Americans of ODA-574. The team Donovan was with knew the men here at the compound so there were greetings shouted back and forth. Within a few minutes they pulled to a stop in front of a still-standing building the ODA was using as a headquarters and all dismounted. Donovan jumped down off the back of the Humvee, stretched his legs and said hello to two of the Green Berets that were sitting on the edge of the porch in front of the building.

"Hey," they replied very nonchalantly. "How's it going?"

"Good, how you guys doing?"

"We're frosty. Who are you?"

"Pat Donovan, Air Force FAC, just helping your bros out with air support."

"That's cool. That's a valuable commodity out here, much appreciated. Speaking of which, if it's okay with your team, we'd like to borrow you while you're here. We're going to finish checking out the rest of this compound and having some bomb droppers on call would be a plus. You can also give us a hand with the searches and security. That is if you know how to use that thing slung over your shoulder."

"Seems like the default by the Army and the Marines is that the Air Force doesn't do small arms, but yeah, I could probably manage to keep from shooting myself or any of you all if I had to. Happy to help." He tried not to sound offended.

"Awesome, let's go." They grabbed their weapons, which had been leaning against the wall behind them. Boone had heard the conversation. "I'll go with you."

"All right, the more the merrier. Can we take your truck?"

"Sure, it's a rental," Boone replied as he got behind the

wheel. One of the two got in the passenger seat and the other jumped in the back with Donovan. They all shook hands and introduced themselves to each other. The soldier doing all the talking was Silla and the other was Newton. Silla was a guy that looked like Conan the Barbarian and Newton looked like Isaac Newton. They drove away from the front gate, deeper into the compound and out a hole in the back wall. They drove up to a disabled anti-aircraft artillery piece and parked about thirty feet away. It was a ZSU-2, 37-millimeter. Donovan approached and could tell it took some hits when the compound was attacked from the air. There were spent shell casings all around and the seat was covered with dried blood. Just to the north of the piece Donovan spotted a hole in the ground. The four walked up to it.

"What's that, spider hole?" Donovan asked.

"Kinda. There are miles of tunnels underneath this compound." The soldier pulled out his flashlight and aimed it down the hole. They could see the floor of the tunnel about eight feet down. Donovan kicked one of the spent shell casings from the ZSU down the hole and it thumped as it hit the sand at the bottom. They slowly walked in different directions, searching the area for anything significant. Donovan walked to the east and saw what looked like a dry creek bed. He descended down into it and looked back to the west. He saw the entrance to a cave and slowly approached with his rifle leveled at his hip. He reached the entrance and could see a hookah pipe, surgical tubing, a syringe, ammo and a torn Koran. He slung his rifle and pulled his Berretta 9-millimeter pistol from its holster, cocked the hammer and entered the cave, going in about fifteen feet. He saw piles of file folders, documents and a dozen cardboard boxes. At this point he thought that this was outside his job jar and the best thing for him to do was to get the intel experts after this stuff. He backed out of the cave and linked back up with the others. They assembled back by the ZSU, discussing what they'd seen.

Donovan was telling them about the cave… Ziiippp! A rifle round ripped past their heads. None of the four ducked or ran, they just turned and faced the direction they thought it came from.

"Sniper," Silla said, and pointed up at the ridge to their west. He raised his rifle and looked through the scope. Donovan was waiting to react how everyone else did so he just stared back up at the ridge. It was at least a couple of klicks away. "Savages." Silla walked back toward the truck. They drove for several minutes and stopped a few hundred meters away from a huge steel door that secured the entrance to a large cache in the side of the mountain the compound was built up against. "We've already explored that. Lots of weapons, ammo, Intel; impressive."

They looked at it for a few minutes before driving back to the headquarters building. Donovan told Paul about the cave. He got pretty excited and recruited a few of the Green Berets to go with him and Jack back to the cave. They left Paul and Jack there at the compound and the rest headed back to the airport. The return trip was uneventful.

By the time they got back to the airport it was starting to get dark. Donovan wanted to check in with Captain Casey. He'd asked around and found out the Captain was set up in the control tower. He climbed the several flights of stairs to get to the main control room where he went through a large green metal door. There were half dozen Marines in the room. Casey was on the radio and one of his NCOs was looking through their Special Operations Forces Laser Marker. The SOFLAM was capable of designating targets out to eight kilometers. The NCO was in the process of ranging the target and passing the information to Casey. It became apparent to Donovan that Casey was getting ready to hit something in the ridgeline on the opposite side of the runway. He listened to the back and forth between Casey and a flight of F-15Es. When he heard that the target was an SA-3 he became much more interested. He knew he wasn't the one in charge, but he also knew that there were a few things that didn't seem to be making sense. He waited for a pause in the transmissions.

"Captain Casey, what's up?"

"What do you mean what's up? I've got an SA-3 I'm getting ready to schwack!" Casey shot back, irritated.

"Have you checked with SOLAR yet?"

163

"Who the fuck is SOLAR?" he asked, more agitated.

"SOLAR is the Special Operations Air Component. They're running all the air support for all of Afghanistan. They've probably got some intel you might want to have before you start dropping bombs."

"Uh, well..." It was obvious a lot was racing through Casey's mind, mainly that he was ready to kill a bunch of people with confidence ten seconds earlier and now he realized he hadn't thought it through. "Well if you want to call them, go ahead." Without missing a beat he keyed the mic. "Viper 5-4 flight, standby."

Donovan had the radio Boone lent him in his ruck, spun it off his shoulder and took a knee on the control tower floor. He pulled out the mic and control head for his radio, keyed in the Satellite channel for Solar and tried to raise them,

"Solar, Solar; Solar Zero-Six-Alpha."

"Solar Zero-Six-Alpha; Solar, go ahead," the answer came back.

"Solar, we've got a potential target here, north of Kandahar airfield, say when ready to copy description, over."

"Zero-Six-Alpha, send it."

"Solar, target elevation is 2390 feet, SA-3 battery, twelve personnel, target location is 31.56, 65.81, how copy, over?"

"Zero-Six-Alpha, elevation 2390 feet, SA-3 battery, twelve personnel, location is 31.56, 65.81, over."

"Solar, that's a charlie read back, over."

"Zero-Six-Alpha, what's your request, over?"

"Solar, are you showing any friendlies in the area and do you have any intel on that target, or that location, over?"

"Zero-Six-Alpha, rodger, standby."

"Captain Casey, I've got Solar looking into that target, continue to standby." Donovan spoke at high volume so everybody understood that this was not a confirmed target. Two minutes went by.

"Zero-Six-Alpha, Solar, over."

"Solar, Zero-Six-Alpha, go ahead."

"Zero-Six-Alpha, those are friendly forces in possession of the captured SAM system, repeat, those are friendly forces in possession of the captured SAM system, acknowledge, over."

"Solar, Zero-Six-Alpha copies, friendlies. SAM system in possession of friendly forces, over."

Casey had heard the transmission and waved off the flight of F-15s. Once he confirmed they were in positive receipt of the message he cleared them back to the tanker and signed off. He walked toward Donovan; there was a very slight pause and then he stuck out his hand. "Hey man, thanks for the backup. Holy shit, I guess I got my dauber up and…well, again, thanks. Fuck." He was obviously shaken up.

"Okay man, no sweat, that's what we do. I'll pass you all of Solar's info. You should give them a call on the landline and keep in close touch with them. The guy running the show, Stacks, is my bro. He's one squared away dude. Check shit with him, he'll be in the know."

Donovan could tell Casey appreciated that info. His eyes were locked on Donovan's. He just had his head deflated a couple of hat sizes and he knew it. Donovan knew he was the better for it, but he was shaken up a bit too. He felt like he'd had four cups of coffee without eating anything, but he was also excited he'd saved the lives of those men out there. He couldn't wait to tell Stacks.

He waited until Casey left the area and tried to raise Stacks on the radio. "Solar, Solar-Zero-Six-Alpha, for Solar-Zero-Six."

"Zero-Six-Alpha, Solar Zero-Six is off shift, anything else I can do for you, over?"

"Solar, no thanks. Thanks for the help earlier, really appreciate it, over and out."

"Zero-Six-Alpha, no problem, Solar, out."

He started back toward his bunk feeling like he'd done something. As he walked down the metal stairs of the control tower, he got weak in the knees and sat halfway down the stairs. He put his head in his hands, ran his fingers through his hair, took a deep breath and let it out forcefully. He sat thinking about the engagement off the highway; it was all starting to catch up with him. He took another deep breath and slowly let it out. He ran his fingers through his hair again and again. He needed a drink. Within 24 hours he'd become a killer, took lives and saved lives. He pushed himself back to his feet and finished walking down the tower stairs. He reached the bottom, got his bearings and made his way back to his bunk. He gently dropped his ruck, trying not to wake up his team; he swung around and sat on the edge of the bunk, rotated on his butt and laid back. He reached under his bunk, waving his hand around until he located the little desert-camouflage pillow Nikki had given him. He pulled it up and stuffed it behind his head. He slept.

It was light before he woke up. Most of the team was already awake and kitted up. He laid motionless with just his eyes open and waited for about five minutes before he righted himself on his bunk, scratched his head, then rested his chin on his hands, elbows on his knees.

"Hey man, you look like shit," Boone informed him.

"Thanks, you actually look pretty chipper. What's up?"

"We're going on a mission, heading to Osama's house! Yeah, that's right!"

"No shit…no shit." Donovan was still waking up. "That's, uh, that's good, right?"

"Shit yeah, we're going to the man's house."

"All right, let me get my shit together."

"Cool."

"Uh, Major, you'll be sitting this one out," Hanson interrupted. "This will be a routine SSE and it's pretty close to here so if we need air support we'll call back to the Marine HQ. Besides, as you can imagine, we've got a shitload of strap-hangers that want to go on this one."

"Hey Sergeant, didn't you ever hear the phrase, 'Dance with the girl you brought to the dance'?" Donovan asked him. "I'm your girl."

"Well sir, if you're making some kind of reference to your sexual orientation, remember, 'Don't ask, don't tell.'"

"Okay, let me put it this way, fuck you and good luck," Donovan said with a smile and extended hand.

"Sure, we'll bring you back a souvenir."

"That would be awesome, but seriously, be careful, and

166

if you need real air support call me direct, Boone's got my freq." Donovan shook Hanson's hand and as he turned back toward his bunk he saw Sergeant Buress. "Bob, when did you get here?" He was thrilled to see a familiar face. "Are you going with these guys?"

"Hey sir, got in last night while you were sleeping. Yep, we're about ready to roll. You okay with that?"

"Hell yeah. I feel a lot better knowing you're going with them. That's great. Be careful. How long are you supposed to be gone?"

"It's right around here, Tarnak Farms, or something like that, just south of the airfield. Should only be a couple of hours depending on what we find."

"Okay, man, like I said, be careful. See you when you get back."

"Okay, sir, see ya." Buress swung his ruck up over his head and it slammed down on his back. His knees buckled slightly under the weight before he grabbed his weapon and walked out the door with the rest of the team.

Donovan was relieved that the team would have quality support by an experienced ETAC like Buress. He realized he hadn't found coffee yet and he was yearning for a cup. He walked through the terminal to the ops center the Marines had set up there because he knew they'd have coffee and they did. He grabbed a cup and walked outside the terminal. There was a huge bomb crater right out the front door and he walked toward it. As he did his foot kicked something that clinked across the concrete and skidded to a stop. It was a piece of a bomb fragment, no doubt from the bomb that made the crater, jagged with razor sharp edges. He'd been a bomb-dropper his whole career but never really had the opportunity to see the business end aftermath of a bomb run.

Holy shit, he thought. *That's fucking brutal.* Off to the side of the crater several Marines were standing around a pile of captured munitions and small arms. It looked like they were cataloging them. There were mortar shells, artillery shells, rockets, AK-47s, rifles, and boxes of ammunition. He looked it over for a few minutes and then walked to his left, away from the front of the terminal. He sat on the curb and looked out toward the airfield and drank his coffee; it was harsh, strong, but it was hot. He took a few sips and thought about what he should do next. He noticed a group of five Marines walking along the edge of the runway, from right to left. He watched them as he drank his coffee.

Wham! A small explosion erupted in front of the second Marine. It was a mine. Donovan sprang to his feet and started running. He'd gotten about fifty yards when two things occurred to him, there were at least a dozen Marines between him and the ones that were hit, and there were more mines out there. Just as he had that thought he heard faint shouting; one of the NCO's was directing everyone to freeze. He stopped too, backing away onto the tarmac. The other Marines in the group that hit the mine were administering first aid. It was apparent the NCO had taken charge; he was on his radio and within a few minutes, maybe just seconds, a LAV moved in the direction of the fallen Marine. They got him in through the back hatch and drove the LAV directly to the medical area on the north end of the field.

Donovan found out later that the second Marine in line had stepped on a "toe-popper." He lost his foot and four fingers from his right hand; the shrapnel had continued past him and hit the third Marine in line and killed him. When he heard the news, anything positive he felt about what he'd done up to that point disappeared.

CHAPTER THIRTEEN

K2

Donovan eventually made contact with Stacks and got the order to get to K2. He got on a C-130 flight that night and flew to K2 and eventually made his way to the CJSOTF TOC. Stacks wasn't on shift but Donovan got directions to the tent his guys were staying in, found a bunk and racked out. He didn't wake up until after daylight. He looked around the tent; there were about a dozen cots, a third of them occupied with guys from the night shift. He sat up quietly on the edge of his bunk and just stared for a while.

After a few minutes, Stacks threw open the tent flap hunching over to get through the opening. Once he cleared the entrance he stood up and immediately spotted Donovan at the opposite end of the tent and whisper-shouted, trying not to wake the rest of the guys. "Dude!" Donovan snapped out of his daze and burst into a big smile.

"Hey sir! Great to see you!" Stacks motioned for Donovan to come outside and he turned around and went back outside the tent. Donovan put his boots and fleece on and made his way around the cots to the door of the tent. He pushed the flap back and stood up on the outside, squinting against the daylight. It wasn't sunny but it was a lot brighter than inside the tent. He had noticed when he came in the night before how much different the weather and terrain were in Uzbekistan than Afghanistan; it was a lot colder, muddier and damp. As he stood up, Stacks stuck out his hand,

"Hey buddy, how the hell are you?"

"Hey sir, I'm awesome. How are you guys doing up here?"

"Oh, this place is a shit hole but I'm loving it! We're doing great work."

"I know you are. Thanks for the help. That was a fucked up situation."

"Yeah, but Dude, you were in the shit man!"

"I know. Glad to see you! How are the guys?"

"Okay, great, great. Hey, why don't you find something to eat and get cleaned up and then come over to the JOC and I'll get you read in."

"Okay, where's it at?"

"Uh, just walk up around to your left here, then get up on that kinda road and keep moving to your right. Eventually you'll see a long tent, you really can't miss it. We've also got a spot up in one of the old hangars. Some of our guys are in there. I'll get you working a shift tonight if you're good with that."

"Hell yeah, I'm good."

"Ok... Dude!" Stacks laughed as he walked away. Donovan went back in the tent. He opened the flap, ducked through and stood up on the other side. He noticed a few of the guys were waking up.

"Hey sir, whazzup?" Zondo asked. Senior Airman Zondo was one of Donovan's favorite troops. He was on the quiet side, nice guy, good sense of humor and friendly. He was average height; his black hair was shaved down to stubble.

"Hey Sean, great to see you." Donovan walked up to Zondo at his bunk. Zondo stood up and Donovan gave him a hug. "You look good. How was the trip over?"

"Sucked."

"Well, all right. Who else came over with you?"

"Starling, Ski, Don, Knight, Rogers, Fairlane...uh, I might be missing somebody, but you'll see them all. Glad you're here sir."

"Me too, I'm glad I'm here too. So, where's the shower, shitter, chow hall, golf course..."

"Funny sir, ha ha, there are no showers here..."

"Oh, nice, touché..."

"Yeah sir, keep your French to yourself would ya?"

"Okay man, alright, well I'm going to get cleaned up and get to the TOC."

"Okay sir, head out the tent, hang a hard left and circle back behind the tent, just as you reach the back of the tent go 90 right and keep walking on that path, about halfway from our tent to the runway there's a shower tent."

"Thanks man, see you later."

"Roger sir."

Donovan went back to his bunk, grabbed his shaving kit and a towel and headed to the shower. He found it on the first attempt. He hadn't had a shower in a couple of weeks so it was great – cold and short – but great. He eventually met back up with Stacks at the TOC and got spun up on operations. He sat in on a couple of the targeting briefs and pulled a few shifts as an OIC, working the air desk. He was getting into the swing of things and really appreciated being back with his guys. He didn't personally meet the CJSOTF leadership but Stacks had briefed Colonel Longstreet and Lieutenant Colonel Bullock that Donovan was on board and integrated into ops. Donovan got Colonel Longstreet's email address and sent him a note as feedback on the ODA he'd been working with:

> *Colonel Longstreet, sir, I was recently linked up with ODA 548 and provided them close air support and rounded out the team wherever they needed me. It was a great honor to work with such a great bunch of Americans. They were squared away and were the ultimate professionals. Very Respectfully, Major Patrick Donovan*

To which Colonel Longstreet replied:

> *Major Donovan, thanks for the note, I appreciate comments like that coming from a great fellow Irishman like yourself, Colonel Longstreet*

Donovan was happy to get the response; he shared it with Stacks. Things were slipping into a routine mode. There were few requests for close air support that went "kinetic," but he was getting to know the bigger picture: who was where supporting who. He was getting to know the broader team also. Who was working in the JOC, who ran the special ops aviation support, who to talk with to get things done and which NCOs made things happen. Stacks kept him as a "floater" after pulling a few shifts so that he could have as much overlap as possible. What Donovan didn't know yet was that Stacks's dad was sick. He was making sure Donovan could handle things until, if he had to go home, they could get another Lieutenant Colonel in to replace him. Stacks had him go to the targeting meetings, the change-over briefs, any ops and intel briefs; basically, if something was going on, Stacks wanted Donovan in on it. So, even when off shift, Donovan hung out in the JOC and also went on a couple of AC-130 flights as a ground liaison, assisting the aircrew in communicating with the controllers on the ground. On one of those missions he ran into and flew with an old bomb squadron mate, Major Dan Rice. As he flew on those missions he was getting yet another perspective on the fight, flying with one of the engaging aircraft.

Donovan was sitting next to Stacks's station listening to the coordination that was occurring in the JOC and to the radio calls that came in to the air desk. In between everything, the two of them talked about ops, about home – anything. Stacks was leaning forward, sitting with his elbows on his knees holding a spent water bottle, now half filled with tobacco spit, each sentence punctuated by a spit into the bottle. As he talked to Donovan, little pieces of snuff roamed around his teeth. "Hey Dude, would you watch the desk, I gotta go take a shit," he said as he put the spit bottle down next to the field table leg his laptop and radios rested on.

"Sure, you bet."

He stood, smacked Donovan on the shoulder with one hand and strolled out of the JOC. Donovan got up out of his chair and swung Stacks' around back facing the field table and took a seat. As soon as he sat down a radio call came into the ops desk, which was right behind the air desk. He listened up to see if there'd be a need for air. Staff Sergeant Sweeney was working the ops desk. He'd just come in from the field two days earlier. He and Donovan had chatted on several occasions and had a good rapport. Sweeney went back and forth with the ODA team on the other end. Several times he stood up and located the sets of coordinates that were being passed on the map hanging behind his workstation. Several times he told the ODA to "standby" as he went into the command section to discuss with Bullock. After a few minutes the conversation was over.

Donovan waited until Sweeney had finished writing in his log, then asked, "Sweeney, what was all that about?"

Sweeney swung around in his chair to face him, not initially tracking who was talking. Just as he looked at him he stopped and put up a finger,

"Hang on a sec, forgot to write something down." He spun back around, jotted another set up notes and then turned back to Donovan.

"Sorry, sir, what was that?"

"Just wondering what that was all about."

"Oh, I guess really nothing. The team called from their safe house. They'd been approached by somebody through their Northern Alliance bros that said they represented a bunch of Al Qaeda who said they wanted to surrender. Like a thousand, with family, wives, kids, the whole enchilada."

"No shit, that's great."

"Yeah, well, they smelled a rat. They thought it felt like a set up and they'd be walking into an ambush. The contact said they wanted to meet at a crossroads about 20 klicks from their safe house. They actually started out in that direction but changed their mind. They called us to see if we had any intel but we didn't. Sounds fucked up."

"Well, they ought to know; they're out there, we're in here. Actually, you just got back from there right?"

"Yep, was out there for a month, we're rotating between the field and the desk to get a break once in a while and keep somebody with some savvy on the desk."

"That's cool. Okay man, thanks, anything else going on? Seems kinda quiet."

"Nah, nothing really... oh, I got invited to a skinning the day before I came back in."

"What? No shit?"

"Yeah, they captured an Al Qaeda guy that they said shot some kids in the nearby village. They were going to start by cutting a slit at the base of the back of his neck, pull the skin back away from the backbone and pour hot tar down his spine."

"Motherfucker! Geez!"

"Yeah, I didn't go though, didn't think a US troop attending something like that would be a good idea."

"Uh, yeah, good call. Son of a bitch."

"Hey, we ain't in Kansas anymore, sir."

"Ain't that the truth?"

Donovan spun back around and wrote a note regarding the proposed surrender, highlighting the location and time. Then he sat back in the chair, still thinking about the conversation with Sweeney. Stacks came back into the JOC. Donovan saw him approaching and stood to vacate his chair. Once Stacks sat down, Donovan pulled the other chair around and sat. "Well, how'd everything go?" He asked Stacks.

"Just fine. Gotta like those porta-potties. I almost had to hover over it. It was so full."

"Yikes."

"Yeah, how about in here?"

"Just a call in from the field, I wrote up the details in the log. They were approached by a rep who said he spoke for about a thousand Al Qaeda members and their families that wanted to surrender. They weren't buying it."

"Yeah, that sounds too good to be true. We have been knocking the crap out of them though."

"Yeah, they thought it was an ambush."

"Well, they ought to know."

"That's what I thought."

"Whadya say we get some chow then head back to the tent and play some cribbage?"

"Okay, sounds good to me."

"Astro should be showing up any minute – yup, there he is." Stacks spotted Captain Mullens walking through the tent flap just as he was speaking. "You go ahead. I'll give him the changeover brief and meet you at chow."

"Okay, see you there."

Donovan got up and went to chow. Stacks met him there. They ate and then walked back to their tent. It was dark and it was starting to snow. Stacks led the way into the tent; the Airmen greeted them. "Oh…here come the bosses." They were sitting on their bunks, some were listening to music, a few were writing letters and there was a group of four that were playing cards on top of a foot locker positioned between two bunks. Two of the card players were sitting on folding metal chairs.

Stacks took off his gortex desert camo jacket and shook it out over top of the card game, "Whoa, incoming!" he laughed.

The guys were less amused.

"Okay men, we're going to shift to playing cribbage. Are you guys at a place you can stop?"

"Sure, sir, whatever you say," Ski replied, rolling his eyes.

"All right, Dude's joining us tonight and he's still a rookie so we'll have to explain it again. Just remember, it's all about the counting." Stacks went over the basic rules of cribbage, stopping on occasion to ensure Donovan was tracking. When he got to the scoring, Stacks entered into a melodic rhythm, demonstrating how to add up the points, "15 for 2, a run of five for 5, flush for 4, for 11…or in this case," he rearranged cards on the foot locker, "15 for 2, 15 for 2, 15 for 2, pair for 2 for 8…" He saw the counting as an assessment of the skill and experience of the player. As they started playing, Stacks would laugh at each of Donovan's attempts to add up his scores.

As Stacks shuffled for the next hand Ski pulled out a bottle from his ruck, which he had beside the chair he was sitting in. Donovan looked at the bottle, then slowly turned his head to look at Stacks to see how he'd reacted. He was aware he was new to the crowd and that Stacks was the boss. Ski pulled the bottle up into plain view, Donovan turned back to watch Ski, who reached between his legs and grabbed a paper cup, put it on the footlocker, then reached down again between his feet and lifted up a plastic bottle of orange juice. With one hand, he poured the orange juice, with the other he poured in what now was obvious to Donovan, the vodka. As he sat silent, he turned back again looking for a reaction from Stacks. Stacks had finished shuffling the cards, put them in the middle of the footlocker and then leaned over to grab his spit bottle from beside the leg of his bunk. As he leaned over to his left he extended his right hand, which now contained an empty paper cup. Ski repeated the screwdriver-process and filled up Stacks's cup. Stacks took a sip, "Ah… that's harsh."

"Where'd you get that, Ski?" Donovan asked.

"There's a guy I meet at the fence that sells it to me, the finest former Soviet State bootleg vodka. You want some?"

"Sure," he responded. Ski handed him a paper cup and filled it half way with orange juice and then topped it off with the vodka. "Thanks." He took a swig, "Wow, that's like avgas!"

A couple of the other guys brought out their canteen cups or water bottles, or used paper cups and Ski topped them all off. That finished off that bottle. He reached into his ruck and pulled out another. Ski screwed the cap off and it made a different snapping sound that Donovan was used to hearing when opening a liquor bottle.

"Can I see that?" he asked. Ski passed him the bottle and he looked it over. "Huh, looks like they used a piece of scotch tape versus an actual seal. I'm sure this is top quality hooch."

"Best we can get around here. I'm not complaining," Ski replied.

"Me neither," Donovan quickly answered, followed by everyone else one by one in the tent. They all laughed.

They continued to play cards for hours, getting to know each other a little better than they ever had a chance to back home. Donovan thought to himself that this is what he thought going to war was going to be like: with your comrades, bonding in the lulls between fighting and eventually becoming a stronger unit because everything would become personal. You'd be fighting next to and for your buddies. This was a lot different than his first foray into combat, alone, but he did eventually form those bonds with his ODA comrades. They talked about their families, wives, kids, hobbies, cars, home.

"This ain't a bad job," Don stated. Donovan sat upright and made sure there was a lull in the conversation so he knew all were listening.

"Job? It has been said that there will be no more war." He had everyone's attention. "We must pretend to believe that. But when war comes, it is we who will take the first shock and buy time with our lives. It is we who keep the faith. We are called mercenaries on the outposts of an empire. We serve the flag. The trade we all follow is the give and take of death. It is for that purpose that the American people maintain us. Any one of us who believes he has a job like any other, for which he draws a money wage, is a thief of the food he eats and a trespasser in the bunk in which he lies down to sleep."

They all sat silently staring at him, barely breathing; he

stared back, stone-faced.

"Shit Dude where'd that come from?" Stacks broke the silence.

"It's a line from my favorite movie." They all let out audible sighs or took a drink of their rotgut vodka.

"Hell sir, we thought we had an Audie Murphy here in our midst," Ski said.

"Just 'cause it was said in a movie doesn't mean it ain't true, right? I believe it," Donovan answered back.

"Here's one of my favorite quotes," Stacks started. "It is not the critic who counts, nor the man who points how the strong man stumbled or where the doer of deeds could have done them better. The credit belongs to the man who is actually in the arena; whose face is marred by dust and sweat and blood; who strives valiantly...who knows the great enthusiasms, the great devotions, and spends himself in a worthy cause; who, at best, knows the triumph of high achievement; and who, at the worst, if he fails, at least fails while daring greatly, so that his place shall never be with those cold and timid souls who know neither victory nor defeat."

"Amen. Gents, that's us. We're out here getting some for Uncle Sam. You all should be proud of yourselves." Donovan added, they toasted.

"Okay, let's get back to cards; philosophy 101 is done for the night." Stacks could tell a few of the guys were starting to think deep; good overall, but too much could be bad for morale.

They wrapped up the card game shortly thereafter and all hit the sack. It was freezing and the snow and wind had picked up. Donovan put on his sweat pants and fleece jacket and slipped into his sleeping bag. He put on his watch cap and pulled the bag up around his face. He fell quickly to sleep. After about two hours he woke up shivering; the heater that was hooked up to their tent had gone out and was now blowing frigid air directly on his head. He pulled the sleeping bag completely around his head and tried to go back to sleep. It took him quite a while to stop shivering.

By the time he woke up the next morning, Stacks and most of the rest of the guys had already left the tent. He made his way to the shower, slipping on the ice twice, once falling into a mud puddle. He ended up wearing his sweats and fleece into the shower until he could get all the moon-dust mud off and wore the soaking wet clothes back to the tent. He would shiver for half the day. Once he got dressed he stopped by the chow tent, grabbed a box of cereal and got to the JOC. Once he crossed the threshold and immediately felt the heat; he let it wash over him for a second, then he moved to the air desk and plopped down next to Stacks and Ski.

"Morning Dude. Enjoy your sleep in?" Stacks said with a big smile, teeth laced with specks of tobacco.

"Yeah, sorry about that. Guess a little fatigue caught up with me and that damn ice cold air blowing on me all night," Donovan said.

"Not to mention that quality beverage," Ski added.

"Yeah, not to mention that," he replied.

"Hey Dude, as you know 10th Mountain has been plus'ing up here in country. We had the initial company or so for base security but now the leadership is starting to come in. They've gen'ed up a mission for a company under the 2nd Brigade leadership, Task Force Commando. I'm going to send Zondo and Fairlane out with them. The mission is prisoner processing. They've got all the prisoners from Qala-i-Jangi they've got to do something with, so they're using an ancient fort in Sheberghan, which is about 130 klicks west of Mazar-i-Sharif, to run the processing. That company will move to Mazar-i-Sharif and set up an aerial port. Once the prisoners are processed at Sheberghan they'll be moved to Mazar-i-Sharif to fly out to Pakistan and then wherever else they're going to end up. The 2nd Brigade leadership will be running the show and we'll provide a team to be in place in case we have another prison riot or any other such nonsense. How's that sound?"

"Sounds sound. Only thing is…" Donovan paused for effect.

"Yeah, what?" Stacks asked, suspecting the question.

"Sir, don't you think it would be better if those guys had officer leadership? I can make sure they're not getting rolled into some other type of mission, you know, the normal mission

178

creep type stuff. Plus, I've got time on the ground and have been working here with you so if anything does hit the fan... Well, I'll be there to help." Donovan paused. He'd been talking to Stacks while leaning forward with his forearms on his knees. He looked up from beneath his brows for Stacks's response.

"You're shitting me right? You just got back."

"Yeah, but... I really think it's the way to go and I'm kind of an overage here right?"

"Okay, let me think about it. I've got to go take a shit." Stacks got up and left the JOC.

"Dang sir that was ballsy," Ski chuckled.

"Why, didn't that make sense?"

"Yeah, just not coming from you, having just came in from a boondoggle."

"Boondoggle? What's that supposed to mean? I was out there on orders, orders that gave me no specific guidance and I did what made sense."

"Take it easy sir, I'm just giving you shit. I'd be asking the same thing but I'm hoping to roll with an ODA any day now."

"Okay, no shit man, I was making it happen the best I could."

"Really sir, I was just giving you shit. I hear you," Ski said as he placed his hand on his shoulder. Donovan finally understood that he was in fact joking. He let out a sigh and laughed. Ski laughed with him.

Donovan stayed at their workstation and waited for Stacks. He figured Stacks would want to send him back to Kuwait to work with ARCENT again. There were a few routine check-ins from a couple of the guys in the field while Stacks was gone, nothing important. This made Donovan feel even more sure Stacks was going to send him back since that's where Colonel Laredo wanted him anyway. Eventually Stacks came back into the JOC and to his seat, which Donovan again vacated for his boss. Donovan had dragged a free metal chair from another work station up to theirs making an annoying metallic screech across the plywood floor in the process. Stacks pivoted and faced him.

"Okay Dude, you're going." Donovan hoped it wasn't too obvious to Stacks that he was elated – he struggled to keep the corners of his mouth turned down, or at least neutral. "But here's the deal: you're out there to take care of the guys, just like you pitched. Got it?"

"Yes sir, of course. No problem," Donovan said sincerely. He put both his hands on his knees poised to either stand up or stay seated, but he felt he had to do something.

Stacks noticed his anticipation. "Go ahead man, get with our Army bros and get spun up on the mission."

He uncoiled and stood up, but almost at the same time he was turning to head out of the JOC. He caught himself and stuck out his hand to Stacks. "Thanks sir, I'll take care of our guys."

"I know you will man. I know you will."

Donovan exited the JOC and started for the tent the 10th Mountain staff had as their ops center. He hadn't thought much about his day job as an ALO with the 10th since he'd been out with the Marines and the ODA's. He remembered the back and forth they went through to try and get a minimal team with the 10th during the initial planning. He wondered if his going along was going to fly with the Brigade staff and figured they wouldn't, really couldn't object to the TAC Team, Fairlane and Zondo. He kept walking and thinking as he wound his way through the camp. He got to the TOC and went in; the large tent system was abuzz with activity. He went from station to station until he found the S-3, Major Will Fredrick. Fredrick was average height, dark, close cut hair and was stoic. He was busy typing on a laptop. Donovan stood silent in front of Fredrick's field table hoping he'd notice him in his peripheral vision.

"Major Fredrick…" Donovan said, waiting for him to look up. He didn't. "Will, Pat Donovan. We met during the planning sessions for 'Freedom Bridge." Fredrick glanced at Donovan briefly then kept typing. Donovan stood there, unable to think of anything else to do, and waited.

After another minute or two Fredrick stopped, picked his hands off the keyboard slightly, then put them back down and turned to him.

"What do you need, Donovan?"

"Nice to see you too Will. I've got a TAC Team and myself ready to head out with you and I'm ready to get read in on the plan."

"We're not going to need close air support."

"You're kidding right? I've been out in the field for the last couple of weeks and it's still Indian country out there. CAS is something that's better to have and not need than need and not have. Am I right?"

Fredrick drummed his fingers on the space bar of the laptop. "Okay, I'll have to discuss it with the brigade commander and we've got a strict limit on how many soldiers we can use for this op."

"If you need me to I can brief the Colonel. Again, I'm not sure what other firepower you might have but not only can we provide you fire support, if all hell breaks loose at this prison like it did at Qala-i-Jangi we can flatten the place in a couple of minutes. Just saying."

"All right, yeah okay, I'll brief the boss. In the meantime go talk to Master Sergeant Stevens. He'll give you the basics, the timeline and anything else you need to know." Fredrick had an obvious change of heart and now sounded enthusiastic. "Hey Pat, thanks for hunting me down."

"Sure thing Will. We're here to support, Climb to Glory." Donovan ended with the 10th Mountain's call out.

"To the Top," replied Fredrick.

CHAPTER FOURTEEN

TASK FORCE COMMANDO

Donovan stayed involved in the mission planning over the next couple of days. The force was called Task Force Commando after the 2nd Brigade Commandos. Colonel Rapier the Brigade commander would head up the operation, Fredrick would be his second as his S-3 and a few other members of the brigade staff would round out the team. This leadership slice would actually lead just about a platoon's worth of troops, about forty. The plan was to fly into Mazar-i-Sharif and set up an aerial port to fly the processed prisoners into Pakistan for further movement to other locations, some going to Camp X-ray, Guantanamo Bay, Cuba. The bulk of the Task Force would then move to Sheberghan and set up processing operations at the old fort there. There were survivors from Qala-i-Jangi, and there were also hundreds of Taliban and Al Qaeda prisoners and that number was growing. The departure date was set for 24 December. Donovan worked with Fairlane and Zondo to get their equipment and supplies right and to talk through what they were going to be doing while waiting for the possibility of a prison break or riot; they didn't know.

The 24th arrived. That morning Donovan used one of the phones in the Dagger JOC to make a quick call to Nikki. He didn't have much to say and couldn't tell her about the operation. He did tell her he loved her, missed her and wished her a Merry Christmas. She took it all in, wished him the same and stayed chipper, just glad she had a chance to talk to him, then she hung up and bawled her eyes out. He also called his folks. They only chatted for a minute or two. His mom told him they loved him. His dad told him to stay safe, good luck and good hunting. He knew how proud they were of him and how proud they were that their son was one of the first to avenge the US after 9/11.

He was glad he got a hold of them but he was also glad the calls were over. At this point he felt it difficult to focus on anything but what was going on there downrange. He, Fairlane and Zondo got their gear over to the assembly area early. Zondo stayed with it. Donovan went back and checked out with Stacks and verified frequencies and call signs and the next couple of ATO's worth of aircraft that would be flying. They were ready. He got back to the assembly area when it was pitch black and snowing. There were yards and yards of gear strewn across the cracked tarmac. Soldiers were sitting on the cold concrete and leaning back against their rucks. Colonel Rapier stood with a cup of hot chocolate, surrounded by three of his primary staff; Fredrick was one of them. He reached into his cargo pocket, pulled out a stack of papers folded over lengthwise. He started distributing them to a couple of soldiers and then two of his primaries grabbed the stack and took over. After a couple of minutes one of them came around to the Airmen. Donovan was standing with Zondo and Fairlane was sitting, leaning against his ruck. The soldier handed Donovan a sheet. He flipped it right side up and found it was a song sheet of Christmas carols. He looked at Zondo, turned the sheet so Zondo could quickly read it, and then looked it over again.

"Wow, no shit, are we going to sing?" he asked Zondo. Zondo didn't answer; he didn't know what to make of it until...

"*Silent night, Silent night, holy night,*" the Colonel started singing. "*All is calm, all is bright.*"

Donovan looked at Zondo, shrugged his shoulders, smiled and started singing.

"*Round yon Virgin Mother and Child, Holy Infant so tender and mild, Sleep in heavenly peace, Sleep in heavenly peace...*"

Zondo looked at him and shook his head with a crooked smile forming on his face.

The singing only lasted a couple of minutes. They only did a verse or two of Silent Night, Jingle Bells and Rudolph the Red Nose Reindeer. Donovan shook Zondo and Fairlane's hands and a couple of the soldiers in their immediate vicinity, wishing them a Merry Christmas. He thought this would make a great story someday, singing Christmas carols before heading into combat.

A few hours passed and then it was time to start loading. It looked like dawn was going to break soon. They were going to move via a French Air Force C-160, the French loadmaster made the announcement. "Attention, attention, prepare to load."

The US Air Force logistics personnel then directed the soldiers onto the plane. The C-160 looked like a smaller, two engine version of the US C-130. All the rucks and bags and cargo pallets were placed in the center of the cargo area and the personnel were strapped into aluminum-framed canvas seats along the sides. Donovan had a seat toward the left-forward crew door. He dropped his gear then got ready to strap in. Out of force of habit he didn't secure his lap belt. In the B-52 he learned to never secure the belt until after successful engine start; with eight in the BUFF that took a while and afforded plenty of opportunity for an engine fire.

He looked to his left and one of the French aircrew was strapping in. He was huge, he looked like Ivan Putski the Polish Pile Driver, the professional wrestler from the '70s and he was eating a big sausage. He and his comrades were wearing heavy black flack vests with extremely high protective collars that covered their necks up to their helmets. The man strapped in and stared out the open ramp at the back of the plane watching the Americans load. He slowly shook his head as he took big bite after big bite of that big ring sausage. Donovan looked him over but was hesitant to strike up a conversation unless it was to ask him *how he was* or *where the library was.* He ran French joke after French joke through his mind. He'd never been to France and hadn't met any of the deployed French troops or aircrew so his mind ran with the stereotypes. Then he thought, what the hell.

"Bonjour mon ami," he said, overplaying his New Jersey accent.

"How's it going?" replied the Frenchman with his best John Wayne imitation. They both laughed. The Frenchmen held the remaining nub of the sausage toward Donovan and gestured for him to take it.

Donovan instantly held up a hand and said, "Gracias." He'd had a brain fart and that word just came out. The Frenchmen stopped in mid-chew, arm still outstretched and stared at him. "Non, Merci. Sorry, I'm tired my friend. No thank you though."

"Roger," replied the Frenchman as he chucked the last nub into his mouth, then reached for his shoulder straps and buckled up. He motioned to Donovan to do the same. He did.

The aircraft taxied for what seemed like thirty minutes. It then made a sharp left turn of about ninety degrees and came to an abrupt halt. Donovan said a quick Our Father. The French aircrew double-checked their chinstraps and flack vests. The crewman sitting near Donovan gave a thumbs-up and then spoke into his mic, words no one could hear over the now roaring engines. At once the brakes were released and the aircraft lurched forward and began to accelerate. They were heavy; Donovan could feel it. The aircraft lumbered down the dark runway. They all could feel that they were going faster and faster, but then everything instantly sounded and felt the same; the changing speed and changing noise had stopped. Now it was a steady speed, loud roaring engines and the vibrations of the wheels in the pitted runway and the loose nuts and bolts of the 1967 airframe. The pilot was holding it down on the ground before he yanked back on the yoke. Everything was pushed toward the floor; the angle of attack kept increasing. Now everyone was leaning hard toward the nose of the aircraft. Within a few minutes they stabilized in a steady climb. They climbed for about five minutes and then leveled off. The engines spooled down to a loud hum. Donovan was heading back into Afghanistan.

Donovan had nodded off. He awoke to a loud shrill coming from the aircraft PA system crackling to life. Words were said in a long string but nobody could understand them. He thought he might start a business retrofitting speakers on military aircraft when he retired. He figured they were entering into Afghanistan. The aircrew moved back to their original positions. An aircrew member was positioned in front of each window to spot for SAMs. His thoughts were correct; they were crossing the border. A few seconds after the announcement the aircraft nosed over and everyone lifted up off their seats, restrained by their seat belts. A few loose items floated momentarily in the air, some hitting the ceiling of the aircraft. They were pulling negative Gs. He thought to himself, *Shit hot.*

The aircraft continued to descend. It was a few minutes before the pilot started to dish out and level the plane off. Then he aggressively banked to the left, leveled, then banked hard to the right. They were flying nape of the earth. The pilots were aggressive, banking, diving, short climb, pushover, level off, bank, pull up and over. Donovan smiled, this was his kind of flying. He loved low-level in the BUFF. With the smile still on his face he turned to his right to see how the soldiers were holding up. Not well. There was a half dozen with their faces pushed hard into puke bags, getting an aggressive ab workout; another dozen or so were green as frogs and most of the rest just sat still facing forward with their eyes closed. They didn't know what was going on and most of them weren't used to that kind of flying. Donovan loved it and he had a newfound respect for the French flyers. The American heavy cargo aircraft tactics in Afghanistan was to spiral climb up over the departure airfield until getting to a safe altitude and then cruise at high altitude out of the range of any expected enemy air defense system, any that the Taliban could have, and then spiral down over the destination airfield, which maintained or tried to maintain a safety zone around the field, into a landing; all at night. Here the French were, broad daylight, yanking and banking in the heart of the engagement envelope of EVERY system the Taliban could have including AK-47s. As he thought about it, he realized he did respect their guts and flying ability but they weren't just putting their asses at risk; there were a couple dozen guys in the back that were along for the ride. As an Airman he felt the way he did about the flying but he did realize there's more to it. He thought back to his flights with Bud at Fairchild. He had the same mindset, it was fun, but Uncle Sam wasn't paying the military to have fun.

After another thirty minutes the aircraft stabilized and configured for a landing at Mazar-i-Sharif. The landing was smooth. Once they taxied in and parked they unloaded and the Brigade leadership was picked up by an SUV and whisked away. Donovan and his guys and the rest of the soldiers got to setting up tents, digging a slit trench and getting their equipment squared away. During this process he met Captain Nelson, company commander. He was a good natured, easy going individual with a great sense of humor, and he knew his stuff. Donovan quickly connected with him. Donovan, Zondo and Fairlane bunked with Nelson and another dozen or so soldiers in one of the tents.

As it started to get dark the SOF guys who were in the area made contact with the Brigade leadership. They were set up in a school near downtown Mazar-i-Sharif. That night they had planned to lay on some food for the "conventional soldiers." A couple of trucks waited near the aircraft ramp. After the tents were set up the soldiers, who wanted to, boarded the trucks and headed to the school. Donovan and his team went along. The trucks turned off the main hardball and headed to the school, down along a dirt road and surrounded by a few mud huts. There were about fifteen from the Brigade group total. They were met by two SOF soldiers at the door of the school who invited them in; they headed into a classroom. There was a TV set up and there was a 60's car-chase movie playing, dubbed in Farsi. There were two long tables set up off to the side with three metal food bins. Most of the food had already been eaten but there was some rice, a few pieces of an unknown type of meat and some bread. Next to the metal bins were three cardboard boxes marked with shipping information that came from Jordan. There were apples, oranges and plums. Each soldier took a pass through the line.

Donovan took a scoop of rice, a piece of bread and a plum. As he was walking back to find a seat in front of the TV he took a bite of the plum. It was soft; he continued to chew then looked down at the plum to see it was full of worms. Without making a big deal about it he raised his plate to his mouth, looking around to ensure he wasn't going to offend anyone, he let the uneaten piece of the plum fall to the paper plate. He sat in one of the metal chairs lined up in front of the TV next to Zondo and ate the rice. He looked at Zondo's plate, noticed a plum on it, and got Zondo's attention. They made eye contact and he looked down at Zondo's plum then looked back up at Zondo and shook his head. Zondo raised his chin in acknowledgement. Fairlane stood behind the both of them. Donovan looked back over his shoulder and checked Fairlane's plate. He had no fruit.

They all ate and appreciated the food. Donovan especially grew fond of the bread. After about 90 minutes they loaded the trucks back up and headed back to the camp. They got back to the tents and everyone not on duty climbed into their sleeping bags. For minor comfort, each tent had a kerosene stove. They were a little complicated to set up and the first night the tent filled with black kerosene smoke. Some of the soldiers were so tired they didn't wake up before being all but pulled from the tent.

The next day Donovan got the lay of the land. There were several distinct sections of the airfield. Where they pitched their tents was an open plot of dirt, a few hundred yards away were hard structures that made up the bulk of the airfield. In between were remnants of the Russian Air Force, dismembered hulks of MIG-21s and an MI-24 Hind helicopter. He was eager to climb around the wrecks. He'd done numerous target studies for his nuclear mission that referenced the MIG-21 Fishbed, but had never seen one. On the walk over he and Zondo linked up with the Brigade lawyer who was an aviation aficionado. He and Donovan talked airplanes and capabilities and struck up a fast friendship. Once they got to the aircraft, they went their separate ways in exploration. By the time Donovan and Zondo were through, they had extracted the control sticks and two ejection handles from two MIGs and a control stick and a minigun from a Hind. They slung the bootie over their shoulders, walked back to the camp and stuffed it all in their rucksacks. Zondo carried the minigun and he was careful to keep it under wraps, knowing that just because he had it didn't mean he'd get to keep it.

Planning went on for another day. Donovan had gone through many sessions of the Military Decision Making Process but this one was going down in his green notebook. The team that would go out to the prison the next day was called to assemble on the runway nearest their tents. Everyone gathered at the edge of the blacktop at 0800 and waited. After about an hour, Major Fredrick and the First Sergeant pulled up in an SUV. They had been waiting for the locally contracted trucks they'd use for the movement the next day to show up, but they never came. Fredrick got out of the SUV, looked at the gaggle, put his hands on his hips and started to slowly pace back and forth. Several of the soldiers, who'd been sitting in the dirt got to their feet and moved in his direction. Soon they all stood in a semi-circle around Fredrick, Donovan and his team too.

"All right, bring it in," Fredrick shouted to the crowd who were all within 20 feet of him. "The First Sergeant is going to read the manifest by vehicle. I want you all to take your positions on the tarmac in vehicle order, in position and standby for further."

"Johnson, Jacobs, Malone and Phillips," the First Sergeant barked out. Those four individuals looked at each other and slowly walked out onto the blacktop. They looked slightly confused but stood in vehicle-position-order facing away from the Major. This went on until all of the names were called and all of the "simulated vehicles" or "chocks" were manned. Now Fredrick gave further directions,

"All right, we're going to rehearse our arrival at the prison." The team was going to proceed to the Sheberghan prison and set up processing operations. There was an element of Northern Alliance soldiers on site guarding the prisoners. Per a previous discussion between Donovan and Fredrick, Donovan would be responsible for external security, which included keeping outside elements out and keeping the prisoners in, and in case of a prison-wide riot or revolt he'd bring in the airpower. Fredrick would run ops inside the prison, primarily focused on processing and he'd retain overall operational control and Colonel Rapier would be in command. This was an unusual and unprecedented role for an Airman, at least as far as Donovan knew. But, with the help of Fairlane and Zondo, they had a solid plan.

"Chock one, you depart on my command and proceed for approximately 20 yards and then make a left arcing 180 degree turn to where the First Sergeant is standing. Chocks two, three, four and five follow in sequence. Once chock one arcs back after his second 180 degree turn back to his original heading this will simulate the approach to the prison gates. After he regains his present position, he'll make a 90-degree right turn and proceed to where I'm standing. This will simulate final parking. Chock two will turn left and proceed a matching distance. Chock three evenly space between chock one and the intersection. Chock four, turn left and evenly space between chock two and the intersection. Once each chock halts, dismount and take up firing positions. Chock two with the 240B will position along the main entrance road, back 50 meters with a field of fire to cover the front gate and right and left flanks. TACP element as chock five will proceed to the far right approximately 200 meters and set up fields of fire covering the east and south sides of the prison. The Northern Alliance elements will cover the north and west sides of the prison. Any questions?" He paused for a few seconds. "Okay, execute."

The first set of four soldiers walked through the directed path, each maintaining their relative sitting position as they made their maneuvers. They were following in sequence by the next chock and so on. Zondo was "driving" the fifth chock vehicle and simulated having trouble getting it in gear, but he simulated fixing the problem before Fredrick saw what he was doing. Donovan looked around and saw face after face struggling to stay straight.

"Close it up Air Force!" he shouted and Donovan and their team jogged forward to gain their spacing. They all had big smiles on their faces and Zondo started to giggle a few times. Donovan saw that Fredrick saw him so he motioned to Zondo to knock it off, laughing as he did. Although he and Fredrick were of equal rank, Fredrick owned the ground and was in charge.

They ran through the walking simulated vehicle movement no less than six times. After the sixth, Fredrick called the group back together, gave a few motivational words and dismissed them. It was sunny. Donovan, Zondo and Fairlane stayed in place. Donovan laid back against the slanted earth near the tarmac. He put his hands behind his head, tipped his hat back and closed his eyes against the sun.

"You guys ready for tomorrow?"

"Sure sir, we're ready, just hope we get that difficult driving maneuver right using actual vehicles," Fairlane said sarcastically.

That night nearly saw the first casualty of Task Force Commando. In the pitch black of night a second lieutenant female intelligence officer stumbled out of her tent, groped through the darkness and found the wooden post that was driven in next to the slit trench, but was disoriented and instead of stepping to the right side of the post she stepped to the wrong side and plunged into the excrement-filled hole. She was small enough that as she fell face first her shoulders got wedged between the sides of the trench with her head under the sewage. She panicked. She thrashed, totally confused, but eventually broke her shoulders loose from the wet earth and got her knees underneath her and burst through the surface of the muck. She screamed like no one in the camp had ever heard anyone or anything scream – it was a high pitched, but guttural, primordial shrieking of terror, anger, relief and frustration that would echo in the ears of all who heard for years to come. Everyone got up and burst from their tents, armed and ready for action. The first to get to her were the soldiers pulling watch. Two got to her within a couple of seconds of her outburst. The first reached for her arm but stopped just short of the trench; she was still in it, thigh deep. He didn't know if she'd been hurt, but when the second soldier got there a second or two later his first reaction was to laugh. With that, the first soldier then grabbed her by one of her arms, which were both extended skyward. She pulled away. He grabbed her hand.

"Come on Lieutenant, you've got to get the fuck out of there and get that shit washed off you." The second soldier laughed again, thinking the first was trying to make a joke. He wasn't. "Come on, grab my hand and pull yourself up out of there," he insisted.

"Hey man, just have her walk out the backside, it's sloped," said the second soldier.

"Oh, yeah, okay. Ma'am, about face and walk on out of there. Come on move!" he shouted. She turned around with her arms still in the air. She didn't want to even touch herself. She then started retching as she slowly slogged up out of the hole. By now the whole camp was around the trench.

"Okay everybody, break it up, back to your racks. On the double!" Captain Nelson ordered. "Son of a bitch. Hey Grasso, go get the doc. He's over in the hard billet. Move!" he directed the second soldier.

"Sir, I'm on watch."

"I got your watch. Go."

The lieutenant was sobbing, snot streaming from her nose and she was dripping in shit, piss and vomit. A couple of soldiers came running with arms full of bottled water. Without a word or a question they started opening them up and pouring them over her. At first she shrieked and then stopped, realizing they were helping. She went down to one knee at first and then down on both. The water dousing started to reveal her blond hair which had been muck-brown.

"Jamie, stand up so we can get most of that off of you," Nelson directed. She stood back up slowly and let her arms hang limp at her sides. "You'll be okay."

The Captain medical officer came running up and as he tried to stop short of the lieutenant, planted a boot in in the mud and slid into her at a relatively high speed. He knocked her and himself over onto the wet ground. That pushed her to a new level of anguish. She shrieked again and rolled over on her back in the mud.

"Jesus Jim!" Nelson yelled. He reached down to pull the doc to his feet as he tried to help the lieutenant back up.

"I'm sorry Jamie, I'm sorry. Let's get you over to the aid station and I'll get you fixed up."

"Nelson, can you have somebody grab some of her clean clothes and bring them to me?"

"Sure," Nelson replied, shaking his head. Donovan and his guys had been watching the whole thing in stunned amazement. They wanted to help, but so did everybody else, so they stayed out of the way. The doc took his patient under one arm and walked her in the direction of the aid station. She got cleaned up; the doc checked her for injuries and then he gave her handfuls of antibiotics and a couple of shots. It would take days for her to recover, emotionally.

****

Uktam had been captured shortly after the engagement on Highway 1. He and two of his comrades endured a long and brutal trek to Sheberghan. They were kept bound and confined in the back of a jingle truck, a fancily decorated heavy cargo truck, that took them over rough roads and across shallow rivers with little water and no food. Once they got to the prison they were thrown in the area reserved for the hardcore foreign fighters. The prison had two main sections, one for the local Taliban and one for the foreigners. Uktam had survived mainly through word of his valorous acts against the Americans. He didn't know what to hope for; he was in a foreign land with no friends and now he was in an ancient prison.

****

Morning came quick with the middle of the night interruption. The Task Force would split up, leaving a logistics element at Mazar-i-Sharif and the forward element staying outside Sheberghan in a compound, driving back and forth each day to the prison. Donovan and his team skinnied down their rucks to lighten their load. Zondo had transferred the liberated minigun from his ruck to an A-bag, and Donovan and Fairlane piled their stuff on top of it, hoping no one would mess with or steal it. The forward team loaded into the trucks and they moved out. It was 150 Kilometers and would take between two and three hours. They left the airfield and headed into Mazar-i-Sharif. After weaving through the crowded streets they popped out the west side and back into the desert. They drove along the hardball for another twenty minutes and then to their north they saw the ancient city of Balkh. It looked ominous from the roadway. The terrain climbed toward the city, which was topped by a tall wall. That's all they'd get to see of it as they pressed on toward Sheberghan.

Everyone in Donovan's vehicle took turns nodding off except for, thankfully, the driver. After two hours they drove to a small compound consisting of a half a dozen buildings outside the city, located next to a dirt airstrip. An Army Military Intelligence (MI) team was there, waiting to join the Task Force and ride to the prison with them. There were six members of the team. The convoy pulled into the compound and stopped to pick them up. The MI team also had two Afghan interpreters with them. The convoy unloaded their gear into the allocated buildings; there were about fifteen per room. Each staked a claim to a patch of concrete floor. Donovan, Zondo and Fairlane took spots against the back right wall, away from the door and stuck together.

After everyone got situated, they remounted the vehicles and the convoy continued. Donovan's vehicle held him and his two Airmen, an MI soldier and one of the Interpreters, Sahir. Zondo and Fairlane started calling him "Zamphire." Sahir tried several times to correct them, but he obviously didn't get the joke and eventually let it go. Sahir was twenty-five, very slight and he dressed in clothes that looked more western but from the 70's: pants, shirt, coat and shoes, instead of the traditional garb and sandals of his countrymen. His black hair was short compared to his countrymen, long compared to the US military and his teeth were in bad shape. He still had them all but they looked horrible from years of neglect and no dentists. Unfortunately, the crowd he was about to spend a lot of time with were pretty merciless when it came to ribbing and, more unfortunately, Sahir didn't quite get American humor and took it all pretty hard.

They moved out and within thirty minutes could see the edge of the city as they continued to approach. Everyone was wide-awake. Just before entering the city, off to the left of the main roadway was the hulk of a Russian T-72 tank, its long unusable gun pointing at the road. They drove down the main street. Face after interested face starred at the occupants of the small convoy. They passed an open-air market with what looked like the side of a skinned camel hanging from scaffolding, dozens of flies buzzing and walking across the meat. There was a

194

mixture of old and new; motorcycles and donkeys shared the road. They eventually came to the center of the city and s-turned through a large square and turned back west again. As they traversed the square, Donovan noticed three young girls in azure blue school uniforms, heads uncovered. They could have been students anywhere in the western world. Passing them heading in the other direction were two women in head to toe burkhas in the same color blue.

Within two minutes they were at the turn into the prison. Now they'd execute their rehearsed vehicular maneuver. It was flawless. Donovan's team took up positions on the far right and they maneuvered their vehicle to point toward the wall of the prison. There was a metal door at the bottom of a tower capping the corner of the compound. To their immediate left was a mud-walled building with a door with bars across the window. To their right was an open field and a small creek. There was a path that led along the field to another wall and behind that were small houses. There was a break in the wall that allowed pedestrian traffic to come and go. Zondo pulled out the radio and put it on the tailgate of the truck. He established communications with Solar. Fairlane walked around to the right to look down the length of the east wall. He took a look and came back to the truck. Zondo put the radio in the driver seat and he and Fairlane looked at Donovan as if asking, "What next?"

"Okay gents, we've got this little slice of heaven for the next couple of weeks. I figure we'll keep our heads on a swivel and make sure nobody comes out and nobody approaches us from out here. We'll get a daily check-in set up with Solar to remain in contact and get any updates and I'll find out what the Task Force battle rhythm is for meetings, updates, whatever. We good?"

"Yes sir," said Fairlane.

"So, sir, now what?" Zondo asked.

"Well Sean, let's reconfirm our coordinates. Get a set for each corner of the compound; use the towers. And get to the front gate and once we get inside, pick a couple of spots in the middle of the prison that we can use to ruin a riot. Okay?"

"Yes sir; sounds good," he stated. He liked having something to do. He pulled his military GPS out and got to work.

Donovan pulled out his commercial GPS to get a rough comparison to catch any big errors in their measurements. As he was looking over it he picked up movement in his peripheral vision and turned to his left. A young Afghan man was approaching him. He was impressive looking: young, bright eyes, mustache, mushroom hat, and colorful vest over a brown ankle length over shirt. He had two ammunition belts crisscrossed over his chest and an AK-47 slung over his shoulder. Donovan put his GPS in his pocket, took off his nomex glove and extended his hand to greet his ally. Then he realized he should offer the traditional greeting first and abruptly pulled his hand back. The approaching Afghan stopped in his tracks and the half smile he'd been sporting vanished. He stood still as if he'd been short-circuited, Donovan put his hand to his heart.

"Asalam alaikum," he said with his best attempt at masking his accent.

"Asalam alaikum," replied the Afghan as he reenergized, a broad smile coming back to his face. Donovan then extended his hand, met by the Afghan's; they shook. As they were shaking, Donovan glanced at Sahir over his shoulder toward the front gate; he was talking to one of the soldiers.

"Sahir!" he yelled to get his attention. Sahir excused himself from the conversation with the soldier and walked toward him. Donovan held up a finger to ask the Afghan to wait and a puzzled look came across his face. Luckily Sahir had arrived. "Sahir, please ask this man his name."

"Okay sure." Sahir began to speak and a short conversation ensued. Donovan was anxiously awaiting the opportunity to chat but the conversation went on for a few minutes. Sahir then turned to Donovan.

"It's all okay."

"What do you mean, it's all okay?" he asked, trying not to show his irritation.

"I've made it all okay."

"What are you talking about, Sahir?"

"I've made it all okay, he's our friend now."

"Okay, let's start over. What is his name?"

"His name is Niyoosha."

"Ni-oo-sha?"

"Yes sir, Niyoosha."

Donovan turned to Niyoosha and looked him in the eye. "Niyoosha." he stuck his hand out and shook again. "Donovan," he said, pointing to himself. Niyoosha made a pretty good attempt at pronunciation, and then Donovan realized that was his first name so he corrected himself. "Pat," he said as he put his hand to his chest.

"Pat," Niyoosha repeated perfectly.

"Okay Sahir, what was all the rest?"

"Well Pat," Sahir had taken the liberty of addressing him with more familiarity; when they met at the compound it had been "Major Donovan." Donovan tried not to again show his annoyance with Sahir, but he did raise his eyebrows at the phraseology. "I told him that we are here for the prisoners. We are here to take them away and that we will not need their help."

"Oka, Sahir, first off, try to let me do the international masterminding and translate what I ask you to, and secondly, translate what I ask you to. Kapish?" Donovan threw the last part in just to mess with him.

"I kapish," Sahir replied to Donovan's surprise and amusement.

"Okay, okay," he said, laughing slightly.

The three of them chatted for a few minutes. Donovan asked him how many men he had and what his orders were at the prison. He had seven men; they were to assist the Americans in any way that was needed. They were members of the Northern Alliance. There were dozens more local Afghans inside and around the prison who were strictly guards. They shook hands again and parted ways. Sahir went back to the main gate and started chatting with the same soldier again. Donovan went back to their vehicle; Fairlane was sitting in the passenger seat. Donovan opened the driver side door and sat with his legs still hanging out of the vehicle, the thought occurred to him to break out his hand sanitizer.

"Hey Ian, don't forget to use the hand sanitizer early and often," he told Fairlane.

"Sir, I'm not shaking anybody's hand."

"Come on now, you can shake hands, just don't stick them in your mouth when you're done. You know, TB and all that. But you gotta be friendly."

"Nah, I'm good. I don't want to bring anything home to the wife and kids."

"Oh, don't worry, you probably won't make it home alive anyway."

"Huh?" Fairlane asked, incredulous.

"Just kidding man. This is easy duty; we'll be fine. Just guarding some prisoners, shakin' some hands, kissing some babies..."

"Sure sir, whatever."

Zondo came back and approached Donovan. "Hey sir, got all the data."

"Okay Sean, great. I'll crosscheck with what I got for this tower. That's all I got a chance to do."

"Yes sir, I got just the two front towers and the main gate and then estimated the center if the inner compound."

"Okay, that's good. What about the two rear towers?"

"Yeah, sir, I didn't get those."

"Why not?" asked Fairlane with a snide tone to his voice.

"Well, didn't look safe to go that far."

"Okay, I'll run down there in the next day or two. Let's set up a routine here. We're going to be here for a few weeks. Any suggestions?"

"Well sir," said Fairlane, "We can take shifts."

"Like what?" Donovan asked.

"Maybe me and Zondo can do a day or night shift and you can float."

"Well, we're probably only going to be here for about twelve hours a day, maybe more, but we won't be here overnight. Let's think more along the lines of what we'll be doing all day. I think we'll all be on while we're here. Why don't we go through today and see the battle rhythm then decide tomorrow?"

"Roger sir," Fairlane replied.

"Roger," said Zondo.

They all settled into positions around the vehicle. Fairlane stood off to the right, Zondo to the left as they faced the prison and Donovan sat in the passenger seat of the vehicle as he jotted notes in his green notebook. He wrote for ten minutes.

"Gents, I'm going inside to see how they're doing."

"Roger," they both replied in unison.

Donovan walked toward the main gate. There were soldiers positioned around the left and right sides of it. To the left of the gate was a long table, with a few chairs next to it. Up the drive back toward the road was the 240B team, having a smoke. Donovan walked up to the small door that went through the massive wooden doors of the main gate and knocked; a yet smaller door inside the small door opened and one of the 10th MTN soldiers stuck his face in the opening. Next to it was an Afghan face.

"Hey, can I get in? Just want to chat with Major Fredrick."

"Sure sir, standby," the soldier replied and then shut the smaller door. There were several clinks and clunks and then the small door opened. Donovan went in, having to duck slightly to get through without hitting his head. Once he emerged on the other side he stood up straight and scanned the courtyard. There were several tables to the left, up against a whitewashed mud building. Several soldiers were sitting in chairs behind the tables, which had file boxes or equipment on them. At one of the tables two soldiers had rubber gloves on and they were taking DNA swabs from each prisoner. Another table had a camera set up at it. Each prisoner who was routed to that table had his mug shot taken. Straight ahead was a long open courtyard that led to numerous cellblocks. To the right there was another courtyard where about a dozen soldiers milled around. Near the tables was the JAG and one of the senior NCOs. He approached Fredrick.

"Hey Will, how's everything going?"

Fredrick looked up. "Good Pat, how's everything outside?"

"Good, no issues. Hey do you have a battle rhythm established?"

"No, not really, other than showing up and leaving. We'll show at about 0700 and leave to get back before dark, about 1900."

"Okay. You got no meetings or anything like that you want me at?"

"Well, we'll do an update brief, maybe about 1700. I'll let you know, haven't established that yet. Pretty much we're going to process thousands of these prisoners, as long as it takes."

"Roger, got it. Thanks." He turned to head out of the main gate and reached into his pocket for a piece of gum. One of the US soldiers, a Private, was escorting a prisoner back to the holding cells and they crossed paths. Donovan and the prisoner locked eyes. On an impulse he reached out to the prisoner with a stick of gum. The US soldier yanked the prisoner away from him. Donovan interjected, "It's okay; hearts and minds, Private."

"I don't know sir…" The Private held firm to the prisoner's bicep.

"It's cool Private, really. What's he gonna do?"

"Rip your throat out sir."

"Okay, all right," he said, but handed the prisoner a stick of gum, then reached into his cargo pocket and pulled out a bottle of water and handed it to him. The prisoner looked at the Private and the Private hesitantly motioned to the prisoner to take it; the guard was becoming impatient.

"Hey sir, enough of the kumbaya already, all right?"

"Yeah, just a sec." Donovan held up his hand to hold the prisoner in place to drink the water; he knew it wouldn't be a good idea for anybody if he went back into "gen pop" with a fresh bottle of water.

****

Uktam had been swabbed, fingerprinted and photographed. He didn't like it but he was glad to be out of the holding area. He was being escorted back and an American officer stopped his guard and handed him a stick of gum and a bottle of water. Uktam had only seen Americans from a distance as he was firing an RPG at them. He knew his sister was in America somewhere. She didn't come home so maybe she liked it. Maybe she saw something in the Americans that he and his comrades hadn't seen. He drank the water with gusto; it was delicious, clean and fresh and clear. He was parched and had never tasted water that wonderful in his life. He placed his hand over his heart and nodded to the American.

****

Donovan nodded to the appreciative prisoner and went out through the small door and ran into Niyoosha and two other men. He paused and greeted Niyoosha; one of the other men looked directly at him and rendered the traditional greeting. The other kept his head down but also rendered the proper greeting.

Yusef had arrived at Sheberghan several weeks earlier. He was recruiting foreign fighters for the cause and did not know that both Uktam and Donovan were at the prison. He recognized Donovan at the last second when he approached Niyoosha and kept his gaze averted. He thought about what to do with this opportunity.

Donovan headed back to the truck. As he approached the vehicle, Zondo and Fairlane were surrounded by little kids. They were passing out something.

"Hey guys, what's going on?"

"Well sir, I gave a pack of Charms to the little one right there." Zondo pointed to a tiny little boy in a white pillbox hat with a runny nose. "And he must have passed the intel to his bros 'cause next thing we know all these little fellers came ambling up."

"Okay, great. Well, don't run out or you'll have a riot on your hands."

"Actually sir, you mind if we bust into the MREs and pass out whatever candy is handy?"

"Let's hold off on that right now. I don't want to set their expectations too high. Actually, let's start shutting down this local chapter of UNICEF and get back to standing around."

"Yes sir," replied Zondo. "Okay kids, vamoose." He waved his hands in a shooing motion. Not understanding his words but understanding his gestures, the kids fell back to a low-slung mud wall behind the vehicle and sat and starred at the Americans.

Days of the same routine went by. The soldiers and Airmen would get up before dawn, load the vehicles, drive to the prison, unload, take up their positions, perform their duties, eat breakfast, lunch and dinner MREs, secure everything, load up and drive back to the compound.

There were several incidents that made their time a little more interesting. After the first week, the group of small children had grown to nine. They would show up first thing in the morning, hang around until lunch, then disappear until just before dinner and leave once the Americans were done eating. In addition to the kids, several of the Afghan soldiers, Niyoosha's men, had started hanging around the Americans. They were all in their mid-twenties with the exception of one who was about fourteen. It was always cold in the morning, nice during the day and cool again in the evening.

One afternoon about two weeks into the operation, the fourteen-year-old Afghan soldier approached Donovan with his AK-47 at the ready. Sahir happened to be killing time with Donovan's crew. Donovan saw him coming,

"Sahir, ask this kid what's up," he said while climbing out of the vehicle, his Gau-5 in hand.

"He wants to talk about weapons," Sahir translated.

"What about them?" Donovan asked. Sahir translated. By this time the young soldier was standing, squared off with Donovan.

"He wants to compare your weapon with his."

By now Zondo and Fairlane had joined the small group. The young soldier with the AK-47 kept his weapon aimed off to the side, lowered the barrel and released the magazine. He pushed the top round out with his thumb and put the magazine back in the weapon. He held it upright for Donovan to look over. Then he gestured for him to do the same. Donovan got the hint; so far no words were exchanged and Sahir stood in rapt attention like the others. Donovan pointed the muzzle of his weapon at the ground and released his magazine and ejected a round. He held it up, mirroring what the AK-armed soldier did. The Afghani slowly reached for Donovan's round. He waited until it was clear Donovan understood what he wanted. He slung his weapon over his shoulder to hang muzzle down behind his back before he took both rounds and held them side-by-side, smiling. Donovan turned to Sahir,

"Tell him size isn't everything."

Zondo and Fairlane laughed.

"Yeah Zamphire, translate that," Zondo urged.

"I am Mr. Sean, that is my job," Sahir replied. He did. The Afghani soldier rocked his head side to side.

"Sahir, tell him that the 5.56mm round is much faster and has a greater range." He did. The Afghani responded.

"Sir, he said the 7.62mm has greater penetration and hits harder," translated Sahir. As he was translating the second piece, the soldier clenched his hand around the two rounds and punched his other hand. Donovan turned to Zondo and Fairlane,

"Dang, this kid knows his shit huh?" They both nodded in the affirmative. "Okay Sahir, tell him that we respect his weapon; at close range it is highly effective. However, and take your time on this part, tell him that the cyclic rate, uh, just tell him it fires faster. And tell him that in the full automatic mode, if I pull the trigger and hold it, all of the rounds will be out of the magazine before the first shell casing hits the ground. Do you understand that?"

"No sir, not that part. Please explain."

"Okay, so, you can shoot the weapon one round at a time or you can make the weapon shoot very fast. This weapon," Donovan patted the side of his rifle, it rattled like a can of marbles, "Can shoot so fast that if I pull the trigger and the bullets start coming out, and the empty shell casings eject and fall to the ground, tell him that all the bullets will be out of the weapon before that first shell casing falls to the ground." Donovan turned to his guys. "I don't know any other way to explain it; it's a pretty simple concept."

"Yes sir, but Zamphire doesn't know jack about weapons. I think the AK-guy will get it," Fairlane offered up.

Sahir translated. The young soldier must have gotten it. He seemed impressed and shook his head up and down, then thrust his hand out to Donovan, raised his chin and jutted his lower lip out a bit, in pride, having had a conversation with an American and held his own in talking about weapons. After they shook, Sahir stuck his hand out to the soldier, but the soldier turned and walked away. Sahir slowly and awkwardly lowered his hand and headed back to the main gate.

A few days later the regular group of kids was flocking around Donovan's vehicle. He and his men had tried to be consistent when handing out candy, food, water, anything. The crowd had grown and a few older kids had joined in. There were now also four regular Northern Alliance soldiers that milled around the Americans all day.

On this particular warm and sunny day it became obvious that after three weeks things were starting to get tense. Donovan, Zondo and Fairlane were into their normal routine when off to their right they heard raised voices. Donovan was sitting on the stone half wall behind the vehicles interacting with a couple of the very young kids. He stood up, put his helmet back on and met up with Zondo and Fairlane on the other side of the vehicle. The four Afghan soldiers were on one side of the congregation and two older boys were on the other. The lead soldier, medium height, lean and wild brown hair, was yelling at the taller of the two boys, he wore a long white ankle length shirt, brown hair and a ruddy complexion. Donovan figured it was about territory. The soldiers didn't want to split whatever the Americans were giving out with the kids and now that the older kids showed up, it aggravated the situation. The two continued to yell back and forth until, with lightning speed, smack! The adult had had enough and slapped the kid across the face; he stumbled to his right, but didn't go down. Donovan and his guys started moving in the direction of the confrontation. Again, the soldier smacked the kid as hard as he could, again the kid stumbled but didn't go down; all of the on-lookers kept moving with the two.

Donovan had seen a lot in his time so far in Afghanistan and he believed he'd deduced a pecking order. Men were at the top; there were lots of subcategories and stratifications within that realm. Then came beasts of burden; they had it rough, but they were necessary equipment to get things done. Then it appeared came boys nearing manhood, then dogs; they were guards, weapons, tools. Next were kids, then women. It appeared that rank ordering shifted depending on the situation and the subject. They watched a very young boy tend sheep every day in the field next to the prison; his method of herding the sheep was to throw rocks at them. He'd throw a rock at them to get them to move. He'd throw a rock at them to get them to turn. He'd throw a rock at them to get them to stop. The kid's arm was impressive; he never missed.

By now Donovan's instinct to intervene was kicking in but he knew this was a cultural thing. The kid was a threat to the man and he'd resisted being told what to do. This guy was a soldier and it looked like he was one of the leaders, he just looked tough. He slapped the kid one more time and this time the kid went down hard to the ground in a heap making a hollow thud, stirring up a small cloud of dust. Donovan moved faster, trying to think faster than he was moving to come up with what to do before he reached the crowd. As soon as he hit the ground, instinct kicked in for the kid; he bounced up and charged for the man. He got within about two feet when the soldier butt-stroked him with his rifle in the face. The kid went straight down but he wasn't out. That was all Donovan could take,

"Hey! That's enough!" He couldn't remember any Afghan words and didn't know what to say; he was furious and nervous, He noticed Zondo to his right with his weapon at chest level, "Sean! Lower your weapon, now!"

As he told Zondo to stand down and secure his weapon so as not to provoke an escalation to an international incident, he realized he'd put his right hand on the grip of his pistol and immediately raised both hands in the air. "Stop, stop, stop!" he knew they couldn't understand him but he had to try something. The soldier who struck the boy hadn't looked over at Donovan yet but two of the three other soldiers did and maneuvered their weapons from slung on their backs to at the ready. Donovan made a motion with his arms, like when you wave at a car to slow down, trying to get everyone to calm down.

"Ian, go get Zamphire!" he yelled at Fairlane, using Sahir's nickname unintentionally. "And get the doc! Sean, back me up man, okay?" he said to Zondo in a low voice.

"Yes sir." Zondo said back in a low tone.

"Okay, okay, okay, everybody take it easy."

He again tried to communicate through gestures to calm down, trying to get between the assaulter and the boy. The Afghani soldier had already turned his back on the boy and was walking away from him. He was still lying on the ground, up on one elbow, dazed, blood running down his face from just below his eye where he'd gotten hit on the edge of his eye socket. His cheekbone was broken and blood was starting to come out of his mouth. Donovan gently grabbed him by the shoulders and tried to lay him back but the boy resisted. Donovan eventually got him to relax and lay back. That was a mistake. Blood started to pool in his mouth and run down the back of his throat; he started to gag and tried to sit up. Donovan helped him. He leaned forward and a large gush of black blood fell from his mouth. Donovan waved to the boy's friend to come help. He wouldn't. Just then Fairlane ran up with the doc and Sahir. The doc knelt down next to them.

"What the hell happened?"

"He got butt-stroked."

"By one of our guys?" he said in a high tone.

"No doc, the tall dude over there pacing back and forth." The Afghan soldier didn't appear nervous; he was annoyed, probably by all the fuss the Americans were making.

"What did you do that for?" the doc yelled at him. "What are you hitting a kid for with a weapon? What's wrong with you?" The doc was furious. "Translate that Sahir." he insisted.

"Belay, I mean don't translate that Sahir!" Donovan directed. "Take it easy doc. You focus on the kid; I'll take care of international relations. Sahir, ask the man who hit the kid what they were fighting about."

He slowly approached the man and exchanged a few sentences, Sahir talking, the soldier yelling. Sahir took the few steps back to Donovan.

"He said he is his uncle. The boy wasn't doing what he told him to and then when he argued with him, he made him stop."

"I don't get these people; to them life is worthless," the doc said.

"Yeah doc, haven't you been keeping up with your *National Geographic*? Different cultures. Now the guy shouldn't have butt-stroked the kid, that's for sure, but really isn't much different than home. Elders figure they need to be obeyed," Donovan said.

"No different than home? What nightmare community did you grow up in?"

"Uh, that'd be New Jersey. And seriously doc, lighten up. Guy hit the kid with the butt of his rifle. Shouldn't have done that. Got it. Agree, but let's lose the self-righteous indignation would ya? Where did you grow up? Let me guess, Iowa or California, oh and I bet you attended Our Lady of Perpetual Motion Seminary."

"Okay, he's good for now. I'm going to take him back inside, maybe give him a couple of stitches," the doc stated, not acknowledging Donovan's comments; the doc actually was from California. He helped the boy to his feet and walked him back up and through the front gate. Donovan and his team thought long and hard about what had happened and tried to come to terms with it all.

A couple of days later, again going through their same routines, it was time to feed the prisoners under Donovan's watch. There was a metal door near the base of the tower. Each day at about noon two kitchen workers would bring food and pass it through that door. Donovan noticed there were hundreds of prisoners in that section and there was only one guard that unlocked the door and then stood guard; he was unarmed except for a stick while the workers brought in the food. He'd directed his guys to stand at the ready whenever that door was opened. He stood with them. He figured if the prisoners rushed through that door, with three GAU-5s on full-auto they could certainly slow them down. Over the previous few days there were times when things got pretty stirred up in that section of the prison. Nobody knew what was going on but there were a couple of incidents a day that drew the guards in the tower out onto the ramparts. Normally they were never seen. Donovan had mentioned the situation to Fredrick and asked him for some additional manpower if he could spare it. He kicked that decision over to the Sergeant Major. The Sergeant Major told him he could have three troops for a couple of days. Donovan positioned them with Zondo and Fairlane to create interlocking fields of fire; no area the prisoners could come from or run to would be uncovered.

All was quiet on the first day after the additional manpower was positioned. The next day, before lunch, there was again a lot of commotion; again the tower guards came out from inside of the tower. This time they got real excited and started yelling down into the courtyard of the prison. One guard came out with a hand held radio and spoke into it. A few minutes later, the kitchen crew pushing the empty wheelbarrow they normally used to bring food, plus two local Afghan soldiers, hurriedly moved toward the metal door. Donovan directed his men.

"Okay fellas, they're going to open the door. Take your positions."

Fairlane was sitting in the passenger seat of the vehicle and had just nodded off. He woke up and looked at his watch. "Hey sir, it's not lunchtime. What gives?"

"Not sure, take your position – move!"

The team moved to their positions and stood ready. The man pushing the wheelbarrow pulled up short of the metal door. One of his escorts looked up at the tower. The guard at the tower gestured impatiently for him to open the door. He pulled a key on a lanyard around his neck from out of his shirt and unlocked the big padlock, opened the door and stepped back. Two prisoners emerged with a white sheet between them, like a hammock, heavy laden. The burden was a dead body. They moved around the wheelbarrow, one on each side, and gently placed the body wrapped in the sheet into the basin of the wheelbarrow. The kitchen crew quickly turned the make shift hearse around and headed back toward the main gate. Just as they made the gate there were three loud pops from inside the prison.

"Was that gunfire?" asked Zondo, who had moved up next to Donovan after the door had been secured.

"It was something." Donovan moved toward the vehicle. He reached into the cab, grabbed the radio and called to the ops station inside. They didn't know what the noise was either. "Sean, Ian, you guys stay put and keep things under control here. I'm going to go walk around the fort and see what I can see."

"Sergeant, you should go with the boss," Zondo suggested to Fairlane.

"Boss has got it Zondo, he's got it." Fairlane was slightly annoyed at the suggestion.

"Come with me," Donovan directed Leavitt. He was one of the members of the additional security the Sergeant Major had provided. Private Leavitt was five foot six inches, blonde hair, brown eyes and weighed, maybe 120 soaking wet. He had been standing in the background, back against the low wall during the excitement. He pointed to his chest and looked to the next ranking soldier, Sergeant Miller.

"Sarge?" he asked Miller very quietly.

"Get going," Miller answered.

Leavitt jogged to catch up with Donovan. "Sir, what are we doing?"

"Just going for a little walkabout. That sounded like a large caliber weapon." They approached the corner of the wall under the tower and made a left turn. Donovan stopped. There was a worn dirt path that roughly followed the length of the east wall with green grass on either side. There were overlapping circles of very closely cropped grass surrounded by taller grass. About thirty yards up the path off to the side away from the wall was a goat grazing, tied to a stake.

Leavitt again looked over at Donovan. "Sir, what are all those circles?"

Donovan looked back at him, grabbed the front lip of his helmet and rocked it back and forth to scratch his forehead. "Well Leavitt, those are the result of a poor man's mine detector."

"Huh?" Leavitt grunted, his nose crinkled in confusion.

"The Afghan's tie a goat to a stake in an area they think there might be mines. The nature of the goat being to constantly graze, so he grazes; he grazes in one spot then he keeps moving to eat the tall grass, and since he's always grazing he'll eventually cover every inch of the area that stake keeps him in. Then they move the stake and nature again takes over."

"What happens if the goat steps on a mine?"

"They eat what's left of the goat and go get another goat."

"So, sir...you're saying we're going to walk down this path and the only thing ensuring we're not going to get our legs blown off are these goat holes?"

"That sounds about right, Leavitt. Let's go." He started down the path; after about twenty yards he felt that something wasn't right and turned to look back up the path. Leavitt hadn't moved. "Yo, Leavitt, let's go. We need to stay together." He waved him forward.

"Sir...sir...sir, I'm going to go check on Zondo." He turned and walked quickly back around the corner and out of sight.

Donovan didn't have the time or desire to go after Leavitt or get one of the others to accompany him. He knew Zondo would have been by his side but he didn't order him to go with him because he knew he would. And, he wasn't all that sure of what he was doing anyway. He cared about all the guys but recognized he may have, without really realizing it, been protecting Zondo. That thought annoyed him a bit; he'd have to get over that habit if things were going to get worse. He couldn't think along those lines. He had to be more logical.

He made it to the end of the wall and turned the corner. There was a guard standing at the entrance to the tower; they looked at each other, then the guard held his hand out toward the door. Donovan nodded in the affirmative and entered the tower, walking up the winding mud stairs until he reached the top. There were three Afghan soldiers manning a PKM light machine gun, which was on a bipod propped up on some ammo boxes and overlooking the courtyard where the prisoners were milling about. Donovan nodded a greeting as he put his hand to his chest.

"Asalam alaikum."

They did and said the same. He kept smiling and slowly walked around the machinegun; as he got near the barrel he got a whiff of burnt gunpowder. He moved over near the muzzle and felt heat off the barrel. He backtracked, reversing his direction so as not to walk in front of the recently fired weapon. Once he got back behind it he checked to see if any of them were looking at him. They all were so he picked the oldest and made a gesture toward the machinegun and then made a motion with his hands like he was shooting it. The man who he was addressing, who was much older than the others, with a long white beard and a deeply creviced face, slowly moved his head left and right, signifying, no. Donovan thanked them and reached out to shake their hands; he shook each and then walked back down the stairs and out past the guard.

He continued to move forward around the fort. As he cleared the guard he looked ahead. There wasn't a clear path and there weren't any "goat holes." He pressed ahead anyway and shortly got to the next tower. At the corner there was no door so he figured it was around the corner. He made the turn and immediately recoiled and fell backwards as a huge Afghan dog lunged for his throat. He snapped just short of Donovan's leg, restrained by a chain that looked like it came off the anchor of a battleship. Donovan backpedaled as fast as he could, his heart going a mile a minute. Once he'd gotten clear, ten feet from the still snarling, barking and slobbering hound, he got to his feet and dusted himself off, never taking his eyes off the dog.

He now had a chance to see more than just teeth. The dog looked like it had been repeatedly beaten. There was blood coming out of his nose and his snout was covered in it. He was scarred all over and that huge chain had worn all the fur off his neck and was now wearing sores into his skin. One of the claws on his right front paw was ripped out. He had a big tail that curled back on itself but the last six to eight inches of it had been cut or bitten off and the end was festering. He looked like he was brown but it was hard to tell. Donovan thought this dog made Cujo look like a foo foo poodle, his emotions went from fear to pity. He'd still shoot the dog if it went for him again, but he loved dogs and felt sorry for this one's plight, knowing it would never change, he might do it a favor if he shot it between the eyes.

He thought of Steve, his dog, as he looked for what the end of the chain was secured to. It was the hulk of an old tractor. He made sure there was enough room for him to get to the door, there was so he went in and started climbing the stairs. The dog never stopped barking and snarling. Donovan got to the top and there again were three men, two young and one old, seated at a small round table. The old man was missing an eye; no glass eye or patch or glasses, just an empty eye socket. The two young men looked alike and may have been brothers with thick black beards; both were seated with AK7's across their laps. The old man was sitting in a bigger chair. On the table were a teapot and three glasses. The old man reached behind him and pulled out a dirty glass. He poured tea into their three cups and then made a motion with the teapot to ask if Donovan wanted some. He nodded yes and the old man poured in the tea. Donovan took the glass and held it up to the men as to say "cheers" then raised the glass. As he did he surveyed the glass and its contents; there were black flecks swirling around that he hoped were tea leaves but figured the thing to do was drink it. He kept his lips closed, letting the tea hit them before lowering the glass. He hoped they didn't notice and weren't offended. He'd drank a lot of weird concoctions our of grog bowls, but this one, he was going to pass on.

Nothing was said, no further attempts were made by anyone to communicate. Donovan gave the experience about five minutes, then put his tea glass down, offered a greeting and a thanks gesture and walked back down the stairs, past the dog and around to the front of the fort. He made the fourth corner and was glad to see a few soldiers standing around outside the main gate. As he got closer he noticed they were all talking to a woman and stopped slightly off to the side, close enough to hear what was being said. It quickly became obvious she was a reporter; she was taking notes on a small pad and was focusing her attention on one soldier, then quickly shifting to another, taking notes and then reengaging with the next in line. She turned back to her left. Donovan could see on the front of her windbreaker: CNN. The small door in the main gate opened and a soldier popped out then stood to the side of the door. Colonel Rapier came through, walking straight for the reporter. The other soldiers parted to let him pass. Once he cleared their line he stuck out his hand, shook the reporter's, then diverted her off to the side. The soldiers went back to their duties. Donovan continued past the gate and headed back to the vehicle and his guys.

"Hey sir, we were just about to come looking for you." Fairlane was obviously glad to see him.

"I'm good. In the northeast tower there's a freshly fired PKM. I figure that's what those reports were. I'll radio it up to the head shed. I would have stopped in but there was a media frenzy going on at the front gate."

"Really? Who's over there?" Fairlane asked excitedly.

"I saw a reporter from CNN; that was it. She was talking to Colonel Rapier."

"Oh, CNN-6." Fairlane referred to the news channel and Rapier's rank, Colonel, an O-6.

"Is that what they're calling him?"

"Yes sir, seems like any time there's any press around he pops up."

"Well, that's funny. But who do you think should be talking to the press? He's the man, he's got the answers and this op is his responsibility, right?"

"Don't look at me sir, I'm just telling you what they call him." Fairlane got defensive.

"Yeah, I know, that's okay. That's one of the things I love about the military – everything is actually funny – or I guess our sense of humor, I should say." He paused to think about what he just said. "You know what I mean. Anyway, Rapier's a good guy. He appreciates what we bring to the fight and he's been including me as a member of his staff."

"Okay sir, yeah, sure. You guys can be on the same bowling team when you get back to Drum."

"Yeah Ian. I'm sure my Uzbek wife and he will get along famously. I'm gonna give it another ten minutes and then I'll head up front and talk to Fredrick. I want to see how we're doing up there with the processing anyway."

"Hey Major," the Sergeant Major shouted to Donovan.

"Yeah Sergeant Major, what's up?"

"Hey sir, your boss is coming in tonight."

"Which boss you talking about Sergeant Major? Colonel Laredo?"

"Yes sir, that's it," he said as he turned and walked back toward the front gate.

"Wow, what's the boss coming here for sir?" Zondo asked.

"Beats me, but it'll be good to see him," Donovan replied.

Colonel Laredo wasn't coming to Sheberghan; he was transiting through it to pick up a load of processed prisoners and then head to Pakistan. The Airmen would later find out that while inflight one of the prisoners broke loose and Colonel Laredo jumped on him and quickly "subdued" him before he could put the aircraft at risk. The word was, the subduing part was done masterfully with his fists.

Donovan found out through Fredrick that this was their last day. They'd processed over three times more prisoners than they had planned and the rest would be left in Sheberghan, taken care of by local security forces. They were mostly local Taliban and weren't seen as a terrorist threat. Hopefully they wouldn't see them again in the near future on the battlefield. At the end of the day the crew gave away a box of MREs and all the candy they had left to the kids who'd been their companions for three weeks. They got back to the airfield after dark, walked into their crowded room, threw their gear down and started talking about starting up a card game.

"Major Donovan?" A soldier had just entered the room after the group.

"Yeah?"

"Sir, Colonel Rapier wants you to join him for dinner with the local Afghan General at 1900 and bring your interpreter too."

"Okay, sure. What about my guys?"

"Negative sir, just you and Zamphire."

"Okay, got it. Sorry guys, I tried," he said to Zondo and Fairlane.

"No problem sir, I don't want to eat the local food anyway. Don't feel like bringing Achmed the parasite home with me," Fairlane joked.

"Okay, well I'll bring you some leftovers if you change your mind."

"Uh, no thanks," Fairlane said as he slumped down on his sleeping bag.

The dinner was an interesting affair. The Afghan General was in charge of the airfield, the prison and the area surrounding Sheberghan. He was about 5'7", black hair and clean-shaven. He wore a black shirt decorated with embroidery around the collar and sleeves, when Donovan saw him he thought he reminded him of a young Omar Sharif. Colonel Rapier had been coordinating and working with him throughout the entire operation so they had a working relationship. The General had several of his staff also attend. There were twenty people at the dinner. The meal consisted of some type of small bird way too small to be chicken; it could have been dove or pigeon. There were dozens of them, all roasted and assembled in the middle of a large metal tray surrounded by vegetables. There were trays of bread and hummus. Everyone chatted, ate and drank bottled water and Pakistani Coke for about an hour and a half.

Donovan had thought about being cautious with the food but decided to dive in. About three in the morning he realized he'd made a mistake. He was back and forth to the porta-potti a half a dozen times; he had bad cramps and could barely stand upright all the next day. He didn't eat anything throughout the day, knowing they were flying out that night. He didn't want to have a physiological incident on the plane. He'd gone eight years flying B-52s and never had one so he was determined to keep his record and the plane clean.

When the time came the Task Force packed up their tents and hauled all their gear down to the runway. Zondo was still humping the minigun in his ruck. The aircraft was floor-loaded, all the passengers sat directly on the floor and a long cargo strap was put across the waists of groups of nine or ten at a time. Donovan thought about what would happen if they had a hard landing or worse. It would be a mess. It was an American crew that was flying them out and they were in a hurry to get off the ground. Once everyone was strapped down, the aircraft rapidly taxied to the end of the runway, spun around, hit the brakes and the pilot pushed up the throttles. The aircraft rocked in place and then the pilots released the brakes. Everyone lurched back toward the back of the airplane; it rotated after a few seconds and they were airborne, heading back to K2, Uzbekistan.

****

Yusef had bought his way into the prison and paid to have several prisoners released when the Americans left. Unbeknownst to him, he had Uktam released. He decided not to take action against Donovan at this time, but he knew their destinies were intertwined.

****

Task Force Commando recovered uneventfully into K2 late that night. Donovan, Zondo and Fairlane were picked up by Gennaro in a truck. They hauled their gear back to the tent and racked out until mid-morning the next day. It would take Donovan the rest of that next day to recover from the social. Once he was up and around, he took a shower, the first in three weeks, went back to his bunk, propped up a bag of dirty clothes on his bunk to lean on, leaned back and started listening to music on his CD player. The Bee Gees' song that was blaring during his firefight en route to Kandahar started playing. As soon as he got it queued up, Stacks came through the tent flap.

"Hey buddy, all cleaned up? How was it?"

"Good sir, interesting."

"Love to hear all about it but I've got to get back for a big planning meeting. Hey, boss wants you heading back to Kuwait."

"Oh yeah, what am I gonna do there?"

"Don't know, but that's where he wants you, so you've got today and then we're going to try and get you out first thing tomorrow morning. Cool?"

"Sure, I'm here to serve at the discretion of my leadership."

"Okay. We'll play cards tonight," Stacks said as he headed back out of the tent.

"Sounds good sir, thanks." He turned his music back up and started thinking about that intense day.

The next morning he wandered around, spent a little time in the JOC, ate with the guys and packed his gear. He'd fly out that afternoon, the earliest flight back to Kuwait. When the time came Gennaro pulled a Gator up in front of the tent and Donovan loaded his stuff. Stacks showed up just as he threw in the last bag. He directed Gennaro to go on to the check-in point without him; he'd walk with Stacks.

"Okay Dude, well, it was great to work with you and have fun back up there with the boss."

"Will do, thanks for the opportunity. Hey, how's your dad?" Donovan asked his friend.

"Not too good. I'm actually thinking about seeing if I can get back home; actually starting to work on some of the details."

"Sorry to hear that; really sorry. Why don't you get the boss to leave me here? Hell, I'm as spun up as I can be, been on the ground, in the air, know most of the main players."

"I asked, he said no. He's gonna send Sandman out here within a couple of days."

"Shit, okay. Well, I hope your dad gets better."

"Okay man, thanks. I'll see you later." Stacks hurried off.

Donovan got on a C-17 a few hours later and headed through Tashkent back to Camp Doha, Kuwait. He was the only one in the back of the empty plane.

Nikki was enjoying not hearing from Yusef for several weeks. She was happy to just worry about how Donovan was doing, get an occasional letter from him and focus on taking care of Buck and Stinky. She really began to explore her emotions, how much she missed Donovan and how excited she was to start a normal life with normal problems, but she knew Yusef would be back and in some way she or those who loved her would have to deal with him.

CHAPTER FIFTEEN

BAD PENNY

17 February 2002, Camp Doha, Kuwait.

Donovan had only been back a couple of days when the call came in to the ACE detachment. Lieutenant Colonel "Rosie" O'Donnell picked up the phone and got the gist of the conversation and then handed it off to him. It was Lieutenant Colonel Bob Lee. He started to lay out the basics of a plan they were working on, initially tasked to the CJSOTF to develop. He said they were just getting set up, having been tasked to move the Division staff forward from K2 to Bagram, Afghanistan. They were calling themselves CFLCC-Forward.

"Pat, we're working up a plan, Anaconda, and we need an ALO and since you're our ALO you should be here. I'll send over some slides on the SIPRNET."

"Okay, sir. What else can you tell me?"

They talked for a few minutes and then ended the call. Donovan digested what he'd heard and started to think about options

"Hey Rosie, had you heard anything about this?"

"Well, I know the Colonel went to a VTC the other day and came back and mentioned Anaconda but not much more than that." Rosie shuffled through the papers on his desk.

"When is he getting back?"

"I think he's going to be a couple of days. He was up at Prince Sultan Air Base meeting with the CFACC, Lieutenant General Moseley."

"Fuck. Well, we've got to get moving on this; we can't wait a couple of days." Donovan was already feeling a sense of urgency, based on the feeling he got from Lee's phone call. He also had a slight hesitation as to what to say next, having just come out of the field. "Hey Rosie…" He had decided which way he was going to go and figured to just get on with it. "I know you're senior and you're running the show but I'm the ALO with 10th Mountain. This is my job."

"You just came out of the field."

"Yeah, I know, but like I said, it's my Division. I know these guys; it should be me." He watched Rosie's face for a reaction, figuring he was going to pull rank, but was counting on this catching him off guard and that he'd have to wrestle with the fact that he was running the show while the Colonel was gone.

"Okay, you're right."

"That was easy," Donovan thought to himself.

"Figure out what you'll need and start working transportation," Rosie directed.

"Rog." He got to his feet. "Are you going to get a hold of the boss?"

"Yeah, I'll give him the rundown and pitch the idea that you'll lead the effort, whatever that ends up being."

"Okay, I'm going to check on flights." It was going to be tough to get there. Airlift was still pretty limited going into Afghanistan; it only flew at night, which cut the window of opportunity to catch a flight in half and each missed flight could cost up to 24 hours. Donovan started thinking that he would have to leave ASAP, hopefully first thing in the morning if not sooner. It was 1900. They could improve their position and move from Kuwait forward during daylight and then fly in from one of the forward bases. He figured he'd better get his shit together.

"Hey Rosie, I'm gonna lean forward and figure the boss will give the go ahead and go pack my gear. We're gonna need to move ASAP and I need to get reorganized. Could you have somebody look at lift for us? First thing you can get. I'll need a little time after seeing those slides to figure out who and what to bring, at least a TAC kit and a couple of dudes."

"Okay, go ahead. I'll see what we can get and I'll get a hold of the boss."

Donovan went back over to the 332nd ASOS facility. Since he had been there last they had added additional bunks around the bay to hold the transient TACP personnel flowing into Afghanistan as the troop numbers went up. He opened the smaller door next to the large overhead, as always it was dark inside. He found his bunk and used the small push light he had attached through the buttonhole on his collar to look through his rucksack to find his headlamp. He found it, put it on, adjusted it and turned on the light. He started looking through his A-bag when he heard a rustling above him from the top bunk. He didn't look up; he knew it was Senior Airman Reed and he didn't want to blind him with the light.

"Hey sir," he said groggily and with a hoarse voice/ "What's up?" Reed worked the night shift and still had a few hours to go before he came on.

"Nothing, man. Go back to sleep."

"Waddya doing with your stuff?" Reed cleared his throat between words.

"Nothing, go back to sleep," Donovan urged him again.

"All right sir, but if you're going anywhere you're taking me with you." He rolled back over. After about two minutes he was breathing deeply.

Donovan pulled out his Night Vision Goggles and several other pieces of equipment and his FAC kit; the kit was customized by individual controller. Usually it contained tools for working with maps: plotters, compass, pens and pencils, checklists, measuring devices, etc. All controllers carried one. Usually the kit contained Cyalume sticks as a marking tool; there were visible and infrared versions. On occasion they were broken open and drunk. The test was to see if you could pee in glowing Technicolor. Donovan finally grabbed his six magazines of 5.56mm and three of 9mm ammunition. As he was getting the gear together he paused; what else did he need? A plan. He took everything he pulled out and put it in a smaller assault pack and shoved it under his bunk, then got up and navigated to the door. He opened it to the sound of the generators and the smell of Camp Doha. He let the door go, forgetting about the spring closer. The metal door slammed against the metal frame with a loud bang.

"Shit," he said out loud as he winced in sympathy for the dozen or so guys he just woke up out of a dead sleep.

He got back to the JOC and logged back into the SIPR computer. There was an email from Lance Baker, Lee's number two, who Donovan made the pitch to deploy with back in the General's office at Fort Drum. The PowerPoint slides were titled, "OP ANACONDA V12." He double-clicked on the slides and hit the slideshow button, reading over the commander's intent and mission statement slides a couple of times. The slides covered the basic concept and looked pretty skeletal. He thought about how best to set up the air support for this operation but caught himself dwelling on the concept and realized he'd better get to the logistics of getting a team and gear together to get to Bagram ASAP.

The current intelligence reports indicated there was a concentration of enemy troops in the planned area of operations. CJOSTF-North had begun developing a plan to rid the country of what was believed to be the last pocket of organized resistance comprised primarily of Al Q'Aeda fighters, mostly Arab. Eventually this plan, Operation ANACONDA, would be turned over to the newly formed Task Force Mountain, led by Major General Hacker.

Task Force Mountain moved to Bagram Airbase in mid-February. The Task Force was comprised of conventional forces, approximately a brigade of 101st Airborne Division Infantry, a battalion of 10th Mountain Division Light Infantry, US Army SOF forces, coalition Special Operations Forces, Navy SEALS, Other Government Agency personnel and Air Force ETACs supporting every SOF team and Army unit to the company level. There were 37 ETACs fielded for the operation. The Area of Operations (AO) was the Shah-i-Kot Valley, approximately nine by fifteen kilometers, about the size of a typical Civil War battlefield. In general, the plan was to set up blocking positions in a half-moon to the North, West and South. The Anti-Taliban Forces of General Zia accompanied by US Army SOF teams from CJSOTF North would drive in from the North and East to act as a hammer on the blocking position's anvil. The plan then would be to have the Anti-Taliban Forces, or ATF Afghans do a house-to-house search of the three villages in the valley for Al Qaeda and Taliban and/or weapons stores. Any enemy that attempted to flee from the advancing ATF would be forced into and captured by the blocking positions.

The operation was set to kick off on 28 February 2002.

The sun was going down and Donovan knew he wouldn't be getting much sleep. He hated that thought considering he knew with getting positioned and set up, not to mention the op itself, sleep would be scarce. He had been through enough Army exercises to know the standard TOC environment: tar-like coffee, chew, spit bottles, pale faces, sunken eyes and a heavy stench from a combination of B.O., gas, bad breath and burnt coffee. He was looking forward to it.

He had to assemble the list of guys he'd be taking with him. He needed radio operators, another ALO at least, a couple of techs, intel maybe. He figured six to eight would do it. He went through the roster they had and started going over names. TSgt Hughes walked into the room just as Donovan scrolled past his name on the roster. *A sign?* he thought.

"Sergeant Hughes," Donovan called to him. "Come here would ya?"

"Yes sir," he answered cautiously. "What do you need?"

"I'm putting together a team to go forward for an upcoming op."

"Okay." Still somewhat sheepishly.

"I need you to be on that team."

"Uh… well, I work for Colonel Rosie so you'll have to discuss it with him." Obviously thinking of what to say while he was saying it.

"Yeah, consider that discussion complete. You're coming with me, copy?" Donovan said.

"Yes sir."

"Great. Who else is with you?"

The two went over the list and got together seven names. He had one other officer in mind. "Sonic" was a fighter pilot; he hadn't really met him yet, just in passing when he first showed up. Donovan got Sergeant Hughes to start assembling the equipment and letting the enlisted guys who were going know what was up and what the timeline was. Rosie was just getting off the phone.

"Rosie, any word from the Colonel?" He got up and moved next to Rosie, notebook in hand.

"Not yet. He's still in that damn VTC."

"How about travel?"

"Well, I've got two options for you but I need name-lines, you know, full name, rank and social security number, for all your guys. Have you picked your team yet?" He didn't look up from the computer screen that had the travel info on it.

We just got that together. Here's the list" Donovan passed him a sheet of yellow legal pad paper with the information.

"All right, you should probably get your personal gear together."

"Yep, I will."

"You're running out of time." Rosie pointed to his watch.

"Rog, I'll get it."

Donovan got back to the squadron about 0045 and started organizing his gear. After about 45 minutes he shoved everything back under his bunk and rolled into it. He stared at the slats and springs of the top bunk and listened to the drone of the generators. After what he guessed was about an hour he felt someone push on his shoulder.

"Sir," the voice whispered.

"Yeah?"

"Sir, we got a flight plan for tomorrow." It was Sergeant Grasso; he took a knee next to Donovan's bunk and read him the details. They were going to go out of Ali Al Salem again so they'd have to drive there, catch a flight to Seeb, Oman, and then into Bagram from there.

"Thanks. Make sure everybody knows," Donovan directed.

"Okay."

Donovan thought to himself, *We've got that part taken care of.* He ran a few more things over in his mind and then went back to sleep.

He got up with the first series of door slams from guys coming in and out of the squadron, grabbed his toilet kit and towel and headed to the showers. The showers and bathrooms

224

at Camp Doha were little trailers parked at the end of each row of warehouses. They stunk and were huge Petri dishes, but they were something close to porcelain versus the porta-potties, slit trenches and diesel barrels forward. So, after shitting in holes dug with an E-tool or using an Afghan version of a toilet, it wasn't bad. It resembled civilization, not necessarily "better" but more like home, if home was a bus station. Everything became relative. By most standards the showers were rank; the drains usually backed up and forced jizz and piss and soapy water up over your shower shoes, but again, after not taking a shower for a month or two, they were "nice." Donovan shit, showered and shaved and headed back to the squadron. He opened the door, held it back from slamming, thinking to himself, *How the fuck hard is that?* As he turned the corner and headed to his bunk he looked down and saw Sonic sleeping a couple of bunks down from his.

"Fuck!" He said in a loud whisper. He had forgotten to let Sonic know what was going on and that he was going with them in less than 90 minutes! "Hey Joe." He used Sonic's real name instead of his call sign, somehow already setting up for his apology.

"Yeah, what's up sir?" He squinted against the one ray of daylight slicing through a crack in the boarded up windows.

"Joe, did you get the word about moving out today for an op in Afghanistan?" Donovan asked hoping he had but knowing he hadn't because it had been up to him to tell him.

"Nope." He still squinted one eye but had a definite change of expression on his face. "What's going on?"

"Get up and start getting your gear together and I'll brief you as we go. We're heading to Ali Al Salem in about an hour and a half. Bring your tactical gear and you need to be prepared for a couple of weeks in the field," Donovan told him, still pissed at himself for forgetting to tell him the night before, and he was going to be his number two. He thought, *What a way to kick off an operation.*

Everybody did what they needed to get ready. Gear was loaded in the vehicles and the departure time was rapidly approaching. Donovan sat on the edge of his bunk trying to think of what else he had to do before he left Camp Doha.

A voice broke the silence, "Sir...sir!" It was Airman Reed.

"Reed, what's up buddy, how you been?"

"Good sir, you about ready to go?"

"Yep, I'm ready – hey are you gonna spend the whole war ferrying guys back and forth to Al Salem?"

"Not if I can help it sir. I need to go get some."

"Are you current?" he asked, not looking up from his notebook.

"Shit yeah sir! Of course I am."

"Okay then, go find somebody else to drive us ASAP. And do you have your gear ready?"

"Yes sir!"

"I mean, ready-ready, like move out ready, like right now grab-n-go ready?"

"Yes sir! I can grab my stuff and be in the truck in less than five minutes."

"Good, 'cause that's about how long you got, plus go find...hang on..." Donovan stood up and looked around the bay. He saw a Staff Sergeant walking toward the door. "Hey Sergeant!" The sergeant stopped in his tracks and looked in his direction.

"Yeah, whadya want?"

"Yeah sergeant, Major Donovan here-" Before he could continue the sergeant interrupted.

"Sorry sir, I couldn't see who it was and since you didn't have your blouse on, couldn't tell your rank."

"No sweat. Where you heading?"

"I was on my way over to the PX."

"Okay, new plan. I need you to drive us to Ali Al Salem to the airfield. Can you do that?"

"I've never been sir."

"That's okay, we've got a guy going with us who has and you'll have another guy going along for security that's done the trip before."

"Then I guess I can," the sergeant said as he nodded.

"Great, we'll be leaving in about four minutes."

"Okay sir, got it. I'm ready."

"Outstanding."

"Reed!" Donovan turned back to the young Airman.

"Yes sir." Reed stuck his head up over the lockers.

"You're in the war. Let's go."

Reed let out a muffled "Whoop!"

Everything was loaded and the small convoy of three vehicles made the serpentine journey out of the base and headed to Al Salem. Reed was now in a passenger seat and he was going out on a mission. He leaned his head against the window. He was sitting behind the driver. Donovan was sitting in the front passenger seat and happened to be looking back and noticed Reed wiping his eye, obviously trying not to be noticed. He thought to himself, *Go ahead kid. I feel the same way.* Reed hadn't bothered to ask the Major what the mission was. Donovan knew that he didn't care, he just wanted in. He knew Reed had a million thoughts going through his head as they turned onto Sixth Ring Road. He would be proud he was one of the first to deploy after 9/11 and he knew he wasn't sure what he was going to tell everyone back home. Donovan thought that everybody back home would be expecting them all to come back war heroes with great war stories, changed men. Most of them up to this point had been playing video games and in Reed's case, about twice a week made the shuttle run to the airfield at Al Salem. None of them were sure yet what, but they knew now they were going to do something, maybe something big. Donovan knew that for all of them that hadn't gone to war before that this would be a unique experience for each of them. This was a big deal. He knew everybody wasn't a "trigger-puller," most of the military are support troops, mechanics, supply, chow slingers, but he also thought that the moms and dads of the sheet-metal-benders and the cooks and the mechanics aren't less worried or less proud than the trigger-pullers' moms and dads. He knew his folks were worried, he knew Reed's folks were worried and he knew at that moment, that's what Reed was thinking about. And now, they've got something to worry about. Now Donovan started to wish he'd been able to call home before he left. Maybe he wouldn't be able to ever say good-bye. Maybe they'd never know how much he loved them and what great parents they were to him.

The small convoy arrived at Al Salem, went through the usual routine getting through security, got to the PAX terminal, unloaded their gear and started the long wait. They palletized their gear and settled into the rows of metal chairs. Donovan sat in one of the chairs at the end of a row. Sonic grabbed a water bottle and was heading a couple of rows behind.

Donovan stuck his hand out to the side to catch his attention. "Sonic, sit over here."

"Sir, you mind if I get about an hour's worth of shut eye? My brain is scrambled."

"Sure, go ahead. We'll talk when we get to Seeb."

"Okay sir, great. Thanks." Sonic pulled his floppy hat down to his eyebrows and shuffled away.

Reed had gotten a water bottle during Donovan's brief exchange with Sonic. "Sir, you mind if I sit there?"

"Sure, be my guest."

"Thanks sir, how you doing?"

"I'm great, how's about you? You hanging in there?"

"Oh yes sir, I'm stoked."

"Oh yeah, what are you stoked about?"

"Sir, about getting in the shit."

"Okay man, but don't get too fired up. Not sure how much shit we'll be getting into."

"Don't matter sir, I'm not driving that stupid truck back and forth to the airfield, I'm doing what I've been training for."

"Great, that's great. Are you ready, to get into the so-called shit?"

"Hell yeah sir."

"Okay, but if there's not enough shit for you don't say I didn't try."

"Okay sir, you got it."

"Hey, you want to call your folks?" Donovan knew that the eighteen-year-old had to be homesick and probably pretty nervous.

"Whadya mean sir? Can we do that?"

"Sure, hang on a second. Let me go see what the deal is

228

around here and we'll see what we can do."

"Sir, that'd be awesome. Thanks a lot."

"Okay, let me check first. Be right back." He put both hands on his knees, paused for a second like he was building strength. "I'll be right back."

Reed's eyes never left the Major. He watched him walk up to the counter and talk to the Airman working the desk. They talked for two or three minutes before Donovan walked back to his seat.

"You're in."

"Cool!"

"Okay, but listen up. You gotta watch OPSEC, operational security, you know?"

"Yes sir."

"Here's the thing. You can't mention anything to your folks about traveling, where you are, where you're going, what you're doing, where you've been, nothing. Just talk to them, about how they're doing. If they ask what you've been doing or what you are doing, just redirect that question to them. Ask them how's it going, how they're doing, what they've been up to. If they ask you again, tell them you've only got a minute and you just wanted to tell them you love them, you're fine, yadda yadda, got it?"

"Yes sir, got it."

"Okay, go up to the guy behind the counter, he'll point you to the phone."

"Okay sir, great. Thanks a lot."

"Don't mention it; you just own me a Coke when we get back to Doha. Actually, make that an ice cream."

"Okay sir." He sat like a coiled spring looking at Donovan, waiting to see if he was done.

"Go!"

Reed all but ran to the counter and on to an office in the back where the phone was. Donovan smiled and put his hat on and pulled it over his eyes, leaning back in the metal chair.

18 February 2002:

The flight to Seeb was uneventful; they arrived in the early evening. Once they all got into the terminal and verified everyone had their gear and weapons Donovan checked for the next flight to Bagram; they'd be leaving in about twelve hours. He grabbed the three other members of his team. "Hey gents, after we drop our weapons at the armory let's sit down in about an hour. We need to talk a few things over."

"Okay sir," Sonic responded for the other two. "We'll meet you over in the pavilion by the PX."

Seeb was an international airport in Muscat, Oman where the US had a small compound near the runway. There was an area crammed with tents for billeting, a dining facility and a small PX for sundries; near the PX was a small pavilion. When military processed through the PAX terminal they were issued a ration card, two beers a day: you get a beer, you get a check mark on the card. An hour later the three, led by Sonic, showed up at the pavilion. They saw Donovan sitting at a small table and approached.

"Hey sir." Sonic, Reed and Hughes sat down.

"You guys, not you Reed, want a beer? Figure we might as well, right? Don't know how long we'll be downrange." Donovan wondered how the other two would respond.

"Sure why not," Sonic replied and Hughes nodded and shrugged in concurrence.

"Okay, Reed hold the table. You want anything?"

"No sir, well...how about a Coke or something?"

"Sure, you got it."

After a couple of minutes, they came back to the table and sat back down with Reed. Donovan handed him his Coke and the other three had 16-ounce cans of Murphy's Irish Stout. Donovan poured his and watched the beer roil up the side of the glass, forming a creamy head.

"That's good beer." He leaned forward, both elbows on his knees and stared closely at it.

"Jeez sir, get a room," Sonic quipped. They all laughed, especially Donovan.

"I do love good beer. Okay, let's get started."

"Sir, what are we doing?" Sonic asked.

"Well, I've been thinking about how we ought to set up our operations and how things ought to work to prioritize the close air support requests and to deconflict fires." He took his napkin out from under his beer can and pulled a pen out of the front of his uniform blouse. "We've already got CJSOTF-North and CJSOTF-South operating out there, but we're going to be with Task Force-Mountain, the 10th Mountain Division guys that have the lead for this. So, the way I figure it, we need to subordinate those two HQ's as far as air requests and fires are concerned, and all of that has to come through us. We don't know what we don't know yet, but we do know that piece; TF-Mountain's in charge and we've got two SOF Task Forces in support. If the decision maker is at Mountain we need to control the air requests and deconflict fires. What I saw of the plan, right now anyway, was more of a policing action and it's concentrated in a pretty small area, less than a 10 by 10 kilometer box. Just considering how the requests are flowing now, through the two CJSOTF's, we've got to work to reestablish the hierarchy. So that'll be me working with the CAOC."

"What's the Chaos sir?" Reed asked. Sonic and Donovan laughed.

"Well you're more right than wrong Reed; it's pronounced, 'K-ock,,' Combined Air Operations Center, where all the airpower decisions are made, the ATO..." He spelled it out for Reed without waiting for his reaction.

"I know what an ATO is sir. I knew what an AOC was, just never heard of it called the CAOC," Reed defended.

"Well, yeah, I guess we always just referred to it as that in all of our training. Sorry, Reed, I know you're squared away."

"Hooah sir," Reed said with a stern look on his face.

"Okay, so I'll work that piece as soon as we hit the ground, then we've got to work to set up comms and then we've got to work on integration. I know we've all done this stuff in exercises before but it's a lot more complicated, trust me. And it's going to get even more complicated when we start changing things up with guys that have been doing this already for a few months. So, we've got to figure out the best way to ensure, if we get into a big scrap, that we don't frat anybody – that's job one.

Well, killing the enemy while not killing friendlies is job one." They all looked at Donovan wondering what he had in mind. "We've got to make sure everybody's on the same page. We'll get LNOs, liaison officers."

He started spelling everything out, knowing that they all had different levels of experience. He used what he thought Reed's was and explained everything, like he was explaining it to him. "Each element will have a man in the TOC, and whenever we get a target and even during a troops-in-contact situation whoever is taking the request will call out, 'Attention in the TOC' and then shout out the coordinates. We gotta make sure everybody's listening, then they compare their front-line-trace, where their troops are, and if they're good, they give a thumbs up, or better yet, ID themselves by their unit and let us know they're clear. If not, they better be raising holy Hell to let us know. Obviously with a TIC we'll have friendlies in the area, but we need to make sure we account for everybody, you know, fog and friction of war. Everybody got it?"

"Yes sir," they all said in unison.

"Okay, we'll work out the specifics when we get there and we've also got to figure out the nets, radio frequencies, priority of fires with 10th Mountain and a billion other things. I hope we've got enough time." He lifted his glass to his mouth and downed the last few swigs.

"Do you know when it's supposed to kick off?" Sonic asked.

"Not for sure. I think we've got a few days. We'll find out when we get there. Okay, everybody, better get some rack time. I have a feeling we won't be getting much over the next couple of days."

"Yes sir," they said again in unison as they all finished the last of their drinks.

"Hey sir, we've still got another beer on our ration card," TSgt Hughes said as he raised his eyebrows, beckoning for approval.

"Sure, go ahead. I'll tell you what, after this is over, if we come back through here, I'll throw my card in the kitty," Donovan offered.

"Sir, you're not going to want to do that," Sonic interjected.

"Yeah, you're right, forget that. We'll take Reed's card! How about that Reed?"

"Sure sir, good by me."

"All right gents, we've got us a deal." Donovan slapped Reed on the back. The three elders went up and got another beer and brought another Coke back for Reed. They chit-chatted for another 30 minutes and then they headed to their tent for what was left of the short night.

The next morning Donovan and Sonic ran into each other in the latrine, shaving.

"Morning Sonic."

"Morning sir. How'd you sleep?"

"Not too well. I got up and double-checked our flight; sure enough, it doesn't take off till this afternoon. I should have known but I guess I wasn't thinking. Everything goes in at night. I think the flight to Bagram from here is about four to six hours, something like that, so we've got to take off this afternoon."

"Okay." Sonic tapped his razor on the side of the sink.

"It's a 1300 show, probably take off at 15-1600. They couldn't give me anymore specifics yet."

"Okay sir, I'll let the guys know. Any plans till then?"

"No, let's meet up for lunch at around 1100. I'm going over a few more things and we can chat about the unclass stuff then. I'm also going to try and get some calls into the CAOC before we take off."

"Okay sir, you need any help?"

"Not sure yet, but I'll let you know, thanks Sonic."

They had lunch, then at 1300 they rallied in front of the main billeting tent, all their gear piled up next to the small dirt path that led to the black top road about two hundred yards away. It was hot, about 98 degrees, and the sun was directly overhead. Donovan sat down on the ground, leaned against his ruck, pulled out his green notebook and started writing. Sonic picked up a few rocks and tried to hit the pole of a sign across the path. He missed three times and then dropped the rest of the rocks and sat on the ground, leaned against his ruck and pulled his hat down over his eyes. Hughes and Reed were talking about the NFL and the Super Bowl.

After about twenty minutes Donovan looked up at the sound of a muffled engine coming from the direction of the road. It had been so quiet and there had been so little traffic he figured it was their transportation. The noise got a little louder but then faded away. He stood up and stretched. "Hey Hughes what was the deal with transportation?"

"Sir, they said there's a shuttle bus that makes the rounds every twenty minutes or so and goes to the PAX terminal."

"You don't figure that bus is going to drive up this dirt path do ya?" He took off his floppy hat and ran his hand through his hair, looking up at the sun and squinting.

"Uh…" Hughes looked at his feet.

"Okay, looks like we're going to hump our stuff to the road and find the bus stop."

"Sorry about that sir." Hughes slapped his hat against his leg then pulled it down hard on his head.

"That's okay man, I shoulda had that revelation twenty minutes ago; must be the sun. Let's move out to the hardball, that's a blacktop road pilgrim," Donovan said with a John Wayne accent, looking at Reed, who smiled.

They threw their rucks on and slowly walked the 200 yards to the road. The bus stand was right next to where the path met the road. After a few minutes, they loaded the bus, stopped at the armory to pick up their weapons and were dropped off at the PAX terminal. They waited, drank water, chatted, nodded off, and wrote letters; anything to pass the time. At about 1800 they loaded and took off at about 1900 for Bagram. They landed at midnight and got situated. They would billet at a place whose current residents called, "Motel Six." It was a Russian-built two story brick and stucco building with the roof blown off. Donovan made sure the guys got bedded down and he went looking for the JOC. After about a half a dozen questions and an hour he found what he was looking for. In the morning, they would show up and get to work.

CHAPTER SIXTEEN

BAGRAM, AFGHANISTAN

19 February 2002, Bagram Air Base, Afghanistan:

When the team arrived the TOC was under construction. The sound of hammers and saws filled the tent. The TOC was being erected with sections both inside and outside of an enormous, old Russian hangar built during their occupation. The main area was under tents just outside the hangar. Military field tables were set up in rows facing what was going to be the front of the TOC where three large video screens and speakers would be erected on an aluminum frame, looking like the set up for a rock concert.

As he walked into the TOC, Donovan looked around and saw Lieutenant Colonel Lee, who he knew from Fort Drum and had talked to about the operation just a few days ago. Lee was about five foot seven inches and sported a blonde-white flattop. He had a somewhat subdued southern accent. They had trained together on a couple of occasions back at Drum, right after Donovan had arrived just prior to 9/11. Lee had tried to establish his "Alpha Male" status right off the bat, screaming directions at Donovan's team during one exercise for no apparent reason, other than to assert his rank and status as the MFWIC. Always a source of amusement for Donovan and his guys, every Army officer in these exercises would exert a lot of energy just going around marking their territory.

"Colonel Lee," Donovan said, waiting for him to look up, but of course there was the obligatory, look-at-how-important-I-am pause.

"Donovan!" Lee barked out. "How was the trip? Glad you're here." He seemed sincere.

"Not bad, glad we're here too. Where do we stand?"

"Well, as you can see we're getting things squared away. You guys need to set up next to Fires, which will be over there." He pointed to the left of where he was standing. Soldiers were laying down plywood flooring, erecting tent poles and stringing electrical and communications wires.

"Okay sir, sure, sounds good. We brought our radios and some of our equipment but we don't have everything we need." Donovan looked to him for help.

"Get with the Sergeant Major and see if he can get someone searching for the stuff you need."

"Awesome, thanks."

Donovan was seeing Lee in a different light. Seemed like he did want him and his guys as part of the team and he also seemed to genuinely want to help. Donovan turned to Sonic, Hughes and Reed to start them working on getting set up. "Sonic, get our turf established. We'll need at least two tables, electrical connections, phones, etc. You know what we need."

"Roger sir, we'll get on it," Sonic replied. He put his arm around Tech Sergeant Hughes' shoulder and started giving him specific directions as they walked deeper into the tent.

The initial few hours of set up were rough; the Sergeant Major changed direction and the layout several times. Sonic tried twice to drive a decision but it looked to him that whatever his suggestion was the Sergeant Major would do something different, just to do something different.

Eventually, the Airmen got set up next to Fires, but off on a wing of the JOC to the left of the big screen set ups, which was fine with Donovan. They had a couple of field tables, a stack of their radios, but no phones. He'd been roaming around trying to figure out who'd be sitting where and looking for any points of contact he could connect with early on to start establishing relationships. However, most of what was going on was being done by all the element's respective minions. As he walked around the still under-construction ops center he felt like something else was missing.

"Hey Sonic!" he yelled across the tent. Sonic moved in his direction.

"Sir?"

"Can you see if you can track down a piece of Plexiglas or a whiteboard, or something like that?"

"Sure, I'll see what I can come up with."

Donovan spotted the Sergeant Major in charge of the

JOC set up checking items off on a clipboard. This looked to him to be a good time to make contact and see where the Air Force stood with the Sergeant Major. He got within a yard, but the Sergeant Major wouldn't look up even though Donovan was obviously in his peripheral vision. He waited. The Sergeant Major kept writing. Donovan kept waiting. Finally, he broke the awkward silence.

"Sergeant Major."

"Hold on."

He knew if he'd waited a hundred years the Sergeant Major would tell him to wait longer. He waited.

"Sergeant Major, if this isn't a good time I can come back later."

"Ain't gonna be a good time, so why don't you hang on a second," the Sergeant Major said without looking up. Donovan was sure he wasn't actually calculating anything, writing anything down, wasn't really doing anything at that moment at all.

"What can I do for you…sir?" the Sergeant Major asked with as much disdain as he could squeeze into those words. Donovan looked at his nametag: Hertog.

"Sergeant Major Hertog, how you doing? Major Donovan." He stuck out his hand. The Sergeant Major looked up from his clipboard, peered over his glasses, paused and then shook his hand. "Just wanted to see if you could help us out with a few things we need to get set up."

"Everybody's got the same problems sir. What makes you so special?"

"Ain't asking for special Sergeant Major, just lookin' for a couple of things to help us help the Division out, you know, air support and all that."

"Oh don't start getting smart with me, Major."

Donovan scanned around the tent as if he were looking for something. "Sergeant Major, not gettin' smart, just looking for some help with a few things, that's all."

"Well, I've got a million things going on sir, so like I said, what makes you so special that I gotta put you at the front of the line?"

"Fuck it. Jesus Christ, you know why we're here right?

237

You know what, I'll take it up with Colonel Lee." He walked away from the Sergeant Major and went looking for Lee. After a few minutes, he found him in the main hangar talking to a couple of Majors. Donovan walked up, waited the obligatory arbitrary time period and then got Lee's attention.

"Hey sir, can you help me out?"

"Sure, what do you need?"

"Well, I was looking for some hookups for phones and a field phone – we don't have one – maybe a piece of Plexiglas, SIPR hookup, and a couple other things."

"Did you talk to the Sergeant Major?"

"Well, I tried to."

"You gotta talk to the Sergeant Major. I can't help you if he can't."

"Won't"

"Hey, just go back and work it out with the Sergeant Major. He'll help get what you need."

"Uh huh. Ok sir, thanks." Donovan walked away, pissed off. He knew how things worked back "in garrison" but he didn't figure that would apply out here. They were days away from combat and he was pissed that he had to play these games at this point to try and do his job. He went back to where his team was setting up. Sonic was under one of the field tables running wire.

"Sonic."

"Yes sir."

"Make sure we've got a complete list of everything we need from the Army. I don't want to have to go ask twice."

"Sure, we're about there I think."

"Okay great, thanks."

Donovan figured at this point the most important thing to get done next was to make contact with the CAOC and get the information flow going. He was not able to connect when they were still at Seeb; now he was feeling the time crunch. Over the next few hours the buzz of activity continued. The large compartmentalized tents were erected, electrical lines were run from the large generators positioned outside toward the flight line and communications lines, telephones and computers, were run and set up. He needed to get some papers he'd grabbed before he left Kuwait out of his ruck, which was back in "Motel 6." He checked out with Sonic and left through the hangar. It was the first time he'd gotten a good look at it in the sunlight. It was shot full of holes but he couldn't tell if they were made by US or Soviet or Afghan weapons.

He made his way across the concrete floor and out the open end of the hangar, heading to the dirt road that led back to Motel 6. He thought how nice it was to stretch his legs, after standing all day. It was a beautiful February day, cool but sunny. He took his time up the road until he got to his billet. He walked through the doorway; there was no door. He went down the hall to the room where he and about a dozen soldiers and his team had their gear. He pulled his ruck out from under his cot and started looking for the papers. On the bunk next to him a soldier was sitting on the edge of his cot staring at the floor. Donovan looked up at him, and then looked back inside his ruck. As he looked through his clothes and gear he had the urge to look back at the soldier; just as he did, the soldier looked up at him. Once their eyes met the soldier quickly looked back at the floor. He appeared to be in his early twenties at the oldest, wearing one of the ubiquitous black fleece jackets over his tan T-shirt and desert pants. He had short black hair, all pulled straight forward and he was dirty. His face was dirty, his hands were dirty, and his clothes were dirty. He was very skinny and his face was gaunt. He looked like he hadn't slept in a week.

"What's up soldier?" Donovan asked.

"Nothing…" he said while starring at his feet. Then he glanced up and noticed Donovan's rank on his collar. "…Sir."

"You okay?"

"Right as rain sir." He now looked Donovan in the eye, very intently. Donovan stopped routing through his ruck and sat up on his bunk facing the soldier.

"Don't look right as rain dude. What's going on?"

"We're at war sir."

"Rog, got that part, how about with you?"

"Whaddya mean sir?"

"You look beat, you doing okay?" Donovan looked into

his eyes and he could tell he was exhausted.

"Well sir, I can't sleep. I'm on the line all day and I come back here at night and I just lay here, I can't sleep." He started to shake his head, staring at the floor again.

"What's your MOS? 11B?" Donovan wondered if he was constantly on patrol, infantry.

"No sir, I'm a 12B, combat engineer. I've been inching along on my belly with this for almost a month." As he spoke he lifted his hand, Donovan hadn't noticed he had anything in his hands until then. He showed him what looked like a fiberglass wand, or a conductor's baton. "I know I'm going to poke the wrong mine the wrong way and blow my face off one of these days. The flail is broke and we've got to clear the areas between the runways and the taxiways. We just keep finding more and more mines. There must be billions of 'em or they're breading or something. I've found 58 myself and there's a bunch of us. I know when I hit 69 I'm done, blown up. I've used that number for everything. If somebody asked me how long it was gonna take me to do something, I'd say 69 seconds, or 69 minutes, or 69 hours... how many of something I had, it was 69...how many times I've seen a movie..."

"Yeah I get it soldier, 69. Man you can't think like that. When are they going to get the flail fixed? That's that tractor type vehicle with the rotating drum with chains on it, right?"

"Shit I don't know...sorry sir, I don't know."

"What's the hold up?"

"Sir, with all due respect and pardon my French, but how the fuck am I supposed to know? I'm the grunt slithering through my part of the war on his belly waiting to get blown the fuck up."

"How much longer you figure you got the duty?"

"Sir, ain't my call. I don't know."

"Well, you're right about that. This might sound stupid, but is there anything I can do?"

The soldier laughed for a couple of seconds, then straightened up and got serious. He reached into his fleece and pulled out a piece of paper. "Sir you got a pencil and a piece of paper?"

Donovan pulled out his pen and green notebook. "Sure, shoot, whadya need?"

"Can you make contact with my folks and girlfriend-"

Donovan interrupted. "Come on man stop thinking like-"

The soldier interrupted the interruption. "No sir, not for that, well... at least... no look, I want you to make contact 'cause I ain't got no phone and I'm not sure if my letters are getting back...and I figure being a Major and all, you gotta get to a landline sometime right?"

"Sure, sure, be happy to." Donovan copied down the two numbers. "Any particular message or just that you're doing fine?"

"Well, I sure as shit ain't doing fine."

"Yeah, but you don't tell your folks that. All that's gonna do is worry the shit out of them. Look if you get blown up, which you won't..."

"You don't know that sir."

"Okay, well, let's assume you won't, okay? If you do get blown up, which you won't, they'll have the rest of their lives to feel like shit. If you don't get blown up then you've made them feel like shit from now until you get home. So don't tell them you're not doing fine, tell them you love them, tell them something positive. I'm not saying bullshit them, but again, telling your folks back home too much truth about what's going on in your daily life...well...it's almost cruel. They're proud of you and they're proud to be telling their friends about their hero son – and you are, kid. Your buddies back home ain't clearing any mines in East Bumfuck, Kentucky."

"How'd you know that's where I was from?" the soldier joked without smiling.

"There you go, just make fun of the whole situation. Bottom line is tomorrow morning you gotta get back out there and get on your belly and stick your rod in the dirt."

Now the soldier laughed, kinda choked, kept laughing and teared up a little. Donovan slapped him on the shoulder.

"Okay kid. Hey, what's your name by the way?"

"It's Reynolds sir. Hey sir, thanks for helping out and the

chat."

"Don't mention it Reynolds; it was a pleasure meeting you and thanks for that dangerous shit you've gotta do."

"Thanks sir. At this point I've got no choice, but thanks."

Donovan got his papers, tucked his green notebook back in his trouser leg and headed out the door. The soldier lying next to Reynolds sat up in his cot, apparently having listened to the whole conversation.

"Hey Reynolds, if that wasn't a typical load of officer crap rah-rah bullshit, I've never heard any."

"Yeah, but at least the guy checked up on me. When's the last time you've seen one of our fucking officers – I don't even know who or what that guy was, but he talked to me for five minutes and he's gonna call my folks and Stacey."

"Yeah, I guess...yeah, I guess you're right. Hey, I'm going to run him down and see if he'll call my folks too."

"Shit, go for it dude, I'm sure he will." The other soldier ran out the door, tripping over the edge of Reynold's bunk.

Donovan returned to the TOC with his paperwork. He'd printed off copies of the ATOs for the last few days before they left and their Standard Conventional Loads, SCLs, each aircraft's weapons loads. As he approached their workstation he noticed things had gotten done. The computers they brought were set up and running, their stack of radios was assembled and at the end of the table was a telephone. Reed and Hughes were lying on their backs running and bundling wires. Sonic was on one of the laptops.

"Sonic, looking good. How's it going?"

"Good sir; got a good start. We've got power to the computers; we're still trying to get connected to SIPR. We've also got a hook up for NIPR but neither one's running yet. We've got the radios stacked up but we've got to run all the cabling and power. We've got this phone, it's a STU," Sonic picked up the hand set and held it up toward Donovan, "but it's not hooked up. Should be DSN and secure though."

"That's great. Great work." Donovan leaned over and voiced his thanks to the guys under the table and gave them a thumbs-up. "Okay gents, let's huddle up here real quick and see where we stand." The small team gathered around the radio stack. "Sonic just gave me a rundown on what's hooked up and what's not. Again, great work in short time; outstanding. Okay, logistics; I think we need to try and get as many of us bedded down in this area as we can. When I was walking out of the hangar earlier I noticed a couple of guys that looked like they were just returning from getting cleaned up walking up a metal staircase to what looked like a second floor so there might be billets up there. I want Hughes and Reed to split shifts, 12 hours a piece, and me and Sonic will split 12 and I'll float on and off of that. I don't need 12 hours of sleep. I know we brought MREs but I'm not sure we've got enough to last more than a couple of days."

"Yeah, sir, we're supposed to get those from the Army," Hughes pointed out.

"Roger that Hughes. See what you can do about that or find out if they're going to bring in chow, mermites or something like that."

"What the hell's a mermite?" asked Hughes.

"Chow containers. They cook the food someplace else and bring it in in these cans and plastic deals, mermites."

"Oh, okay." Hughes scratched his head.

"Okay gents, I'm going to find a phone and see if I can raise somebody at the CAOC. What's today?" Donovan asked.

"Sir, it's 20 Feb, it's Wednesday," replied Hughes.

"Okay fellas, get back at it. I'll see you in a bit."

He headed across what would be the TOC floor back toward the main hangar to where some makeshift offices were being set up. He saw Colonel Black, the Division Director of Operations, G3, sitting inside a plywood-constructed office behind a laptop on a field table. Colonel Black was about medium height, blond hair, blue eyes, and sharp features. He had an overall calm demeanor, never appeared to Donovan to be an overly happy guy, but he was generally cordial, very professional. Donovan knocked on the doorframe. "Colonel Black?"

"Yeah," he replied without looking up from the computer. "What is it?"

"Sir, you got three minutes?"

He looked up for a second, then looked back down and typed for a few more seconds, then stopped and looked up at Donovan. "Sure, what do you need?"

"Sir, we're getting set up and could use some help."

"What do you need?"

"We're trying to get comms with the CAOC and we brought what we had, which was primarily tactical equipment, radios and a couple of laptops. We need help getting the right connections and maybe getting somebody from the 6 to help us."

"Have you talked to the Sergeant Major?"

"Yes sir."

"Well, what do you want me to do that he's not doing?"

"Sir, I just feel like we're running out of time, just getting in line."

"You figure you should go to the head of the line? Why's that?"

"No sir, but we can't be at the back of the line. My small team is all things airpower, specifically close air support, which we might need-"

Colonel Black interrupted. "Look, got it. Go work it out with the Sergeant Major or Fires or whoever, just go do whatever it is you need to do to be full up when we need you."

"Yes sir." He figured that was going to be a waste of time and left Black's office.

Just as he turned to go back into the TOC he almost ran into the Division Chief of Staff, Colonel Moriarity. Moriarity had a round face, brown hair, was a little less than average height and on the stocky side, not on the out of shape pudgy stocky side, but the tough-I'll snap your neck in the blink of an eye-kind of stocky. He was one of the officers on the Army staff that Donovan tried to have as little to do with as possible because he wasn't a big Air Force fan. It seemed to Donovan and all the guys back at the 20th who had anything to do with him that the Air Force could do no right. There was an incident back at Fort Drum that helped shape the Airmen's opinions. A storm was coming in and the weather guys in the 20th had warned the

Division through an update directly to Colonel Moriarity of potential high winds. He ignored the warning; the winds hit the post as forecast. A bunch of the Division Helicopters weren't tied down or parked in hangars and they were damaged. There were millions in damage done to dozens of airframes. At the end of the day Moriarity managed to blame the Air Force for not making the weather call.

"Oh, hey sir, excuse me," Donovan apologized as he tried to side step around the Colonel.

"ALO," Moriarity said. "What are you doing?"

"Sir, just getting set up and ready."

"Are you going to be ready?"

"Yes sir, we'll be ready."

"Where's the TALO?"

The TALO was the Air Force officer aligned with the Division to provide airlift and logistical support. Those guys didn't spend much time at the squadron back at home. He was just realizing; he'd never actually met any of the TALOs.

"Sir, I'll track him down."

"We need a lot of logistical support for this operation."

"Sir, has any of that been pre-coordinated?"

"That's what we've got you Air Force here for isn't it?"

"Well…" Donovan was going to start explaining the request process, going through Army channels to the COAC for planning and coordinating, but he thought better of that idea. "Yes, sir, exactly."

Moriarity sidestepped him and continued walking down the corridor past the makeshift offices, reviewing his clipboard as he walked.

Donovan started to get more of an uneasy feeling that he was missing something. He hadn't thought about the TALO; normally that wouldn't be his job. Those guys are snap-linked with their Army counterparts by design, by doctrine, but he began to realize he was *the* Airman on the scene and he'd better make sure he'd got everything covered. He started second guessing who all was in on the plan. He'd gotten the plan at ARCENT headquarters in Kuwait. He got the briefing slides sent to him from Bagram a few days ago and had left them there with the ACE. Colonel Laredo knew and he was certainly talking to the CFACC about it. He then figured he better not assume a thing. He'd coordinate with everybody at every level.

The first thing he had to do was make positive comms with the COAC. He turned back around and went back into Colonel Black's office, knocking again on the doorframe. "Sir…Colonel Black?"

"Yeah, what is it?" He looked up and saw it was Donovan. "Yeah?"

"Sir, do you have a phone I can borrow for a few minutes?"

"Sure, I was just getting up to find the Deputy G3. Help yourself."

"Thanks sir." He tried the normal DSN prefix and dialed the number he'd gotten back at Camp Doha for the CAOC. The phone he was using was obviously only non-secure capable. He still needed to make contact and hopefully get a secure line soon. The phone rang. After five rings there was an answer.

"Combat Plans, Major Richardson, unsecure line, how may I help you, sir or ma'am?"

He hated that way of answering; he thought there was no point in saying that phrase versus just answering the phone, telling whoever was on the other end it was an unsecure line and then saying, "how can I help you?" After you spoke you'd have the "sir" or "ma'am" part wired.

"Hey, Major Pat Donovan. I'm the Division ALO here with Task Force Mountain. I've got some coordination to do but right now I don't have access to a secure line. What I'd like to do is get some names and numbers and then hopefully within a couple of hours I'll call back on a secure line and get some work done. Can you help me with that?"

"Okay, you're gonna have to tell me again who you are and what you want."

"Sorry, what part of that didn't you get?"

"I guess the 'who you are' and 'what you want' part."

Donovan could tell this guy was a tool. Probably some schmuck that got stuck with a 120-day rotation to someplace, in this case Prince Sultan Air Base, Saudi Arabia, or P-Sab as it was "affectionately" called, that he didn't want to be.

"Okay man, look, I'm borrowing this phone and I'm not going to get to use it for very long so let's take notes this time okay? I'm Air Force Major Pat Donovan. I'm the Division ALO with Task Force Mountain and I need some Points of Contact, P-O-C's," he said snidely, "And some contact numbers on secure lines; got that?"

"Look is there any way you could call back in about ninety minutes? It's coming up on lunch time and they've got pretty strict hours here. This sounds like it's going to take a while, so if you can call back…"

"You gotta be fucking shit'in' me. Look Richardson, can you put your mom on the phone or something, 'cause I'm about done fucking around with-" *Click*.

He felt the blood rush to the top of his head and force the short hair on top to stand at attention. He could literally feel the color red on his neck and face. He was sure that the phone handset now had his palm and fingerprints permanently indented into it. He wanted to punch someone or break the phone or throw something. He got madder because he didn't have any options; he had to call back, had to. What else could he do? But he knew he was going to lose it. He put the handset down on the base station and waited. He picked up the phone and redialed the number like he was trying to put his finger through the back of the phone through each button he speared. He waited, after about six rings,

"Combat Plans, Major Richardson, unsecure line, how may I help you, sir or ma'am?"

Donovan paused, still boiling. "Hey, Donovan here, I need your help on this, I don't think it'll take that long and I'm sure you can still get your second helping of rice pudding at the chow hall." *Click*. He couldn't believe what was happening. Before he gave himself too much time to think he dialed again.

After no less than twelve rings, "Combat Plans, Major Rich-"

Donovan abruptly interrupted, now in a rage, his voice was raised and he was leaning across Colonel Black's desk, supporting himself with his non-phone hand. "Look fuckstick, I don't know who the fuck you think you are or what you're trying to fucking prove, but I'm in the middle of fucking Afghanistan trying to get ready for an operation, you're not my fucking girlfriend I'm having a fucking tiff with. Get your fucking shit together and pay attention to what I'm telling you and what I'm asking or I swear to Christ when I see you I will bash your fucking face in. Are you hearing me!!?"

The voice on the other end of the phone was as calm as could be, soft tone, low volume, "I have a phone roster I can send you over the NIPR if you can pass me an address."

Donovan was incensed. "Sure, address is Patrick-dot-donovan-at-centcom-dot-mil" He asked for several other items and some documents to receive over the SIPRNET. When complete he put the receiver down and walked out the office just as Colonel Black was walking back in. "Sir, thanks for the use of your phone."

"Sure, you can use it anytime I'm not."

"Thanks sir, appreciate it." He walked back through the TOC to his team's workstation and paused at the end of their field table. He saw the guys were still working wires and connections and doing comm checks, so he figured they were well on their way to getting things full up. Sonic was sitting at the table behind one of the laptops. Hughes was sitting next to him on the other.

"Bingo, we're connected!" Sonic said enthusiastically.

"All right!!" Huffman shouted from under the table.

"Hey sir, you've actually got an email from…looks like some guy at Combat Plans in the CAOC."

"Halle-fucking-lujah" Donovan said as he walked around to the other side of the table. He looked over Hughes' shoulder at the email inbox and spotted the one from the CAOC. He reached past Hughes and grabbed the mouse and double clicked on the email. He read for a second, let go of the mouse, pulled out his green notebook and wrote down several numbers then patted Hughes on the back. "Thanks man."

He walked away from their workstation without another word and made his way through the maze of working soldiers still putting together workstations and stringing comm wires. He was headed for the G2 section and pushed through a plywood door marked, "A2-Top Secret." He scanned the area. The room was fairly large, half of it walled by existing infrastructure, brick and steel; the rest was fresh plywood, field tables, computers and large monitors. There were several shredders and side tables lined with coffee pots and paper cutters. The walls had dozens of maps on them; some had friend/foe symbology written on them and others were fresh, having just been nailed to the walls. Most of the activity, like everywhere else, was focused on setting things up and assembling the Intel section of the TOC. He saw a female soldier seated at one of the field tables and noticed there was a phone next to her with a red label across the handset; from there he guessed it said SECRET. That's what he was looking for. He moved away from the door and wound his way around the various obstacles until he reached the female soldier; he couldn't tell her rank because her back was to him.

"Excuse me," he said, in a conversational voice. Just as he spoke some type of power tool operated and drowned out his voice. "Excuse me!" he shouted. Of course right then everything went unexpectedly silent and his voice boomed throughout the room. The female soldier started and turned, looking up at him.

"What the fuck! Holy shit man you're like two feet from me, whadya screaming for?!" She was obviously startled and upset that she'd been surprised and that some guy was yelling at her. He was embarrassed but laughed it off.

"I'm really sorry. Shit. I was trying to get your attention and all the noise… sorry. I'm Pat Donovan." He'd noticed as she turned after being startled that she was a Major also. "I'm looking for a secure phone. I've got to make a couple of quick phone calls back to PSAB to work some coordination." As he was talking to the Army Major, he saw that she was chewing tobacco. As he stated his need for a secure phone, she spit about four times into an empty plastic water bottle.

"Uh, who are you? I know, Pat Donovan. I guess I should say, what are you?"

"I'm the ALO," he stated.

"Oh, cool." She extended her hand to shake. "Sure, you can use this phone and when you're done I need to talk, actually

I need you to talk to one of our guys. We've been getting some cross flow of info from the Air Force Intel folks I – we – need to ask you about." As she was talking he couldn't take his eyes off her teeth. They were infused with bits of snuff and every word she spoke rearranged how the pieces were dispersed. Maybe she was related to Stacks. He barely paid attention to what she was saying.

"Uh, Okay, sure, great, just let me make a couple of calls and we'll chat about that. Is there a phone that I can use that won't disrupt what you're doing?"

"Oh, don't worry. I'm going to go take a shit. That'll take me at least fifteen minutes."

"Okay," was all Donovan could say. As the Major got up, she pivoted in her seat forward and started to lift off the chair, paused, farted and continued to rise. She walked away at a brisk pace. He thought she *had* to be related to Stacks. "Shot out!" she said.

Donovan half-smiled at her and descended into the cloud of flatulence. He tried to breathe through his mouth as he sat in her chair and pulled his green notebook out, looking down the list of numbers he'd gotten off the email Major Richardson sent him. He decided the first call would be to the Director of Combat Operations. He dialed the DSN number and waited.

After four or five rings: "Combat Ops, Tech Sergeant Lemon, unsecure line."

"Hey Sergeant Lemon, this is Major Donovan, how you doing?"

"Good sir, what can I do you for?"

"Who's the boss there and is he around?"

"Sir, it's Colonel Solaris and hang on, let me see if he's around. Hold on sir."

"Okay, thanks." Donovan rotated the handset, keeping the earpiece against his head. He held the phone upside down with the mouthpiece up in the air and leaned forward on his elbows, letting his head slump forward. That was a mistake. His position now funneled the still wafting odor of the seat's previous occupant into his face. He rapidly lifted his head and leaned back. "Holy shit…that's rank."

"Colonel Solaris," said the voice on the other end of the phone.

"Hey sir, Major Donovan here."

"Hey Donovan, what's up? How can I help you?" the Colonel said with a hint of impatience.

"Sir, I'm the Task Force Mountain ALO. Sir, can we go secure?"

"Sure, I'll initiate." After the series of beeps and squeaks Donovan's phone display read – SECURE: SECRET – COAC – Combat Ops – PSAB. "Okay, I got you secure. Can you hear me ok?"

"Yes sir, how me?"

"I got you five by five. Okay, what's Task Force Mountain?" the Colonel asked. Donovan cringed.

"Sir, it's a SOF and conventional ground task force led by the 10th Mountain Division staff and contains elements of 10th Mountain 1-87 Battalion, 101st Air Assault Division 1-87 Battalion and elements of CJSOTF-North and CJSOTF-South and OGA and Coalition forces and a large Afghan force. We're doing the planning for Operation Anaconda." He paused for effect and to see if the Colonel was tracking any of this. There was a lengthy pause. He waited…

"Okay Donnelly…"

"It's Donovan sir."

"Okay, sorry Donovan. Can you give me any more details, some more specifics?"

"Sure sir. Big picture, the operation is scheduled to kick off on 28 Feb, it's targeting what the Army Intel is stating are about one to two hundred Al Qaeda fighters in and around the Shah-i-Kot Valley. Afghan led forces will drive into the valley and force the enemy against coalition, mainly US, blocking positions where they'll be captured and processed – 'hammer and anvil.' The estimate is a 72 hour operation."

"So, what do you need from us?"

"Well sir, a lot. I'm looking at the ATO, it's a couple days old, but if this is what we're flying right now, I'd ask for some changes."

"Go ahead."

"Well, we're flying two-ships of fighters. We need to make that four-ships to give us more flexibility and coverage if we get into a CAS fight. And we're showing only sporadic bomber coverage; we need to increase that to 24/7 so we've always got a bomber vulnerability period and we'll have to adjust the SCLs so we can ensure we've got the right weapons for the targets we'll be going after. So, we'll need more tankers and we've got to ensure we've got C2 birds up 24-7 also. This is probably coming in through Air Force channels via the Army side or the Army coordination detachment there in the CAOC but we need gas for the assault force, the helos and for the Apaches that will be in support. If we can get increased ISR coverage and more armed predators that would help with the IPB and CAS. Sir, we're gonna need the ATO increase for the planned 72 hours of the operation, plus I'd like to get 48 hours before also."

"Okay Donovan, first off, we were just about to stand down bomber operations to give the crews a rest. They've been going at it since early October. Next, not sure we're going to be able to give you the coverage you want and I'm actually not sure you need what you're asking for. On the C2 piece we've only got a couple of birds a piece for AWACS and JSTARS and again, don't think you need all that. And we don't own the armed Predators."

"Sir, you can stand down the bombers after this operation. We're looking at a couple more weeks of flying tops. I'm building this CAS plan based on the worst-case scenario and I actually think these are minimums. I gotta have 24/7 coverage or if I commit one flight, I'm done. If I've got more engagements I'll have to split flights unless I've got overlapping coverage."

"Oh now you're talking about overlapping coverage!" the Colonel said with a gruff laugh.

"Yes sir, 24/7 fighter four-ships and 24/7 bomber coverage, and the C2, and the Preds and the gas. And like I said sir, those are minimums. We're also going to need pre-assault fires in the form of strikes on deliberate targets and robust CAS coverage for D-Day."

"You're asking for a lot, Donovan."

"Sir, all due respect this is a big operation. What else you got going on?"

"Let me check into this and I'll get back to you."

"Sir, this isn't my phone. Let me give you my NIPR email and you can shoot me a note and I'll find a secure phone to call."

"Okay, go."

Donovan passed his information. He closed out with the Colonel, put the receiver down and sat thinking for a couple of seconds. He wasn't sure he was going to get what he needed; if not, then what? He had a bad feeling about the operation. He put his pencil in the spine of his green notebook, closed it, put it in his cargo pocket and just sat there for a few more seconds. He was afraid people were going to get killed, or not, based on that phone conversation. Had he been clear enough? Should he have stopped with the DCO or tried to get to the DCFACC or the CFACC – right to the three-star?

He walked out of the G2 section and back to the ALO workstation. On the way he ran into Lieutenant Colonel Lee. They chatted for a few minutes on the need to work up targets for the pre-assault fires. Lee told Donovan there was going to be a meeting in a few minutes to flesh out a first hack at what those targets would be. He told him the G3, G2, Fires, CJSOTF and Coalition reps would attend and that he "should probably be there too." Donovan understood that the Army owned the deliberate targeting process but he always thought it was funny that the Air Force, the ALO, was kind of optional.

He continued on to the ALO section to check up on the guys and see how things were going. The team was still hard at it making progress. Donovan felt good about that. He went back to the G2 area to meet back up with the tobacco-chewing gas-passing Major to follow up with her request to talk with one of her guys. He walked back to where he'd used the phone and the Major was standing by her desk, leaning over with both hands on the edges of a map laid out on top. He came up to her right side and as he got within a few feet he stepped into her peripheral vision; she looked up and smiled at Donovan, yellow teeth full of snuff.

"Everything go okay out there?" he asked.

"Whew...yeah, barely though, man. I almost blew an O-ring"

"You mentioned earlier you wanted me to talk to one of your guys."

"Yep, he just stepped out but we can discuss the broad strokes." She looked down at the map as she spoke. "My guy has been talking to one of your Air Force Intel troops at PSAB and they've been discussing the threats and the Intel estimates. Two things: on the enemy estimate we're pretty far apart on the number. Here and up through the Army Intel channels we're estimating 150-200 enemy pax. You guys are thinking it's over a thousand, maybe twelve to fifteen hundred."

"Yeah, that's pretty far apart. Can I tell you why I think the Air Force guys are right?"

"Shoot."

"A few months ago I was working with TF-Dagger out of K2 and I was on shift one night when a call came in from one of the ODAs. They'd been approached by some locals that were acting as intermediaries for what they said was a group of about two thousand Al Qaeda fighters and family members that wanted to surrender. It was right in the area we're getting ready to assault. Dagger didn't pursue it; they felt it smelled too much like an ambush. Now that could have actually been a ruse or it could be the guys we're gonna be dealing with in a few days."

"Huh, interesting. Well, our official Intel estimate is still the lower number. The second thing was we were working up threats to the Helicopter Landing Zones, the HLZs, and we've got some imagery that looks like it's a DShK heavy machinegun positioned right over top of one of the primaries. Some special operators are going to check it out within the next couple of days. I'm not sure how much you know about our targeting process but if we've got imagery that confirms we've got a target, we've got a target, but if we don't have the luxury to fly a satellite or an ISR bird leisurely over the battlefield we template additional targets. That means we figure, if we were the enemy, where would we put what type of weapons systems? You follow?"

"Yeah, I'm a bomb dropper by trade, I get it."

"Okay, so this morning we had the one DShK via imagery and right now we've templated three more. Your Air Force guys are helping us with this and we're working to get another sweep of the Named Areas of Interest, you know, NAIs by tomorrow. So, I just wanted you to be aware and we might need you to help if we need more ISR support."

"I'm working on that right now. I've asked for more of everything. If I can use your phone once in a while, that would help."

"Sure, whenever you need, as long as I'm not using it!" she said jokingly.

The targeting meeting was to convene in a small room off the G2 section Donovan had just been in. He brought Sonic with him. It looked like the meeting was about to begin; he scanned the room to see who was there and if he knew anybody. He saw the G2 rep he recognized from Fort Drum, CWO Adams; he was medium height, stocky and sported a black crew cut. The Chief had a round face and wore silver rimmed round-lensed glasses. He was quiet but knew his business. The G3 rep was the Deputy G3, Lieutenant Colonel London; he was about 5 foot 10 inches, with a short blond flattop and always had a wad of chewing tobacco in his lip. He was what Donovan considered a "regular guy." He was a good soldier but he was capable of communicating on a personal as well as a professional level. He also recognized CWO Hart from CJSOTF-North and walked across the room and shook his hand. The Chief didn't recognize him at first but then remembered him. He greeted Donovan but it was obvious that he was trying to get some notes done before the meeting started. Donovan noticed that and broke contact with him, saying he'd talk to him later. Chief Hart was tall, red hair, very pale skin. He was wearing a brown fleece top over his desert trousers. All the others at the meeting were in the desert combat uniforms, DCUs, except for someone Donovan had never seen before. This man had a green canvas shirt and blue jeans and leaned back against one of the field tables with his arms crossed. He carried a nickel-plated Colt .45. Donovan heard someone call him Jimmy. Everyone else, including Donovan, carried the standard 9mm Berretta in a various array of holsters in different configurations. Everybody was prepping for the meeting but everybody was also busy checking everyone else out. This was the first meeting of several of the many elements that were part of this operation so there was a lot of butt-sniffing going on. Colonel Black walked in. Chief Adams, who was closest to the door, called out, "Room tench-hut!"

"As you were," replied Black.

"Okay Chief, what do we got?"

"Sir, gentlemen, ma'am, we've looked at possible targets and have come up with twenty-one nominations."

The group went over the twenty-one targets as they were individually briefed to Colonel Black. He took in the information about each one; occasionally a team member would inject some additional pertinent detail. The targeting officer chewed his nails throughout the brief, even when answering questions, making faces like an angry beaver. By the conclusion of the meeting the targets were "racked and stacked," prioritized and listed in order to be reviewed by the Commanding General, Major General Hacker. Colonel Black would take the list to the General; at some time in the future the team would be given back the prioritized list as approved.

The meeting took just over an hour. As it was breaking up, Donovan moved to try and catch Black before he got out the door. There were several others with the same idea and a small logjam formed and Donovan was at the back of it. Lieutenant Colonel London had stayed behind to talk to Chief Adams. Donovan moved to position himself far enough away from the two talking so it didn't appear as though he were eavesdropping, and to set himself up to intercept London if he made a dash to the door after he finished with the Chief. He sent Sonic back to keep the preparations going. He waited. London looked up at him a few times during the conversation. A bit to Donovan's surprise, when London was done talking, instead of heading for the door he headed to him.

"Hey sir, how you doing?" Donovan asked.

"Fair to middling. What's up?"

"Sir, I wanted to float something by you, see what you think before I elevate."

"Okay, go ahead." London crossed his arms. He had a small clear plastic water bottle about a third of the way full of spit. He tucked it up under his opposite arm.

"I can give you all the details, but to the point: I think you ought to let me lay on about three days of an 'air campaign,'" he made air-quotes, "so that we can suppress or destroy any threats to the HLZs and take out fighting positions, LOCs, whatever we come up with. We've got differing Intel estimates of enemy numbers and threats. We could be looking at a lot more than we're planning for."

"Okay, thanks, let me run that by the leadership. Do you think you can get what you need if we decide to go that route?"

"Yes sir, we're the only game in town right now and there's talk of scaling back the overall air support. If we were looking at a fight I don't think we'd have any issue getting everything we asked for. Now that's me talking but it's what makes sense."

"Well you don't ever want to rely on that!" London joked. "I'll get back with you. Thanks."

"Okay sir, thanks." He left the room hoping his pitch would bear fruit.

He weaved his way through the outer offices and into the main JOC area. As he headed to the ALO workstation he saw Sonic nose to nose with an Army Captain yelling at each other right in the middle of the floor. The Army Captain was Captain Sullivan, the Division "Battle Captain" charged with running the JOC floor. He'd share shifts with a "Battle Major" to cover 24/7. Captain Sullivan was about 6'4" and Sonic was 6 foot. They were both animated, arms flailing at their sides, faces as close as they could get without touching.

"Look, I don't give a shit how you do this back at Fort Drum; this is how we're gonna do it here!" shouted Sonic.

"I don't give a shit if you give a shit or not. Some Air Force Captain's not gonna dictate TOC procedures. Whaddya out of your fucking mind?" Captain Sullivan shot back, leaning a little extra forward.

"Hold it fellas," Donovan interrupted as he got within arm's reach. He realized immediately what they were fighting about. If Sonic was arguing with the Battle Captain it had to be about the change in clearance of fires procedures they'd talked about on the way in from Kuwait. He also realized he hadn't gotten around to discussing this important change with the Army leadership yet and created this obviously bad "relationship-situation." Neither one stopped talking or broke their stare. He put a hand on each one of their shoulders. "Gents, listen… Knock it off!" he shouted. This caught Lieutenant Colonel London's ear and he started moving toward the center of attention with a purpose.

"Captain Sullivan…Captain Sullivan," Donovan said, trying to break Sullivan's lock.

"Yes sir," Sullivan said, still staring daggers into Sonic.

"Captain, this is my bad. Because of the number of agencies and different units involved in this operation we've got to implement a modified clearance of fires procedure and I hadn't gotten around to running this through the leadership, so obviously you didn't get the word. Captain Latch was moving out on what I told him to coordinate. Sorry about that. I'll go discuss this with Colonel Black or Lieutenant Colonel London and get this all squared away. We got two good officers here just trying to do their jobs. No harm, no foul? We good Captain? Sonic?" Donovan looked them both in the eye. He knew he got through to Sullivan when he actually met his eyes and broke the eyeball death-lock with Sonic.

"Yes sir," Sullivan said, still with a bit of acid in his voice.

"Yes sir," Sonic replied.

"Okay gents. Shake so we can move on to bigger and better things."

They shook. London had stopped within earshot but didn't interrupt while Donovan was trying to straighten things out. He was both giving the Major a chance to fix things but he was also gauging how he operated. Donovan turned to walk back to the G3 offices and as soon as he pivoted he saw London leaning on one of the field tables, chewing on a toothpick.

"What was that all about?" London asked him.

"Well sir, my fuck up. The Captains are good. If you got a minute, I'll fill you in and actually address an important issue that was behind the whole thing."

"Okay, let's go outside and get some air," London said as he stood up and led the way outside the tent.

It was a sunny day. Both men squinted against the harsh light of the Afghan sun neither had seen in days. As they walked toward where Donovan's crew's antennas were set up he looked out toward the runway. He saw areas between where they were and the taxiways beyond roped off where the mine clearing was going on. He saw in each section several objects that he quickly figured out were combat engineers crawling, inching their way from one end of those boxes to the other, lane by lane. He still didn't make the call he'd promised.

"Hey sir, can you give me thirty seconds? I'll be right back." Donovan broke contact without waiting for an answer. He ran back into the tent; within less than twenty seconds he was back with a black object in his hand. As he approached, London saw it was a satellite phone. Donovan wanted to put it in his hand so that he wouldn't forget to make the call he'd promised the young stressed out engineer. He sat back down next to London.

"Okay sir, here's how it would go: 'Attention in the JOC! Immediate CAS request from Warrior 01, or whatever the call sign is, grid x-y-z,' and then all the LNO's would check the front-line-trace of their units and confirm they've got no friendlies in that area. We'd pass that on to the requesting unit and the supporting aircraft, then pass the supporting aircraft to the requesting unit and then they've got it, should only take a few seconds. I'm concerned with all the ETACs we've got, all the different units and the close battlespace that we could end up calling in air on ourselves." He was ready to battle it out with London.

"Shit, makes sense to me," London said immediately. "Go ahead."

"All right, great. Sir, would you make sure your guys know?"

"Yeah, sure, but if there're any questions tell them I said we're good."

"Okay sir, thanks. We'll get back to the battle drills."

Over the next 48 hours the Task Force worked around the clock to get ready for D-Day.

CHAPTER SEVENTEEN

BUDDIES

23 February 2002, Diego Garcia, British Indian Ocean Territory, US Air Base, Wing Operations Center:

"Sir, I got a call from the CAOC asking for you," the desk sergeant told Lieutenant Colonel Voss, the Operations Officer for the Expeditionary Bomb Wing as he passed him the handset.

"Lieutenant Colonel Voss."

"Colonel Voss, this is Colonel Don Thompson, Ops desk at the CAOC."

"Yes sir, go ahead."

"Voss, what's your call sign?"

"Bison, sir."

"Okay Bison, this is Spaceman. I've got an update for you."

"Okay Spaceman, go."

"Okay, we've got an operation cooking off soon and we're going to need you guys to shift to surge mode. We're going to need 24-hour bomber coverage, full weapons loads, multiple refueling, the whole works. The ALO on the ground is a bomber guy, you might know him: Dude Donovan."

"Oh hell yeah, his old unit is here in strength. We all know Dude. Happy to bring in some fire and steel for him. Okay Spaceman, copy. I'm guessing we're going to get a draft of the ATO or something to start working off of? I'll alert the crews and get the max number in crew rest, ready to go."

"Okay Bison, thanks. I'll talk to your sergeant there and get all the particulars sent to you ASAP."

"Okay Spaceman, copy all, Bison out." Voss handed the phone back to the desk sergeant to coordinate the flow of information. He waited until he hung up. "Sergeant, get Major Bunke up on the horn will ya?"

"Yes sir," the sergeant replied and started dialing. After a few seconds he reached the phone out to Voss. "Sir, Major

Bunke's on the line."

"Hey Craig, what's going on?"

"Hey Jim, looks like Dude Donovan has got something big going on and we're gonna surge. Can you get your crew ready? Actually, you guys are in crew rest right?"

"Yep, we'll be ready. When's this thing kick off?"

"Within the next 24 to 48; I'm waiting on the details."

"Okay, I'll get a hold of Emmett, Leo, Ken and the rest of the crew, we'll be ready to go."

"Great thanks, Jim. We'll get a hold of you with the details when we get them." Voss handed the phone back to the sergeant and started looking over the schedule.

Jim Bunke was Pat Donovan's best friend. They'd gone through officer training school together and both had their first assignments at Fairchild in the B-52. Like all other aviators Bunke went through Air Force Survival School, which was run out of Fairchild. He'd spent a week learning survival skills in the woods of the Pacific Northwest just north of Fairchild. Donovan had thought it would be a good idea one day to rent a small aircraft and drop supplies to his buddy while he was trudging through the field portion. He'd coordinated with Bunke to lay out a signal and Donovan would drop a few bags of food down on the marker. When the fateful day came, Donovan flew a Cessna 150, a two seat, single engine light aircraft over the target area. He'd put together six bags of food and made four "high-drag-salamis." This was his invention, tying a loose garbage bag to the end of a three-foot salami. The idea was that the bag would catch air and slow the salami down, preventing it from exploding on impact.

When he was over the geographic spot they'd worked out, he reduced power and configured the aircraft for slow-flight. The stall warning horn was blaring as he searched for the signal marker. After the third orbit he saw it. There was a white X laid out on the ground and he could see Bunke and a couple of his comrades just off the mark in the bushes. He did one more orbit before pushing the door open and dropping two bags. They tumbled to the ground, missed the X but hit in the general vicinity. Donovan came around again, this time armed with the salamis. As he rolled out and leveled the wings, he opened the door and threw down the salami like a spear. The "chute" ripped right off and the salami went "slick," burrowing into the soft ground. Still in the turn, he looked back down and saw Bunke and his team heading for the garbage bags of food. Right behind them he saw the cadre of instructors in hot pursuit, eventually tackling the students and confiscating their loot. Bunke would tell Donovan later that the instructors made the students sit there and watch while they ate all the goods by the campfire. Bunke figured a guy that would go through that much trouble to try and get him some snacks deserved some top-notch air support.

CHAPTER EIGHTEEN

FINAL PREPARATIONS / SAME AS IT EVER WAS

27 February 2002, Bagram Air Base Afghanistan: The Evening Battle Update

It was D-2 and the final preparations on the JOC were almost finished. Donovan's Air Force team was complete with their physical set up and had a few more communications issues to solve. The Fires team opposite them was also good to go. The JOC had transformed from a construction site to an operations center. Sonic ran a few more CAS battle drills, yelling out "Attention in the JOC!" every fifteen minutes or so. All the liaison teams Donovan had recommended be positioned in the JOC were all set up: the coalition SOF forces, the SEALS, reps from the 101st and 10th Mountain maneuver elements, Task Force Dagger, Task Force K-Bar; they were all there ready to deconflict their positions from potential targets. The main sections of the JOC if seen from above would have appeared orderly and neat, but there were miles of cables snaking around the plywood flooring taped to table legs, under rubber mats, through holes in the floors, up along the tent support poles and across the top of the tent. Some ran to the humming generators, some between equipment; they ran everywhere. Field tables lined the walls of the tents facing away from center. These were mainly the liaisons. A VTC was about to begin with the ARCENT commander, Lieutenant General Mikolashek and Major General Hacker and the TF Mountain staff. Donovan was off to the side of the screen, focused on finishing up some of the last minute details at his workstation. He'd listen in while continuing to work.

"JOC tench-hut!" bellowed the Sergeant Major.

"Carry on," replied Hacker in a normal speaking voice.

"Carry on!" shouted back the Sergeant Major.

Major General Hacker approached his center seat facing the screen; he was flanked by Colonel Moriarity and Colonel Black. He took his seat and opened a blue folder with some notes in it and began to review. Colonels Moriarity and Black did the same. The various staff members positioned themselves so they could see the screen and hear the General. One of the technicians that was working the setup of the VTC reported that the "bridge was up" meaning they had connectivity with Kuwait.

"About two minutes General," stated the tech.

The General didn't look up from his notes but Colonel Black did. A few seconds later the screen popped up an image of the ARCENT headquarters conference room with Lieutenant General Mikolashek and his staff assembled. He looked up and saw the connection was made.

"Hey Phil, how do you read?"

"Loud and clear sir," Hacker replied.

"Phil, you ready?"

"Yes sir. If we fail, it's the Air Force's fault."

Donovan reacted without thinking, "You gotta be fucking shitting me!" he said out loud. Several of the nearby staff turned and looked at him in shock and one or two of the head table looked in his direction also.

Hacker continued, "Sir, they're telling us they can't get us the fuel we need, they can't get us the transport to get Task Force Rakkasan's troops and equipment here in time and they can't hit the targets we need hit for our pre-assault fires. We're ready. We've got a solid plan. We're just lacking the necessary support from the Air Force."

Donovan was amazed at the General's comments for a couple of reasons. He thought to himself, "Here's an Army Division Commander, the 10th Mountain Division Commander on the eve of battle and the first thing he gives his commander in response to the question, if he's ready, is an excuse; pre-blaming the Air Force, and that he'd do that in front of his staff." He thought about picking up the phone right then and there and making contact with the CAOC but he'd wait to see what else was said. He looked over at Sonic who was sitting at one of the computers.

"Sonic, you fucking hear that?"

"No sir, what? I wasn't listening," Sonic replied without looking up from the computer screen.

"Never mind, I'll tell you after the brief."

The VTC continued for another forty-five minutes. Donovan didn't remember much of anything else that was said.

It was a few hours later, now minutes before the Update Brief was set to start. Donovan checked that each of his team members that had a speaking part in the brief were ready to go. He was going to brief the ATO. Lieutenant Colonel Lee was going to brief the pre-assault fires, even though one hundred percent of those fires were coming from the USAF; it was still his brief. Donovan also had his weather guys from back at Fort Drum with him. They'd brief the projected weather and the impacts it would have on each weapon system. Being late February, it was obvious to everyone that the weather would be a factor. All the arranging, rearranging, the hammering, wiring, everything that went into prepping the JOC was finished. Colonel Moriarity was directing traffic, giving last minute guidance and corrections, operating at full throttle as the Chief of Staff.

There were several other generals in the JOC, some just showing up prior to the brief. Two would take on the roles of Deputy Commanding Generals, Brigadier General Harvard; he walked with a noticeable limp from wounds sustained in Somalia and wore his nickel plated .45 automatic with the hammer cocked on his hip. He was a little over six feet tall, stocky, about 220 pounds. He was in charge of SOCCENT. He'd participated in the invasion of Grenada and the actions in Mogadishu in 1993 that became the legends of Black Hawk Down. Brigadier General Jameson was the military liaison to several government organizations; he was also a renowned and well-respected special operator. Colonel Longstreet would also be sitting up front for the brief. Donovan had taken advantage of a lull in the activities a couple of days prior to approach the Colonel and reintroduce himself as Stacks's lieutenant and remind him of his prior service with TF Dagger.

General Hacker didn't attend the brief. The Battle Captain started the brief with a time hack – everyone synchronized their watches. Colonel Moriarity would be taking the brief. The briefers were lined up in chairs, in briefing order off to the side of the screens. After a few of the staff sections presented their portion of the brief it was the G2's turn. They briefed the current intelligence estimates. The weather section fell under the G2, Army Intelligence. Tech Sergeant Hartman, one of Donovan's squadron mates from Fort Drum, would brief the weather and its potential impacts. Hartman was about five foot nine inches, a little on the heavyset side, real closely cropped black hair. He sported an in-regulation, but by any other standard, ridiculously cheesy mustache and he wore his gas mask inserts for eyeglasses. The gas mask inserts had optical lenses but were in a plastic and rubber frame, almost like a scuba diving mask but not near as big. He stepped up to the briefer's spot. His cover slide was showing on the screen.

"Slide" Hartman stated, directing the slide flipper to move on to his first slide. "Sir, the next several slides depict the weather factors over the next 72 hours and the effects they'll have on each weapon system. Sir, this first slide shows the freeze line is currently at 9000 feet and is projected to be 9000 feet for D-day. There's a front moving in that will bring with it periods of low visibility at lower altitudes with the possibility of snow and freezing rain. Slide. Sir, you can see the effects for each of the weapons systems." He paused to let the Chief of Staff absorb the information. Colonel Moriarity stared at the slide for a few seconds.

"Go ahead," he directed.

"Slide," called out Hartman. He went through the remainder of his slides and finished with the standard closing. "Sir, pending your questions, that concludes my brief." He started to move off the briefing position back to his spot in the briefer's chairs.

"Hang on Air Force," Colonel Moriarity said, holding up a hand while writing a note in his notebook, not looking up from the page. Hartman stopped in his tracks and moved back to the briefer's spot. Donovan looked up from his notepad, listening for the questions the Chief would ask.

"So, with all of what you've briefed me here, considering the effects on our aircraft and weapon systems, the potential weather effects – all that – what would you recommend for the operation?"

Donovan got to his feet and moved toward the screens. "Sir, that's not on him; he gives you the information and you make that call," he stated, trying not to sound disrespectful.

"Bullshit. He just briefed all that information; I'm assuming it's accurate. I have to go make a recommendation to the Commanding General and I want to know what our weather expert recommends. What do you recommend Air Force? Go or no-go?" He looked back at Hartman. Donovan had thought about directing the Sergeant not to answer that question but he did not interrupt.

"Sir, I'd call it a no-go for D-Day and I'd recommend a 48-hour slip," Hartman said, one hand grasping his other wrist, his arms hanging in front of him. He said it with absolute confidence and sounded extremely sure of himself.

"Okay, noted," Moriarity told him.

Donovan thought to himself, "Good for you Hartman!" He'd tell him that later, but now the next briefer, one of the G3 staff started briefing the operations portion of the brief.

"Slide."

Donovan thought if the CG went with the weather recommendation, it would be a blessing. Everyone was still sprinting to get ready and the JOC staff was still running battle drills to get their processes down. The slip would give 48 more hours to get elements positioned, fuel, weapons, everything. While the briefing continued he went back over to his workstation. He was going to call Colonel Solaris and let him know what was happening. They'd gotten their hotline hooked up so he gave it a shot.

"Chief of Combat Ops, Master Sergeant Walko."

"Hey Master Sergeant Walko, is the CCO around? This is Major Donovan."

"Sir, something I can help you with?"

"I'd like to speak direct to Colonel Solaris if he's around."

"Sir, standby one, let me check." After about a minute, the Sergeant came back on the line. Sir, he's in a meeting and will be probably for the next couple of hours. Can I leave a message?"

"Yeah, tell him to call me on this line when he's able. I've got some updates on Operation Anaconda."

"Okay sir, will do."

"Okay thanks, out here." Donovan picked up the STU phone and tried to reach Major Richardson, who he hadn't heard from in about three days. He was still waiting on some of the products he'd promised. He dialed the number. It rang about four times before someone answered.

"Combat Ops, Major Wright."

"Hey Major Wright, Major Donovan here, Pat. How's it going?"

"Hey Pat, Dave. Not too bad, how 'bout yourself?"

"Good, hey, I called three or four days ago and got a Major Richardson. He was going to send me a bunch of products and phone numbers, etcetera. I got one roster but I've not heard back from him. Sorry, it was Dave right?"

"Right, Dave Wright."

"Dave, what do you go by?"

"Orv, how about you?"

"Dude."

"Okay Dude, yeah, on Richardson. He's been off the last couple of days."

"Off? What do you mean off?"

"We're working five days a week, we get two off, some have the weekend, we spread it out and his was over the last two days."

"You gotta be shitting me," Donovan laughed.

"Nope, that's the deal. Not bad."

"Yeah, I guess. Hey, any chance he handed off his tasks to anybody there?"

"Nope, I guess not since that would have been me and he didn't say anything or leave any notes in the log; nothing."

"Son of a bitch."

"What do you need, Dude? Maybe I can help you out. Where you calling from by the way?"

"I hope so. I'm at Bagram getting ready for Op Anaconda. It's just I can't fucking believe we're on the eve of battle here and this clown goes on a weekend pass without a care in the world. What the fuck are you gonna do in Saudi Arabia anyhow?"

"Most guys just hit the gym, read, hang in their quarters, watch TV, movies, whatever. Anyway, what do you need?"

He went over the list; Wright gave him everything he'd been waiting for in about ten minutes. He hung up and figured he should call the Special Operations Liaison Element. From the list of numbers Wright gave him he quickly found the SOLE's main number and dialed.

"SOLE, Master Sergeant Karpas," came the voice on the other end.

"Hey Master Sergeant, Major Donovan here, how you doing?

"Good sir, how the hell are you?" Karpas answered back in a very cheery and enthusiastic voice.

"I'm good. I wanted to run my plan by you for a sanity check."

"Yes sir, shoot."

"Okay, here it is…"

Donovan explained his bar napkin plan to Master Sergeant Karpas and Tech Sergeant Mark Luck, both were well renown in the TACP community and were working in the Special Operation Liaison Element. After the call, Donovan felt a lot better, at least about his plan, having run it by someone who'd been doing the air to ground business for a living for years. The brief had ended during his call with Karpas. Just as he hung up Staff Sergeant Fairlane and Senior Airman Zondo showed up at his workstation. He stood up, moved from around the field table and gave them both a handshake and a hug.

"Great to see you guys, how the hell are you?"

Zondo answered first. "Good sir."

"We're good sir, just wanted to swing by and say hi. We're up the road at Motel 6," Fairlane added.

"Great, so what's the plan for you guys?"

"Sir, I'm obviously with 1-87," Zondo replied.

"Sir, I'm not sure yet, but I'll be happy to work here with you if you need me," said Fairlane.

"Okay, we'll see, we will need some help. I've got a couple other guys I've heard are in the area I might grab but I'll keep you in mind. Hey gents, we could be looking at a 48-hour slip due to the weather. Actually, get this, the Chief of Staff put Hartman on the spot about his weather brief, he actually pressed him to state whether or not he recommended go or no-go. He said no-go for good reason; the weather's shitty for the next two days and they went with his recommendation, so you guys will probably be sitting around or rehearsing for a bit. You should try and get as much rest as possible. How you fixed for gear?"

"We're good sir," Fairlane answered.

"Okay, I gotta get back at it. I'll check on you later. If you don't see me, come by here before you head out if you can." Donovan shook both their hands, Zondo saluted. Sonic had been talking with the G2 staff and had just returned after Zondo and Fairlane had left. "Sonic, you just missed two of our dudes, ETACs. They're staying down at Motel 6."

"I'll swing by and see them when I get a chance later," said Sonic.

"What's up?"

"Sir, I just got back from G2; you need to go talk to the Warrant."

"Why, what's up?"

"Sir, I'll let you get it from him but you need to go talk with him. There's some concern over one of our targets."

"Okay, I'll go talk to him right now. He still there?"

"Think so."

"You got it. I'm still waiting for a phone call from Colonel Solaris, the Chief of Combat Ops."

"You want me to send someone to get you if he calls?"

"Yup."

Donovan left for the G2 Section. One of the target nominations was near Gardez and the Army intel folks believed if it was hit as part of the pre-assault fires it could kick up a hornet's nest and start another front to the operation.

****

28 February 2002, Gardez Afghanistan:

Ski had been chopped to augment the SOF TACPs. He was in position near Gardez with a team that was in a safe house just east of the city. They'd been working out the details of their support to the operation and were ready to go. He was riding with three other team members in an SUV heading away from their safe house when they all noticed someone running toward them and readied their weapons.

"What's that guy doing?" Ski asked.

"I don't know but he's not armed," the team leader said. "Okay, let's see how this plays out."

The man slowed down a few meters from the truck and approached as the team members dismounted the vehicle. He was breathing heavily.

"Don't bomb us! Don't bomb us! My brother runs this whole area and he is not helping Al Qaeda at all and I got lots of weapons, mines and RPGs. I will turn them all in to you right now, just don't bomb us! Don't bomb us!" he pleaded as he leaned on the truck, out of breath.

The team brought the man into the back of the vehicle and drove to his compound. There was a flatbed full of mines, RPGs, mortars; the whole truck was full. They gave it all to the Americans.

"Gents, we better pass this info up the chain so these guys don't get hit after they just surrendered all these munitions to us," Ski suggested to the ODA commander.

****

The target was removed. Donovan called the CAOC and told them of the rationale, then went back to his workstation.

"Sonic, get one of the guys to hang up that piece of Plexiglas and start filling it out like a tally and tracking board.

"Sure sir, we're all over it. I got a draft I just finished writing out and I'll have Huffman make it happen."

"Okay, great, thanks." As Donovan was working he caught someone approaching in his peripheral vision and looked

272

up to see a solid looking Captain, blond hair, light complexion with a red tint. Trailing one step behind was an Army Major, tall, dark hair. As Donovan was searching his memory to figure out if he'd ever seen them before, they arrived at the edge of his desk.

"Hey sir, Rex Aykroyd," he said without expression as he and Donovan shook, and then rotated his shoulder back an inch in the Major's direction. "And this is Major David Bates." Bates stuck out his hand.

"Hey, David, nice to meet you. How you doing?"

"Good David, thanks. I'm Dude, or Pat, whichever you'd prefer. Nice to meet you."

"Okay Dude, nice to meet you too. We're the Fires team with Rakkasan."

"I'm glad you guys came by. First, what can I get for you? I can give you a brief rundown of our ops plan, freqs, ATOs, SCLs, whatever you need," Donovan offered. "I'm assuming you guys are here for the sand table brief too, right?"

"Sir, yep, and what you've offered up, that's awesome, just what we're looking for," Rex said, now with a very slight smile.

"Okay, oh, hey, this is Sonic, my right hand man."

"Hey Sonic."

"Sonic, get these guys whatever they need. Once you've got what you're looking for we'll sit down with you for a few minutes and go over our plan and processes." He sat down at the laptop.

"Okay sir, that'd be great," replied Rex.

The Captain and the Major spent about fifteen minutes with Sonic getting the latest information form the CAOC, ATOs, rosters, call signs, all they could get their hands on. Rex then approached Donovan.

"Sir, we've got what we need. What else you got?"

Donovan got up and stood in front of the piece of Plexiglas. He grabbed a dry erase pen.

"Okay, here's how we'll operate." He drew a rough outline of the planned battlespace, "With as many ETACs as we have out in the field we could easily overload the available freqs. We've got AC-1 and AC-10 channels for SATCOM; both belong to the CAOC and are used primarily for comms between the CAOC and the AWACS, call sign 'Bossman.'" He then drew a straight line horizontally through the middle of his depiction of the battle space. "We're going to use a north freq and a south freq for UHF. Anybody north of that east-west grid line will use this freq," He wrote it out on the board above the line. "And anybody below the line will use this freq." He wrote it out on the board below the line. "I've also set up five control points and some IPs to funnel and flow the aircraft in logically. We'll be the traffic cops up here and push aircraft as necessary to either you guys or straight to the ETACs, but we'll be keeping track and deconflicting. You guys got mortars right?" He asked, knowing the answer. "Well, if you're going to shoot you've got to call it in to us with the max ord and all the pertinent info, so we can push aircraft out of the way. Priority of fires is Troops-In-Contact, TIC. I've got the CAOC to basically double the ATO and double the coverage, so you guys should get all you need." Donovan went on for about thirty minutes, covering the specifics of the plan and ensuring Rex and David knew the plan as well as they could in the few minutes they had to talk.

"Sir, thanks for the info and thanks for the rundown." Rex shook Donovan's, then Sonic's, hand.

"Yeah Dude, it was great meeting you and if we need anything else we'll go through Lieutenant Colonel Lee or we'll contact you guys direct. What's your call sign?" Bates asked.

"Tombstone. 'Tombstone Actual' if you need to talk directly to me." He pointed to himself with both thumbs. The two turned and snaked their way around the field tables and out of the JOC.

Donovan, Bates and Aykroyd attended the sand-table brief. Several soldiers had built a replica of the battlefield out of wood, plaster of Paris, sand, paint, sticks and rocks for use during the brief to the commanding general. It was quite a sight. It was a packed house and the key leaders pointed at significant objectives, lines of communications, phase lines and terrain features during their portions of the brief. The battlefield ran north south, bounded on the west side by a pair of north-south high ridgelines interspersed with a series of peaks, the eastern edge was defined by the rounded ridge rising from the valley floor known as the "The Whale." At the south end was a prominent peak that would be called "The Finger." In the middle were the valley floor and the three villages of Marzak, Serkhankhel and Babulkhel. Donovan was starting to sense the significance of what was about to happen. This was going to be a full up battle. He knew that because of the insight he got working with Dagger and the Air Force Intel. He started to feel like this was going to be important, historic. He felt important.

Donovan couldn't believe how lucky they all were that the weather, and the weatherman's recommendation, delayed the operation to the point now all were feeling more confident in their processes and procedures. Based on how he felt, he was pretty sure there were many more in the JOC who felt the same way.

It was approaching midnight. The next day was D-minus 1. Donovan wanted a full day to tie up any loose ends before D-Day so he knew he'd better try and get a couple hours of sleep. He'd sent Sonic out to do the same a couple of hours ago.

"Reed."

"Yes sir?"

"I'm going to hit the rack for a couple of hours. I want you to make sure I'm up by 0430. And call me or Captain Latch if you need anything before then, okay?"

"Yes sir, I got it. 0430 and call you or Captain Latch if anything important comes up."

"Right, and don't hesitate; if you have to think about it just wake me up, okay?"

"Yes sir."

1 March 2002, Bagram Air Base Afghanistan:

Donovan got up to his rack, put his head down, and after what felt like ten minutes...

"Sir...sir! Reed here, sir, it's 0430."

"Uh, oh, okay Reed thanks, I'll be right down." He

hadn't taken his boots off. He leaned forward, ran his hands back and forth across the top of his head, and then stood up. He wavered back and forth for a couple of seconds, grabbed his hat and started moving. He got to his workstation within a few minutes but was still waking up when he saw Sonic sitting in front of the laptop.

"Hey man, you get some rack time?"

"Yes sir, all I needed. How about you?"

"Yeah I got about a good hour in the last couple of days. Fresh as a daisy," Donovan said through a yawn. "I'm going to head over to the Dagger-Forward JOC and see what's going on, if there's anything new, just check in. Sonic, call the CAOC and see if they've got any updates would ya?"

"Sure sir, will do."

Donovan wanted to talk about the use of the AC-130 gunships. Since they operated in direct support of Special Forces, he wanted to look at the ability for them to also support conventional forces if they were dealing with troops-in-contact situations when they were flying. To Astro it seemed reasonable but he couldn't make that call. Donovan looked up toward the front of the tent and saw Lieutenant Colonel Bullock. He approached him, broached the subject and came away with a conditional "yes" to the use of the gunships in situations where they weren't otherwise tasked to support SF ops.

He went back to the main JOC. The night sky was clear so he stopped after leaving the Dagger JOC and looked up at the stars for a few minutes. The majority of that side of the hangar was full of holes or missing as a result of airstrikes, allowing ample moonlight to come in and fall on the concrete floor. It felt great to just stop and look up, and not think, but it started to make him sleepy so he shook it off and moved back into the cover of the hangar and tent. The rest of the day was filled with rehearsals, drills, phone calls, meetings, chow, coffee, trips outside to the porta potties, discussions, slides, briefs, coffee, water, charms candies, coffee, coffee, coffee…

"Huffman," Donovan said as he noticed Airman Huffman who was working on the radios.

"Yes sir." Huffman spun around to face Donovan.

"We've got a VTC set up with the CAOC tonight and one with the Carrier Strike Group after that and I need some info put together. You got a pen?"

"Yes sir, shoot."

He dictated a list for Huffman to work on. "Then, let's see, it's almost 1700, you all need to go get chow, bring it back here and we need to run some more battle drills. I'll man the fort until you get back."

"Sir, we can't bring chow back into the JOC. Sergeant Major's orders."

"Okay, well you guys take fifteen, then come back ready to get back at it."

"Okay sir."

Fairlane had been helping out with the set up and was working on the radios at the time.

"Ian, you too," Donovan directed.

"Okay sir, roger."

Huffman, Reed, Hughes and Fairlane left the area and headed to the main hangar where the chow line was set up.

"Sonic, you go ahead too."

"Sir, how about I go with you when they get back?" asked Sonic.

"Sounds good. Can you put a framework up on the board so the guys just have to fill it in? Also, get a map posted up there that we can draw the control points and IPs on."

"Yes sir I'm on it." Sonic grabbed a dry erase pen and the ATO sheet.

A few minutes went by. Donovan looked up and saw Fairlane moving toward him with a purpose.

"Sir, the Sergeant Major is trying to make us serve chow."

"Huh? Did you tell him I wanted you guys back here to run battle drills?"

"Yes sir. He didn't care and said if we don't serve we don't eat."

"Holy fucking shit. You gotta be fucking shitting me." He stood and moved from behind the field table, maneuvering around the desks as he headed out of the tent. Fairlane followed.

Once he cleared the makeshift security area he was in the main hangar. It was still light and the main hangar door was open. He saw dozens of soldiers lined up at the chow tables, slowly flowing through the line. His guys were standing off to the side, getting talked to by a soldier. As he approached he recognized the soldier as one of the Division's First Sergeants. He walked up and stood next to his guys as the First Sergeant went on. After a few minutes of listening to the lecture about "being part of the team" and doing "their fair share" he'd had enough.

"Hold on First Sergeant, I-"

"You hold on sir, I've got this. This is none of your concern," the First Sergeant interrupted.

"What? What do you mean this is none of my concern? These are my men and I ordered them to get chow and get back into the JOC ASAP so we could continue preparing for combat. D-Day-"

The First Sergeant cut the Major off again. "Oh, here we go, this is gonna be about how the Air Force is fucking special and you don't have to pull your weight." He exaggeratedly rolled his eyes and tilted his headway back.

"Sergeant!"

"FIRST Sergeant," the First Sergeant interrupted again.

"Okay, First Sergeant. First off, I haven't heard a goddamn 'sir' outta you yet. Second-".

"Look '*sir*,'" the First Sergeant said as snidely as possible, "I already told your little Air-Men here, they don't serve, they don't eat." Just as he was finishing his sentence the Division Command Sergeant Major, the enlisted top dog, came up on his right shoulder and injected.

"What's the problem here Major?"

"The problem is the Air Force is special and they don't have to do anything but eat, use the showers and shit in the latrines," the First Sergeant offered up.

"Sergeant Major, the problem is I told my guys to get their chow, eat and get back into the JOC to continue to run battle drills. D-Day kicks off in a few hours and we've got lots of work to do to be ready to provide Close Air Support. I need them back working, not serving chow." Donovan felt better that he was allowed to finish a sentence, make his point and be able to make it to the Command Sergeant Major.

"Well Major, we're all getting ready for combat and we're on the same timeline you are and you don't get to operate under your own set of rules. So, your guys are serving or they ain't eat'in. You don't clean the shitters and the showers; you don't use the shitters and the showers! Questions?" The Sergeant Major stood with his hands on his hips, looking up at Donovan with a sneer pasted on the face of his round, shaved head perched atop his 5' 6" frame.

"Holy fucking shit," Donovan said to no one in particular through a slight chuckle. "Go ahead guys, back to work." Fairlane tossed his empty tray in a trashcan next to the chow tables. They all walked back into the JOC and retook their positions around their workstation.

"Ian, head out through that tent opening right there," Donovan pointed to a flap behind and to the right of their workstation. "Grab everybody an MRE and give me a count of how many we've got left. Looks like we're going to have to stretch the supply out over a couple of days, at least until the op is over."

"Yes sir." Fairlane headed for the tent exit and came back with a half full box of MREs. "Sir, we've only got two more boxes."

"Okay Ian, thanks," Donovan said, shaking his head.

The Airmen took turns eating their MREs outside the tent by their vehicle. The work continued and eventually all the pieces and parts of Donovan's plan and set up were complete. He held the VTC with the CAOC and the CSG. It was uneventful and it was obvious to him that nobody there was getting too spun up about the operation but he'd gotten all he asked for.

The TALO, Captain Ken Abbott, had gotten there a couple of days prior and rolled up into Donovan's team. Donovan knew of him from back at Fort Drum but they'd never met. He was flown out from Drum to the CAOC and on to Bagram. When he arrived he was spent after getting run ragged and beat up repeatedly during the nightly Battle Update Briefs. He was working the positioning of fuel for the helicopter lift force and for the FARPs, Forward Arming and Refueling Points, which would also be used by the Apaches. He also worked the airlift to get the main body of the assault force, the 101st Air Assault Division elements, from Kandahar to Bagram. He was six feet tall, shaved head and a light complexion that was now pasty white. He took all the stress and demands and barbs in stride, and just as D-Day was approaching got everything when and where it was supposed to be.

The CG came into the JOC just before he was going to get some rest before D-Day and the staff ran a TIC battle drill while he was there. Sonic called out, "Attention in the JOC," and ran the drill. No one responded; the JOC was dead silent. The CG turned and walked out. Donovan felt a baseball-sized knot in his stomach.

"Fuck," he said out loud. That night the gunships and predators flew up and down the Shah-i-kot valley. As H-Hour approached, he got up from a couple hours of rack time at about 0300. The operation would kick off at 0630. It was 2 March, 2002.

"Hey Reed, what's the latest from the Gunship?" He asked as he stretched his arms over his head.

"Sir, they checked in for updates from us about an hour ago. They said they spotted several small fires along the Whale and down in the villages. Seemed like just normal activity."

"Let's get them up on the radio."

"Sir, I'm pretty sure they're in support of Mako 31."

"Okay, that's great; don't bug them then. I'm just looking for the latest. I'm sure if they spot something they'll pass it on. How about the Predator? Any chat reports via mIRC from them?"

"Sir, nothing significant."

"Ping them anyway and keep your ears peeled. I'm going to give the CAOC a call to check the launch status of our pre-assault strikers."

"Sir, got that a couple of hours ago, everybody's in the green and en route. Current estimates are on time to the TOTs."

"Great, thanks for the follow through. Go get some coffee while I review the email real quick."

CHAPTER NINETEEN

FIRST CONTACT

1 March 2002, Marzak, Afghanistan:

After the fateful engagement along Highway 1, Uktam had regrouped with two other survivors, but had been captured by an American Special Forces patrol. He was sent to Sheberghan Prison where he stayed until the Americans conducting processing operations left. Once they were gone the local Northern Alliance soldiers took over security. When that happened some of the prisoners were treated harshly and others were released via the dealings of Yusef. After his work in Afghanistan was done, Yusef made his way back to the US. Uktam was one of the lucky ones. Once he was released he and a few others made their way back to Lashkar Gah. He was shaken, physically and emotionally. At Lashkar Gah they were taken in by a local Taliban element and had a few weeks to recover. There he was reunited with his friend from home, Babur, who was tall, clean-shaven and had red hair. Babur had grown in importance over the months since they left home, telling his friend of his exploits and accomplishments. He was now directed to prepare to move to another location as the anti-coalition militias were trying to consolidate. He would drive through Kandahar, Ghazni and Gardez to the village of Marzak to recruit fighters and he wanted Uktam to go with him. As they drove they talked about home and about what they would do when they got to their destination. They did not know what they were going to do but Babur was instructed to get followers that could operate heavy weapons.

"Uktam, brother, can you fire a heavy machine gun?"

"I'm sure I could. I have received the training."

"How about an RPG?" Babur asked.

"Yes," he answered, forlorn as he remembered the pride and happiness he felt when he'd hit the American Humvee with his first shot, quickly followed by the loss of his friends and comrades. "Yes, I can operate an RPG."

"Okay, brother, I'll say I can shoot the Dshk, you the RPG."

Days passed and the two made it to Marzak. The trip was nerve-wracking. They constantly worried that they'd be hit from above at any minute. They were met there by a local leader and given their assignments. Babur would man a heavy machine gun to protect the southern entrances to the valley they were now in; Uktam would stay in Marzak to help guard the leaders. Babur was outfitted with western style cold weather gear he'd drawn from the supplies provided at Marzak. Those going to the high terrain were given the first opportunity to use the limited gear they'd assembled.

Babur made his way with four comrades up to the top of a prominent ridge that overlooked the valley just to the west of Marzak. They'd taken two days to cart the heavy machinegun, ammunition, tent and supplies to the top and set up on the northeast edge. They watched and waited. Their leadership had learned that a column of vehicles commanded by a General of the Eastern Alliance, Zia Loden, was to enter the valley soon and had positioned their gun so it would cover the valley for one or two kilometers. Their primary targets were American helicopters, which they were sure would be bringing American troops in to support the Eastern Alliance. The anti-coalition militia knew who the 10th Mountain and 101st Air Assault Division soldiers were and were prepared to counter their air-mobility advantage. The team of five was confident and anxious to do their part. Babur and his companion Chenglei, a fighter from China, stood alongside their tent and looked out into the valley while the three others slept. It was 1 March, the Shah-i-kot Valley.

Lieutenant Colonel Paul Lavoire was the Advanced Force Operations (AFO) commander in charge of reconnaissance operations in the valley. He was in on the planning of Operation Anaconda from the beginning and had made his recommendations and voiced his concerns. He saw what he knew the enemy saw and directed one of his Special Forces teams to set up an OP on the top of the "Finger," a piece of high terrain that oversaw the southern end of the Shah-i-Kot valley and its approaches. "Mako 31," the team of SEALs and an Air Force Combat Controller made their way to near the top of the ridge. Two crawled further forward. As they looked over the final lip of terrain before they could see down into the valley they spotted a tent and a heavy machine gun wrapped in a blue tarp. They took pictures, marked the position's coordinates and carefully made their way back to the rest of the team, moving far enough away from the site to avoid accidental detection. The information was passed back to Lavoire and then on to TF Mountain HQ. The team recommended eliminating the threat just prior to H-hour of D-Day, which was only a few hours away. Lavoire gave the approval.

Babur spent most of the day working up aiming points, picking a spot that could be a potential avenue of approach, aiming as best he could, estimating the distance, adjusting for the range and writing down the azimuths and elevations of the Dshk. He had copied dozens down in the brown notebook he kept in the cargo pocket of his Russian-made army trousers. He and Chenglei neatly stacked ammo in the tent and near the gun. The other three of their group were a Chechen and two Saudis. They didn't speak much to each other but they understood their mission and felt a camaraderie that transcended the language barriers. They ate a stew that Chenglei prepared that night and headed off to get some sleep, anxious for a fight. One of the Saudis took the first watch. Babur would take over in the early morning hours. It was cold at night and the other men stayed in the tent except for an occasional trip to the rocks to relieve themselves.

2 March 2002, Hills above the Shah-i-Kot Valley:

Shortly after midnight the Mako 31 team made their way carefully back toward the enemy site. At a point about 500 meters from the site they dropped their rucks. The leader of the team, "Happy," directed the Airman and his explosives expert to stay with the rucks. He also wanted them out of hearing range of any radio transmissions since they had Grim 31, an AC-130, supporting them and they would be making routine radio calls to gain any situational awareness the gunship could pass. The two stayed at that spot and the leader with his two comrades crawled forward toward the enemy. They arrived at the point they'd been the previous day and stopped to do a weapons check and wait until H minus one hour. Then they would attack. As they waited a figure approached their position. The Special Forces leader thought this was it. The foreign fighter stopped feet from their position and gazed out to the west.

Babur had taken his shift. He was restless but also proud. He accomplished each task with a sense of purpose and thought of the glory and praise he and his comrades would get for their work over the next few days. He wondered how Uktam was doing and whether or not he was up for the task he'd been assigned. Babur gave him the choice of which duty to take. He felt that the RPG would require closer contact with the enemy and half-hoped that Uktam would take the Dskh position and allow him to take the more dangerous job, but he left that decision to his friend. "Glory to him," he said out loud at that moment.

Happy heard the foreign fighter say something he couldn't understand; one of his teammates looked at Happy for a confirmation to attack or wait. The call was to wait. They stayed hunkered down behind the rocks and hoped they could wait until the established time before they engaged.

Babur walked back to the tent. He took a drink of water from the canteen he'd rested against the side of the tent, stretched, crossed his arms across his chest against the cold and walked back to the high ground.

The Special Forces team waited.

Babur walked away from the tent, back to the west. He walked back up to the ridge above and behind the tent. He again

285

looked out to the west and strained to see any movement. At the crest of the ridge he saw something.

The three Americans were momentarily exposed. They saw that the foreign fighter had seen them; he yelled a warning and sprinted back in the direction of the tent.

Babur ran toward his comrades, trying to get to the Dshk; he knew if he could get to it and swing it around he'd have fire superiority and be able to fight off the Americans. He ran as fast as he could, yelling another warning to his fellows.

Happy gave the word and the three Americans crested the ridge and charged toward the tent.

Chenglei grabbed his AK and pulled and held the trigger, emptying an entire magazine in the direction of the enemy he'd not yet seen. Only two shots initially came back from the Americans; two of their guns had jammed. The third was firing with effect.

Babur reached the tent and yelled a brief situation report to the crew as he grabbed more ammunition. All five emerged from the tent. One of the Saudis rushed straight at the Americans, firing as he charged. With their weapons cleared the three Americans shot precisely; the Saudi dropped with three shots to the chest. In unison the three Americans turned on the next closest man, darting to their right, and cut him down with three round bursts. A third tried to escape over the far side of the ridge on the backside of the tent. He also fell. Babur and Chenglei made it over that ridge as the Americans sprayed the tent with bullets. Happy ordered the team to fall back. The Airman had been in contact with Grim 31 and on Happy's direction cut the AC loose on the enemy below.

Babur and Chenglei stumbled down the ridge out of breath. They helped each other up and trudged forward.

Grim 31's sensors picked up the bodies in the snow, confirmed the location of friendlies and saw two retreating "squirters" heading away from the tent. Having received clearance from the Combat Controller, they went to work.

Babur, glad to have escaped, thought they should make their way back to Marzak. He communicated as best he could with Chenglei a plan to continue to move until it got light and then see where they stood by morning. As he was communicating with Chenglei, he heard the low drone of aircraft engines overhead.

Uktam was standing outside the mud hut he and twenty of his fellow fighters were occupying in Marzak. While he smoked a cigarette he thought about his sister Nika. He heard the muffled sounds of the AC-130 firing; he had heard that sound before. He'd learned to fear it and so did all of his comrades. One of the others emerged from the hut.

"Do you hear it?" he asked.

"Yes of course," replied Uktam as he drew on his cigarette.

"It's the Spectre gunship, the inescapable death."

"Yes, the only thing that can stop the gunship is the sun," Uktam stated.

"I wonder who they are shooting at," the fighter said.

"I don't know, but I pray for them." Uktam threw his spent cigarette to the ground and crushed it with his foot. He turned and went back into the hut and laid on his blankets. He lay with his eyes open, unable to sleep. He heard more reports from the Spectre's guns.

CHAPTER TWENTY

D-DAY
NO TURNING BACK

2 March 2002, Shah-i-Kot Valley, Afghanistan

In the darkness of the early morning the Chinooks started their motors and accomplished their systems checks. After a few minutes the troops were waved ahead to load. Heavily laden, the soldiers slogged forward, breathing the combination of cold morning air and burning aviation fuel. Their platoon sergeants yelled for them to hurry up. The helicopters were loaded and sat idling, waiting for the final go ahead. The Apache crews were loaded and their rotors spinning as they too waited for the go. The fighters and bombers flying in support of the pre-assault fires were on their final legs; some were Initial Point inbound for their targets, the beginning of their target attacks. Donovan and his crew were ready. The radios were silent. The airstrikes were planned 40 minutes prior to the first chocks hitting the HLZs and would end 10 minutes prior. The patrolling gunships were now reporting that they were seeing movement on the ridges overlooking the HLZs.

The mood in the JOC was tense but the concerns there were different than those of the soldiers waiting to assault, the aircrews flying in support of the operation preparing to strike their targets and the special operators who were positioned all around the battlespace. The tension in the JOC was about decisions and how they'd affect the operation and people's lives. The tension in the field from those physically going into battle was about their lives and the lives of their buddies next to them.

The order to attack was given. The engines spooled up on the helicopters and their occupants felt the lift off, their burdens heavier as they were pushed deeper into their seats with the force of the upward thrust. Every man's thoughts were his own at that moment. Some prayed, some rehearsed their duties again in the heads, some thought about killing or being killed. It was still dark but a thin ribbon of light started to emerge at the horizon to the east. The assaults would occur during daylight as planned to give the crews the maximum visibility to land safely on the untried terrain. They were all committed; there was no turning back.

The operation began; a flight of F-15Es hit the first targets. They dropped the as yet un-combat-tested thermo baric bombs designed to create a fire and blast effect unlike a conventional bomb. They could be dropped at the entrance of a tunnel or cave and clear the entire enclosed area, around corners, killing everything inside. They called in to Tombstone and confirmed their TOT. They were right on time and confirmed they were still a go, "As fragged" was the response they got back; they were cleared to strike as planned. They hit cave complexes both in the north and the south ends of the battlefield successfully and looped around for another attack to hit their third target. A B-1 was also cleared and hit additional caves and re-struck the ones the F-15s had already hit. A B-52 laid a string of weapons across the back of the "Whale" where Lavoire's AFO troops had seen significant enemy activity.

Then a weapon got stuck in the B-1's bomb racks. They couldn't release it and requested permission through the AWACS back to the CAOC to jettison it in the target area. They waited for the reply. As they waited, the B-52 with more bombs to drop was forced to hold outside the box. Donovan knew the clock was ticking.

"Sonic, let's push the B-1 out of the way and let the Buff drop the rest of their bombs while we're waiting on the COAC to make a decision," he directed.

"Yes sir." Sonic immediately called to the B-1 to move out of the area and hold at a set of coordinates he gave them.

The column of General Zia's forces was approaching the valley; they were led by a SOF team in several vehicles. The spirits were high amongst the Afghans. One of the AC-130s patrolling the area radioed down to the team's HQ that they were observing a massed formation that appeared to be in a position to block the allied advance and it was in a position that matched a location the intelligence reports had predicted opposition would be. The commander in the HQ ordered the gunship to open fire. The gunship began firing. The SOF team leading the Afghan column, the "hammer" of the operation, started receiving incoming. They called for close air support. The Afghans were taking casualties. A round hit directly next to one of the SOF vehicles and a US soldier and three Afghans were killed. The column stalled and started to break apart as everyone ran for cover. General Zia ordered his men to break and pulled them out of the fight. The plan did not survive first contact.

As this was happening, the F-15s called in that they'd gotten the "knock it off" call.

"Sir, just got a call from the Eagles that they got a knock it off call," Sonic passed.

"Who called knock it off?" Donovan asked.

"Looks like one of the ground units."

"Shit. How many targets did we service? Shit. Okay, let's re-role them all for CAS. Get how much station time they've got left and we'll hold them all outside the box."

"Roger; on it." Sonic put the handset back up to his ear.

The Chinooks carrying 1-87 Battalion passed the summit now occupied by Mako 31. The Mako team looked at each other now that the full significance of what they had done a few hours earlier settled in. The helicopters passed easily within range of the Dshk; one of the SEALs raised his weapon, aimed at the passing Chinook and followed it through his gun sights for a few seconds, then turned to the others and mouthed, *Holy shit.* The assault force approached their landing zones. The Chinooks were ten minutes out and were passing abeam Marzak.

Uktam had come back out of the hut to relieve himself; two others emerged at the same time for the same reason. He moved away from the hut toward the valley, lit a cigarette and then urinated. As he puffed and pissed he heard the distant beating of helicopter rotors. It was almost light. The other two men who'd left the hut with him approached while looking skyward. Each had taken their weapons out. Uktam unslung his AK-47 and cycled the action to chamber a round. With the cigarette dangling from his lower lip, he watched as the helicopter drew closer and raised his weapon. By now the others had done the same. As the Chinook passed they aimed and fired.

With ten minutes from their LZs 1-87s first two Chinooks took fire from Marzak. It was ineffective. Charlie Company's bird came in for its final approach, flared and as soon as the back wheels touched down on the rocky terrain the 1-87 troops exited off the rear ramp and formed a wedge as they moved away from the helicopter. Zondo was the left anchor of the wedge; he lumbered forward under the weight of his 120-pound ruck. The engines of the Chinook spooled and it departed, sending dust and debris over the soldiers. They formed up and began their movement to the objective, Ginger. As they moved out they noticed individuals on the ridgeline to their right. One of the NCOs asked the Australian liaison officer with them if they were theirs.

"They're not ours," was the reply; he raised his weapon and started firing.

The company started taking fire from three directions, heavy machineguns; AK-47s and RPGs. Zondo heard the order, "Drop your rucks!" He dropped his, hit the ground and put it between him and the enemy and returned fire. A burst of machinegun fire impacted within inches of him. He turned around to see if anyone saw where that fire was coming from and there was nobody there. Zondo quickly assessed that his interpretation of the order to "Drop your rucks!" was incorrect; apparently it meant drop your rucks and run for cover. He got on his radio and tried to call the Apaches that had escorted them to the HLZ. No good. He tried "any aircraft" on the common frequency. No good. The rest of Zondo's chock had gone down into a natural terrain depression, a bowl, and began returning fire.

Don Gennaro had come in on the second Chinook in the first wave. Once they were dropped off Gennaro moved to link up with the battalion commander, Lieutenant Colonel LaFontaine. He moved as fast as he could under the weight of his ruck. What appeared to him at that moment as a cylindrical object, moving in slow motion, caught his attention out of the corner of his eye. He thought during this stretched out time period, "This is going to hurt." He wondered if he should dive to the ground or keep moving… it hit the ground and skipped within ten feet of him and hissed and fizzled. It was an RPG, a dud. Gennaro kept moving. Only half of the Chinooks were able to offload their troops because of the stiff resistance. Once Gennaro got to cover he looked up over the lip and saw Zondo stuck out in the open, pinned down by the enemy fire. Gennaro got Zondo up on the radio and told him to stay put until he could get air support. Zondo reluctantly agreed. An enemy emerged from behind a large rock and fired at him; he returned fire and ducked back behind his ruck, which at that point was looking pretty small. Just as he ducked back behind the ruck, an incoming mortar round exploded within feet of his position and threw him through the air several feet to his right.

I'm dead, Zondo thought to himself; he didn't want to look down fearing he wouldn't be there. Once he realized he was still in one piece he got mad, returning fire with his weapon, and tried again to contact air support.

"Tombstone, Tombstone, White Lightning Zero Three, how copy!" Zondo shouted into his handset. He heard nothing. "Tombstone, Tombstone, White Lightning Zero Three, how copy… Any aircraft, any aircraft, White Lightning Zero Three!" He stuck a finger in his other ear and listened hard to the earpiece of the handset. It was dead. "Shit." This was a far cry from the operation the Company had planned when they spent a couple days building signs directing prisoners to processing points to place at the blocking positions. He knew the Battalion needed air support; he needed to get linked up with Gennaro and share his radio, but for now they were all pinned down.

Gennaro tried to reach the Apaches, the AWACS, Tombstone, anybody, but had no luck. The battalion Fire Support Officer, Captain Taylor, was able to reach the Apaches and got two to come help out. Within a few minutes an Apache flew by to the west and drew heavy fire.

With the enemy gunners now firing at the Apache, Zondo took a deep breath and dashed out in the direction of the company, enemy rounds striking all around him.

"Zondo, are you nuts, what the hell are you doing?"

Gennaro yelled as Zondo dove down at his feet.

"Sitting out there in the open wasn't my plan Sarge. My radio's shot up, we need air," he replied.

"No shit."

Zondo and Gennaro worked together to get his radio operational. Zondo called again for help. "Any aircraft, any aircraft, White Lightning Zero Three."

"White Lightning Zero Three, this is Exxon 23, go ahead." The tanker aircraft had received Zondo's transmission; they were in business.

"Exxon, I'm in need of immediate air support, push aircraft to this TAD ASAP." Zondo relayed his tactical frequency and position. The tanker relayed the message to "Bossman" the AWACS.

Back in the JOC, "Sir, White Lightning 03 is troops-in-contact, requesting immediate air support through Bossman," Sonic passed to Donovan.

"Roger, push one of the initial strikers to him until we get something else lined up."

"We coordinated with Bossman to send Blade 01 to White Lightning until he's bingo, a B-52, he's got 27 bombs, Mk-82s," replied Sonic.

"Sir, we've got a call in from Mako 31 requesting air; he's got targets on the Whale!" Huffman shouted from his station by the radios.

"Okay, check on the station time left on the Buff. If he's got more than 30 minutes send him. What's next up on the ATO?"

"Sir, we've got another TIC called in by Dragon One Zero, one of the 101st ETACs".

The radio calls kept coming in. Donovan worked the sequencing and deconfliction, Sonic and Huffman were on the radios; Sonic worked with the AWACS and Huffman took in the calls from the ETACS.

The Apaches that had escorted the assaulting Chinooks were duking it out toe to toe with the Al Qaeda and Taliban fighters. The Apache crews knew they couldn't hover; if they hovered, they were going to die. They executed multiple gun runs, spraying enemy positions with 30mm, and once they identified a weapon system or dug in position they fired salvos of rockets. They were taking a beating, each airframe absorbing multiple hits, but the crews were staying with the infantry. The running gun passes kept the enemy's heads down for a few moments at a time, allowing the ground-pounders to maneuver and in Zondo's case, call in airpower. But the battle damage was mounting. Flight by flight, the Apaches had to exit or risk becoming a rescue effort.

Sergeant Anton found and grabbed Zondo and put him in the middle of the formation. "Let's keep you alive so you can keep us alive."

Sergeant Lepore, who'd been with Donovan, Captain Nelson, Fairlane and Zondo at the Sheberghan prison, and his squad were taking heavy fire from a machinegun positioned in a rock crevice. He couldn't fire with effect on the enemy from where they were so he maneuvered his squad as best he could, then passed Zondo coordinates. He only passed a five-digit grid. For Zondo, that would leave too much room for error that close to friendly troops. He needed eight or ten-digit grids. Just then Captain Nelson approached Zondo and Gennaro.

"Okay Air Force, what you got available to take some of this heat off?" Nelson yelled over the sound of outgoing fire.

"Sir, we've made contact and we've got a B-52 inbound but we'll get something going here in a few minutes," Gennaro told him.

"Well hurry up," the Captain said as he maneuvered back, hunched over, to his original position.

Captain Taylor followed right behind Nelson, "Okay guys, what you got available?" he asked the Airmen.

"Sir, we're on it," Zondo replied.

"Then get on it." Taylor ran to his left to cover. The enemy was close enough to yell taunts and wave at the Americans.

The battalion tactical command post; Lieutenant Colonel LaFontaine, Rex, David and LaFontaine's staff took about twenty minutes to maneuver to consolidate 1-87's positions. As they were finishing with their last set of coordinates, the two Airmen saw the battalion commander and his battalion sergeant, Sergeant Major Grippe. It bolstered their morale and it was obvious it lifted the entire company's spirits. Within five minutes of LaFontaine's arrival Gennaro called in the first airstrike.

"Blade 01, cleared hot," Gennaro called to the B-52, "Everyone get down, take cover! We've got 12,000lbs of bombs coming down around us right now!" he yelled to his comrades.

The bombs started impacting the ridge; the earth shook for several seconds. A shower of debris fell down over the soldiers. There was an audible cheer. Now it was the American's turn to jeer, "Take that motherfucker," a soldier yelled as he leapt to his feet. His buddy pulled him down and rolled over top of him to curb his enthusiasm. The strike took the wind out of the enemy long enough for LaFontaine to direct his company commanders to have their men dig in at the bottom of the bowl. There were 86 troops in the confined area. The Americans set up their 120mm mortar two hundred meters to the south of the bowl and started firing as soon as they were set up. They only got off a few rounds before the tube took a direct hit.

"Sir, both the buff and the F-15s are bingo. We've got another flight of F-15s, a B-52 and a B-1 coming on station within five," Sonic relayed to Donovan.

"Okay thanks, great. Let's keep pushing them to White Lightning, Mako and Juliet," he directed.

Most of the rest of the JOC was taking in information and battle tracking while the Airmen in the ACE pushed firepower to the field. The predators that were flying in support of the operation were now feeding live video into the JOC. Donovan looked up from his station and noticed just about everyone in the JOC was staring at the video screens. He went back to work, checking who he'd have available for the next air support request. His team had just worked six simultaneous troops-in-contact situations, getting air to each of the elements that requested it. Lieutenant Colonel Lee approached him at his workstation.

"Pat, Bates, the Fire Support Officer with Rakkasan just called in that they're taking fire from Marzak," Lee stated.

"Okay sir. Yeah, I met Bates. What do you want us to do?"

"I need you to deal with it."

"Okay, let me see what I can do about it. I know we've got Rules of Engagement issues but I get it, I'm with you. I'm on it." Donovan picked up the hotline to the COAC; once the other end answered he asked for the TST cell.

"TST cell, Lieutenant Colonel Jacobs," the other end answered.

"Hey sir, this is Major Donovan at Task Force Mountain. Need some help with a targeting or ROE question."

"Sure Donovan, shoot, what you got?"

"We've got troops taking fire from a village. They're not able to maneuver to respond directly or get a positional advantage and we're looking for a solution."

"Okay Donovan, let me get with the JAGs and I'll call you right back on this line," Jacobs said.

Fifteen minutes went by before the hotline rang. Sonic picked it up, determined who it was and passed the phone to Donovan.

"Donovan."

"Yeah, Donovan, this is Jacobs. Here's the deal. You can deliberately target the village, going through the normal request process which will eventually end up with the Central Command commander, or the commanding general can declare the village hostile and you can attack it."

"Okay sir, thanks. I'll run with that." He hung up the phone and looked for Lee, who'd left the area. He looked over toward the command section and noticed Major General Hacker was talking to Colonel Black. He decided he'd address this directly with Hacker. He walked up to the two and stood within view of Black and waited for a break in their conversation. Eventually, Black looked up at Donovan and shrugged as if to say, "What do you want?"

"Sir, I need a quick word with the general."

"What about?" Black asked him. At that point Hacker

looked over his left shoulder at him. He took that as a cue.

"Sir, it's about Marzak."

"Go ahead," the general said. This was the first time Donovan had been up close and gotten a good look at the General. The first thing he noticed were his hands. He had the long skeleton fingers of an ancient wizard. The fingernails were too long for an Army officer and they were a transparent yellow and seemed thin and brittle. The General's head was lightly sown with very thin wispy hair that was combed way too far on one side to way too far on the other. His skin was pale, a very dull, haunting shade of whitish grey. Donovan lifted his gaze from the General's crossed hands up to his eyes, they were deep, sunken and they were the bright shade of black marbles. His frame was like a wire mannequin adorned with DCU pants and a black fleece jacket. Donovan was momentarily transfixed, but he broke lock and got back to the task at hand.

"Sir, there are two ways we can attack Marzak. One is for you to declare it hostile, and-"

Hacker interrupted him. "It's hostile." He turned back and resumed his conversation with Colonel Black. Donovan hurried back to his workstation.

"Sonic, what do we have available for air that's not working TICs?"

"Sir, we've got a Buff and a flight of F-15s."

"Work up some rough coordinates for Marzak and have Huffman generate a 9-line."

"The village?" Sonic's look was questioning.

"Yes. Dead center mass will work. We'll push abort authority down to one of the White Lightning elements, but I'll make the 'cleared to engage call.'" Donovan thought it was unbelievable that the US Air Force was getting ready to attack a town in 2002. He figured the village was about half the size of his hometown. The coordination occurred and at the right time he took the mic from Huffman.

"Bongo 52, Tombstone Actual, you are cleared to engage."

"Tombstone Actual, Bongo 52, roger cleared to engage. We'll lay it on heavy on behalf of the Lilac City."

297

Jim Bunke was piloting that bomber and the Lilac City was a reference to Spokane, Washington, one he knew Donovan would understand. The bomber proceeded to the target and released 27 Mk 82s. The village disappeared in a roil of smoke and fire.

CHAPTER TWENTY-ONE

CONVERGENCE

Uktam had just climbed into one of the SUVs that were loading to move fighters to reinforce the west. The column of three vehicles proceeded along the path that led away from Marzak toward the valley. They had just crested a knoll and started to descend into the valley when their vehicle began to bounce. They thought they were driving over a rocky portion of the roadway but they were vibrating up into the air with each impact of the 500lb bombs released from the B-52. The hut they had stayed in, along with most of the village, was now a pile of smoking rubble.

Zondo noticed that rounds were impacting close to his position. He figured he and Gennaro were now being targeted by a sniper and called up a set of fighters, F-15Es. He passed the enemy and friendly positions, confirmed the axis of attacked and cleared the two aircraft "hot" to attack the sniper position. As they rolled in for the final attack the enemy launched a SAM.

"Break right!" he yelled into the handset. The aircraft made a high-G maneuver to keep the SAM from tracking, it broke lock and fell to the valley floor. The aircrew quickly passed their appreciation for the call, reoriented and strafed the enemy position. Zondo had saved the aircraft and they were now taking out the enemy that was specifically trying to kill him. The aircraft had descended below the "hard deck" of 10,000 feet. The altitude was established to keep the aircraft safe but the crewmen realized to effectively employ they'd have to come down on the deck, which they did. The aircrews were flying at whatever altitude it took to maximize the effects of their weapons.

Charlie Company had now taken over two dozen wounded. Zondo and Gennaro were taking turns controlling the air as the situations changed. They were down in the bowl and couldn't get a good fix on the enemy. They gave the fighters a general area; 'top of the ridgeline to our east' and target description; 'group of five guys with small arms.' The aircraft confirmed the position of the friendlies and did whatever they could to hit the targets, sometimes actually seeing the enemy and other times dropping on the terrain feature the ETACs had described.

Zondo finally got frustrated and ran up to the lip of the bowl with his radio. As he was trying to get a fix on an enemy mortar position rounds were impacting all around him. Then he saw several enemy fighters moving to his left. In a few minutes he started taking fire from that direction. He couldn't get to where Sergeant Lepore was, or to a position he could get more accurate coordinates, so he ran back down into the bowl. He was glad to be back with the company. At that moment he realized when they dropped their rucks they'd left the laser range finder. He needed that vital piece of equipment if he was going to be able to call in air strikes with any precision and with the enemy as close as they were; that's exactly what he needed.

Again under heavy fire he got himself as close as he could to the rucks under cover, then took a deep breath and made a serpentine sprint for the ruck. He rifled through the contents quickly; he had positioned the LRF at the top. He also grabbed his NODs, night vision equipment, and darted back to cover, the whole time with rounds impacting all around him. He made his way back to Gennaro.

"Ok Zondo, let's work up some grids," Gennaro instructed him.

Together they used the Mk-7 laser range finder coupled with their GPS and started marking enemy positions and likely avenues of their approach if they were going to attempt to overrun their position. He handed the radio work back over to Gennaro and helped move the wounded to the casualty collection point. In between trips he ran to plug a hole in the defenses as the medics continued to move the wounded.

As he moved to fill the gap, several enemy troops came up over the ridge. He stopped in his tracks, raised his weapon and fired. He had three fighters charging and firing directly at him. He could see their faces. He fired three rounds at the one farthest to his right; the man crumpled in midstride. Zondo swung his weapon to his left and fired at center mass of the second man, the enemy fighter dropped his arms to his sides, dropping his weapon and ran a few steps forward collapsing to the ground. Zondo swung his weapon further to his left as he watched the second man fall; at the same time he felt two hard punches to his chest. He lined up the third man and fired five rounds into him. That fighter had stopped to fire two well-aimed shots into Zondo's chest but his body armor saved him. Every 10th Mountain soldier who saw the group come at them fired with effect; ten of the enemy went down. Zondo didn't have time to absorb all of what just happened. He assisted with getting the rest of the wounded to a safer position.

The enemy continued to rain mortar rounds on 1-87. They had cemented the base plates of their mortars just outside of cave entrances. If they heard aircraft or helicopters approaching, they would pull the tube up off the base and run into the caves. The mortars were the American's biggest threat.

Information was now beginning to flow into the JOC. Enemy mortar fire hit General Zia's forces and they were taking casualties. The word was quickly passed through the JOC that they were turning back. Donovan remembered a conversation he'd had with Colonel Longstreet: these troops were Minute Men, they were local militia, they couldn't afford to take heavy casualties and their leaders wouldn't remain leaders very long if they lost a large portion of a village. But their initial presence did turn the heads of the enemy. What 1-87 and 1-187 were facing in the south was stiff but localized resistance. The enemy, like the coalition, considered the Afghan forces as the main effort.

Sergeant Rogers supported A-Company. Their Chinook landed, offloaded the company and dusted off without taking enemy fire. The company consolidated and began their movement to their assigned blocking position. Each man was carrying an 80-100lbs load. Rogers's ruck, like Zondo's, with the additional radios and batteries, weighed in at over 120lbs; he weighed 150lbs. After several hours of hard rucking through the rough terrain on the way to their blocking positions, the column took a knee. As they were catching their breath the enemy opened up with heavy machineguns, AKs and RPGs. Everyone dropped their rucks and ran for cover. The Americans returned fire, maneuvering for a better position. Rogers emptied several magazines at the enemy. He marked their position and got on the radio.

"Tombstone, Tombstone, White Lightning Zero Four!" he yelled into the mic.

After several attempts he realized he had a faulty handset. After shooting, moving and communicating their way to a defensible position, the company realized key equipment had been left behind with the rucks. Rogers had carried his ruck as long as he could and it was the closest to their position. He made a run for it. Under heavy fire he retrieved a replacement handset and made it back to cover. As he was replacing the handset, several enemies charged the company's position. Knowing he couldn't yet contact air, Rogers raised his weapon and shot at the attacking formation of enemy fighters. He hit three who fell dead. Three reversed course and ran back over the ridge they came from; the company soldiers felled a dozen more.

"Tombstone, Tombstone, White Lightning Zero Four," he called several times. The radio was working but he couldn't raise the JOC. He tried "any aircraft" and made direct contact with the AWACS. He requested air support.

"Sir, White Lightning Zero Four is calling for TIC support through Bossman," Sonic relayed to Donovan.

"Okay, let's push him the F-15s, Twister Flight," Donovan directed Sonic.

Sonic contacted the fighters; passed them Rogers's TAD and pushed them his way. Rogers got the F-15s up on the net and within a few minutes cleared them hot on the enemy position. The aircraft screamed overhead and released their weapons. The detonations created a pair of mushroom clouds. The attack silenced the foe for a few minutes; then the enemy fire flared up again. Rogers cleared the fighters in for another pass. As they approached the enemy launched a shoulder fired SAM; it snaked skyward toward the fighters.

"Missile launch, break left!" Rogers yelled into the mic. The aircraft pulled up and hard left, contrails streaming off its wingtips the higher aircraft of the two reacted visually to the missile and broke right, streaming contrails from his wingtips as he pulled hard and then rocketed straight up. The aircraft rejoined and came around for another pass. The third attack seemed to have driven the enemy back under cover.

The company continued to move through the rough terrain. They had dropped their rucks during the first attack and had maneuvered away from them during subsequent attacks. They were now in dire need of equipment and supplies.

"I'll go make a run to retrieve the gear," Rogers told the company commander. "I need pieces of my TAC kit anyway."

"Okay Rogers, go ahead. Specialist Fine, Stevens and Howard." He pointed to three of his soldiers close to him. "You go with him to provide security and to help mule some of that gear back." The three looked at the company commander and each other, then looked at Rogers and slowly rose to their feet.

"What the fuck Air Force, be a hero on your own time!" Specialist Fine said in a low enough tone that only Rogers could hear it."

"Sorry man, let's just get the job done," he replied.

The three moved out from the direction they'd just come, back past the rest of the company toward the abandoned rucks. They hiked back to a point that overlooked the rucks, the three soldiers refused to go further.

"Okay Rogers, we can see the rucks from here. You go get what you need and bring back whatever you can. We're staying here," Fine said, as he sat down.

"Well, all right then." Rogers turned and jogged down toward the rucks. As he reached the halfway point between the three Specialists and the rucks, rounds started impacting all around him. An enemy sniper was zeroing in on him. He got to his ruck, grabbed his gear, went through three others, jammed what he could into his ruck and started back up to his starting point. He made it to the top, still under fire, and dropped down in front of the three soldiers.

"Okay, you all ready to head back?" He was breathing heavily.

The number of TICs Donovan and the ACE were handling continued to mount. Donovan's team was getting the "got-to-have" TIC requests and the "need-to-have" immediate requests. Each request for air was answered with the call, "Attention in the JOC," the coordinates for the requested air support were yelled out, usually with one of Donovan's guys standing on a chair or booming out the info. All the liaisons that were tasked to be in the JOC checked to make sure their elements were cleared. The required responses were 'by exception' so silence was consent. If one of the elements had people in the area, they'd pipe up. It was a non-technical way to ensure the numerous elements sprinkled throughout the battlespace weren't going to drop bombs on each other. They flowed the aircraft through which was now an obviously incomplete request structure. To complicate matters, the COAC, the all-knowing airpower entity at Prince Sultan Air Base, far, far away from the battlespace, had grown accustomed over the years of prosecuting an uncontested interdiction campaign supporting the No-Fly zones in Iraq. Now they were all in a close-combat CAS battle and the clunky mechanisms of the CAOC were rusty.

Donovan had to keep in mind the balance between supporting the requests that had already been made with the request that may be made. Every time he committed an aircraft or flight of aircraft to a maneuver element his team had to monitor to ensure that if that flights first pass took care of the problem for the ground troops; they'd be re-tasked to help out their buddies taking fire from another location. Donovan had to decide which aircraft with which munitions to send to which controller. If sorties were executed within the first five minutes of their vulnerability period, which for fighters would be approximately 90 minutes to two and a half hours, the remainder of that period could go uncovered. Immediate requests had to be monitored closely and all factors weighed to determine when to 'push' an aircraft to an ETAC. He realized that squeezing all that air into that small battle box put the aircrews in danger. However, both the aircrews and the ACE realized Army, Air Force and Navy lives on the ground were at stake and there was never a moment's hesitation. Donovan held aircraft at the predetermined control points and sequenced them into the fight as able. It was now obvious to everyone involved that this was not going to be the detainee roundup that was expected.

As the situation was intensifying, an incoming mortar round hit Lieutenant Colonel LaFontaine's TOC on objective Ginger, wounding everyone except him, Gennaro and a couple of his troopers.

Colonel Moriarity approached the ACE desk. Donovan and Sonic were catching their breath in between air support requests.

"ALO, come here," Colonel Moriarity put his arm around Donovan's shoulder and led him to the center of the JOC. Once there he pointed to the video screen. "See that truck?"

"Yes sir."

"That truck is resupplying the enemy that is engaging our troops. You need to kill that truck."

"Sir, we've had dozens of troops-in-contact situations. That's our priority..."

"Listen ALO, I just told you to kill that truck. Kill it. It is resupplying the valley and hindering operations"

"Sir, if I pull aircraft off a TIC it's going to put our guys at risk." Donovan warned.

"Do it."

"Yes sir, we'll roll some aircraft against it when we get a chance." He started to turn away.

"I just gave you an order to kill that truck; *that* is the priority." Moriarity's face turned bright red. His face looked like there was a bigger, meaner Colonel Moriarity inside trying to burst out. It seemed like his face was stretched to the maximum, his lips were tautly stretched over his small yellow teeth. His eyes were like seeker heads off of a sidewinder missile, constantly scanning, detecting and at exactly the right moment, locking on to whoever's eyes dared to look into his. At this moment it was Donovan's. Donovan walked back to his station. The feeling of accomplishment that he and Sonic just shared for providing air support to the troops-in-need faded fast.

"What was that all about?" Sonic asked.

"He wants us to target a truck," Donovan said as he looked at the Plexiglas board.

"A truck? Haven't we just been schwacking Al Qaeda?" Sonic was indignant.

"Yep. Look, I'll push something against it as long as we're not competing with a TIC."

"Okay, sir, we've got a flight of F-16s."

"Sure, let's get after it. You can get rough coordinates off the Predator feed."

The next few hours were frustrating for the Airmen. Colonel Moriarity called Donovan back out to the front of the JOC.

"Okay ALO it's been hours and you haven't killed that truck." Moriarity was angry.

"Sir, if we're going after that truck we're not providing close air support. What you're talking about, that's interdiction."

"You mean to tell me it's going to take you four hours to get air support to my guys bleeding out there?"

"No sir! We've responded to every troops-in-contact situation within five minutes, to every call for fire we've gotten and killed the enemy and saved our guys. What you're talking about is re-rolling CAS assets off a CAS mission to go and interdict something we don't have coordinates for. It's a fishing expedition." Donovan stayed as respectful as he could.

"Every time I talk to you it's another excuse. Blow up that truck!"

"Yes sir."

After a relatively brief time period Colonel Moriarity came back to the ALO station.

"ALO, come here," he commanded. Donovan moved again back to the center of the JOC. "I'm going to put up a clipboard here near your work station. Every time I point to something on that screen and tell you to kill it, I'm going to hack a watch, write the time down and see how long it takes you to get it done."

"Yes sir."

He went back to the radios. Sonic had been working several more TICs, pushing air and sending available aircraft against the trucks. Donovan got frustrated after sending flight after flight of fighters in search of a second stake-bed truck. The only means the F-16s and all the fighters had to find those vehicles was the 'Mark-One-Eyeball,' using their own vision, no electronic sensor, to try and locate a small truck in rocky terrain from 25,000 feet. After yet another set of fighters 'bingo'ed' on gas in search of the truck, he approached Sonic.

"Sonic, listen, I heard what the Chief of Staff said but we're not wasting any more air looking for that fucking truck. We're going to support the troops on the ground. I'll try and get the COAC in on the interdiction op but we're not going to use CAS to search for that truck.

As he was talking to Sonic, Brigadier General Jameson approached him.

"Hey Pat, you all are doing great work and saving lives. Now look, the CG wants you to kill that truck, that's a viable target. Is there anything I can do to help you take it out?" General Jameson said with a genuinely concerned tone.

"Sir, no sir, thanks though. Sir, here's the deal: our aircraft have a tough time picking that needle out of a haystack from 20,000 feet and we're really focused on the close air support piece, saving trooper's lives."

"I know that Pat, but see what you can do. That vehicle is-running around the AO providing supplies."

"Yes, we'll do what we can."

"Okay Pat, keep up the great work," the General said.

An hour or so later Donovan was on the hotline to the CAOC trying to work out the time sensitive target, TST, rules of engagement, ROE, to see if he could get some help in setting up some interdiction sorties. Just then Major General Hacker strode with a purpose toward Donovan who saw him coming and pulled the handset away from his ear. The general grabbed it and pushed him.

"Who do I have to call to kill that truck!?"

"Sir, nobody sir, we're on it. I'm working with the CAOC to treat this as a TST or deliberate target or a preplanned to get non-CAS assets dedicated to this interdiction effort."

He realized he was still holding on to the handset as the general was tugging on it. The general starred him in the eye, released the phone, turned and walked away. Donovan also realized he had balled up his fist; he immediately and exaggeratedly opened his hand and dropped it to his side.

As night fell, Gennaro handed the mic over to Zondo; he was exhausted. Zondo orchestrated a gunship and fighter attack that destroyed numerous enemy positions and facilitated the extraction of the wounded. During the gunship strikes, Gennaro actually fell asleep to the sound of the 40mm. After the strikes the Chinooks were cleared in to extract 1-87. Zondo helped load the wounded while Gennaro coordinated for strikes on their own positions. Once they lifted off the Airmen cleared the attacking aircraft strikes, 'sanitizing' their previous positions.

In the ACE Donovan and his crew worked every aircraft on the ATO. In addition to supporting the TICs, the team started receiving requests to hit fixed targets from the field. Donovan started putting together information for the CAOC to set up an air interdiction campaign, hitting those fixed targets and pummeling the 'Ratlines' the enemy was using for escape and resupply. As reports came in on caves, bunkers, mortar positions, vehicles and weapons, Donovan directed strikes against them or called them into the CAOC to be added to the target list on the ATO. The entire area around the Shah-i-kot Valley was revealing itself as a marshaling area and a base of operations.

The whole JOC was glad to watch the last Chinook lift off on the Predator feed, bringing out the last of 1-87. Donovan was concerned about all the soldiers in that small force under fire all day but now he had time to think about his guys. He knew they were in the thick of it, but their calls had to be relayed so he hadn't heard from any of them directly.

The initial shock experienced by the Task Force from the stiff resistance knocked everyone back on their heels. Lieutenant Colonel London moved up toward the screens at the front of the JOC. Donovan saw him and was curious what the word was from leadership and came up alongside him.

"Hey sir, any updates for us?"

"Hey Dude, yeah, we're going to declare victory and get the Hell out of here." London turned and walked back to the G3 office. Donovan felt relief; he thought now they might be able to have a chance to hit the reset button, keep the soldiers out of the way and pound the enemy positions.

3 March 2002, Bagram Air Base, Afghanistan:

Within the next few hours, Major General Hacker got input from his staff and subordinate leaders. Lieutenant Colonel Lavoire radioed the general. They talked about the decision to pull out. Lavoire recommended against it. He thought they'd have a great opportunity to continue to fix and kill masses of Al Qaeda and foreign fighters. Some of his staff thought it was a good idea to log the enemy killed and reset for another operation. Hacker made the decision to reinforce in the valley and press the attack.

A couple of hours had passed since the 1-87 Chinooks departed the valley. Other elements had managed to get into position with little resistance and were still there. 1-87 would be relocated and the other elements would be reinforced and the reserve would be committed. The conventional forces were now the main effort and the SOF forces were going to the O.P.s and to the blocking positions.

Donovan coordinated with the COAC for pre-assault strikes to support the reinforcements going in at dawn. He's just hung up the phone and looked up. Zondo and Gennaro had entered the JOC and were heading his way. He got to his feet.

"Holy shit, great to see you guys." He stuck out his hand. Zondo just stood there looking at the Major. Donovan put his arms around him and hugged him. "Great work Sean, glad you're okay, Don, awesome work. You guys okay?"

"Sir, I sure the fuck hope we don't have to go back out there," Gennaro said sternly.

"Well Don, okay, hang on a second. Sean you okay?"

309

"Yes sir, I got shot," Zondo told him as he showed him the two impact points on his body armor, "but I got 'em." It was obvious he was full of emotions. He stood there looking at Donovan.

"Holy shit, glad we got body armor instead of those piece-of-shit flak vests, right?" Donovan didn't really know what else to say.

"You and me both sir." Zondo was charged up.

"Sir, I'm not going back out there," Gennaro reasserted.

"Okay Don, what do you mean?" Donovan noticed the conversation was being listened to by several of the soldiers within the Fires area. He put his hand on Gennaro's shoulder and guided him toward a kerosene stove near the back exit of their tent section.

"Sir, I'm just saying it was fucked up out there, it was fucked up. I'm not saying I won't go if I have to, just, you've got to... well, it was just fucked up." He looked Donovan in the eye.

"Okay Don, if I need you to, you'll go, I know that. The fight's just started."

"Yes sir. I will." He nodded.

"You're hyped up right now, take a knee for a few. Go make sure Zondo's okay and you guys are both squared away ready to go again as soon as you can. Let me think on this a minute."

Gennaro rejoined Zondo who was talking to some of the Fires guys. Sonic approached Donovan.

"What was that about?"

"Well, Don's shook up. I know he'll be okay; he's just really amped up. I'd really prefer not to send those guys back out there, but shit, I'm not going to pull an audible on the Army at this point. They're solid, just first day in the war – shit, what'd we expect right. Okay, let me think on that a minute."

"Okay, sir. I'll go."

"I know you would. Let's see how it plays out with 1-87. I might need you out there as an option as it is. We haven't started taking JTAC casualties yet but the way it's been going, shit, we'll see. You've been critical to this part of the operation." Donovan replied. They both walked back over to their workstations.

"Sean, Don, you guys go get some shuteye. The plan is to put 1-87 back in tomorrow, up north, so get some rest. Don, come back in a few hours," Donovan directed.

"Okay sir," both Zondo and Gennaro said in unison.

Donovan sat back down at this laptop and answered several secure emails to the COAC. He looked over at then walked over to Senior Airman Reed who was filling out the request log. He waited until he finished his last entry.

"Hey sir, what you need?" Reed looked up at him.

"You current?"

"Yes sir,"

"You ready to go?"

"Yes sir." Reed's eyes got bigger and he stood up.

"Okay, here's the deal. I need you to go in for Tech Sergeant Gennaro. Go get your stuff together, find him. Do you know who he is?" Reed nodded in the affirmative. "Tell him to get back up here so he can get you spun up and have him walk you over to the company commander, introduce you and make sure you're where you need to be when you need to be there. Got it?"

"Yes sir, got it."

"Okay, thanks for stepping up. I gotta have Gennaro's seniority in this JOC and plus this is going to get a lot more complicated since we're going to be introducing interdiction sorties, preplanned targets, all that, and Gennaro's been doing this for almost twenty years. This all right with you?" he asked.

"Yes sir." Reed just about came to the position of attention.

"Good man. Thanks, go get after it and good luck." He walked over to Sonic. "I'm sending Reed in. He's current and ready to go. We'll keep Gennaro here in the JOC; we'll need his experience."

"Riiiiiight," Sonic stretched the word out for sarcasm.

"Anyway, that's the way it will be, okay?"

"Sure sir," Sonic replied as went back to typing.

"Oh, I'm going to call the CAOC and talk through the pre-assault fires with the CCO." He picked up the phone. After a few attempts he made contact with Colonel Solaris, the Chief of Combat Ops, CCO. "Sir, Donovan here. Have you all gotten our requests?"

"Yeah Donovan, we're working them to put in tomorrow's ATO right now."

"Okay sir, great, appreciate it…"

"Hang on Donovan, you still there?"

"Yes sir, I'm here."

"Look, we're putting a lot of effort into building this ATO with these targets. We'll be running the interdiction piece. Just wanted to make sure you understand."

"Sir, I understand, but we've got to control those strikes. We're in a seriously condensed battlespace. But, yes sir I get it." Donovan didn't completely understand what the Colonel meant.

"Ok, out here." Solaris hung up.

3 March 2002, Bagram Air Base, Afghanistan

The ACE continued to push CAS to the teams who had eyes on the enemy and to strike targets that had been called in throughout the day. Donovan and Jimmy, Lavoire's deputy in the JOC, talked several times about getting as much air to Mako and Juliet as they could. Donovan established the routine for his guys to push air to troops-in-contact; then to the SOF observers; then hit the preplanned targets, and then they'd dropped any remaining munitions on Marzak or the Ratlines. The gunships were "winchestering," using up all of their ammunition; hitting enemy formations, cave entrances and vehicles.

The night was busy. Donovan and Sonic didn't have time to sleep. As morning approached some of the key leadership started coming back to the JOC. Colonel Moriarity was one of them. He walked right up to the ACE.

"ALO, what you got lined up to support the reinforcing assaults?" Moriarity asked Donovan.

"Sir, we've got a B-1 and a B-52, they're set to strike at twenty minutes prior to wheels down."

"Have you made contact to confirm?"

"Sir, I've been in contact with the CAOC and they

haven't passed anything to indicate otherwise."

"So you haven't confirmed they're good to go, that their strikes will proceed as planned! That's what you're telling me right?"

"Sir, the CAOC knows these sorties are to prep the assault. I've got a hotline to them and it's their duty to inform me if there are any issues."

"Okay ALO, so it's taking you guys hours and hours to get air support to my men and now you have no idea whether or not the pre-assault fires are going in or not? Once I launch that force and they cross the mountains around Bagram, I can't call them back."

"Sir, right now, at this moment, those aircraft took off on time, they refueled, they're heading this way and they haven't radioed that they have any problems making their TOTs or that they're not coming."

"Listen ALO, you're not getting it. I've got to make the decision to launch the assault force based on the pre-assault fires going in or not. So, you tell me, is this mission a go or a no-go?" Moriarity put his hands on his hips.

"Sir, it's a go!" Donovan said confidently.

"Okay ALO, but if any of my guys get killed their blood is on your hands," Moriarity said as he stepped closer to him. Donovan did not reply; he started back to the ACE workstation. When he'd gotten about halfway there Sonic saw him, put the handset to his side and yelled across the JOC.

"Attention in the JOC, Bone 01 just checked in; as fragged!"

"Roger, thanks." Donovan took the news like a shot of hot coffee. He turned back around and moved in Colonel Moriarity's direction. He knew he had to have heard that announcement but he thought it appropriate to make sure the Chief of Staff got the information directly.

"Chief, pre-assault fires just checked in, they're good to go."

"Okay ALO thanks," Moriarity replied without turning back around to look at him.

The bombers hit their targets right on time. The

reinforcing assault force got into position without much enemy resistance. The soldiers moved to sweep the valley. The preplanned attacks were approaching their targets. Within minutes of their TOTs, the Rakkasans started taking heavy small arms and mortar fire.

"Sonic, grab those sorties going against those preplanned targets and re-role them to support those TICs," Donovan directed.

"Roger, on it," Sonic replied.

A B-52, a flight of F-15s and a flight of F-16s were pulled from hitting fixed targets and were pushed to the ETACs with the troops-in-contact. This happened twice more over the next few hours. Then the CAOC called.

"Sir!" Huffman yelled to Donovan. "CAOC's on the line, need you ASAP."

He grabbed the hotline. "Task Force Mountain, ALO, Donovan," he said with a finger in his other ear.

"Donovan, this is Colonel Solaris, CCO."

"Yes sir, go ahead."

"I told you that we were putting a lot of effort into coordinating an interdiction campaign; those sorties that are dedicated for that purpose are not for you to use for CAS, do you read me?" The voice on the other end of the phone was obviously pissed.

"Sir, I get the concept but we've got an established priority of fires and we've got troops-in-contact, that's number one."

"I told you Donovan, let those preplanned sorties proceed to their assigned targets, that's an order!" Solaris barked.

"Sir, I copy all." He had barely got the words out of his mouth when he heard the phone on the other end hang up.

After another hour or so, the same situation arose; one of the Rakkasan elements was taking fire from three sides, Rex was calling to get more air and the most readily available was another interdiction sortie.

"Sir, we've got two more TICs. I just got off the phone with the CAOC and I guess they just told me what they told you: hands off the preplanned sorties," Sonic relayed to Donovan.

"Push the sorties to the TICs," he directed. Sonic complied.

Within three minutes the hotline rang again. All the Airmen around the workstation starred at the phone. Donovan put up a hand to let everyone know he had it. He picked it up.

"Task Force Mountain, ALO, Donovan."

"Donovan, Colonel Solaris. You pull one more aircraft off of a preplanned target and I'll have you court martialed!" he warned.

"Roger sir, copy." Again he heard the click on the other end.

"Sir, you want me to still push those aircraft?" Sonic asked him.

"Absolutely," Donovan said. As he sat back down at his workstation, he looked up and saw Colonel Laredo and Rosie walking in their direction. He was surprised and got back to his feet to await their approach.

"Hey Pat." Laredo shook his hand and slapped him on the shoulder. Donovan reached over and shook Rosie's hand too.

"Hey sir, glad to see you."

"Okay, so give me the rundown," Laredo directed.

Donovan handed over the duties to Sonic who was giving Rosie an overview of the operation and what had been going on. He talked to the Colonel for about thirty minutes then introduced him around to several of the Division key players. Several others had come with Laredo from the CAOC. Colonel Reed was from the Battlefield Coordination Detachment, the Army liaison element in the CAOC. Colonel Garibaldi was Air Force from the Master Air Attack Plan cell and Lieutenant Colonel John "Hound Dog" Harper was an A-10 pilot working at the CAOC and he was going to help out with the operations and also help integrate the A-10s that were moving from Al Jaber to Bagram to help with close air support. Colonel Mike Steinbrenner was leading the detachment of A-10s. Donovan was now spending a lot of time spinning up all these additional players, half of which were working on the interdiction piece.

Later that evening Laredo told Donovan he needed to

get some rack time; Donovan said he was fine. That quickly turned into an order and Laredo had Rosie take over running the ACE. Donovan hit the rack but was back up at 0200 and spelled Rosie. It was early in the morning, 4 March 2002.

4-5 March 2002, Takur Ghar, Bagram Air Base, Afghanistan:

As part of the shift in strategy, SOF teams were being put out on Observations Posts, OP's around the battlefield. One of those, a SEAL team, was inbound to a ridge near objective Ginger at 0300. Razor 03, with its ramp down, was about to touch down on a point called Takur Ghar. The enemy opened fire with small arms, machineguns and RPGs. The crew started to abort, the pilots spooled up the engines, the helicopter lurched up and forward; rounds hit several hydraulic lines and fluid sprayed over the ramp. The first man in line to exit was Petty Officer First Class Roberts; he slipped on the hydraulic fluid and slid out of the back of the Chinook. One of the crewmen grabbed for him and got his foot, but with the acceleration of the aircraft and the heavy combat load of the SEAL, Roberts slipped from grasp and fell back to the ridge. Once they found out they had left a man on the landing zone, the pilots tried to return, but the helicopter had taken too much damage. The pilots limped the helicopter to a spot on the valley floor. When the JOC received the situation report regarding Razor 03 and the need for a Search and Rescue mission they ordered a Predator to the area. The JOC watched the feed. Donovan moved over to see the screen and saw what they all thought was one of their own being dragged down a path, surrounded by enemy fighters. The gunship moved into the area.

Razor 04 had just dropped off its team at another OP; they were now heading to Razor 03's position. In 45 minutes Razor 04 arrived and picked up all of Razor 03's personnel and flew them back to Gardez. Everyone involved wanted to go back after Roberts. Hacker ordered the QRF, a team of Rangers, to assist with the rescue effort. The QRF was on standby to address situations just like this and they immediately got ready; they had about an hour flight to get to Takur Ghar.

As the clock was ticking the sun started to come up. Donovan was in contact with the gunship crew; they wanted to stay into daylight hours. He worked to see if they could land, refuel and rearm at Kandahar; he figured they could at least gas up since 130s were routinely operating in and out of there now. At the same time the special operations air element at Misirah was giving it other orders. They were sticking to the standard operating procedures, which was to not fly during daylight hours. Laredo got on the phone and tried to influence the decision; it was no good, the gunship departed, out of gas and out of time. Donovan's team pushed a set of fighters overhead, but with no one on the ground yet there was nothing for them to do. Razor 04 was heading back to Takur Ghar with the SEAL team. The QRF, Razors 01 and 02 were en route.

At 0500 Razor 04 landed almost at the exact same spot Razor 03 had; the enemy opened up with everything they had. The team exited the aircraft, absorbing a hail of enemy fire. The feed in the JOC showed the events unfold. As the team exited the ramp three fell. The enemy fire increased. The JOC watched as the remnants of the team maneuvered down the backside of the ridge, dragging two of its wounded. The third man was not moving.

The enemy now moved to pursue the team. Watching from his position, Donovan discussed the option of using the Predator to coordinate close air support. Everyone was desperate to help but that small team, for now was on its own.

The sun was now fully up; it was 0630. Razor 01 flared for its landing. One of its engines took a direct hit from an RPG and fell straight down to the ground like a dead fish. There was an audible gasp in the JOC; hands were rung through hair, fists were clenched. Razor 01's door guns immediately began to return fire. One of the gunners was hit and killed. Three Rangers died exiting the helicopter; those that got out tried to set up a perimeter. Other Rangers and several of the helicopter crew were wounded. Two Airmen survived the landing and the first moments of the firefight and began coordinating CAS. The shot up team couldn't egress down the side of the ridge. They couldn't move the wounded. Now the Rangers were returning fire.

The thermal images of the fierce fighting locked most eyes on the screen at the front of the Mountain JOC. Donovan was working additional air assets to flow to the ETAC and Combat Controller that were with the QRF. The direction to Razor 02 was clear: "Don't land on that ridge." Razor 02 maneuvered to a position out of the line of fire, about 2000 feet below the summit, and dropped off the other half of the Ranger QRF. They would have to climb to link up with their brothers.

A Ranger Captain was the officer in charge on top of Takur Ghar. He knew he had to do something. He, Tech Sergeant Valentine, the Air Force ETAC and two other Rangers rushed an enemy strongpoint while the M240 machine gunner provided covering fire. The strongpoint turned out to be a bunker. Valentine teamed with SSgt Geoff Barnes to coordinate air support. He directed one of the Rangers to get his ruck to Barnes since it had the radio in it. Valentine continued to return fire. He stood up and fired at the bunker to cover the squad leader who was firing his M203 grenade launcher at the same bunker. The first set of fighters they had were F-15s loaded with LGBs and their 20mm cannons.

Valentine yelled to Barnes, "Have them execute gun runs from our right to left!" As the first fighter made its approach, Valentine wasn't sure if the fighter was targeting them or the bunker.

"Abort! Abort! Abort!" he yelled to Barnes.

"Abort! Abort! Abort!" Barnes yelled into the mic. Valentine had him reorient the fighters and have them come in from a different angle so they could confirm which direction the aircraft's gun was pointing. The fighters made several gun runs. The enemy fire continued from the bunker. Valentine discussed using bombs since they were so close to the enemy. Initially they decided not to; now they needed the firepower. Valentine directed Barnes to have the fighters drop long of the bunker on the backside, then they'd walk them in closer and closer to the bunker. The first pass dropped long and impacted on the downward slope of the ridge behind the bunker. The team walked the bombs closer. The next one they directed at a tree that was up against the bunker. The fighters lined up, were cleared hot and the 500lb'er hit the tree and split it in half. The firing from the bunker stopped. The Captain decided they'd wait for the other half of the team before they'd make an attempt to overrun the top of the hill.

As the other half of the team was slowly making its way to the summit the enemy dropped mortar rounds around them. Donovan's team kept pushing aircraft to the Americans on and around Takur Ghar. An Australian Special Air Services team was in a position overlooking the enemy firing on Takur Ghar. Aircraft were pushed to them; they controlled the strike and took out the mortar position that was firing on the reinforcements trying to make the summit. The second team made it to the top and joined their comrades. The Ranger Captain directed an assault on the top of the ridge where the bunker was; they took it with no further casualties.

Once they consolidated their position the officer's concern turned to getting the wounded medically evacuated. He made the assessment that it was safe to bring in medevac airlift to get the seriously wounded off the mountain and radioed that assessment back to headquarters. Just as that call was made the enemy reemerged and launched a determined counterattack. The Rangers quickly fought off the assault, killing all of the enemy fighters. Two more Americans were wounded, one seriously, Senior Airman Cunningham, who had been fighting and caring for the wounded throughout the day. He was now fighting for his life. The team then directed F-14s to drop on several positions around the area. Several calls came into the JOC to authorize the medevac. They were all denied until about 2000 that night. The Chinooks showed up on the Predator feed. All watched nervously as they touched down and picked up the Americans off of Takur Ghar. Each second seemed like an eternity. Donovan watched as his ACE team continued to push air to provide as much cover as they could. Once they lifted off and quickly moved from the Predator's view, quiet filled the JOC. The total wasn't known yet but all knew that Americans had been killed.

Hundreds of bombs were dropped and every AC-130

sortie winchestered that night. Donovan took a 90-minute break and was at his station when Lieutenant Colonel Lee approached him.

"Pat, I need you to take a look at something."

"Sure sir, what you got?"

"Well, read it over and talk to me about what you think but keep this between us okay?" Lee asked. He handed Donovan a sheet of paper as he looked him in the eye.

"Okay, sir, I'll get right on it."

Donovan took the paper and sat back down. He started to read. He read the subject, "Lack of Responsive Close Air Support by the USAF" and only the first few lines before he knew the purpose of the memo. He read it through completely, twice in order to give Lee an accurate, professional assessment. He walked over to Lee who was seated across from him in the Fires section.

"Sir, this is…" He checked himself; he wanted to add his oft-used adjective, "fucking," but knew Lee was a Southern gentleman and he liked him so he didn't want to offend him. But Donovan's ire couldn't be completely contained. "This is bullshit; absolute, unbelievable bullshit." Lee didn't interrupt, so he continued. "Sir, we're in the middle, smack in the middle, of combat operations and we're writing memos? And sir, whether or not it's the right thing to do, it's inaccurate! The response times in here…obviously this was penned by Colonel Moriarity, refer to that God…that damn truck. That's not Close Air Support! Look, we've been knocking the living crap out of the enemy and it ain't with M-16s or Apaches, it's with airpower…and…"

"Okay, got your thoughts Pat, thanks." Lee took back the memo.

"Sir, do you agree with what that says?"

"Well, I believe we could be doing better and there are some valid points," Lee said unconvincingly.

"Okay, sir. So, does the boss or the Chief want my input?"

"You just gave it. But I don't think we're going to be able to work it into the text."

"Well sir, could you at least shoot me a copy of that so I can give my higher ups a heads up? Sir, if the Division Commander stands by those words what difference would it make if my leadership got a heads up? What are we going to do, start providing responsive CAS?" He added sarcastically.

"I'll confirm we're going with these words; then I'll send you a copy," Lee said.

Donovan made his way back to his workstation. He sat back down at his laptop and stared at it for a few seconds. Sonic stood at the radios.

"Hey sir."

"Yeah man, what's up?" He snapped out of his funk.

"Sir, one of our units is taking fire from Serkhankhel."

"Okay, let me get with the CAOC to see if we're still good with the approach we used for Marzak."

Donovan called and put the request to the CAOC staff before he approached the Army leadership. At the same time, he asked about the other village in the valley, Babulkhel. The answer he got back was the same: if the commanding general declares the villages hostile they would be valid targets. Donovan presented the situation to Hacker; he made the declaration.

"Sonic, we're going to run the next bomber, a B-52, against Serkhankhel. We'll push the abort authority for the strike down to whichever of our guys has eyes on," Donovan directed.

"Roger sir. We just got another troops-in-contact call. Taking fire from Babulkhel."

"Okay, the B-1 in the next vul period will hit Babulkhel," he replied.

Within the next two hours both villages were rubble. Air strikes increased. Donovan now approached the different elements to look for target nominations. No solid nominations were offered up. He was feeling energized by the increase of airpower and a little cocky that they now had more weapons than targets. The A-10 contingent had also just arrived, led by "Moses" Steinbrenner, increasing their air support capability. He continued to push any "excess" air to Jimmy for Juliet to use across the valley. Any weapons that weren't expended were routed to and employed on the 'ratlines' to hopefully kill any enemy trying to egress the area or at least to discourage them from trying. Nobody wanted any aircraft to bring bombs home and the Navy aircraft couldn't land back on the carrier with bombs so Donovan coordinated with the CAOC to set up 'dump targets' and a 'bomber box.'

The first were areas around the ratlines; they then created coordinate boxes over Serkhankhel, Babulkhel and Marzak. The CAOC called Donovan within a few hours of establishing these options and corrected the terminology to 'Special Engagement Zones,' SEZs; the other terms, he was told, were 'not appropriate.' He passed that information on to his Airmen.

"You can't execute effective combat operations unless you use the correct terms," one of them replied.

"Yeah, I just hope they're as careful in spelling my name correctly during the war crimes trial," he said in reference to the attacks on the villages.

The battle continued for another ten days with the tide turned in the favor of Task Force Mountain. Eventually the Afghan forces conducted clearing operations supported by US and coalition special and conventional forces. Air power assaulted the valley day and night and as Donovan worked hard to ensure all the weapons were being expended he got a call from Kermit, who was working in the MAAP cell.

"Pat, Kermit. How's it going?"

"Hey sir, good how are you?"

"I'm good. Hey look, you've got to slow down on expending those JDAMs," Kermit directed.

"What do you mean sir? We're killing the enemy."

"Yeah, that's good but if you're not, you gotta let the weapons come home. We're gonna need them." Kermit spoke softer now over the secure phone.

"What do you mean? For what?"

"Just use what you need, but if you don't need to expend a weapon don't dump it, got it? That's all I can tell you. Gotta go – out here." Kermit hung up.

Donovan passed the new guidance to his team. Just then a large earthquake hit the region and all personnel were evacuated from the JOC. Calls were still coming in for close air support; Donovan stayed. He thought to himself, *What the fuck else can happen?* After 30 minutes the JOC was repopulated.

Colonel Laredo and Rosie reentered the JOC and approached him.

"Pat, why don't you take a walk with me?" Laredo asked.

"Sure sir, where we going?"

"Gonna go up to the tower where our weather guys are set up. Rosie will cover for you."

They walked down the dirt road to the old control tower. Donovan hadn't seen the sun in over a week; he squinted the whole way. They walked up the rickety stairs and through a makeshift plywood door. They entered and were greeted by a Master Sergeant.

"Hi Colonel Laredo, how you doing sir?"

"Great, great, how about you? You getting all you need? How you holding up?" the Colonel asked with genuine concern while he continued to shake the Sergeant's hand.

"I'm good sir, thanks. Sir, I understand you need the room?"

"Yes, just for about ten minutes, thanks."

"Okay sir, we'll see you later." The Sergeant left out through the plywood door. As he was leaving, two others came in through the same door. It was Staff Sergeant Valentine and the Ranger Captain.

"Hi sir, how you doing?" Valentine asked.

"Never mind that, how you doing? It's great to see you. And Captain it's an honor to meet you too," said Laredo.

The three talked for ten minutes. The conversation was focused on the captain's desire to keep Valentine as part of his team. Laredo wanted to rotate him out, back to the rear. The Ranger wanted to keep the Airman with him who fought by his side and had been a part of his team back in the States. The conversation ended with the Colonel allowing Valentine to stay but just for a few more days. Laredo and Donovan left the tower and headed back toward the JOC.

"Pat, you need to get ready to head back to Kuwait," said Laredo.

"Sir, what, we're still in the thick of it here. I put this thing together and we've got it humming-" Donovan blurted out.

"Sure, yeah, great work, really, but I've got Rosie here and I need you back on task for your original mission."

"Sir, really, this is going to be winding down within a few days-"

"I'll give you a couple of days to make sure Rosie is spun up but you need to get back to Kuwait, copy?"

"Yes sir, got it."

Donovan went back into the JOC and the general officer's section was crowded with several dozen personnel, all staring forward at the video screens. He walked around the mass and made his way to the ACE workstation. Rosie was seated in front of the laptop with a phone in each ear. Donovan looked over at Huffman.

"What's going on, Huffman?"

"Sir, we're tracking a convoy egressing the battlespace. It stopped for a couple of minutes and some of the personnel got out and walked around. One of them was a tall Arab-looking individual. And when I say tall he was well over six feet," Huffman added. "We're scrambling to get F-16s overhead. The staff thinks it may be Bin Laden."

"What? No shit?" Donovan turned and looked at the screen.

"No shit sir," Huffman smiled.

"Boy, they can guess that from that black and white Predator feed?" He didn't expect an answer. Huffman had stuck a finger in one ear and was pressing the radio handset against the other. Rosie was still having a two-phone conversation. He decided to slide to his right and see what everyone was looking at. On the screen three SUVs had just started to move again.

"Sir, Oreo flight, two F-16s is five minutes out!" Huffman yelled across the JOC. Rosie put down one of the phones and repeated the message at max volume. One or two heads turned in the direction of the Airmen, the rest were riveted on the screens.

Over the course of the next few minutes, the F-16s

reported on station and began searching for the vehicles. After about ten minutes they called in that they'd spotted it. Rosie got the go from the Army leadership to attack; he cleared the F-16s hot. They tried several strafing passes with no effect. Then they tried to drop their bombs but they couldn't get close enough to the moving targets. At about that time Bone 11, a B-1, checked in with Tombstone.

"Sir, Bone 11 just checked in!" Huffman alerted the JOC. "He's got MTI, Moving Target Indicator!" None of those staring at the screen knew what that was, nor seemed to care. Donovan and Roz did.

"Huffman, push the F-16s out of the way and roll the B-1 in on that convoy," Rosie directed.

The B-1 was capable of identifying and tracking moving targets with its radar. Everyone who was in the JOC who wasn't on a radio was now crammed around the Generals and staring at the screens. The B-1 flew out away from the convoy, turned back around at a far enough distance to allow its radar systems to go to work. Rosie cleared the bomber to engage. The video stayed fixed on the moving vehicles, then the screen went white. The flash of the explosions whited out the thermal images. After a second the picture built back in; there were burning hulks in the riverbed. The entire JOC exploded with cheers, clapping and high-fives. It wasn't Bin Laden.

Later that night Donovan kept flowing aircraft to support requests. When there were none he ran attacks against the villages and the ratlines. There was a lull late so he got up and went over to the stove next to their station. He grabbed a cup of bad coffee and sat down, warming his hands by the stove.

"Sir," Huffman called out.

"Yeah Huffman, over here."

"Sir we've got movement detected on one of the ratlines by a gunship."

"Okay, coming right over."

Donovan got the details from Huffman. A predator also reported tracking the movement so he went over to the screens to see if he could spot it on the feed. He walked over to the front of the JOC with his cup of coffee and looked up at the screens; there were four bright blips on the dark screen, individuals moving through the mountainous terrain far to the west, heading further west.

"Attention in the JOC!" Donovan ran the battle drill for clearance of fires. None of the liaisons had personnel in the area. He looked back up at the screen. The four dots moved slowly across the dark terrain, the infrared highlighting their body heat.

"Kill them sir, that's a valid target," the Battle Captain offered.

"They're in a free fire area," the Ops Major added.

Donovan took a sip of coffee. He looked to see if any of the Generals were in the JOC; they weren't. The Division lawyer approached him.

"Sir, according to the ROE, that's a clean kill."

"Okay, thanks," he replied. "Huffman, what's the gunship call sign? Did you pass them a 9-line?"

"Sir, it's Grim Five One. Yes sir, they've got it." Donovan walked over to Huffman and stuck his hand out. Huffman handed him the radio.

"Grim Five One, Tombstone Actual."

"Tombstone Actual, go ahead," replied the gunship.

"Roger, Five one, the target you are tracking, four personnel on foot. You are cleared to engage."

"Roger Tombstone, cleared to engage, Grim Five One."

Donovan walked back over to the screen and took another sip of coffee. The screen began to light up with splashes; they looked like neon-filled water balloons bursting against the terrain. They got closer to the bright dots. The dots moved faster, two more shots. One of the dots became a human being, cut in half, being thrown through the air streaming bright blood in a wide arc. In a few seconds all of the dots stopped moving; the brightness spread out across the ground and slowly faded in the cold night.

CHAPTER TWENTY-TWO

LOOSE ENDS

Colonel Moriarity approached Donovan, clipboard in hand. Donovan caught him out of the corner of his eye and started to his feet while finishing off the email he was writing.

"Colonel Moriarity," he greeted the Chief of Staff.

"Air Force, I still don't think you fully appreciate what it's like to be on the needing end of close air support..." Donovan started to interrupt. "Ah, ah...I'm speaking. Now, it just occurred to me that in order for you to become a better officer, no wait, that might not actually be possible, maybe in order for you to do a better job of providing my soldiers better support you should go out on this next patrol. You'll only be gone for about five or six hours..." Again, Donovan tried to interject. "Ah, ah...I'm speaking. Grab your gear and meet Sergeant Major Wallace right there, you'll go out on one of the mop up patrols." The Colonel pointed to the tent flaps at the rear of the JOC. "Is that all clear to you Major?"

"Crystal sir," he replied. He was exhausted and frustrated with his inability to make any headway with Moriarity and the Colonel's insistence in whipping him like a rented mule.

Donovan hadn't put two and two together and was surprised when he met up with Sergeant Major Wallace at the prescribed time. He approached Wallace who had his head down, adjusting his gear.

"Sergeant Major, long way from Watertown isn't it?" He stuck his hand out.

"Well, at least you're not skipping toward me on the parade field." Wallace looked up and recognized him and remembered their conversation from months earlier. "I told you sir, I wasn't interested in dating. You following me all the way to Afghanistan is kinda creepy."

"Well I see you're as friendly as ever. How about when we get home you buy me a beer this time?" Donovan slapped him on the shoulder. Wallace smiled back at the Major. Donovan was just glad not to be doing the same thing with the same people and felt a little happy.

They joined the squad that was going on patrol and he was paired up with two Specialists, Franks and Cordova. They loaded the Chinook, took off and headed for their objective. He stared out the window, admiring the lush green valley and the beautiful snow-capped mountains in the distance. He was tired but didn't sleep; he enjoyed the view and being out in the sun. He chatted with and got to know his teammates.

An hour later the helo touched down just long enough for the teams to unload. All cleared the chopper within sixty seconds and took up initial defensive positions before moving out. The location was on the eastern edge of the battlespace. Donovan moved with his squad as it swept the valley, hoping to drive any Taliban or Al Qaeda forces into the awaiting SOF-manned blocking positions. The squad broke into three-man elements. They were following a creek bed, moving through a ravine with high steep walls on both sides. Every few dozen yards the creek bent to the left or right, creating corners that had to be scouted.

Donovan took his turn. The two soldiers he'd been paired with, who were now his friends, followed him closely. He walked on the right side of the creek. As he slowly rounded the bend what had been hidden by the terrain was slowly revealed: trees, rocks, the side of the ravine and three foreign fighters. He used hand signals to direct Franks and Cordova to stop and seek cover. They leaned against the embankment of the creek, hugging the earth. The three foreign fighters detected the Americans' movement and ran toward the opposite side of the creek. They splashed across, churning up sprays of water, firing as they moved.

As they went to the left they negated the Americans' cover. Cordova caught all of a five round burst from the first fighter's AK in his torso. He went down. Franks swung his weapon and fired; his three rounds struck the first of the three men in the face, sending a spray of red mist, bone and brain fragments shooting from the back of his head. Franks' action locked open; he was empty. He lunged for the spare magazine he'd just positioned in the dirt in front of him.

The second man in the enemy stick fired and hit Franks in the left hip, shattering his pelvis and folding him in half. The enemy now shifted direction and headed right for the Americans, almost in single file.

Donovan had been firing but hadn't hit anything. A fraction of a second before the enemy attempt to overrun their position, his weapon went empty. With no other options he surged toward the enemy fighters. Badly hit but still in the fight, Cordova fired from his prone position and knocked the first enemy to the ground with a three-round burst. Donovan side-stepped around the body, took three more steps and swung the butt of his GAU-5 up and caught the cheek of the second fighter square. He felt his face cave in like a ripe pumpkin. He kept his momentum going forward, past that man and his muscle memory from playing football kicked in, he sprinted toward the third fighter and lowered a shoulder into his chest and lifted the man off the ground and onto his back. Donovan righted him self and swung his weapon at the enemy's head. The fighter ducked, rolled over and scrambled to his feet, struggling to regain his balance, but started to fall. Instinctively, he tried to catch himself and took his left hand off the fore stock of his AK and stayed on his feet. The weapon's weight pulled the muzzle downward, removing Donovan from its kill zone. The American was already back on his feet and now tried to come back at his enemy again with his weapon's butt plate. Neither man could think ahead; it was all reflexes and muscle memory. One each of the Americans and the foreign fighters were dead or dying, a second of each lay thrashing on the ground in pain.

The struggle between Donovan and the third enemy fighter climaxed. The foreign fighter still had rounds in his weapon; he was now focused on trying to push back from the American enough to level his weapon at him and kill him with a burst of 7.62mm rounds. Donovan kept surging forward; he couldn't let his opponent get more than a few inches away. He pulled him in. Both men fell to the ground. Donovan went for his knife, attached to his body armor, but it was pinned between him and the enemy. *Fuck!* he thought for a microsecond. He'd let his weapon drop, realizing he couldn't use it anymore as a club. The enemy was strong; Donovan was losing his grip, both hands pulling him in. He tried a head butt but caught the thick rolled up rim of the enemy's 'mushroom' hat. He tried again and put the curved portion of his Kevlar square on the bridge of the enemy's nose, breaking it and flooding his face with black blood. This blow dazed the foreign fighter enough for Donovan to let go of the grip he had with his right hand. He squeezed his hand into a fist and targeted the enemy's crushed nose, punching the area over and over as fast and as hard as he could. The enemy loosened his grip on his weapon and dropped it.

The American's mind shifted from reactive survival to deliberate attack – he could now think and he kept striking. As he continued to strike the face of the now incapacitated and nearly unconscious enemy Donovan's mind shifted again. *Fuck!* he thought. He realized that he had no idea what was going on around him, where the rest of the patrol was; he'd lost all situational awareness. Except for what was within a few feet of him over the last few desperate minutes he'd been aware of nothing; were more enemy coming? It was another terrifying moment.

He let go of the enemy, picked up the discarded AK and moved to the right, back toward the embankment. He stayed low and barely moved as he slowly looked past the terrain to where seconds earlier the enemy was attacking from. He saw nothing, did a quick 360-degree visual check of the area and moved back past the pile of bodies in the opposite direction. He now thought about the man he'd just been locked in mortal combat with. If his mind hadn't caught up with his body's actions he knew he would have continued beating him until… he didn't know until what. He stopped breathing? His head caved in? He pushed those thoughts out of his head and moved back toward the fallen Americans. He checked Cordova first. He was seriously wounded but conscious. Donovan saw the rest of the patrol moving in their direction.

"Hey man, you saved my life when you nailed that first guy," he told Cordova, who was writhing in pain. Two of the five shots hit below his body armor and hit cloth and flesh.

"No problem, glad I can help. Now, can you get us out

of here?" Cordova asked.

"Sure man, I'm on it," Donovan replied. He grabbed Cordova's bandages off his body armor, opened them and pushed them against the entry wounds. "Keep the pressure on there man, okay?" He pulled Cordova's hands up over the bandages and pushed down hard. He went to check on Franks.

Franks was still breathing but he was bad. He grabbed Franks' bandages and took his own and tried to slow the bleeding. When he pressed against the wounds he felt shattered bones grind and give way to the pressure like crushing a bird nest. His stomach dropped.

"Oh man, fuck… Franks, you with me?" he asked, hoping but knowing Franks was unconscious. He secured the bandages to Franks' wounds as best he could. He carried a PRC-148s; he ran the MEDEVAC checklist through his head as he pulled out the radio and tried to remember how to set it up.

"I know this, I know this," he said out loud. "Motherfucker." He frantically looked for the laminated MEDEVAC 9-line checklist in the radio pouch and found it taped to the radio.

"Any aircraft, any aircraft, this is Tombstone Actual with a MEDEVAC request-litter urgent," he barked into the radio.

The MEDEVAC request was rapidly processed and a USAF HH-60 was cranking engines as the crew completed their final pre-mission checks. The bird was off the ground within eight minutes of receiving the request.

Donovan put down the AK and grabbed Frank's M-4, making sure it was loaded. He had the newly arrived soldiers from the other elements of the patrol continue to tend to the wounded. He moved to the fallen enemy fighters. He got to them in the same order he'd met them in the fight, in line. The first was dead. The second was on the ground writhing in pain. The third was unconscious, blood streaming down the sides of his face from his nose, mouth and head. Donovan took off the man's hat and propped his head up. He moved back to the second man, who was in excruciating pain and knelt down next to him. The man looked up into Donovan's eyes; they were telling him something. He wished he knew what it was. He thought for a second and shot to his feet when the image matched a recent memory.

"Jesus!" He knelt back down near the man and reached for his canteen, which was behind his right hip. The fighter put his hand up with his palm toward him, then turned his head to the side.

"It's okay, it's okay. I'll take care of you. We've got help coming. Here, here's some water. Water." He moved slowly, put his hand behind the man's head and lifted it enough so that he could take a drink. "That's it. Water," he said. Then he brought his hand to his chest. "Pat. My name is Pat," he said slowly. "What's your name?" Donovan brought his hand to his chest again. "Pat." Then he moved his hand to the fighter's chest and touched it. "Your name?"

"My name is Uktam," the fighter replied in English.

"Uktam? Did you say Uktam?" He leaned back, dazed.

CHAPTER TWENTY-THREE

WINDING DOWN

Donovan returned to Bagram. The next day he saw Colonel Rapier and Major Fredrick, whom he'd been with at Sheberghan walk through the JOC. He chased them down.

"Hey sir, how you doing?" He followed as they continued to walk away. Rapier was in midsentence with Fredrick, but Donovan's words caught his attention and he turned to look and saw him.

"Donovan, how the Hell are you, how's things going?" He shook his hand. Donovan was shaking Fredrick's when he answered.

"Great sir, how about you? What's going on?"

"This is great I ran into you. We're putting together a plan to assault the Whale, and I need you."

"Shit hot sir, I'm in," he said without thinking about Laredo's orders for him to leave for Kuwait.

They talked over the basic plan and the timing. Donovan did work the air support piece but told Rapier he'd have to get permission from his boss to be part of the assault. Rapier offered to engage direct, Donovan asked him to give him a shot first. He discussed with Laredo to no avail. Donovan then recommended Sonic be the ALO for the operation and Laredo agreed. He handed off the rest of the planning to Sonic.

In a few days Donovan's original team was replaced in the JOC and he was scheduled for lift out that night. Once he was relieved for the last time by Rosie, he packed his gear and took a walk down the dirt road that passed in front of the JOC. He walked in the opposite direction he'd gone before, away from the billeting area toward the outer gate. He saw at the end of the road a Northern Alliance T-72 tank, which was used to guard the entrance. Civilians were walking on and off the base past that checkpoint. There didn't appear to be any significant security. There were venders selling bread and hats and Soviet bayonets. Donovan approached one of the bread venders and gave a dollar for a piece of bread; the US military presence created a boom and inflation. He ate the bread, which was delicious, and walked further toward the tank. Off to his left a young man approached him.

"American, American, come here American…"

Donovan approached. "Hi," the man continued to beckon him. "American, you want to buy a Makarov pistol?"

"Where is it?" he asked. The man reached into his pants pocket and pulled out the black pistol.

"Right here American, look, good quality." He displayed it for him, tipping it side to side. Donovan looked at it from a few feet away while he ate his bread. The man reached for the pistol's slide, pulled it back and let it spring forward. As it reached the closed position, "Pow!" it went off.

Donovan felt an impact to his left leg. He stopped in mid chew and froze with a piece of bread hanging from his mouth. He started reaching for his 9mm but realized it was an accident. At the moment the round went off, the guard on the tank swung his machinegun mounted on the turret in the man's direction. Donovan put up both his hands.

"Halt, halt, it was an accident, it was an accident," he yelled in the guard's direction.

The guard raised the muzzle up into the air. Two other Northern Alliance soldiers ran toward the man who froze in place and tried to cycle the action on the weapon again.

Donovan warned him. "No, no, just put it down on the ground."

He ignored the demands. The soldiers grabbed the weapon and the man and moved toward the tank. Donovan looked down at his leg; there was no blood. He reached into his cargo pocket. The bullet had gone through his trousers, creasing his green notebook. Donovan opened the book, pulled out his pen and wrote himself a note.

16 Mar 02, almost shot by a guy trying to sell me a Makarov

He folded up the book, put away his pen and finished eating his bread as he walked back to his tent.

He was moved out of the hangar and put in a transient tent. He lay on his bunk and waited for dark when his lift to Kuwait would load up. He stared at the ceiling of the tent, barely blinking for hours, digesting what had happened over the last several months. When the time came he walked to the checkpoint before the runway. The Airman there checked that he was on the manifest then walked him to a C-17 waiting with its back ramp open. He climbed on board. He was the only one in the entire cargo section, which could hold one hundred. Eventually they took off. As the aircraft spiraled up out of Bagram, Donovan had a similar thought to the way he came into Afghanistan. *You shouldn't leave the war by yourself either.* He laid down across three web seats and slept.

He got back to Kuwait. After a few days back in the 332nd, with the slamming metal door and the smell of the desalination plant, he was told that Colonel Laredo was back and wanted to see him. He'd just heard on the news that Operation Anaconda was over. It was 18 March 2002. He was down about not being there those last two days, but according to the news the operation was over a week ago. He walked over toward the ARCENT JOC, about halfway there he saw Colonel Laredo with two other officers.

"Hey Pat, follow me," the Colonel directed as he continued to walk. The four went another twenty yards to a parked SUV. The Colonel told them all to get in. Once the doors were shut he gave them the news. "Gentlemen, we're preparing to invade Iraq." Donovan thought to himself, *Holy shit. Ah, no wonder they told me to save the JDAMs.*

Yusef entered the bar, walked up and sat at his usual spot. The bar was completely empty; he was the only customer. Nikki was behind the bar drying glasses. She saw him come in. "Motherfucker," she said under her breath.

"Hello Nika my dear. How are you these sunny days?"

"Are you going to buy something?" She picked up a glass and started cleaning it with a bar towel.

"All business I see. That's okay; we can do that too. I need to speak with you in my car, now."

"I can't leave the bar untended I'll lose my job."

"There's not a soul in here. Come, now. I won't ask you again" Yusef got off the barstool. Nikki grabbed her purse and they went out the back door to the alley to Yusef's car, a maroon, 1989 Chrysler Lebaron. He opened the door for her; she sat in the passenger seat with her bag in her lap. He went around to the driver's side, got in, and turned on the radio.

"I must see a true sign of your loyalty." Yusef waited for a response.

"I am not loyal. I do what I do because you threaten me. You threaten me by threatening my family. That's it; please leave me and my family alone. Do you not see that we have nothing? My family struggles to survive, like everyone. I got out."

"You didn't get out. You were sent out. I know your story Nika, you remember? I got you out. Don't think I don't know your story. You got sent out as an imitation Russian whore. Then you broke your deal and were lost to us all, until I found you."

"You have killed me. You have taken my life. You killed my only friend. What more could you want from me?" She looked at him as tears ran down her cheeks. She didn't sob. "I have done everything. When will it ever end?"

"Now Nika, it ends now. This one thing and I will let you go to live your amazing and wonderful life here in America." He twirled his finger in a circle at the side of his head.

"I just want to live my life with my new husband and-"

"Oh... hsss," he sucked air in through his teeth. "That part, may be difficult."

"What do you mean?" Nikki rose up and turned toward him in her seat.

"Well, you know our boy Donovan just married you because, well, he's, how do they say here, a schlub. He doesn't love you, he's just a schlub."

"He loves-"

Yusef cut her off. "It doesn't matter, it doesn't matter. We have your lovely brother Uktam in a safe place back home and if you don't kill our boy Donovan when he gets home – he is on his way home, I know that – then we will kill your brother

336

and not in a nice way."

"No."

"No? There is no no. You will do this, I will get you into Canada and then you can go wherever you like. We need to show our ability to reach out and touch any American, anywhere, and especially in America. Remember, and I mean this, and I say this very strongly, we will kill your brother and maybe your whole family, so it's your choice my lovely Nika. Now get out."

CHAPTER TWENTY-FOUR

HOME

Donovan was seated on the left side of the airplane. As they maneuvered for the approach he looked down and saw familiar landmarks and started to think. He was home. It was green down there, lots of trees and lakes and shopping malls and gas stations. The whole experience started to wash over him. He came home too fast. Thirty-six hours ago he was on a military base in Southwest Asia' now he was on short final to Syracuse Airport and after that, home.

The pilot greased the landing and a round of applause erupted throughout the plane – there were a lot of guys coming home, the first returnees. They'd had their piece of the war. Some were admin geeks who did the necessary paperwork associated with the war machine. Some smelled the last breath of the enemy he shot through the chest. To America there was no difference, they were all "heroes."

Donovan didn't make a dash for the door when the fasten-seatbelt-light went out. He sat and stared at his tray table, stowed in the full upright and locked position. He waited until he felt he couldn't wait anymore; it wouldn't be fair to Nikki.

He grabbed his helmet bag and headed down the aisle and off the plane. He went through the loading ramp and out the gate door. As he approached security, he could see Nikki's head bouncing up and down; she'd spotted him. As soon as he cleared the security checkpoint she ran toward him and left the ground about three feet from him. He caught her and held her up in the air, her grip around his neck was crushing his windpipe but he could take it... for a couple of seconds. Finally he had to say, "Okay hon, give me a second to look at you!" He held her at arms-length, "You look gorgeous!"

She grabbed him by both shoulders. "Oh my god, you must have lost 20 pounds! You look fantastic! Are you hungry?"

"No." He said laughing, "I'm good. Let's get home."

"Where's your stuff?"

"It's coming down through baggage claim."

"Okay, well, I've got a couple of guys coming to help with it."

"Oh, you didn't have to do that," he said, but appreciated that she had.

"Baloney, you're not going into the base, you're all mine… at least for a couple of days, right?"

"Sure, sure," he said, not really sure.

"I've got a surprise for you." She jumped up and down with excitement.

"I bet you do." He was unable to imagine what she'd come up with.

They eventually got all Donovan's gear and he thanked the two Airmen he'd not previously met yet; they'd arrived at the unit after he'd deployed. He and Nikki walked to the parking lot. Nikki redirected him by a slight tug on his arm and they started to head straight for a limo parked right outside the terminal. She had rented it to pick them up and drive them home. She jumped up in the air and executed a perfect back-double-mule-kick and nailed the landing. She was clapping her hands, smiling and laughing.

Donovan smirked and shook his head. "This is awesome hon, thanks." He was obviously surprised.

"Are you kidding me, I wasn't going to pick you up in the Sebring or your piece of shit Isuzu returning home from war!" But that wasn't all. "Go ahead, get in." She was still grinning from ear to ear. Donovan opened the door and in the middle of the floor of the limo, tail wagging at 90 miles an hour, was Buck.

"Holy Shit! Hey buddy, hey boy, how are you, I missed you." he put his arms around Buck's neck and gave him a hug as long as the dog could stand it. He caught himself briefly looking for Steve. He knew if he dwelled on it for more than a second he'd break down. "This is awesome hon, wow, thanks for bringing him, it means everything. I missed him – not as much as you of course."

"Yeah, yeah…" Nikki knew how much he'd missed her but she also got to talk to him once in a while and Buck couldn't, so for now it was okay for him to get a little of the attention.

There was a bottle of champagne chilling, a sushi tray and some cigars.

"Wow, nice job hon, best homecoming seen to date!" Donovan joked.

Nikki knocked on the glass partition between the two of them and the driver and signaled for him to drive. They had a great ride home, talking, drinking, snacking and just being with each other. Eventually, Buck settled down at Donovan's feet. Nikki's demeanor changed a little as she thought about how he must be feeling. She stopped and looked at his face just at the time he was thinking about how he felt too. He left; the war was still on. Nikki thought about how horrible it all must have been. Donovan thought about the guys that were still there that he went over with and about the ones that weren't ever coming home. Nikki wasn't sure how Donovan would react if he had to go back.

Donovan's emotions were starting to get too much to contain; he put his champagne glass down and turned toward her, putting both hands on her shoulders, looking her in the eyes, "I don't think I can stand it-"

"It's okay Pat, you might not have to go back."

"No wait," he shot back, "I don't think I can stand-"

"Pat, don't think about that now, wait to see if they're even going to send you back before you start worrying about it," she said, trying to be comforting and reassuring.

"No...no... Nikki, listen... I don't think I can stand it... to be here! To be home."

Nikki didn't know what to say. She stared at him blankly.

"I know, I'm sorry, I'm sorry, it's just that... I don't really know what to say." Donovan hung his head.

"Wait, wait, wait," Nikki pleaded as she grabbed his shoulders. "Wait Pat, look, this has been traumatic. Let yourself come home right now. You're home, be home. Please, let yourself, be home. Be with me." She shook his shoulders.

"Yes, yes... sure, you're right, you're right. I'm home. I'm with you, that's all that matters right now... but I have to tell you something. It's about your-"

"Not now." She held up a finger to his lips and hugged

him.

They finished the rest of the ride mostly quiet and holding each other. They arrived at the house and got Donovan's bags in the house. He took a look around to remind himself of home.

"Everything looks great hon."

"Thanks darling. The winter was rough but all is well. Why don't you go on upstairs, take a shower and I'll join you with a couple of Martinis?" She gave him a kiss on the cheek.

"All right, sounds great to me. One Martini might do me in after six months without drinking, well drinking anything good... and, who am I kidding, I'm sure I'll have at least two."

"Great I'll be right up and I'll make you a snack tray too. I bet you're hungry."

"Sure hon, another snack tray, sure, that'll be great." Donovan laughed and climbed the stairs.

Nikki prepared two martinis and put together a snack tray to give her husband some tastes he'd been missing. For one of those she had bought some new lingerie. She turned with the tray toward the staircase and there was Yusef standing in the front doorway. Startled, she let out a short scream. He brought a single finger to his lips to quiet her and moved toward her. Nikki turned her back momentarily toward him as she put the tray down on the counter. As she turned back, she grabbed a knife off of the tray and turned the blade up toward the ceiling, shielding it from Yusef's view with her forearm.

"What the fuck are you doing here?" She stepped back.

"Quiet my dear. I'm here to make sure you do what you need to do." He slowly closed the distance.

Donovan was still in the shower, basking in the hot water, listening to the music coming from his IPod station at full volume. He could hear nothing but the music. As Yusef approached Nikki within a few feet, Buck turned the corner and saw the intruder. He stopped in his tracks and growled. Yusef froze; the three of them were all motionless. Buck very slowly stalked forward toward Yusef, teeth bared, Nikki smiled. Step by deliberate step the 103-pound dog slunk toward Yusef, who backed away at the same rate, he slowly reaching into his pocket.

Nikki knew the time was now.

"Buck, sic 'em!"

Buck lunged at Yusef, but his paws slipped fruitlessly on the linoleum for the first few churns as he started to gain traction, Yusef had pulled out a switchblade from his pocket, activated the blade and arced the weapon toward Buck. Nikki maneuvered her knife to expose the business end and attacked with Buck. Yusef caught Buck in his lunge and went backwards to the ground; he stabbed the big dog in the side and Buck yelped but didn't stop. He shifted from Yusef's left shoulder to his knife arm and bit down to the bone. Yusef cursed. Nikki hit Buck with her shoulder and pushed him tumbling off to the right when she dove on Yusuf. The dog scrambled to get back to his feet, squirting blood across the floor with every accelerated heartbeat.

Donovan finished his shower, shut off the water and started to towel off, Kid Rock, one of Nikki's favorites, blasting throughout the house.

Nikki straddled Yusef with both knees across his arms. He maneuvered to push her off. Buck made it back to Yusef and clamped down on his thigh; he screamed.

Donovan thought he heard something and now started to wonder why Nikki hadn't come back upstairs by now. He threw his towel down and quickly put on his robe.

Yusef freed his knife arm and swung for Nikki; Buck caught his arm in mid thrust and began to thrash and tear. Nikki lurched up and forward and came down with both arms, full force with a knife plunge to Yusef's chest. Air and blood burst from the wound. Buck continued to thrash Yusef's arm until the knife fell free, then he snapped and latched onto his face. Nikki undulated up and down, thrust after thrust into Yusef's chest. She accelerated the rate and, as fast as she could, put dozens of holes in his now still chest.

Donovan came running down the stairs, turning at the landing,

"What the fuck! Oh my God!" He ran to Nikki's side, caught her on a downward plunge and pulled her off of Yusef. "What the fuck? Nikki are you okay, who the fuck is that?" He looked at her face; she had both arms raised over her head, as she looked Donovan in the eye. After a pause she dropped the knife and threw her arms around Donovan. "It's okay, it's over. What the fuck just happened? Nikki, who is this fucking guy? Are you okay?" Yusef's face was torn and bloody.

"Buck!" She had opened her eyes and saw Buck standing still with a continuous stream of blood running from his mouth to the white linoleum floor. Donovan let her go, turned toward Buck and then rushed to his side. When he got there he put both hands on his dog but turned back toward Nikki,

"Nikki, are you okay?" He waited for a response. "Nikki, are you okay?"

She was dazed, but snapped out of it. "Yes." She dropped to a knee and ran one bloody hand through her hair.

"Okay babe, do you have your phone? Can you call the police or give me the phone and I'll call them."

"No, I got it. I'm okay; I'm not hurt. I'm ok, I'll call 911." She went into the kitchen, got the phone and dialed. "Uh, I…"

"Babe, hand me the phone."

She slowly walked over and handed him the receiver.

"An intruder came into our house and my wife and dog killed him, our address is…"

As Donovan finished the call to 911 Nikki went to his side and held onto his arm. Buck had slunk down to rest on the floor, blood pooling beneath him, making a circle of red on the white linoleum. Nikki bent down and pet Buck's head.

"I love you Buck, you saved my life."

Later, after the police and the vet had left, Donovan tried to make sense of what happened so soon after his return to the States. Nikki and Donovan talked for hours. She told him of her life and of Yusef. They agreed that that information wasn't important now for the police. Nikki knew that Yusef was gone but she didn't know if he had people standing by to follow through with his threat if she didn't do what he had ordered her to.

After a few days Nikki wanted to try and reintroduce normalcy and tried to get back the moment of his return.

"You are beautiful," he said softly as he leaned over to kiss her. "I'd almost forgotten."

"And I almost forgot how handsome you are." They kissed, deeply. Donovan pulled the tie on the front of the nightgown and pushed it off of her shoulders.

"Look Nikki, there's something very important I have to tell you, it's about..."

She put her finger against his lips. "No, not now. Now is for us." She kissed him again, grabbing his shoulders and gently but firmly pushing him down onto his back. She was now on top of him as she kissed him passionately.

"Nikki, wait!" Donovan pushed her back as he sat up. "I've got to tell you what I've got to tell you! It's about your brother." He looked her in the eyes and held her shoulders.

"My brother, what about my brother? She quickly sat up. Uktam?"

"Yes, Uktam."

"What do you know about him? He's back home in Uzbekistan. How would you know anything about Uktam? What are you saying?" Nikki's voice rose as she sat up straighter.

"I met...I guess I can say I met your brother in Afghanistan. I have some bad news..."

"What, what, tell me what?" She got up on her knees.

"Well, he was fighting against us. He was wounded but he's okay. But he got shipped off to Guantanamo Bay."

"My brother is not in Uzbekistan? You are sure? And he's okay? Physically okay?" she asked as she tried to figure out what she should do.

"Well, hon, Guantanamo Bay isn't a good thing. I'm really sorry." He tried to console her. She looked down, then grabbed him around the neck and kissed him over and over.

"Thank you for telling me."

CHAPTER TWENTY-FIVE

AIRBORNE

Several weeks went by. Donovan took a few days off after he'd gotten home but Colonel Laredo's conversation in the SUV in Kuwait kept reminding him that they'd all be busy again, and he'd be in the thick of it. Laredo wanted him promoted and he thought he'd be the right guy to be the Director of Operations for the 14th ASOS. The 14th was an airborne unit aligned with the 82d Airborne Division, so it was off to jump school for Donovan. He recently became a 42-year-old and hadn't slept for some time. He kept running over and over again in his head the events of the last few months. They weighed heavy on his mind and he wasn't sure what he could do to feel good about it. He grew up knowing that the problems in your head are meant to stay in your head and it's up to you to figure them out; you don't pay somebody to solve your problems. But Nikki kept reminding him, this wasn't the '60s or '70s and John Wayne wasn't around anymore.

He showed up at Fort Benning in good shape and ready to go. He drove down from Fort Drum and showed up the night before he was to report in. He was staying at a Super 8 motel 30 minutes from Benning. After he checked in he treated himself to a steak dinner and a few beers at a mom and pop restaurant within walking distance of the motel. He bought a six-pack of Old Milwaukee at a gas station he passed on the way back. He had a few more beers while he watched an old John Wayne movie on TV.

He checked in the next morning and found out he was the senior officer for the class, student A001. The training went well. He was already familiar with the Army's hurry-up-and-wait approach so he'd developed the necessary patience for the routine. The ground portion and tower week were complete. Now it was jump week and his portion of the class was ready for their first jump. After hours in the pack shed and all running through their inspections, it was time for the students to load.

Donovan would be the first out the door.

"Everybody up!" yelled the primary jumpmaster.

The students labored to their feet and moved out in single file onto the ramp and toward their aircraft. They marched against the jet wash of a C-141B. As he walked, he was last in line; he was surprised that the Air Force was still flying the 141. They loaded, were seated and strapped in. The aircraft taxied and they were soon airborne. Donovan said as many Hail Marys and Our Fathers as he could get in before both jumpmasters shouted simultaneously "Get Ready!" He thought now about the war, the death, the killing.

"Port side personnel stand up!" the primary jumpmaster commanded. All jumpers on the left side of the aircraft echoed the command as they struggled to their feet; the students helped each other.

"Starboard side personnel stand up!" The starboard side jumpers echoed the command and also struggled to their feet.

"Hook Up!" both jumpmasters directed. All jumpers disconnected their static lines from the carrying handle of their reserves and hooked into the static line cable overhead, steadying themselves with one hand against the outboard side of the aircraft.

"Check Static Lines!" boomed the jumpmaster.

"Check Static Lines" echoed the students.

"Check equipment!" was the next command, and response. The students checked their personal equipment as they'd been trained to do and then they checked the jumper's chute and static line in front of them.

"Sound off for equipment check!" The aircraft filled with the sound of the echoed response. Starting from the front of the aircraft, the last man in the stick, each jumper in turn slapped the outboard butt cheek of the trooper in front of him and yelled, "Okay!" until Donovan stomped his foot forward and put his arm out with an open palm and sounded off with,

"All ok jumpmaster!"

The jumpmaster slapped his hand. The lines of students on both sides of the aircraft stood with one hand holding their static line, waiting for the green light. Donovan was standing just short of the door watching the earth speed by below. The 141 soared along at 135 knots. Everyone was inside their own heads at this point but all that could see it were staring at the red light waiting for the green.

"Standby!" the jumpmaster said and motioned for Donovan to step into the door. He did and looked out to the horizon. The light turned green.

"GO!!" the jumpmaster yelled and slapped his backside.

He jumped and hit the slipstream. The students streamed out behind him; he spun around and saw the next few jumpers come out of the aircraft.

He was counting...

1000...

He was clear of the aircraft. His mind filled with images of death...

2000...

He closed his eyes hard and squeezed his reserve between his arms...

3000...

He couldn't breathe, everything turned red...

4000...

He saw faces, dozens and dozens of faces rapidly changing...

His chute didn't open. His hand was on his reserve ripcord. He was accelerating toward the earth. His muscle memory kicked in; he pulled the reserve ripcord and dropped it off to his right side. The reserve chute streamed from its pack. Donovan heard the sounds of the silk, cords and risers unfolding, but it didn't open. He knew he was close to the ground. Now he braced for impact.

The reserve chute violently opened with a loud POP! and he was jerked to an upright position, the momentum carrying him past vertical; he hit on the back of his heels, then his ass and then his helmet hit the ground with a crack. The deflated chute fell over his body. He didn't move. He opened his eyes, moved his fingers and toes, hands and feet, legs and arms then brought his head up off the ground and looked down toward his feet, still under the parachute.

It was at that point, exactly, that Donovan realized he understood it all. He didn't want to feel better, not about all of this. He wanted to bear the burden; it was supposed to be hard. It was quite a thing to have killed for his country. The weight of it was what he got for it. It was uniquely and forever his. He hoped he would never stop feeling that weight. And he knew he would have to, and he was ready to, do it again.